CHILD OF HAVOC

THE BALLAD OF SORROWS

BOOK THREE

AUSTIN COLTON

For more information, contact: www.austincolton.com

First edition / April 2024
Paperback ISBN 979-8-89412-733-0

Printed in the United States of America
10 9 8 7 6 5 4 3 2 1

Dedicated to Robert Smith.

*Who encouraged me to dream up stories
and to write them down.*

PROLOGUE
FIREBRAND

Ash, wet from last night's rain, covered the ground for a quarter mile in all directions. The stumps of burned trees that dotted the once luscious glade, were small reminders of what I had already destroyed. The glade was across the mountain, and far enough away from Kings Keep that I could relinquish my anger and fury without restraint. This was a good place for many things, and it was growing to be a new familiar destination. It seemed that the more I came, the less time I could withstand the temptation to return. This was the first time I had come two days in a row. Last night's business had proven more frustrating than I'd expected and I needed a place to myself where I could let out my anger. Where I could fully embrace the raging fire within.

Setting down the heavy sack of coal, I rolled my shoulders back and looked up at the sky. The pale blue was neither marked by clouds or birds and the chill which hung on the spring air came with the cool scent of a damp forest. My cloak clung to me, wet from my travel, with several twigs and leaves clinging onto the hem.

Casting off the cloak, I reached into my pocket and pulled out a small box of matches. Shaking them as I slid open the match-box, I listened to the soft tinkling of small matchsticks. Plucking one out, I flicked my thumbnail on the red phosphorus tip, igniting the match. The flame burst alight, sending small wisps of white smoke into the air before the fire settled and began to burn with a warm orange. Letting the flame burn down the match to my fingers, I allowed the fire to enter through my skin.

The burning sensation traveled up my finger and into my hand. The flame lived inside me, continuing to consume the small wood that I clenched within my fingers. Watching as the small match disintegrated, I linked the small flame to a piece of coal within the sack I'd set down. New life was breathed into the small flame and it began to swell within my hand. The fire began to course through my arm, chasing my blood as it rushed up into my chest. As the power entered my heart, my entire body burst with power and life. The sensation was powerful and deliberate. Focusing my eyes on the stump of a tree a dozen paces to my left, I held out my hand and channeled the fire through my body and out my hand.

A column of fire blasted from my palm and struck the already charred trunk. Erupting, the wood lit like a torch and began to burn, the flames reaching up twenty feet higher than the top of the trunk. Within moments the trunk fell over and erupted into a cloud of ash. Embers flitted in the air and smoke rose high, marring the otherwise pristine sky.

Turning to another half charred tree, I blasted it with fire the same way I had the first. As that tree began to burn, I began to cast fire at random. As balls of fire connected with the earth, the ground erupted sending dirt and rocks in all directions. When the smoke cleared, a hundred small craters covered the glade, making the ground look like a pockmarked face. As I looked at the destroyed earth, I realized how my power had continued to grow. It was easier than ever to cast fire and I was destructive as ever.

Holding both of my hands before me, I produced a ball of fire which was as wide as I was tall. The fire was like a bubble that continued to grow in size, the color turning from a brilliant orange to a deep blue. As the flame expanded, I stepped into it and marveled at the ever expanding dome of flame which slowly moved away in all directions. Spinning with my arms stretched out to either side, I began to weave patterns with the fire. At first, the movements were just a way to let out emotion, done without thought. But as my mind began to focus, so did the shapes which were made in the fire. Images began to form within them, and depicted in the flames was a memory which I had suppressed for so long I had forgotten it existed.

Closing my eyes, I let my mind get swept up into the memory. It seemed that a force beyond myself was conjuring the images and helpless to stop them, I decided to embrace them. I suddenly was back, standing on a battlefield, looking at hundreds of haggard soldiers. The Chezek army was fleeing before us, moving closer to their city walls. Blood slicked my hands and my war hammer felt heavy in my hands. A man, his face caved in from the repeated blows of my hammer, lay at my feet. Now unrecognizable, his body fell still, and he died.

"Get your swiving carcass moving Caden! We must not let them retreat into their city."

The voice cut through the din of battle and my attention snapped back into focus. Looking up from the dead Chezek soldier, I saw a group of soldiers rally, turning about and raising their swords to meet me and my companion. The older man, Graham, raised his axe in response to them before barking at me to follow. Graham was dressed in plate armor painted black, and his war helm had a single spike in the front. His dark eyes were full of anger and his hands gripped his axe with a strangle hold.

Together, we ran to meet the six bloodstained men in battle. Their plate armor was sharp and angular, adorned with spikes and blades which turned their entire bodies into weapons. Though their faces were shielded from us behind the visors of their helmets, I could tell that they were looking at me. Lifting my war hammer, I flipped it so the spiked edge was facing down and prepared myself for attack.

"On my mark."

"Ready," I grunted, heaving my war hammer high.

"Go!" Graham shouted. As soon as the words left his mouth, I sprinted to the right which drew the soldiers attention away.

From the corner of my eye, I watched as Graham raised his two handed axe high, then slammed it into the ground. Where the blade struck the ground, the earth cracked and trembled, large chunks blasting upward as the tremor moved towards the enemy. The swelling earth rippled like water, and the Chezek soldiers dropped to their knees, losing balance. Large chunks of rock slammed into the fallen soldiers, denting their spike covered armor.

As soon as the ground stopped moving, I shifted directions and sprinted towards the downed soldiers. Helpless to stop me, one of the Chezek soldiers raised his hand in defense before I slammed the back spike of my hammer into the helmet. The pointed metal barb broke through the metal of his helmet and lodged into his skull. Twisting the hammer to the side, I dislodged the spike and yanked it out. Blood sprayed from the wound as the man fell backwards.

Still kneeling, the others continued to struggle to regain their footing. One of the Chezek thrust his sword towards me, catching me in the side. The blade scraped across my chain mail but did not break through. Grunting, I smashed my hammer into his chin with a back handed blow. The sharp sound of his teeth shattering was followed by the breaking of bone. As the man tumbled back, blood spewed from his mouth, small yellow teeth tumbling out onto his chest. He sputtered and choked. His eyes were crossed and he did not seem to notice as I raised my hammer. The spiked end loomed over him for a moment before I drove it down into his chest with a two handed swing.

The metal spike broke through the armored plate and plunged deep into the man's chest cavity. There was a soft sucking sound as I pulled out my hammer. Watching the man struggle for breath was more difficult than it should have been. I took a step back and swallowed, a lump beginning to form. Before the soldier could suffer more, I slammed the blunt side of my hammer down upon his head. His metal helmet dented and he fell still, blood pooling around his head as it leaked from the corpse.

The other four were back on their feet and another squad of seven soldiers were sprinting towards me, their swords raised. Taking a tentative step backwards, I readied myself, heaving my hammer so my right hand was close to the head. Holding my weapon close to my shoulder, I took a deep breath, preparing myself to attack.

"Get back!" Graham commanded.

Obeying immediately, I leapt backwards, and watched as the geomancer slammed his axe into the ground over and over. The ground began to break apart, large cracks forming which began to swallow the remaining Chezek. As they slipped between the cracks of earth, they screamed, flailing their arms in desperate acts to crawl out of the earth which was swallowing them. Watching their bodies squirm, I listened to their screams, and I forced myself to stay.

Raising my left hand, I took in a deep breath and from the fire which burned a few paces away, I drew in the power. It seared my insides, sending pain through my entire body. Screaming, I closed my eyes and released the fire. The flames burst from my left hand and shot towards the Chezek warriors. As the fire connected with the first man, it hit him with so much force that his entire helmet was blown off. As the fire disappeared, I got a clear look at his face. The man was bald, his skin partially burned from the fire, and his eyes were full of fear. His mouth hung open as if he were going to scream, but no sound came out. I only looked at him for a second before I blasted him once more with a large ball of flame. The fire seared his face, caused his eyes to pop and his teeth to explode. This time, when the fire faded, a skeletal face of scorched flesh was all that looked at me, its mouth still open in a silent scream.

Small flames sprung to life and danced between my fingers before the power left my body completely. The sudden loss of the fire and magic within me caused me to stagger forward. Dropping to my hands and knees, I trembled, losing feeling in my hands. The chill which overwhelmed me made me feel like I was frozen. Forcing in deep breaths, I closed my eyes and felt a slight tremor in the ground. Tightening my grip on the war hammer, I looked up and watched as Graham strode forward and began to decapitate the remaining Chezek with his axe. He killed them quickly and without remorse, striking them where they were, half buried in the ground he had broken with his magic.

My head felt light and my hands shook. What is happening to me?

A wave of guilt slammed into me with full force and I fell to the ground. My breathing began to grow short and rapid. The anxiety made my chest grow tight and I grit my teeth. The emotions cut so deep it seemed as though I had been run through with a sword. Unable to move, I closed my eyes and tensed every muscle in my body. Despair followed, consuming every thought and feeling. The edges of my vision began to darken and the sound of battle became a distant din.

"Get up!" I growled to myself. This was no time to break down. I had to hold myself together, just for a little longer. Tightening my grip on my hammer until it hurt, I got up to one knee, then with all the strength I could muster, I stood. Raising my chin,

I ignored the dead and focused my attention forward at the armored men on the battlefield.

Don't look back. Never look back.

The Chezek soldiers continued to flee towards their city. Glancing behind us, I looked at the line of soldiers who stood on the hill almost a half mile behind us. The Malketh army looked like a wall of silver, the low hanging western sun shining brightly upon them. The large black banners with the silver eagles were still distinct, even at our distance.

Only four other Malkethian sorcerers were standing upon the battlefield. They stood in groups of two, and I watched as the other sorcerers attacked the Chezek much as we had, tearing the earth asunder and burning their victims. Watching them was like watching the destruction of an entire army. Like those who had fled from us, the Chezek that were fortunate enough to survive their onslaught fled back towards the city.

"Come, young one. There are still more we must fight and we cannot let them get back to their city."

I took in a series of short breaths, nodding as I processed the words. Staggering forward, I followed after Graham who continued towards the large city walls in the distance. Giving chase, we pursued the soldiers who sprinted with wild abandon. It was like watching hogs flee from a predator, all full of squeals and frantic movements.

Graham changed his style of attack, waving his hand here and there, causing only small portions of the ground ahead of us to shift. This caused the fleeing soldiers to fall and stumble, making it exceptionally easy for us to catch them.

Rushing up to a fallen soldier, I slammed my hammer into the back of his head, driving his face into the dirt. As the Chezek soldier fell still, I stepped over him and attacked his companion. The second soldier stumbled forward, his feet tripping on a stone which suddenly shot up from the ground. His armor slammed hard against the ground, the spikes which covered it digging deep into the dirt. The man groaned and he turned his head just as I swung down with my hammer. The spiked edge entered his helmet through the slit in his visor, spreading the metal and sinking deep into his eye. Blood spurted from the visor and when I pulled on the hammer, the body jerked forward. Stepping on the soldier's chest, I pried my hammer free. As soon as it was loose, I held it high and saw the blood drip from off the spiked edge.

We continued to slaughter the Chezek as we pursued the enemy to the wall. While we killed dozens, the majority were still able to take cover behind the first line of fortifications. The wooden chevals were sharp and coated in a shimmering black substance that dripped down to the ground. Behind the chevals were small dirt trenches which had small stone walls built above them. These dirt and stone mounds hid many from our sight, but I could hear the sound of their metal armor clinking as they dashed into them.

The walls of the city loomed high above us, but no archers stood atop them. Though it was strange, it made me less hesitant to pursue. However, the lack of archers did make me wonder what they had planned. It was no coincidence that they had lured us onto the battlefield. I shut away the doubts in my mind. They would not be helpful. Not now.

"Stop!" Graham barked.

I obeyed, skidding to a halt fifty paces from the line of chevals. "What do we do?"

"Burn them!"

With hesitancy, I lifted my hand and pointed my palm at the first Chezek trench. Taking in a deep breath, I pulled the fire inside of me. My entire body flared with heat and with pain. Screaming, I forced the energy through me, summoning as much fire as I could. The grass on the field around me turned to ash, the wooden chevals withering and breaking apart into charcoal. As my surroundings were consumed, the energy and the fire within me grew so intense that I felt like it was about to erupt from my skin.

Then the fire blasted from my hand in an enormous column. In horror and astonishment, I watched as the twisting spiral of orange and blue engulfed the soldiers as they tried to leap out of the trench to escape the flames. The sound of screams was drowned out by the crackling of burning skin, the searing of meat, and the popping of bones. Even though the fire only lasted for a few seconds, when the light faded, I had to blink to rid my eyes of the white spots which obscured my vision. When my vision finally cleared, I saw a heap of molten metal, only the faintest outline that they had ever been pieces of armor. What remained of the bodies was unrecognizable and looked like the white ashes of an abandoned campfire.

Choking, I began to take in staggering breaths. It felt as though my lungs were collapsing in upon themselves, unable to bring in air. Again, I collapsed to the ground. As I continued to struggle for breath, small squeaks and groans slipped through my lips. My entire body was cold as ice and with every passing moment, things began to feel more and more numb. Closing my eyes, I gave into the pain, letting it consume my entire being.

The memory faded and I once again focused on my surroundings. The dome of blue flame had expanded in all directions several hundred feet. Closing my fists, I let go of my connection to the fire and watched as it burst apart. Small blue embers rained down from above as the dome vanished. The light was gone and in comparison, the pristine blue sky above seemed duller than it had before. Glancing up at the sun, I felt like it had lost both its warmth and shine.

It was with sad eyes that I looked down at the ash covered glade. Smoke billowed around me. My rage returned and conjuring another ball of flame, I cast it high into the air. The ball of flame soared upward until it was too far away for me to control. I felt my connection to the fire break and as it did, the fire vanished, disappearing as if it had never existed. Filling both fists with fire, I began to throw them at the ground and as I did so, I put all of my anger and frustration into the action. Soon, I was standing next to an empty sack which was now covered in dirt and coal ash. With my resources exhausted, I clung to the small fire which was still burning within me and dropped to my knees.

It had been ages since I had last reflected upon the first time I killed someone with magic. Or at least, the first time I had purposefully killed someone with it. There was something strange about my reflection upon the past. The more I seemed to dwell upon it, the more detailed and distorted the memory became. There were some details that I could recall with such clarity, while there were others that seemed like a fading dream. But there was one thing that remained constant, and that was the pain.

A bitter laugh slipped from my lips and I pulled all of the small traces of fire from my surroundings and conjured a ball of flame which hung in the air above my hand. Once, this simple act would have caused me pain. Now, there was only pleasure.

Is that how I am supposed to feel?

The flame vanished, the energy snuffed out. Looking around at the ash, it was clear there was nothing left to burn. Even the sack which had carried the coal was now gone, black dust in its place. Turning around, I walked through the ash of the glade, following my footprints. It was time for me to return to the city. As I reached the edge of the clearing where the ash stopped and the winterbare forest started, I glanced back, a sad smile coming to my lips.

Another memory bubbled to the surface, and I did not resist it. Instead, I embraced it, and closed my eyes to reflect upon its nature. It was the end of the first day of battle, the first of what would become an endless onslaught of killing and destruction. But it was a beautiful end to an otherwise tragic day.

I remembered laying on the ground, unable to feel my body. I was looking at a burnt orange sky, the clumpy clouds alight with the brilliance of the setting sun. Memories of the battle flooded back and I jolted upright. The shock and anxiety faded after a second, and I rested back upon my elbows. The first thing that drew my attention was the smoke billowing up from behind the large gray walls of the city. The tips of orange flames were occasionally visible through the smoke. The field all around me was burned, the ash covered dirt trodden over by countless footprints. Three people were standing beside me; two men and a woman.

The woman was small and thin, her long brown hair cascading down her back in soft curls. Her eyes were a deep sapphire blue, shining more brilliant than I'd ever seen, and she had soft pink cheeks. She was looking towards the sky as if examining something in the distance. Her companion was a bear of a man, with a square jaw and arms as thick as my legs. He had a short, well kept beard which was black except for a patch of gray to the left side of his chin. Beneath his dark bushy eyebrows, the man was watching me with keen eyes.

Graham was running a dry stone across his axe, working over a new chip towards the blade's lower tip. The others I recognized, but their names were still unfamiliar to me. If they had introduced themselves, I had forgotten what they had told me.

"You're finally awake," the woman said. She was smiling, though the expression did not touch her eyes. "We were about to move you, but Graham insisted you would wake."

Graham nodded, getting up from where he sat.

"I've seen it before." Amod said, his voice rough and scratchy. "They shouldn't have sent him into battle so soon. Not when he's not accustomed to using his power."

"The boy's my responsibility Amod," Graham said, running his stone across the blade a little dramatically.

He tilted the axe and began to examine the edge, thumbing the side as he felt the sharpness. I was distracted for a moment, examining the blade. It should have been more damaged from striking the ground, though it seemed no more damaged than any other battle worn weapon.

Strange.

Graham took notice of my admiring eyes and I instinctively looked to the ground. Waiting to be chastised, I remained as still as possible. When nothing happened, I found myself sheepishly looking back towards the man. To my surprise, Graham was looking at me with wide eyed concern.

No, I thought, he's looking at me with pity.

"How about we go get ourselves washed up?" the woman said. "I am certain we could all use some good food. We've all earned it."

She reached down and extended a hand. At first I made no move, instead looking down to the ground, and then over to Graham. The man was preoccupied with sharpening his axe again and I finally looked up at the woman.

"I don't bite," she said, flashing me a kind smile.

Reluctantly, I reached out and took her hand. She pulled me to my feet and dusted off my shoulders.

"So, what's your name?"

"Caden," I said. "Yours?"

"Lyla. It's good to more formally make your acquaintance. You have a good companion. Graham will look after you, so long as you stay on his good side."

"Like he took care of the last one?" Amod said with a wry laugh.

"That was not my fault and you know it Amod," Graham snapped.

"I'm only giving you a hard time. No need to take it so personally. We all know that Damon was a swiving fool. Nearly got the entire battalion killed."

"We don't need to talk about that," Lyla said. "Let's go."

Looking at the ground, I began to search for my hammer. Not seeing it, I began to look back and forth, my eyes growing wide. Panic began to build up inside of me and then Graham took me by the shoulder. He proffered my hammer to me. It was already cleaned off, not a drop of blood anywhere on it.

"Here you are. No need to worry. You've got us now."

A wave of relaxation flooded over me and for the first time since I could remember, I smiled. The memory faded as I placed my hand against the half frozen bark of a tree. I looked up at the branches, feeling a wave of sadness wash over me.

My first good memory.

Closing my eyes, I let out a deep sigh, a heavy weight settling in my stomach. I could never understand why remembering the sparse good that had happened to me in life seemed to mitigate the bad. Being a warrior for the Malketh army was no longer my life, and like a distant half forgotten dream, I let the memories slip back into the recesses of my mind. It was time to move forward, if only I could find a way to forgive myself.

No, I thought bitterly. There was no forgiveness for what I've done. But perhaps there would be absolution in the things I was about to do. Letting out a slow breath, I took a step into the woods and muttered, "to the burn and blight."

CHAPTER ONE

RED HOOK, BLACK CLAW

C rickets chirped in the crisp night air a few paces ahead and drew silent as Vivienne and I strode past. The sun had finally set and twilight had given way to the darkness of night. A large moon hung in the air, shining down upon the rooftops of the buildings which lined the street beside us. The smell from the river was foul and it splashed up against the banks, wetting the cobblestone street. The grime and refuse that littered the sides of the street had been baked by the hot day which seemed to ripen the stench to the point that I could hardly stand it. A few people darted past us and I stepped to the side, getting a strong whiff from a nearby alley way. Gagging, I choked, and resisting the urge to vomit, I covered my mouth and quickened my pace. I knew the stench of death well and I wasn't in the mood to investigate. I muttered a prayer to the Valon, hoping that soon whomever had died would receive a proper resting place.

The slums of the Raha had taken a turn for the worse now that the city guard was stretched so thin. It did seem that since we began our crusade at the beginning of summer, things had taken a dark turn. I couldn't help but wonder if we were actually helping as Vivienne and I passed beggars on the street. Each raised their pleading palms towards us, but their eyes remained focused on the ground. In my heart I wished I could help them, but I had not come with coins, and it was not my intention to come here tonight to offer aid. These people needed more help than the temporary succor of one small coin. Still, my thoughts lingered on them as we continued deeper into the slum.

I wore little beneath my cloak save a simple shirt, boots, and trousers. The fabric I wore was old and rough, and each piece had the appearance that it had been patched or mended. It was the type of clothing that someone down on their luck might have to wear. That helped me blend in. However, the more people I passed, the more obvious it was that my hands were too clean to make it look like I belonged here and it didn't help that I wore a sword at my hip. Vivienne stalked the night beside me, wearing a worn shawl over her shoulders to conceal her assassin's garb. Her long knife was tucked away and instead of her usual slipper-like shoes, she wore knee high boots. Despite our preparation and disguise, we still attracted more attention than I liked. I couldn't help but wonder if that was due to the general weariness and distrust of those who resided in the streets of the Raha or if they had a sense which told them that we didn't belong. Either way, it put me on edge.

"I can't believe how bad things are getting. It's only been a week since our last visit and things are already worse," Vivienne commented as we turned down a side street. The houses were made from scraps; these put together shacks barely livable. "It seems like the whole city is turning to shit."

"I'm afraid it will only get worse before things can get better."

"Do you actually think that things will?"

"I'm still holding onto hope. Regardless, I am determined to do what I can."

There was a long silence between us as we walked. Slowing down our pace, I ducked down an alley which opened on a street next to the river. We walked along it for a mile before crossing a bridge which connected us to the western bank. The dark mountain loomed above us and the clouds which blocked out some of the stars looked like dark blotches in the night. The sight made me feel small.

Keeping myself alert, I looked down a side street and saw several people huddled together. They were groaning and mumbling to themselves. I paused, taking a step closer. In a bowl which was set beside one of the men, was a thick red residue. The sweet yet acrid stench which filled the air told me the rest. Turning away in disgust, I covered my nose before continuing. Something foul happened to the body when it was high on slush. The slush seemed to settle deep in the body of those who used it and made them smell as though the living were in a state of decay. While it wasn't something I had originally noticed, my sensitivity to the scent was growing steadily worse the more I was exposed to it.

Perhaps another side effect? I wondered. My senses did not seem to work the way they were supposed to. Not since Kori's death. Almost like a foul odor, a darkness had clung to me since the Shantenbose had killed her. It made me wonder if traces of evil still lingered. Shaking my head, I dispelled the dark thoughts and continued forward. *Focus Caden. This isn't the time to let your mind wander.*

Focusing my mind on the task at hand, I led Vivienne through the slums. As we slunk down the streets of the Raha, I saw small groups of people down almost every other alleyway, all in the same state of unnatural euphoria. I felt a sinking feeling in my gut and wondered to myself if what we were doing to rid the slush stockpiles in the Raha was doing any good.

"How much further is it?"

"To be honest, I'm not quite sure." I pulled out the map that Acacia had given me earlier that night and tried to make sense of the streets around me. I usually had no trouble with directions or maps, but on this side of the river, the Raha became a place that was a peculiar mixture of disorganization and growth. Some streets were cobblestone, some were dirt, and some were gravel. To make matters worse, clumps of trees grew in random places, diverting the roads and making them wind in strange ways. New buildings and shacks seemed to be taken down, moved, rebuilt, or all three within a matter of days. Oftentimes, the new construction turned streets into dead ends and as a result the Raha was little more than a maze that clawed its way up the mountain slopes. Turning left down another street, I finally got my bearing and found the landmarker on the map.

"The little camp should just be a few streets ahead," I said, pointing ahead.

Tucking the map back under my belt, I began to walk towards the landmark which had drawn my attention. The strange building was taller than the rest and almost looked like a bell tower but with one exception, the large ballista and guard who stood watch. A bolt was loaded and the weapon was ready to fire. The guard was leaning up against the edge of the tower smoking a pipe. He didn't seem to be paying close attention to anything, but I still kept my eye on him as we passed by.

After we had passed the tower, I kept my eyes out for suspicious entities wandering the street and found myself gripping my sword so tightly my knuckles were turning white. The familiar grip of Burnfinger's hilt gave me reassurance. We turned down another street only to find that a new cluster of wooden buildings blocked our path. I cursed under my breath, taking a moment to decide if it was worth forcing ourselves through the clutter or if we should find another way. Vivienne gave me a nod and motioned behind her with her thumb. Following her lead, we doubled back, and proceeded down another street.

Trying my best to relax, I straightened my posture and slowed my steps. The Raha was growing unnaturally quiet. Watching as several disheveled men retreated into the shadows, I found myself hesitantly moving forward. It was clear that we were being watched, but a strange tingle on the back of my neck provided me with an unmistakable warning. Something else was out there in the night and I couldn't help but wonder if it was watching me.

Scanning the shadows, my eyes pierced the darkness and I was able to make out small shapes that should have been out of view. The enhanced vision only lasted a few moments and afterwards left my eyes watering. Blinking, I looked over the rooftops and found my sight had returned to normal. Scratching the back of my head, I pushed the question of what was happening to me to the back of my mind. I knew that I needed to remain vigilant and focus on the task at hand. I could worry about that later.

I heard the shouts and chorus of laughter several blocks before we spotted the strange Red Hook fort. The first few feet of the structure's walls were built from rough stones hastily stacked together and slopped with mortar. Built atop this were wooden posts, stacked close together, the bark from the trees the posts had been made from not completely stripped away. Some sections of the wall were covered in plaster or roughly hewn sheets of metal that almost looked like they were intended to be shields but had been taken before the blacksmith could finish. The fort enclosed an entire city block. At each of the four corners, guard towers had been constructed that were covered with a canvas canopy. The towers were not constructed well and the one to my left was so crooked I half suspected a strong gust of wind would knock it over.

Vivienne and I paused, lingering in the shadows below a crooked building as we watched them. For over an hour, we observed their movements. Though I did not have an accurate way of telling the time, I guessed that every fifteen minutes, one of the two guards would walk along one of the walls, joining his companion on the other tower. Then one guard would leave, walking along the other side. This rotation kept the guards moving and alert. Each gave the appearance of keeping a close eye on the surrounding streets. But their posture made them seem disinterested. Not a single soul in the time that we were watching approached the wall or stepped within fifty feet of it.

The loud sounds of fighting and screaming continually rang from within. An occasional roar or cheer could be heard as well as the fowl screeches of beasts. I was certain that we had found the right place, though I wasn't sure if it would be worth waiting for their sport to finish. I did consider the strong advantage the distraction would give us and continued to watch for another half hour contemplating my options. When the middle of the night approached and the noise within hadn't ceased, I decided that it was time for us to act.

"I think that after the next rotation, we should try to find a way in."

Looking at Vivienne, I met her eyes and she nodded. She was frowning and her eyes had an intensity about them. She was the first to look away, turning her attention back to the fort. My eyes lingered on her face, studying her soft cheek and dark hair. Even here in the dark she was beautiful. Hiding my smile by rubbing my nose, I turned my attention back to the wall and waited for the guards to begin their rotation.

Ten slow minutes passed before the first guard leaned over the side of the wall, looking down at the street. I followed the guards with my eyes as they began their change, one of the two guards leaving their towers to walk slowly along the wall. Save the occasional glance, the guards didn't seem to look down at the base of the wall. In fact, they spent more time glancing at the commotion within the fort, clearly more interested in what was happening within than without. A few moments after the guards arrived at their new positions, Vivienne tugged on my sleeve and pointed.

Following her finger, I looked up to the northern tower, just across from where we sat. The guards seemed to be arguing with each other, their raised voices not quite discernible. One of the guards shoved the other, causing him to stumble back, disappearing out of sight. The other guard followed after him leaving the path before us unobserved.

"Here's our chance," Vivienne said. "Go."

I nodded to her and without a second of hesitation, sprinted from our hiding place to the wall. Keeping my eyes open for anyone that might be watching, I dropped to the ground and crouched beside the wall. Looking up at the crudely crafted structure, I waited in anticipation, listening to the fighting guards. Still unable to discern words, it was clear that their argument was escalating to additional blows. The thick sound of a body hitting the ground made me pause, then the shouting continued.

Good, I thought. It would only make our assault that much easier.

Creeping along the side, I searched for a part of the wall that had a large enough gap between posts, stone, and metal to let me see within. Passing such an opening, I paused and held my hand up to signal to Vivienne to stop. Peering through the gap, I saw that the landing above which wrapped around the wall was supported by wooden posts. There wasn't much to the structure and I wondered if there might be a way to peel back one of the roughly hewn sheets of metal to slip in rather than risk climbing over.

"Viv," I said motioning to a panel a few feet above. "If I were to lift you, could you slip in?"

She looked up, head tilting to the side as she considered. "I will give it a try."

Lacing my fingers together, I placed my back against the wall and braced myself to lift her to the small opening. She placed her boot on my interlocked hands and I felt the muck on the bottom slick against my fingers as I heaved her up. She was easy for me to lift and my recent training had strengthened my arms and muscles considerably. Patient, I held her as she pulled on the metal sheet, bending it back carefully so she would make as little noise as possible. The guards above us started to argue with each other, their voices nearly screaming. That gave us the opening we needed.

Looking up, I watched her wriggle through the opening between wooden posts and drop down to the other side of the wall. We looked at each other through the gaps and I gave her a smile. Vivienne motioned for me to wait and my eyes followed her as she disappeared to my right. The fighting guards had stopped and a third voice joined the others. After a few moments, the voices above me went quiet and I heard the sound of boots walking away.

As I waited, every second seemed to last an hour, and my heart pounded in my chest. It felt strange to be so nervous, but stealth was key and I couldn't risk using magic to fight tonight, no matter what happened. Cursing myself, I squatted down and made myself as small as possible. While the light from the torches above shined down brightly upon the street, there was more than enough shadow to hide in. My worry was not that I would be spotted from above, but that some resident of the Raha would see me and call out. Perhaps I was overthinking, but that strange feeling of eyes watching me from the darkness was putting me on edge. With every passing moment the feeling was growing worse. Glancing up at the rooftops, I searched them again. As expected, there was nothing looking down at me from above.

Turning my attention back to the street, I glanced around as several people slunk from the shadows and into their homes. Of the four people I spotted, not a single one glanced my direction.

Each hung their heads in pitiful despair and once again I found myself feeling sorry for them. Hearing a soft thump to my right, I looked over and saw a body on the ground. A moment later, I watched another body fall down from the top of the wall and land with a loud thump on the street a dozen paces away. Blood pooled around both bodies and the arm of the second man twitched. I saw a wound in his back which was still oozing blood.

"Great," I muttered.

Turning my attention to the tower, I saw Vivienne's face poke from the top. She waved me over and tossed a thick rope over the side. Tugging on the thick coarse fibers, I pulled it taut before I began to climb the rope. Vivienne took hold of my forearm when I reached the top and helped me over. We were both silent and I looked down the wooden planks that made up the walkway to the opposite towers. No guards stood at the other end, though I was certain that the sack looking objects on the ground were their bodies.

"You made quick work out of that," I said, the left side of my mouth curving into a smile.

"Sorry if I was a little too hasty," she said with a shrug. "But I wanted to get it over quick."

"The way I see it, that's one problem solved." *Or one problem created,* I finished in my mind. Either way, at that moment no eyes would be watching from above. "Do you want to take the lead?"

Vivienne nodded, crouched low to the ground, and began walking along the wall to the southern side. I followed her to the ladder and took the opportunity to look over the small city block that had been barricaded off. The small homes were all one story, with flat or slanted roofs, most of which were hastily built from bricks or stones. Towards the center, where two homes should have sat, was a clearing, fenced off, and surrounded by over a hundred people. Everyone seemed fixated on the commotion and the few people who sat on the buildings around the clearing didn't so much as glance up at us.

Scanning the crowd, I saw three men who had weapons, but they could hardly be considered guards. Narrowing my eyes, I focused on the pen and tried to get a good look at the screeching and howling bodies within. They moved quickly and were rolling atop one another like fighting cats. Their bone white skin shone in the firelight and had an unnatural sickly look to it. As one swiped its claws across the other, an arc of blood sprayed the crowd. The group backed away, people tripping over each other as they attempted to avoid the spray. Through the opening, I caught my first full glimpse of the creatures which had been fighting. Three Ghouls crouched in a circle, clawing and biting at a skinless body that laid on the ground. They were almost human in appearance, but their limbs were too lanky, their mouths hanging too wide, their smiles stretched the width connecting their batlike ears. None of them had any hair on their bodies and this added to the strange sheen of their skin.

One of them looked up and it appeared to catch my eye in the darkness. Its expression looked like that of a man dying in agony. The Ghouls' hollow eyes were too human for my comfort. I froze as it looked at me and my heart leapt into my throat. I waited for the creature to call out, but it didn't. My split second of panic faded as the Ghoul turned its attention to the flesh it was devouring.

"You coming?" Vivienne hissed from below. Looking at her, I climbed down the ladder, careful not to make any noise as my boots touched the ground. The buildings around us were shrouded in darkness and it was easy to move through them.

"Did you see any building that looked like it could be used as the storage?" I asked in a whisper as we stopped at the edge of the first building.

"Nothing that looked like a warehouse, but if I were to guess, there was a building that was under heavy guard. I bet that is where they are keeping it."

Before I could respond, Vivienne darted across the street and I followed, ducking into the shadows behind her.

"I agree," I said, remembering the three guards I had seen in the crowd. "Did you have a chance to count the guards?."

"There were two out front. Perhaps a few inside. It was the only building that had anyone out front."

"Lead the way," I said with a waving motion.

Vivienne was so silent as she moved through the darkness, her feet treading softly over the dirt road so that she made less noise than a cat. In comparison, I felt like a lumbering buffoon as I did my best to match her movements.

"Relax," she whispered, pausing as we rounded the corner of a two story building with empty windows and a broken door. "You are trying too hard to force yourself to be quiet, and as a result, you are making more noise. Just take a deep breath."

I did as she instructed and she gave me a stiff nod.

"Now, when you step, avoid shifting your weight until your forward foot is firmly on the ground."

I nodded and did as she had instructed as I followed her down the street. I still made noise, but much less than I had been making. It helped that the closer we got to the crowd in the middle, the louder it became. We were a few buildings away from the edge when Vivienne paused. The crowd roared with laughter and cheers. In horror, I watched as a new victim was thrown from off a gallows-like platform. The man's screams were so abruptly silenced in the night that I couldn't help but close my eyes and mutter a silent prayer that the Valon would let his life end quickly.

Silently stalking to the edge of the building, I peered down the street on the far side and looked at the clearing; the sounds of chanting seemed to be quieting slightly. The Ghouls were feasting upon the body. The faces of the spectators were vicious and they all seemed to be relishing in the carnage. They were all vitriolic and violent as they chanted and laughed in delight. Now that we were closer, I could see that the spectators' faces were painted with blood and most had twisted and sharp symbols of red hooks drawn on their arms.

On the far side of the pen sat a stage where seven more people stood, a mix of men and women, with hoods over their faces and hands tied behind their backs. A hooded man stood beside them, two slits cut into the brown fabric for his eyes and a chain hanging from his neck. The man was bare chested and he was covered in bloody handprints. This butcher stood beside a woman, knife at the ready to cut her free and toss her into the pen.

I found myself unable to look away from the scene, my eyes once again falling upon the Ghouls as they began to gnaw on the bones of the corpse, the flesh already scarfed down. I counted the creatures and was surprised that the three beasts could look so thin and emaciated after devouring two bodies so quickly. I found myself wondering how many more victims had suffered death before we'd even arrived.

Feeling a tugging on my sleeve, I looked over to Vivienne who was pointing to a squat building on the other side of the Ghoul pen. There were two cellar doors on the outside of the building and it had thick shudders on all of the windows. Several guards sat on three legged stools beside the cellar doors, their backs against the stone walls of the house. I saw that the man positioned at the front door had a large spiked war pick hanging from his belt, and a short sword resting across his lap. The guard by the cellar had a metal studded club which rested beside him, propped up against the wall. While neither looked like guards at first glance, it was unmistakable now that I'd been able to examine them.

"Caden, what do you want to do?"

"Let's destroy the storehouse, leave the mark, then we can wreak havoc on the lot of them." As I spoke, I heard the gang members beginning to chant. Turning my attention back to the pen, I watched the crowd as they began to raise their right hands in the air. They curled their index fingers and the shadows that danced on nearby buildings looked like hooks.

"Kill! Kill! Kill!"

Everyone in the crowd repeated the word together and I watched as the hooded man pulled a woman to her feet, cut her bonds, pulled off her hood, and threw her screaming into the pen. Closing my eyes, I turned away from the carnage. The sound of the cheering crowd quickly drowned out the tearing flesh and screams of the woman who was being torn apart by the feasting Ghouls.

Anger flared inside of me and I almost considered running out to slaughter them and their foul beasts.

"Let's make this quick," I growled.

Darting across the street, we circled around two more buildings until we approached the guarded storehouse from the north. The lights from the square cast long shadows. Creeping up to the side, I peeked around the corner and saw that the guard was still sitting, leaning against the wall, his eyes trained on the Ghoul pen.

Vivienne pulled a small thumb sized knife from her belt and flung it through the air. It whirled end over end and lodged itself in the throat of the guard. It pierced through his trachea and when he gasped, blood spurted out and dribbled down both sides of the knife. Choking, the man reached up and pulled out the blade. He held it out in front of him for a few moments, eyes wide with shock, before falling off the side of his stool. He landed with a loud thump on the cellar door and slid off, his limp body bleeding out on the dirt. As the blood continued to pool around him, something cried out from within the cellar and slammed into the door from the underside. The chains which locked the cellar were loose and the doors opened several inches due to the impact.

Thin bony hands from within clawed out and continued to push on the door. The Ghouls within began to beat against the door, screeching with high-pitched squeals. The noise brought attention from the crowd as several blood-painted faces looked over at us. I watched as they pointed to us and heard others cry out in alarm. Several drew weapons from beneath their blood soaked cloaks and raced to the cellar. Vivienne and I backed away, pulling out our own weapons to greet them.

Shit, I thought, holding my sword out before me.

No one approached us directly, each turning their attention first to the cellar door and then to the dead guard. As the ghouls continued to paw at the opening, I drew my sword and slammed it against the chains. The wood splintered and the gap between the cellar doors opened another few inches. A Ghoul forced his head through the gap, then his shoulder emerged. In one fluid motion, the creature slipped through the gap and then another. As the Ghouls emerged, the wood splintered into dozens of pieces and what remained of the doors flung from their hinges.

The Ghouls crawled over each other and tore into the crowd, biting, clawing, and screeching. The first man who had been standing in front of the doors was knocked down and disappeared as they piled atop him. The second tried to run and before he could turn around, a Ghoul took hold of him and bit deep into his neck. Blood gushed from the wound and the Ghoul drank, landing atop the man as he fell onto his back.

Darting forward, I swung Burnfinger wide, slicing one of the creatures across the back. The steel of my blade cut through the skin like it was made of silk, leaving behind a gaping wound of bloodless flesh. The creature twisted around, splitting its wound open further which revealed the bones of its ribcage and spine. Opening a wide hungry mouth, the Ghoul lunged at me. With a backhanded swipe, I cut the creature's belly open. It fell forward, hitting its face on the dirt with a loud crunch as its body went limp.

Just as the Ghoul went still, another lunged towards me to take its place. The creature's long arms stretched out towards me, mouth hanging open wide. It fell like the first, cut down in a single stroke of my sword, the head rolling backwards and tumbled to the ground. Unlike a human body, the Ghouls had absolutely no interest in devouring the flesh of their own. As several more creatures climbed over the two dead Ghouls, they paid them no attention at all, their eyes locked on me.

One opened its mouth and let out a howl that was similar to that of a weeping child. The Ghouls tongue black and slightly swollen. Had it not been for the unnaturally wide mouth and dropping jaw, it seemed unlikely that it would have been able to eat due to the tongue size. Stabbing this one through the chest, I drove my steel through its body with both hands. The blade passed through with ease and burst out the back. Once the hilt of the sword struck the sternum, I pushed the blade to one side. The sword cut through the beast easily, bursting out the side and severing the Ghouls left arm. Severed from sternum to shoulder, the Ghouls' insides spilled out of the wound as it collapsed to the ground. I watched the creature wriggle for a moment before falling still. Though most of the flesh was bloodless, a deep black ooze seeped from several of the broken bones. As the black ooze pooled around the corpse, the pail organs shone in the moonlight.

One final Ghoul emerged from the cellar, but before it could make a single step out into the night, a blade struck it between its unsuspecting eyes. Falling forward, it landed face first on the dirt, driving the blade deep within its skull, the tip poking out the back.

Looking at Vivienne, I nodded my thanks. Her eyes were wide with caution but she nodded back. Turning my attention to the crowd, I watched for a moment as they struggled to fight the creatures. The majority of the Ghouls had rushed towards easier prey. While most of the red hook gang members had some sort of crude weapon in their hands, most were too terrified to fight, too unskilled, or both. As a result, they fell easily before the two dozen creatures that remained.

My first instinct was to help them. An odd thing, a part of me realized, but it was a feeling that was easy to set aside. Vivienne and I both watched as these swiving evil creations fed on the Red Hook Gang members the same way they had cast their captives to the pen. It only seemed fitting that they too would meet the same end.

Walking around to the front, I dispatched another Ghoul who was feasting on an arm, severing his head and kicking it back. The arm was still lodged in its mouth as the head rolled to a stop. The front door had been left unattended and I saw the guard doing his best to protect a small group of people as they fled away through the buildings towards the wall.

"Watch my back," I said, stepping up to the door. It wasn't locked and turning the handle, I pulled back the latch and pushed it open. The door groaned as it swung open and the room was filled with rows of slush crates.

I paused, looking into the dark room for a moment before entering. Nothing waited inside though part of me was so used to finding unexpected things in the dark that I did not trust it. Reaching out my hand, I pulled fire from one of the torches outside and let it engulf the entirety of my index finger. The light drove away the darkness and revealed rows upon rows of crates. Each crate was painted with several symbols on the side and without looking into them, I knew what they contained. I snarled as I reached out and touched my blazing finger to one of the crates. The flame burned the wood, forming a dark spot which quickly ignited. The flame took to the wood better than any tinder and spread quickly as it burned the straw within. Taking a step back, my snarl turned into a wicked smile as the fire consumed the first crate, then the row, and then the entire building.

Leaving the storehouse as acrid black and purple smoke began to cloud the room, I let out a sigh and groaned. I heard a thud to my right and looked to Vivienne who was plucking her knife from the back of a woman's head. She wiped the blade on the dirty cloak the woman wore before slipping it back into its sheath.

"What?" She asked.

"Nothing."

Glancing to the survivors, I watched as they rallied together and began to dispatch the Ghouls. The man who had been standing on the platform beside the pen was wielding a massive club which proved effective in killing the beasts. The scene was chaotic and as much as I wanted to make sure all these people suffered for the monstrosities that they had been participating in, at least some of them needed to remain alive. Otherwise, there would be no one to spread the word of our presence.

We made quick work of dispatching the Ghouls. They fell to my steel easily and the savage men and women who were saved by our intervention cowered in the corners of the street. The corpses of their fellow gang members mingled with those of the slaughtered Ghouls. The carnage was terrible, but not unfamiliar. I couldn't help but feel regretful for that. It seemed that my life was turning into one bloody fight after another. But so was the life I had chosen. Hunting down evil had its price.

"Let's draw the mark and get the hell out of here." Vivienne said.

I pulled a piece of charcoal from the inside pocket of my cloak and walking up to the burning storehouse, I scrawled a large black claw upon the side of the rock. It was a crude shape but it was recognizable enough. I dropped the charcoal on the ground and wiped my hands on my cloak as we turned to walk away. None of the gang members tried to stop us as we walked past. Each time I looked at one, they turned away and cowered. We fled down the street and into the shadows. It was quiet as we hurried towards the walls of the fort. There was no more screaming in the night, only the sound of the wind from above. It didn't take us long before we were back over the wall and out in the open streets of the Raha.

"That didn't go quite like I expected," Vivienne said once we were out of sight of the fort.

"No," I agreed. "Not in the slightest."

I still felt on edge until we reached the other side of the river. As we passed over the bridge, I felt confident that we had not been followed, though the strange sensation of being watched returned. The soft prickle on the back of my neck made my hair stand on edge.

"Caden, behind you." Vivienne nodded to the rooftop to our left.

Looking up, I saw a figure standing on the building across the street, watching us. With a body draped in a black cloak, I was unable to see their face or frame. Although I could not see the person's face, I could feel their eyes upon me. A shiver ran down the back of my neck and a cool gust of wind blew my hood back.

The figure looked at me for a moment longer before fleeing into the darkness of night. I followed at a dead sprint. My eyes never left the figure who was running along the rooftops. The cloaked figure moved with such agility and speed that it almost seemed as though I were chasing a phantom. As I darted down the empty street, I gained ground and smiled as we reached the end of the row of buildings. There was nowhere for the phantom to go but down.

I watched as the figure paused, skidding to a stop at the edge of the building. The hood turned and while I could not see the face, it was clear the person was looking down upon me. Then, with the sound of a cracking whip, the figure leapt into the air, soared in a wide arc over the street, and landed like a cat on the opposite side. In stunned silence, I watched as the figure continued to run along the rooftops until the shadows of night engulfed them. This time I did not follow. My heart sank low in my chest and I felt a strong despair fill my soul. They had finally come and I did not feel ready to face them.

CHAPTER TWO

DERELICT

My entire body tensed, I clenched my jaw, and turned to look at Vivienne who stood with her knives drawn beside me.

"What the hell was that?"

"They're here." My voice did not waver but my heart began to beat heavily in my chest; the alarm that had filled me began to give way to rage. Remaining at the corner of the street, I took a moment to collect my thoughts and to calm myself. In the cool midnight breeze, I closed my eyes and listened to the wind. In the distance, over the sound of the sleeping city, I could hear a loud thumping in the air. My eyes snapped open and I turned to Vivienne. "We need to get off the street and find a place where we can lay low."

"Where do you want to go?"

"Ravens Cross is closest. We still have friends there and I am going to need a drink."

"We should travel through the underground. Follow me."

I nodded, and without another word, I followed Vivienne through the streets of the Raha towards the canal which ran like a scar through the city. We clung to the shadows, walking swiftly and silently. Vivienne moved with the grace of a swan and the silence of a house cat. I did my best to mimic her movements, feeling cumbersome in comparison.

My mind started to analyze the situation, wondering how long the phantom figure had been following us. Whoever had been watching me had clearly been sent to spy and nothing more. I was certain we would have been attacked otherwise. This thought didn't help reduce my stress, instead it was intensified. I forced my mind to focus only on the challenge at hand. Once we were safe, I knew I could think about this further.

At the end of the street, we reached the bridge which spanned the southern tip of the canal. Water flowed quickly and rapidly through, splashing onto the sides. A layer of mist hung above the water, floating up towards us as it created fog over the bridge. Stopping on the far side of the bridge, I watched as Vivienne stepped down onto the walkway which lined the left side of the canal. The buildings towered above and made it look like a walkway that ran along the side of a cliff. Following her, I made deliberate, careful steps, not wanting to slip on the slick stone.

My anxiety rose as we walked the canal, and I kept as watchful an eye on the rooftops. There were no signs of movement from above, and the moonlight illuminated the roof tiles to the point where they shone in the night. We walked up the ravine for a mile before Vivienne stopped beside a crooked door, set into the stone wall. Instead of a handle, there was a hole and a chain. The chain was not locked, but instead, secured with a single iron spike. She removed the spike and the door swung inward on its own, revealing a dark passage.

I took a step into the darkness, and turned to wait for Vivienne to follow. As soon as she had shut the door, replacing the spike and chain to prevent it from swinging open, I pulled out a match and struck the phosphorus tip with my thumb. The match flared to life and I watched it burn for a moment before letting it jump to my hand. Dropping the match, I held the flame before us, keeping it small. The fire hovered and looked like I was carrying the flame of a candle without the wax or wick. Holding out the light, I let it illuminate the tunnel which descended gradually for a hundred feet before turning sharply to the right.

The damp air smelled of mildew and I had to force myself to only breathe through my mouth. Even then, the foulness was something that I could taste. I examined the wet stone floor, testing it with the sole of my boot. Satisfied that I would not slip, I took another step down the tunnel before pausing once again.

"Do you know the way?" I said, turning back to look at Vivienne.

"Sheyor has taught me the markings. I can read them now, so as long as they are correct, we should be fine."

"I hate this place," I said, my voice echoing loudly down the tunnel. Vivienne gave me a look and I smiled with chagrin. "Sorry. I'll keep my voice down."

"Are you certain you want to go back to Ravens Cross? I can lead us back towards the palace or even the shop."

"I don't want them to learn about the shop and just in case, I'd rather not lead them back to Seraphina's either. Who knows how long they have been watching and it's probably a moot point. Right now, I just want a drink."

"Follow me then. I'll lead the way."

Vivienne slipped past me and hurried down the sloping tunnel. I followed her and when we reached the turn I increased the size of the flame to better illuminate the way. The tunnel continued for another hundred feet before descending in a stone staircase. The tunnel walls were half brick, half stone; all of which was layered atop one another denoting the difference of age. As we descended the stairs and went deeper into the tunnel, the layers of brick stooped, and the tunnel was of a more ancient and worn stone. It was the remnants of a buried city, a place for dark and dangerous things to hide.

When we reached the bottom of the stairs, the tunnel opened up as it merged with a more natural stone formation that was like a large cave. On either side were tunnels that went left and right. There were small clusters of tents and rubbish against the far walls and small fires illuminated the clusters of people who had taken refuge in the underground city.

Shielding my own fire from them so it would look like I was only holding a candle, my eyes did not linger upon them for long. My hope was that if I left them to their business they would offer me the courtesy. Vivienne and I walked side by side as we continued through the cavern. Though every eye turned to look at us, their interest did not last long. There was a cold draft in the cavern which ruffled my cloak. Vivienne shivered and pulled her hood tighter.

We made our way through the camp to the left tunnel and found a metal gate that had been bolted to the stones and locked with thick chains and locks. There were markings painted on the wall which were hard to read in the dim light. Holding up my hand, I put a little more energy into the fire, burning a bit more coal in my belt pouch. Vivienne tilted her head as she read the engravings and nodded.

"That's the way." She motioned through the locked gate. Her voice drew the attention of a vagrant man who had set up camp a few feet from the gate.

The man, dressed in five shirts and two cloaks, sat atop an overturned crate, warming his gloved hands by the fire. Two of the fingertips on the left glove were worn and raw red fingers could be seen beneath. The derelict man looked up from the fire as we approached. His lips parted, revealing rotten teeth which were tobacco stained, with holes near the gumline. His grimace was followed by a snarl. Drawing a curved knife from under his cloak, he slashed it towards us.

"Back, you fiends. Find your own spot!"

Raising a hand, I tried to make a placating gesture. "We don't mean you harm nor do we want to cause you any trouble. We just need to get through that gate."

"No. No. No." The man pronounced each word forcefully, spittle spraying from his mouth. He began to shake his head, his long stringy hair bouncing back and forth. He reached up and scratched the sores on his face. "You can't let them in."

Brandishing the knife, he backed away from the gate, snarling. Narrowing my eyes, I spared a glance to the gate, examining the cave beyond. The floor was covered in dark brown stains, claw marks, and small piles of brown muck. Turning my full attention back to the man, I snarled back at him and drew my sword. Pointing the tip of Burnfinger towards the man's throat, I watched as his wild eyes grew wide in alarm.

"Sit back down before you hurt yourself."

The man opened his mouth in protest, but after a moment, he closed it again.

"Do you have the key?"

He shook his head.

"If it is so dangerous, why camp so close?" Vivienne asked the man. Her tone was much softer than mine.

He raised the dagger again when he looked at her and without thinking, I stepped forward and pressed the tip of my blade against the man's throat. Squirming back, he dropped his weapon, but kept his eyes fixated on her.

"I have to watch. I have to keep them back," he answered.

"Why?" Vivienne asked.

The man shrugged, making me wonder if he had even thought through that himself.

Perhaps it was his way of feeling important, I mused.

The homeless man did seem to take the task with the serious-ness of a hired guard. His eyes darted back to the gate and he shiv-ered. Reluctantly, I pulled my blade away from his throat, but held it at the ready. Watching the man carefully, I waited a few moments to make sure he wouldn't move. Though the man remained still, his entire body was tense, like a cat about to pounce.

"What's your name?" I asked.

"Osbert."

"You have a kingly name Osbert."

The man seemed to relax at hearing his name, his shoulders drooping as he lowered the knife.

"Yes, my mother named me after her father." Osbert scratched his head, his eyes growing distant. "My grandfather was a good man who worked as a stonemason. I...I was a stonemason once."

Curiously, Osbert looked down at his hands. He let out a deep sigh that rattled in his throat like a rasp. Coughing, he turned around and climbed over his mound of trash in search of some-thing. As he rummaged, I watched as Vivienne took a step closer to the man. Her eyes were suspicious, but there was compassion in them. Sheathing my sword, I placed my hand on the pommel, remaining prepared for whatever would happen next.

"Here they are," Osbert said, pulling out a small vial of red slush. He bit the cork and he reached in with one of his exposed fingers. The tip of his finger entered the red slush which began to hiss slightly as it came into contact with his skin. Osbert let out a sigh of relief and rested his head back against the stone. The rasping in his breath stopped and removing his finger, he took the cork out his mouth and hammered it back in with the flat of his palm. His eyes began to water, giving them a glossy look, his pupils growing wide.

"Osbert?" I asked, waving my hand to draw his attention.

He did not respond immediately, and when he looked over, he

seemed surprised to see us. Osberts eyes darted to the dagger which he had dropped. Lunging for it, he crawled several feet, his fingers moving across the ground like a spider. Stomping the heel of my boot against the back of his hand, I prevented him from reaching his weapon. Vivienne snatched the dagger off the ground and held it like she was going to throw it through the gate. Osbert screamed in rage and pulled his hand out from under my boot. I hear the distinct popping of broken bones. Clutching his broken hand against his chest, Osbert crawled back to his mound of rubbish.

"Useless," I said, turning away from the man. "He won't tell us anything more now that he's taken the drug."

Vivienne nodded her agreement. Her eyes lingered on Osbert as she let out a sigh, tossing his dagger into the mound of rubbish behind him. Osbert crawled around looking for the dagger but after a few moments, his movements slowed. No longer interested in letting him delay us, I walked up to the gate and heaved the large lock and chain. Drawing from the fire burning in my hand, I added more fuel to it, burning a large chunk of coal. The sack that hung from my waist grew noticeably lighter as a result.

Producing a flame, I concentrated the energy where my skin touched the metal lock. The sudden heat turned the iron red hot. With one strong pull, I broke the lock, casting the red hot iron onto the ground. The chain which had been holding the two sides of the gate closed fell to the ground, landing on the stone with a loud clang. Taking hold of the gate, I pried it open and cringed as the hinges squealed and grinded as it swung. The gate caught on the uneven stone ground and I had to forcefully push it so it would be open enough for me to pass through. I squeezed my way through the opening, the buttons on my shirt catching slightly. Vivinne followed and I closed the gate, doing my best to attach the chain without the lock.

We followed the markings on the tunnel as we continued

through the underground passages. The natural and manmade formations were similar to my previous experience in the underground. It was obvious when we entered a tunnel which crossed out of the Raha and into the city proper. The roughly hewn tunnel emerged into a sewer tunnel which spanned fifty feet. The water which rushed along went fast and the torrent smelled strongly of winter's refuse. I had a feeling in the coming months, the melt from the snow would flood parts of the city. That made me wonder what would happen to the tunnels? How many people would drown from the flooding? It was a grim thought, but it made me wonder how year after year people had survived down here. Perhaps flooding wasn't as big of a problem as I was assuming.

It took us an hour to make our way through the sewer tunnels to where the underground channels met the River Earn. The grate which allowed for the water to spill out was not large enough for any human to pass through. But there was a small ladder which was built into the side of the wall, leading towards the roof of the tunnel. Vivienne paused, looking at the markings on the wall beside the ladder.

"Caden, this should let us out close, perhaps a few streets away."

"Good enough. I'd like to get out of this place."

Nodding, Vivienne started up the ladder and pushed open the trap door near the top. I watched as she pushed on the latch and began to push on the bottom side of the trap door. It opened only an inch before it got stuck.

"Something is blocking it. I can't see well enough to determine what is blocking the door." Vivienne pushed several more times, grunting in frustration.

"Climb back down, let me try."

Vivienne slid down the ladder, stepped to the side, and motioned for me to give it a try. The wooden ladder was worn with age and wet from where Vivienne's boots had stepped on it. When I reached the top, I positioned myself so I was as high up as possible, and using my shoulder, I heaved.

The trap door caught, bumping into something heavy. I pushed harder, taking another step up so I could leverage more of my weight against it. With my back flat against the bottom of the door, I heaved which lifted the door a few inches. Taking hold of either side of the trap door, I continued to push open, and whatever had been blocking it toppled over. The crashing sound was loud, and the tearing of fabric followed. Grimacing, I held out my hand and let the flame I was holding grow large. The light revealed the inside of a storage shed, filled with an old boat. A broken mast had been propped up over the door and had been the source of the blockage. A new tear in the sail, several feet wide, ran along the middle.

Climbing up out of the tunnel, I looked down and held the light over the entrance. Vivienne climbed the ladder and as soon as she was out, I closed the door. The small storage shed was an odd place for a sewer entrance. I realized where we were standing most likely had been a street, the wooden walls looked less than a year old. There was a small door to the right and without a second thought, we departed from the small shed.

The fresh night air was refreshing, and I took in several deep breaths. Realizing that I was still holding the small flame, I snuffed it out and placed my hands into the pockets of my cloak. Vivienne pulled her hood to cover her face and without a word began to walk down the alleyway. Neither of us said a word to one another as we walked the remaining three blocks to Ravens Cross.

~

The once comfortable and somewhat comforting din of Ravens Cross brought me no comfort. Raising the mug of ale to my lips, I took another long sip. The drink was cold, which was pleasant enough, but the brew was lacking in quality. Vivienne sat across from me, nursing a goblet of wine. Neither of us had spoken for hours, determined to remain in our silence. Everyone's eyes were upon me, though most tried to hide the fact that they were staring.

So much for anonymity, I thought. Not like I'd had much of that these last few months.

The mercenaries chatted among themselves like normal, but each group took turns to stare at me. On a normal night, that would not have bothered me, but there were too many hooded faces for my comfort. As their shrouded faces turned to look, I felt a shiver run down my spine each time. Any one of them could be the figure we'd seen on the rooftops. Any one of them could be a sorcerer in disguise.

It wasn't rational how much fear was coursing through me now that the inevitable had arrived. It was clear from the moment I used my powers that this would happen. The Malketh have long memories and they were here for me just as I had suspected. Grunting, I finished my ale and slammed the mug harder than necessary down upon the table. Those who had been watching from nearby tables jumped in their seats and turned away. This made me smile. At least some shared my fear.

"Do you want me to get us another round?" Vivienne asked, tilting her own empty goblet.

"Yes," I said, *not that it will help.*

She stood and as she strode to the bar, the mercenaries parted for her. It seemed that the fear most of them had for me extended to my friends. I kept a vigilant watch as she reached the bar and waved to Ben, the bar keep.

Ben's bald head gleamed in the candle light and he greeted Vivienne with a wide smile. I watched them as they chatted, but my mind began to wander down darker roads. It was in the middle of these wanderings that a strange noise to my side garnered my attention. My eyes snapped to the table across the room where an unfamiliar face was looking over at me. The woman's cool blue eyes were looking at me with an intense curiosity. Her blond hair curled down past either side of her narrow face and her lips were drawn into a tight line. We made eye contact and she did not look away. Instead, her gaze seemed to intensify.

I heard Vivienne set a fresh mug of ale before me and I looked down just as the frothy ale sloshed over the side. Lifting the mug, I pressed it to my lips and glanced back over to the woman. She was gone, the table empty. Scanning the room for the unknown woman, I was unsuccessful in locating her.

"What are you looking for?"

"Nothing important," I said, turning my attention back to Vivienne.

"Are you sure?"

I nodded. "It's nothing. Just overthinking things."

"Then you are convinced it is truly them?"

"Vivienne, there is not a doubt in my mind that what we saw tonight was aeromancy. I've seen it before, too many times to count."

I took another long drink. The ale was soothing and since I wasn't burning any fire within, my magic didn't immediately burn away the effects of the alcohol. Wiping my mouth with my sleeve, I leaned back in my chair and tried to organize my thoughts. So many ideas and worries were clouding my mind making it difficult to concentrate on any of them.

"What are you thinking about?" Vivienne asked, placing her elbows on the table as she leaned forward.

She tilted her head as she studied my face. Her long dark hair hung down past her face and dragged slightly on the table as she moved. I found the way she looked at me pleasantly distracting. My mood lightened somewhat and I leaned in to answer.

"I am thinking about how much destruction a fight between me and another sorcerer would be. I'm considering how many people might be killed as a result. I'm wondering if I should wait for them to make the first move. Every violent battle, all the carnage and bloodshed is just as vivid in my mind as it was when I lived it." I let out a groan and ran my hand through my hair. "I knew that they would come sooner or later. Though I was hoping for later, I am not unprepared. Still, even with my preparation, I feel helpless."

Vivienne nodded. "It's understandable to be afraid. You and I have that in common."

A wave of guilt struck me as I realized I had not once stoped to think how this was affecting Vivienne. She had just as much cause to be afraid as I did. "I'm sorry. I should have realized that this would be just as terrifying for you."

"I wouldn't go that far. They aren't here to hunt for me, though it would be a lie to say the thought of fighting people like you hasn't kept me awake a night or two."

"What scares you the most?"

I took another drink to delay my answer. Draining almost half the ale, I set the mug back down and looked Vivienne in her dark brown eyes. The thought of losing her made my heart sink. Just considering that she would die was almost too hard to think about. I opened my mouth to answer her question only to close it again. Finishing my ale, I set down the mug and began to run my finger around the rim. Taking a deep breath, I finally forced the words to come out.

"I am afraid of what destruction will be wrought as a result of our conflict. Malkethians are violent people and they do not care how many people will be hurt so long as I am captured. This creates quite the dilemma, since I do."

"What sort of destruction are you speaking of?"

"The destruction of the entire city."

Vivienne's eyes widened and she nodded. Sitting back, she grabbed her own drink and began to sip. "You think they would go that far?"

"That is the worst case scenario. They will start by attacking my friends. They'll go after Seraphina, you, and anyone they think would help me. Nothing will be off limits to them. So long as they get me, that is all that will matter."

"What will happen if they capture you?"

"They will take me back, torture me, force me back into the war. But I will be little more than a chained dog, sent in to destroy and nothing more. I can't go back to that life. I won't kill for them again."

"Something has been bothering me," Vivienne said, setting her half full goblet of wine on the table. "Why only watch us? We were out in the open. He could have attacked at any time."

"I don't think that was the intention. If so, we would have been attacked for certain. No, the aeromancer's intent was to allow us to see them."

"Are you sure?"

"Definitely. The aeromancer wanted my attention. They wanted to show off their power. What happened tonight was deliberate."

"But that doesn't answer why."

"It was to send me a message. They're here and they know who I am. They know my reputation and though I am not what I once was, I am still very capable of performing the same atrocities. Showing themselves to me tonight was a way of telling me they don't care."

"You keep saying they, but we only saw one tonight. How many do you think are here?"

"There will be at least three."

"Three?"

"An aeromancer, like who we saw tonight, is a poor match for someone like me. But I will stand little chance against a geomancer or hydromancer. But aeromancers are better scouts. When you can run on the wind, leap tall buildings, and hear things at a great distance, it's sort of a perfect pairing."

Vivienne's eyes narrowed. "I am well aware of the reputation the Malketh Spies have."

"One thing you should know, many of them rely so heavily on their magic that they overlook the simple things. You are still a better assassin than any aeromancer I've ever met."

"Don't patronize me."

"I'm being honest. You can't imagine how difficult it was for me to relearn how to fight without my magic. It's a crutch that us sorcerors rely on too heavily. But now that I think about it, the years I spent fighting without my magic has more than likely made me a better fighter. It's one advantage that I have that they will not be expecting."

"Do you think that you can fight three of them?"

I lifted my mug to take another drink, forgetting that it was empty. With a grunt, I set the mug back down. Though I wanted to give her an honest answer, I could tell what she wanted me to say from the way that she was looking at me. Before the pause could stretch too long, I answered. "I hope so."

"But you are not certain?"

"There is so much I don't know. Either way, I am already outnumbered. We might have seen only one tonight, but whoever was watching us is not in the city alone. Like I said, it is standard for them to send three. But if it were me, I would have sent more."

"I still don't understand. Why even hunt you down at all? They let you go once. Why does it matter if you use your magic or not?"

"They should have never let me go. It was a strange twist of fate that made it possible. Had my brother not died, I would never have been able to assume his identity and escape."

"Wait, you never told me that. I thought your friend Lyla gave you your freedom."

"She did. I didn't lie to you, but there are a lot of details I have never told anyone."

Vivienne finished her drink, then set her glass on the table. Leaning forward, she brushed her hair over her shoulder then looked me in the eye. "So, what exactly happened?"

"When I was holding my brother, watching him die, he told me to take his armor, to assume his identity, and to escape. Lyla helped in my deception, but warned me that they would figure it out sooner or later. She told me that if I ever used my magic again, word would eventually get back to the Malketh. Once that happened, they would track me down. They don't like people like me wandering the continent unaccounted for."

"Why not track you down before?"

"It's a big continent. But word spreads quick when a rogue pyromancer shows his face in a city like Kings Keep. Had I moved on, I would have had time to assume another identity and disappear. They might not have been able to find me. It's hard to track a sorcerer who isn't using their magic."

"But you stayed."

"I did."

"I'm glad. I wouldn't have wanted you to go."

I didn't know what to say. Part of me felt guilty for being selfish. But continuing to live without love and friendship was not something I wanted to do again. But even that thought roused deep feelings of regret. Thoughts of the friends I had lost bubbled to the surface and I looked back down to the table. Perhaps if I had left, Kori could have come with me and would still be alive. I looked longingly at the bar, the shelves of dark liquor bottles calling out to me. Though I wanted something strong, I stopped myself. *That won't help and you know it.*

"Thank you," I muttered at last, looking up at Vivienne.

She smiled at me, understanding and compassion in her face. In some small way, the way she looked at me made me feel like she understood and was not judging me for the choices I had made. Vivienne got up from her chair, circled the table and sat down beside me. She walked over to me and wrapped her arms around my waist.

Vivienne didn't say anything and neither did I. Holding each other was enough. It was one of those moments that words would be insufficient to what could be expressed through silence. A warmth spread across my chest as I held her. It felt good to still have someone to care about. As we stood, a small part of my mind began to think, planning my next move. No matter what, I would keep her safe.

CHAPTER THREE
PETRICHOR

The hot air smelled of rain. Thunder sounded from above and I looked up at the swirling tempest. The clouds which had only been in the corners of the sky, had rolled in quickly, and the wind which buffeted the trees of the garden seemed like it might topple them. A strange feeling in the wind made me feel the storm in my bones and I saw lightning flash in the clouds high above. I counted the seconds, waiting for the thunder to sound again. When the roll of thunder reached me, my count had reached thirty-seven. *Seven miles away*, I thought. It wouldn't take long for the storm to arrive. We had minutes.

Tightening my fingers around my sword, I focused my attention on the company of soldiers who had organized themselves before me upon the lawn behind Seraphina's Palace. Each looked exhausted, was covered in dirt and grime, and seemed almost unable to hold up their spears. I had been training them for hours during the heat of the day in full armor. As the storm approached, I considered training them in the rain, knowing that the added stress would make everything more difficult. I grumbled to myself undecided; wondering if harsh training would do them any good.

The catapults which launched clumps of packed mud and

straw at them were only a facsimile of what it would be like to face a geomancer. Most of the squad leaders had trained with me one-on-one, which would give them a bit of an advantage against a pyromancer. But, I had seen well trained units like this falter on the battlefield. This left me with the unanswerable question of how to provide them with the right experience that would keep them alive. It seemed that the more we practiced, the less I was convinced our tactics were truly doing anything to help. Now, more than ever, they needed to be prepared, and it was growing clear that they were not quite ready. If I had several more months to work with them, perhaps I could get them into shape. Alas, we were completely out of time.

Raising my hand, I signaled for the catapults to launch. The soldiers formed a shield wall, blocking the debris before parting to let the archers release a volley of arrows. The archers hit the straw targets which had been set up on the mound between the catapults.

Just as the arrows found their mark, another set of catapults launched packed earth and straw at them. The soldiers, tired as they were, had a hard time forming a second shield wall. Several of the slower soldiers were clobbered by the dirt and fell over, but the vast majority of them were able to deflect the attack. As before, the archers nocked their arrows and drew their bowstrings. As soon as the shields came down, they loosed their arrows which shot through the air, striking the straw targets. Sighing, I let my hand drop to my side.

Nila reached out and grabbed my arm. "Looks like you have a lot on your mind today Caden."

"Let's have them go one more round, and then we should call it for the day. We need to get things cleaned up before the rain."

"I'm fine with that." she said, raising her hand to call for one more volley.

Together we watched as the soldiers readied themselves. The

men standing at the catapults finished loading and pulled the levers. In synchronistic thuds, large clumps of packed mud and straw were launched into the air. Narrowing my eyes, I watched as the soldiers raised their shields and prepared to block the projectiles. The clumps of earth struck metal, bursting into thousands of pieces, showering the soldiers with dirt. Together they stood and not a single member faltered.

Good.

Another volley followed the first and again they were prepared. I decided it was time to give them a surprise. I signaled again, and looked to the south where I had set up additional catapults. The men who had patiently stood at attention during the entire practice pulled down on the levers and launched a third volley. With almost no time to turn and react, the large clumps of dirt and straw struck the guards and knocked them to the ground. Falling atop one another, they let out cries of pain and fury.

Terrowin, the soldier who Nila had appointed commander, looked at me from his perch beside the catapults. He gave me a stiff nod and I signaled for him to launch one final volley at the soldiers. In an instant, another half dozen balls of packed earth launched into the air towards them. Scrambling, the fallen soldiers got to their feet and formed their shield wall just in time to keep themselves from being knocked down. As the dirt slid from their shields and their armor, they remained at attention, bracing themselves for another attack.

An idea sprang into my mind and without hesitation, I acted upon it. Rushing out onto the field, I conjured two balls of flame and hurled them at the soldiers. They reacted quickly, though I could see genuine fear in their eyes. This was the first time I had ever attacked them without warning. Drawing upon the fire inside of me, I burned the grass at my feet, and used the energy to produce an enormous ball of flame above my head. The soldiers eyes widened, but they stayed in formation, linking their shields together as they had been instructed.

Thrusting my hands forward, I broke the ball of flame into a hundred smaller pieces and caused them to rain down like darts. The small needle-like flames pelted the shields, singeing the painted steel as they bounced off like sparks. Taking in a deep breath, I drew the sparks back towards me with a wave of my hand. The fire shot through the air, entered in through my fingers, and fueled the rage within. Linking the energy of the flames to the grass upon which the soldiers stood, I held out my hands and raised a wall of fire which encircled us. Meeting their hopeless expressions, I lowered my hands and relinquished my hold on the fire. When the rain of fire subsided, everything was still. The silence was broken by a loud clap of thunder from above.

Turning my attention back to the sky, I gave the signal to the commander to stop and the soldiers all collapsed to the ground to rest. These soldiers had earned a bit of rest and I was in no mood myself to be out on the field in the rain. I had proven my point, and bitter thoughts had begun to invade my mind. Each of the soldiers looked at me with fear filled expressions. Some had tears in their eyes. Guilt and shame filled me as I realized what I had done. Leaving the soldiers on the field, I returned to where Nila stood and was too ashamed to meet her eyes.

"Where did that come from?" Nila asked, her voice cold.

"I'm sorry. I got carried away."

Nila was silent and I looked back at the soldiers. I raised my hand and signaled for them to rest. Several of the soldiers dropped to the ground, letting out cries of relief. I saw that the looks of shock and fear had faded as they removed their helmets, sweat dripping from their faces and hair.

"Will you see that they are given a good meal with extra ale tonight?" I asked. "They've been training hard and I want them to be rewarded for it. Just don't let them get carried away and drink too much. I want them to be in good fighting shape for tomorrow."

"So, not the good stuff."

"Perhaps just a little. They deserve that much."

Nila held up her hand and waved to the commander that was leading the training. She signaled for them to put everything away, motioning at the sky when Commander Terrowin signaled back in protest. Terrowin began to bark his orders and the resting soldiers grumbled as they got back to their feet, though most still smiled.

"Will you be going to our meeting tonight?" she asked, reaching down and gathering her own things.

"I'm not sure that I will be able to attend this evening." When I looked at her I could tell that she was frustrated. I smiled an apology, but I knew that it wouldn't be enough.

"These men will trust you more if you get to know them."

I found myself clenching my jaw. Although I knew that she was right, there was no way that I was going to get familiar with them. They were soldiers, I was one of their leaders. It would be better if I kept my distance. As I looked at the soldiers cleaning up the field, I already felt an ache in my heart. Though I didn't know them well, it still pained me to know that if they had to fight many of them would die. If they were my friends, I knew that loss would be all the more painful.

"I understand what you mean Nila. But it would be best if they saw me only as a leader and nothing more. I'll have to have you apologize to them for me that I was otherwise occupied."

"Did you not know those who led you into battle?"

"Of course I knew them, but those who led me into battle and those who led the army rarely shared the same company."

"Do you think that was right?"

I paused considering the question. It took me a moment to process my gut reaction and put them into words. I looked in her dark brown eyes, then spoke. "I don't really have an answer for you. Battles are won by those who are and who are not on the battlefield for there are two fights; one of body and one of mind. Not all those who lead must fight and not all who fight must lead."

"Though we do not share the same point of view, I get what you are trying to say. I think that the best leaders win the hearts of men by their example and not by their command alone. A true leader should fight alongside their soldiers."

"Trust me, the time is soon upon us when fighting will be a reality. I cannot be everywhere. They need to learn to handle themselves independent of me. I cannot fight every battle and if they expect me to be with them, they will not be ready. But do not think I will not be in the throng of battle alongside my men."

"That is why we need you at our meetings. You are the only one who understands what we are up against. I cannot prepare them for things I do not understand."

"I don't think that is possible."

The look Nila gave me was sharp, her eyes growing narrow and her nostrils flaring. "Then what is the point?" She growled after she spoke and I took a moment before answering. "Why the hell are we doing all of this if there is no way to succeed?"

"Because there is a chance it will help some of them survive. I want as many of them to live as possible and though this may not be enough to help them win, perhaps it will be enough to help them live."

Nila reached up and rubbed the bridge of her nose. "So that is what it is. You're afraid that they are going to die?"

"Are you not?"

"Of course. But that is always the risk of fighting. What I don't understand is why you are doubting the training method we spent hours devising and improving for months?"

"I thought we would have more time. I honestly think that

there is no better way for us to prepare them than what we have done. However, watching them today, I couldn't help but think about how well they would fare if they were attacked today. Based on what I saw today, I worry that it won't be enough."

"You have been so certain that they will be coming for you, that we will need to defend ourselves against other sorcerers. Tell me, did I ever once question you, challenge your certainty?"

"No. You did not."

"Did you ever stop to wonder why?"

She looked at me as I considered her question. *Had I even thought beyond my own selfish worrying?*

Realizing that I had not, I looked down at my boots, slightly ashamed. "I'm sorry to say, but no. I haven't even given it a passing thought until now."

"The reason I believe you is because I have seen first hand what the Malketh will do when they are scorned. I have seen Sorcerers hunt down simple deserters who had taken refuge in my village. Our city was completely destroyed by the Malketh Army, and with nothing left, we abandoned our homeland and fled south. The thought that I will one day have to face such a foe has filled my nightmares. I have spent many sleepless nights worrying about that day."

Nila paused, pushed several of her long black braids over her shoulder, and turned to look over the guards as they shuffled towards the barracks we had set up for them. The new wooden buildings were hidden behind a line of trees at the mountain side of Seraphina's estate. They were now too large a force to be properly housed within the palace and still be prepared to fight at a moment's notice. I watched Nila as she studied the field, her tongue prodding the inside of her cheek as she thought.

"Tell me Caden. When they do come for you, do you think it will be to take you or to kill you?"

"That's the true question, isn't it?" Taking a deep breath, I found myself looking at the ground not wanting to answer. "I have often wondered about that. If I were to give my best guess, it would be that they will want to take me. Should they wish to execute me, that doesn't seem like something they would do here."

"And if they don't want to execute you?"

"Then they will want me back for the war. I fear they have ways to make me do their bidding. I met a deserter once. He had his hands cut off and his tongue removed. Still, because he was a sorcerer, they kept him alive and used him to fight." I shivered. "That is my biggest fear. I don't want to end up like that."

"If it is of any comfort, we aren't going to stand idly by and let them take you." Nila motioned to the now clear training ground. "Is that not what we have been preparing for?"

"I know, and that means more to me than you could possibly imagine." I didn't tell her that if it came down to it, I would turn myself in before letting them get involved. I was done losing friends.

Strangely, I found a small part of myself hoping that would not be the case and that I would be left alone. I quashed the feeling and drove the thought from my mind knowing that I would have to face up to it later. Someone was already here. It was too late for those kinds of thoughts.

We were silent for a moment and a flash of lighting from above, followed by a clap of thunder, shattered the peaceful silence of the afternoon once again. Small droplets of rain began to fall and the raw earthy smell of wet dirt and grass began to fill the air.

"I'm not going to stay here and get wet." Nila took a step towards the palace but stopped when I did not move to follow her. "Are you coming?"

"Go on ahead. I think I will enjoy the rain for a moment."

She gave me a strange look, as if she thought I were mad as a hatter or worse. When the sprinkles of rain began to fall more steadily, she hurried off, leaving me alone on the training field.

At first the rain seemed warm; the hot summer afternoon grew murky and humid as the first drops evaporated on the hot ground. Once the rain began to fall in earnest, it turned cold and as each drop struck me, it felt like being struck by shards of ice. The water streamed down my armor and my face. The lightning flashed every few minutes and the thunder seemed amplified as it came down off the slopes of the mountain. The wind began to blow furiously and soon the rain began to fall at a sharp angle, pelting my face uncomfortably. Closing my eyes, I began to think as the droplets stung my skin. The cold did not bother me. The fire that burned calmly within was like a small sun, providing me with warmth. Taking in a deep breath, I opened my eyes and watched as steam began to rise from my skin, the rain evaporating the moment it came into contact with my flesh. The steam formed a strange mist which began to float around me, drifting towards the ground and hovering above the trampled grass.

I found my thoughts wandering to the large Dryad tree and the small grove which was sheltered below it. I wondered if it too was protected from this storm as it had been from the cold winter snow, or if the rain cascaded down to water the bed of flowers which covered the graves of my friends. I could hardly believe it had been seven months and I had not visited once. Part of me felt guilty for not doing so; but the bigger part of me had no desire to lay my eyes upon that place ever again. It was time for me to find a way to move on. Nevertheless, the pain still remained. The agony of their loss was a burden I could barely carry, but I could not let myself break.

It was with a heavy heart that I slowly made my way from the training grounds, through the garden paths, to Seraphina's palace. The towers and windowed walls loomed darkly above and sheets of water fell from the slanted rooftop. Entering through one of the servants' doors by the kitchens, the steam continued to rise from my semi-wet armor. Within a few moments, I was completely dry and left no water tracks as I went. When I finally did make my way to my rooms, I did so with reluctant steps. I did not want to return to a place where I would have nothing to do but sit around and stew. Though I did have to admit to myself that deep inside I craved to be alone and away from watchful eyes.

Arriving at my room, I locked the door behind me and reaching out my finger, placed it atop the wick of a candle and brought it to life. The flame burned bright blue for a moment before settling down to the familiar orange. From that one candle, I linked the remaining wicks and in the blink of an eye, they all ignited, the small flames brightening the room with a warm orange glow. Rain still beat against the windows and the dark clouds without cast a cool gray shadow over the trees. The constant drumming of raindrops on glass was more soothing than I had expected.

I walked to my closet, taking off my armor and setting it on the stand which I had set up for display. Dressed in dark pants and a loose shirt, I returned to my sitting room where I took a seat on the couch beside the hearth. Glancing over at the unlit stack of wood, I muttered a quick thanks to the Valon under my breath. Stretching forth my hand, I moved the flame from a candle to the hearth and a fire ignited bright and warm in an instant. The room was cool from the storm and the fire helped stave off the chill. While neither heat nor cold affected me, I could still feel them and heat was by far my preference. After a while, I found myself looking around the room, studying the long drapes that hung on either side of the large windows. The rain continued to beat against the glass and water spilled from the roof above, splashing down onto my balcony.

The walls were bare of any artwork though there were several spots where holes were left in the stone walls from previous hangings. I didn't care much for wall decorations, or tapestries in my private rooms and Seraphina hadn't objected when I'd asked her to have them removed. While it was nice to have wonderful furniture and some luxury, I liked thinking without distraction. To me, there was no point hiding away art in my room where it could be enjoyed by others more frequently. Since their removal, the room was starting to feel more like a permanent residence and I was finally beginning to feel at home in the palace.

The sitting area around me was made up of three couches, a table, and an armchair. They were arranged so they were all facing the fire and I quite liked sitting here to think. On the sofa across from where I was sitting was a small shawl which Vivienne must have forgotten last night. Finding myself smiling as I looked upon it, I wondered when she would be getting back. I said a silent prayer to the Valon that she would be safe and I kicked up my feet and rested back on the sofa.

After a moment, I looked over at the large four poster bed that had been tended to and the pillows had been fluffed. The dresser on the left side of the bed was dark polished wood and a cleaned lantern sat atop it, the panes of glass scrubbed of the black oil soot. My eyes lingered on the bottom drawer of the dresser and the brass keyhole in the center. Reaching up to my neck, I felt for the brass key which was safely tucked away beneath my shirt. The sharp anxiety which had raised my heart in alarm was expelled. As I let out a breath, I considered opening the drawer and examining its contents. I felt a little reluctant, but having already checked them this morning, I forced myself to forget about it. Making a mental note to find a new hiding place, I patted my shirt over the key and relaxed back into the cushions.

All the things which needed my attention rattled around in the back of my mind, irritating my peace like a sore on my tongue or a splinter in my thumb. No matter how much I tried to ignore it, there was a relentless reminder that would never leave me be. What was the most infuriating about these intrusive thoughts was how difficult it was to get up and do anything about them. It was as if the walls around me were closing in and if I would just get to my feet and hold out my hand, I could keep them from crushing me. But as easy as it seemed to do so, I could not get myself to get up. And so, I sat and brooded, resting upon the couch cushions which were growing softer and more inviting by the second.

As sleep began to overtake me, a soft humming spoke in my mind. *Soon, my child,* the voice said. *Soon we will be ready.* Then my world was engulfed by darkness.

CHAPTER FOUR
RITE OF AHNIR

The festival had already begun when our carriage pulled through the gates to Shanrice Palace. Once we were past the gates, the smooth cobblestone drive ended abruptly at a set of five marble steps. Waiting for the coach to open the door, I looked over at Vivienne who gave me a sly smile. The door opened and Vivienne stepped out first, the hem of her scarlet dress touching the ground for just a moment. Following her, I looked up at the brightly lit palace and found myself admiring the decadence.

The front of the palace was separated into three distinct parterres, the middle parterre had a long rectangular pool which was shallow and filled with floating lanterns. Nobles, wealthy merchants, and other high born aristocrats gathered together and two noblemen who had been chatting at the top of the steps looked down and glared at me with disdain. They turned away from us and walked away, whispering among themselves.

"As popular as ever," I muttered to Vivienne, whose radiant smile hadn't faded a bit.

"We can make it through the evening. Besides, Seraphina requested that we be here."

"Will Pricilla be here?" There was a slight vibrato in my voice as I asked the question. I hadn't had a personal conversation with the Queen since her coronation and though I was officially pardoned of any culpability surrounding the death of her sister, I felt like I still was on shaky ground. Every time I had attended a social gathering where she was present, I had been ignored or avoided. Part of me wondered if tonight would be any different.

"She will make an appearance."

"Outstanding."

"Caden, at least try to enjoy yourself. No one here is out to get you."

"I will do my best."

Holding out my arm, I let Vivienne link hers with mine and I led her towards the palace. Together we walked up the dozen steps and strode along the square pond, all the while admiring the lights and decorations. All of the guests recognized me, and most were gracious enough to pretend to ignore us. Still, from the corners of my eyes, I watched as they began to feverishly chat and point as soon as we passed. Stiffening, I raised my chin and continued on, determined to pay them no notice.

When we reached the front of the palace, we saw Tristin and Nero standing in a rather sizable group of lesser nobles and city judges. Though some of the faces were familiar, the only other person I knew was Lady Leonora who's red hair was woven into an elaborate braid. Of the nobles who had been supportive of Aveza, Leonora had not shown true loyalty like the rest. It made me wonder if her allegiances now stood with Queen Pricilla or not. As I observed them, one of the women in the group I did not know made a gesture towards us and everyone looked. Flashing them my practiced smile, I led Vivienne to the group.

"We were just discussing how extravagant Lord and Lady Shanrice are with the decorations." Tristin said as we joined.

"Clearly no expense was spared," Vivienne politely said,

"though I am certain that both Valdemar and Riez are honored to hold the festival on their estate."

"Of course," Leonora said, the other group members nodding in agreement. "But to celebrate the Valon of Life, we must do all we can."

"When does the Rite commence?" The man who spoke was someone I did not know by name. He was tall and thin, with shoulder length auburn hair.

"At sunset," Leonora replied. "The Queen means to make a speech and then the celebration will begin. Of course, there will be song and dance until then."

"Where is the Queen?" Vivienne asked.

"The high lords and ladies are all gathered together in private to commence the evening's festivities," Tristin answered. She gave me a narrow eyed look before turning to Nero. She whispered something in his ear and the man nodded. Half of his face was covered by a scarlet mask which was perforated on the left side with hundreds of needle sized holes. The right side was painted with black pine cone like designs.

Nero looked at me and motioned to the side. Leaving Vivienne to socialize with the others, I retreated to the side of the garden path with Nero who was clasping his hands behind his back.

"Something wrong?" I asked. My eyes glanced back at the group we had left and noticed most were still looking at us.

"Tristin wanted me to give you a warning."

"Oh? And this couldn't have been delivered earlier?"

"We only just found out and it's too late to do anything about it. She just wants you to be prepared."

"Fine, what is happening?"

"The Queen is going to ban the practice of sorcery within the walls of Kings Keep, under penalty of death."

"Oh," I said, my blood running cold. "I can't say that I am surprised. But why has she waited until tonight?"

"I haven't the slightest idea. But it makes sense why she specifically requested that Seraphina invite you."

"Why wasn't I told the Queen requested me here?"

Nero shrugged. "Another good question I don't know the answer to. However, I expect the Queen wishes to make a public show of her power by humiliating you. That's why Tristin wanted me to warn you. Make sure you are prepared."

"Will this new law apply to past offenses?"

"I do not know. Tristin doesn't think so. But the intent is to ensure that you know exactly what is in store should you use magic within the city again."

"Shit, that's going to make things rather difficult."

"If we are wrong, and she is planning on arresting you on charges of past instances of sorcery, Tristin has planned your escape."

Nero pulled a small envelope from within his coat. Taking the folded yellowed parchment from him, I saw there was no wax seal. Placing the envelope into the right breast pocket of my own jacket, I ran my hands down the front, smoothing the fabric. The small attempt to quell my anxiety didn't work and I found myself eyeing the guards who stood atop the palace walls. They were looking directly at me. As soon as they noticed I was watching, they turned and looked down upon the party guests. When I glanced at the other guards who were posted around the room, each was looking at me. They too looked away once they noticed I was looking at them. I felt the hair on the back of my neck stand on end and a chill rushed down the sides of my face.

"Whatever happens, we have your back Caden. You know that, right?"

"I do. And it's more appreciated than you know."

As I turned to go, Nero caught my arm. I looked at the man in his dark eyes and saw a severe concern within them.

"Be careful Caden."

"May the Valon guide us all," I replied.

We rejoined the group and Vivienne looped her arm with mine. The conversation felt stilted and forced, everyone going through the motions. If what Nero had told me was true, my presence was most likely contributing to how everyone was acting. I was only able to stand the uncomfortableness of the conversation for a few minutes before I politely excused myself, eager to get a drink.

Vivienne smiled, muttered a polite goodby, and followed me.

"Sorry about that," I whispered, leading Vivienne towards the doors to the palace.

"Not a problem. What did Nero have to say?"

Patting my pocket, I looked down at the ground for a moment before repeating what Nero had told me.

"Unbelievable," Vivienne hissed. "What are we going to do?"

"Well, we will need to be careful and ready to leave at a moment's notice."

"Well, let's get that drink."

The Shandrice Palace doors were tall and thin, the polished white painted wood shimmering in the late evening light. There was a small entryway which opened up into a great square atrium. The roof was filled with stained glass windows and light from the setting sun streamed in, painting the walls with different shades of blue and green. Each side of the atrium had a large marble staircase and at the far end was another set of doors which revealed a packed ballroom.

Servants stood all around, carrying trays of glass flutes filled with white wines. A waiter gracefully strode from the edge of the room and presented a tray of drinks to us. I nodded to him, grabbed a glass flute from the tray, and took a drink. The wine was aromatic and very sweet. Though not my typical drink choice, it was pleasant enough. A small fire which I always kept burning in my stomach ate at the alcohol, burning it immediately.

Though I was regretful not to feel the effects of the drink, I wasn't about to let myself get drunk tonight, not even for an instant.

We sauntered down the atrium towards the ballroom which was already filled with hundreds of people. I was still getting strange looks, but there were enough people inside that we began to blend in with the crowd. Inside the ball room, the sound of music filled the air so strongly that it masked the din of chattering voices. In the right back corner of the ballroom sat a stage where a company of two dozen musicians sat, playing string and brass instruments. There was a row of percussion behind, the large drums and symbols complementing the pleasant melody. In the opposite corner was another stage, filled with dancers. They performed in elaborate costumes of silk, long trailing fabric sashes and dresses accentuating their movements.

We quietly found a spot in the corner beside a pillar and watched. I could tell by the way Vivienne was shifting back and forth on her feet that she was agitated. The left side of her mouth kept twitching and her eyes were narrow as she scanned the room. I found myself smiling at her and when she noticed, her eyes narrowed further. Letting out a laugh, I took another drink.

"You don't seem to be as angry as I am," she said, taking a sip of her own drink.

"Trust me, I'm rather angry. But there isn't anything I can do about it. Besides, there is one benefit to this predicament."

"Oh, and what is that?"

"If I am not allowed to use sorcery within the walls of Kings Keep, then neither can our friends from the north."

"Do you truly think they will care enough to follow the laws?"

"There is a chance it will make them more careful. If Pricilla truly wants to enforce a law such as this, then the entire city guard will have to be on alert. It would be quite difficult to deal with all of them and for that inconvenience alone, I think they will go along with it at first."

"We'll see," Vivienne muttered, taking a much larger sip of her wine.

The music swelled, the soft melody rising in crescendo as the song came to an end. All the patrons erupted in applause and the conductor bowed. Raising his thin batton, he waved to his right and a row of strings began to play, another soft melodic song taking the place of the first. Partygoers began to break off in pairs, entering the dance floor to softly twirl together. I turned to look at Vivienne who was sipping at her flute of wine and looking at the dance floor with longing eyes.

"Would you like to dance?" I asked, setting down my own glass of wine and holding out my hand.

"Of course," Vivienne said, quickly finishing her wine before setting it down on a table.

Taking her hand, I led her onto the dance floor and together we began to sway. Her scarlet dress spun around our legs and as the tempo of the song began to pick up, we began to dance with a more swift pace. Vivienne smiled as we danced and I felt myself enjoying the simple moment.

"A lot has happened since the first time we did this," I whispered, leaning close so my lips were inches from her ear. "Let's hope that this evening doesn't end with a bloody attack."

Vivienne shook her head and the scent of her perfumed hair drifted all around. "Let's hope not."

"Though, I am glad that Seraphina sent you to dance with me."

"Is that what you think happened?"

I raised my eyebrow and gave Vivienne a crooked smile before twirling her. As she finished spinning, I ran my hand along her arm before placing it once more on her waist. "I suppose that is what I assumed."

"Seraphina had asked me to introduce myself during the party and to speak with you. She figured that you would be more open to speaking with me if you didn't know I worked for her."

"So, to spy on me."

"Since that is what I do, it only made sense. But after seeing you rejected several times, I took pity on you."

"I'm glad you did."

"Me too," she said, drawing close. "Though you're still not much of a dancer."

We danced the rest of the song, keeping close together, her head resting on my shoulder. As the music tapered off, a regal figure stepped up onto the platform and everyone began to bow. Queen Pricilla was dressed in a gown of white and lilac, her auburn hair curling past her shoulders. An elegant crown sat atop her head, the golden band looking almost like metal lacework.

My heart dropped and I instinctively began to retreat to the back of the room. Vivienne followed and our retreat was easy since most wished the opposite. Before the Queen spoke a single word, we were in the back of the room standing against the wall. My eyes darted to the door and I calculated how I could make a swift exit. There were no guards standing in wait; as far as I could see.

"Dearest Lords and Ladies, wonderful subjects of the crown, in commencement of this night, I wish to make several decrees to seal my new reign in the blessing of Ahnir."

Everyone remained quiet as the Queen looked around the room. We were far enough away that I could just make out the details of her face. After a moment, her eyes found me and did not waver.

"First, I wish to acknowledge Baron Hutchrish who is now the Lord of his house. May we take a moment of silence to remember his father Deserak who was slain in the vile attack which also claimed the life of my sister, the former Queen."

The room was silent as a tomb and most bowed their heads in

respect. While I lowered my head with everyone else, I kept my eyes trailed on Pricilla who was still glaring daggers at me. The moment of silence only lasted a minute and as everyone raised their heads, Pricilla held up her hands.

"Thank you. May the Valon bless us with renewed life and light!" Pricilla cried.

"Valon bless us with life and light!" The crowd chanted.

"May the blessing of Ahnir be upon us in this new season."

The crowd repeated the chant.

"For my second decree, I would like to announce that Lord and Lady Shanrice will take over the estates which formerly belonged to House Renor."

A series of gasps spread from the crowd, but the voices were quickly hushed. The Queen raised her hand and silence once again descended upon them.

"And for my final decree of this evening, in the best interest and preservation of this city, I hereby declare that any use of magic or sorcery within my domain will be outlawed. Any person caught performing sorcery or aiding in its practice will be put to death."

A chill rushed down my body and I looked up at Pricilla whose face was grave. Her eyes narrowed and she finally looked away from me. She lowered her hands and I noticed that they were clenched into fists.

"If you will all join me outside, let us gather on the field for the Rite of Ahnir."

The Queen was escorted from the stage by several tall guards in full plate armor. She was led through glass doors onto a large lawn. All of the other guests began to file out and I saw Seraphina among them. She was walking beside Lord and Lady Shandrice. Lord Valdemar glanced my way before leaning over to whisper something in his wife's ear. Lady Riez looked my way and nodded. They immediately looked away and Seraphina only spared us a glance.

"What was that?" Vivienne asked.

"Why don't you go try to find Tristin. I think I will forgo participating in the Rite this evening."

"Are you sure?"

"I think it is for the best."

"Alright." Vivienne gave my hand a small squeeze before stalking off, joining the crowd as they filtered out of the ball room to join the Queen out on the field. The far wall was made of large glass windows, similar to how Seraphina's palace ballroom was built. I was able to see the large flags which were set up around the field and the baskets of flower petals which were being passed around.

Leaning against a pillar, I began to think, wondering what I was supposed to do. The Queen's decree had hit me like a stone and I had a continued sinking feeling in my gut. Although Nero had warned me, it hadn't lessened the blow as much as I thought it would. I felt guilty, knowing that I had brought this fate down upon myself. Though it wasn't intentional, the responsibility was mine to bear. I owed the dead that much.

"Good to see you Caden, it's been a while." The gruff voice sent a more profound chill down my spine.

Turning, I looked at the bear of a man who was standing against a wall with his arms folded. His bald head gleamed in the torchlight and he had a short black beard. The man's clothing was exceptionally fine, the deep earth toned shirt and slacks tailored to accentuate his massive form. Hanging from his neck was a necklace of multi-colored stones, each the size of an acorn.

"It's been a long time, Isar. You look well for your age."

"For a dead man, so do you." Isar's lips were pressed to a line and his eyes were still narrow as if he were scowling.

As I looked at him, a deep sense of loathing filled me, making my stomach churn. "I was wondering who they would send. Now that you are here, I should never have doubted it would have been you."

"You have no idea how long I have waited for this."

"So what now? Are you here to take me home?"

"No," Isar said, a devious smile spreading across his lips. "Not tonight."

I froze, unsure how to react. Isar had caught me off guard and I looked around the nearly empty ballroom. Aside from a few servants removing empty glasses from tables, everyone else had filtered out onto the back lawn. Even the musicians and dancers had left, their instruments abandoned on the stage. Rays from the setting sun struck the windows and cast long beams across the polished stone floor.

"If you are not here to take me, why did you come here tonight?" I asked, turning my attention back to the bald man.

"To give you a warning."

I glared at the man, waiting. When he did not speak, I growled.

"What warning?" I asked through gritted teeth.

"That we will make an example of you. That we will break you before we drag your pathetic hide back to Malketh."

"Good luck."

Isar laughed, unfolded his arms, and rubbed his hands together.

"Caden, you have not changed a bit. I'm glad. I was half expecting you to be...docile."

My lips pulled back in an involuntary snarl. "You wish."

"Come, let us join the festivities. I would love to meet that wonderful woman you were standing with. She, by all accounts, seemed lovely."

Isar turned to walk away but I stayed in place. He only made it a few steps before turning around. Isar smiled and shook his head. "Very well, we shall all become better acquainted soon enough." Isar pulled a cigar from inside his pocket. "Would you mind lighting this for me?"

The man smiled wide as he smelled the rolled tobacco. Licking his lips, he placed the cigar in his mouth.

"I forgot, you aren't allowed to do that any longer." Isar tsked, removed a box of matches from his cloak, and struck the tip. He began to light the cigar, slowly puffing out small streams of smoke as he did so.

I willed the fire to burn hot, drawing out the power. The match burned down to the end and Isar cursed, flicking it away. I extinguished the small burning pieces of tobacco leaving Isar with an unlit cigar. He sucked on the end and drew another match from his box. This time when he struck it, no fire erupted from the phosphorus tip. Growling, he looked me in the eyes and I smiled.

"Seems like you're having some trouble there. Sorry, I wish I could help."

Isar glared at me for a moment longer before removing the unlit cigar from his mouth to tuck it away in his jacket. "Enjoy the rest of the festivities, Caden. Consider it a mercy."

Without another word, the Malkethian turned and left, quickly striding out of the ballroom. I could hear the echo of his boots on the polished marble floor long after he had passed from view. I waited and listened until I could no longer hear him. Turning to look through the windows, I was taken aback by the brilliance of the setting sun. The mountains which loomed above the ridge were glowing red like fire. The partially cloudy sky was darkening to a brilliant orange and long purple shadows crawled down the mountain slopes towards us.

As the day's last remaining life began to fade, I felt my remaining hope diminish; a sense of doom settling into my stomach. It was time to fight, and the new monster I faced wasn't one I was confident I could defeat. Retaining a small amount of my composure, I left the ballroom and exited through one of the glass doors which opened onto the back patio. The chanting had begun and as the sun set, the Rite of Ahnir was complete. Cheers from the crowd sounded hollow to my ears and sinking soul.

My eyes scanned the crowd of nobles and aristocrats. Across the field towards the center, standing before Queen Pricilla was Seraphina. She was looking at me, a grave expression on her face. I saw the warning in her eyes, the pleading of a trapped animal. The unspoken moment passed and Seraphina looked away, her regal mask returning.

Cautiously, I turned around and went back into the palace. Finding a secluded hallway, I stopped by one of the wall torches, I pulled out the folded parchment Nero had given me. Opening the note, I noticed the scrawling handwriting belonged to Seraphina.

> *Caden,*
> *Tonight will test the bonds of all our loyalties. What I do, I do for the preservation of all. Enclosed are Tristin's explicit instructions on a method of escape. I wished that they would not be necessary, but what else are preparations for?*
> *Seraphina*

I read the instructions twice over. They were simple and everything I would need had been accounted for. I visualized each step, memorizing them before I folded up the paper and placed it back into my pocket.

Tristin, you're as clever as ever.

The servants watched me, but did nothing as I walked alone through the ballroom and back into the front atrium. No one was waiting for me when I opened the palace doors, and I found the entire front parterre abandoned. The long rectangular pool was lit with the light of hundreds of small lanterns. A breeze from behind caused the water to ripple and the floating lanterns to wobble. The light flickered and I instinctively drew a bit of fire within myself.

The fire coursed through my blood, replacing my unease with tranquil power. Straightening my back, I began to walk along the pool when I heard the sound of footsteps behind me. Turning, I saw Vivienne in her scarlet dress glide out the front doors of the palace as she walked towards me. I stopped, waited for her to join me, my heart sinking. She was so beautiful and my heart began to race. I couldn't help but feel immense regret that there wasn't more time. She deserved better than what was about to happen.

"Where are you going?"

"Back to the palace," I answered.

"Why?"

"I have to go. It's better if I go alone"

Vivienne's eyebrows furrowed. "What's going on?"

"They're here." Removing the letter from my jacket, I handed it to her. "Read and then burn that. It will tell you everything you need to know."

Vivienne took the letter with tentative fingers. "I don't understand. Why can't I come with you"

"It's time I face this inevitable end."

Without another word, I turned and walked away. I suddenly knew what I needed to do. There was no turning from this course. Everything was about to end just as I had always suspected. In ashes.

CHAPTER FIVE

MAW

When I arrived at the end of the front parterre, I descended the stone steps to the gravel drive when I was struck from behind. The force knocked me to my knees and the back of my neck felt cold and wet. Reaching up, I whipped at whatever had struck me. Looking at my hand, I saw only water. Grunting, I climbed back to my feet and turned around. Standing atop the six stone steps was a tall thin man. His brown hair was cut short, in a similar fashion to my own, and his face was cleanly shaven. The man had a square jawline and pronounced cheekbones. However, his most prominent feature was his stone gray eyes.

His clothing was simple and his shirt had no sleeves, leaving his muscled arms bare. On both wrists were beaded bracelets of turquoise stones that shimmered like water. On his back was a large waterskin, the straps criss crossing across his chest. Though I did not recognize the man, it was clear to me what he was. As he took a single step towards me, I took a tentative step backward. Glaring up at the hydromancer, I felt a chill rush down my spine.

So, you didn't come alone after all. Just as the thought entered my mind, I heard footsteps on the gravel drive behind me. My eyes lingered on the hydromancer standing above me and instinctively reached for my sword. My hand felt nothing but air.

"It is a shame you did not listen to me Caden. I told you to enjoy the night."

Whirling around, I watched Isar step through the palace gate. He was holding a large war hammer which was propped up and resting against his shoulder. A short blond woman stepped out of the shadows behind him, a long cloak draped around her nimble frame. She looked at me with cold blue eyes and a knowing smile. I recognized her and an image of the woman sitting across the tavern at Ravens Cross flashed before my eyes. My eyes narrowed and I scowled at the woman.

"Caden, I would like you to meet Malin," Isar motioned to the woman walking beside him, "and Nels," he said, pointing to the man standing behind me.

Malin's smile widened and she waved her fingers at me. Of the three Malkethian's, she was the only one who was not looking at me with hostile eyes.

"We will be your escorts as we take you back to Demoth for judgment. Lyla is most anxious for your return."

I felt a strange twinge at hearing him utter my old friend's name. For a moment I wondered what she would think of me before I realized I no longer cared. That strange and sudden realization helped me regain my composure. Straightening up, I shrugged and let out a sigh.

"Whatever you do, I will not be going back."

"What do you think is going to happen? Do you really think that you have a choice?" Isar scoffed. "You can't fight us. You can't win. Not alone, anyway."

"Isar, have you forgotten who I am?" I took a step towards the man, letting the fire within me grow. With no talisman, no sword, no armor, I was at a severe disadvantage; but not one that couldn't be overcome. If they would make me a fugitive of the city, I could accept that. There were places to run, places to hide. And only a few palaces down, a small army was prepared. I only had to last long enough to make my escape.

"I knew you all too well, betrayer."

"Betrayer? That is one way to see it. But that is far from all I am. You know me as the destroyer of armies, the demon of the north. You have seen thousands fall to my storms of flames. Do you truly wish to bring down that destruction upon yourselves?"

"But would you bring such destruction upon all that you love?" Malin's voice was sweet and sounded almost like a purr. "You care for these people. At least some of them. Would you be willing to let them die just to delay the inevitable?"

I looked at Malin and though her blue eyes were kind, there was a resolve there. She was just as determined as the other two and shared in their desires. I had no clever retort nor did I wish to lie and try to deny the truth of her words. My jaw clenched and I once again reached to my side where my sword should have been.

"We know you Caden, both for who you were and who you have become. The demon of the north is long dead. You are but an imp in comparison." Isar said, walking down the stone steps to join us on the gravel drive. "I have prepared to face you for years, waiting anxiously for this moment."

"Do you not think we are prepared?" Nels soft voice was like flowing water, his accent strange, each vowel oddly pronounced.

I turned to look at him. "If any one of us uses magic tonight, we will find the entire city guard to be our enemy."

Isar chuckled, "Trivial, and you know that."

"Besides," Malin added. "We have a written pardon. Pricilla has been more than accommodating to our needs."

A shiver ran down my spine and the sting of betrayal was

sharper than it should have been. I did not blame her for wanting revenge and I was a fool for thinking it would not come. Scowling, my eyes looked down at my boots. My shame was replaced by a calm anger. With renewed defiance, I looked up at my old friend, setting aside my petty hatred and saw him for what he was. A new enemy in a long line of enemies.

You're not even the worst among them, I thought.

"This is your last chance to submit peacefully. You can still return and enjoy the night."

"So, if I understand. Your intent is not to just take me away from the city tonight."

"No," Isar answered. "There are those who are not done with you here. But if you submit willingly, this whole experience will be more pleasant."

"What other choice do you have?" Malin asked softly. She seemed to be presenting a more kind front, balancing out the overly blunt anger of Isar. "Did you really think there would not be consequences?"

"I did not think that for a moment," I admitted. "You are not the only one who has been preparing for this."

There were only two choices ahead, submit or resist. Either way, I was at an inevitable crossroads that would see my time at Kings Keep come to an end. But I was determined to make it an end of my choosing and these bastards were going to see exactly what I was capable of. Though I was no longer the demon of the north, I was still his shadow and that had to count for something. I made the only decision I could, one that was decided upon years ago, but it was not as easy to follow through with as it should have been.

Drawing upon the fire I still had within me, I conjured a ball of flame and linked the fire to the large trees which stood on either side of the gates to Shandrice Palace. The leaves withered, turning black, then gray, and then crumbled. As the ash fell, the fire in my hands expanded, forming an orb of flame which completely engulfed my body. The Malkethian Sorcerers leapt back from the sudden heat, providing me with an opportunity to act. Holding my hands high, I caused the flames to erupt outwards in all directions.

As they leapt further away, I darted forward, sprinted through the gate and onto the road. Glancing over my shoulder, I watched as Nels waved his hands, bringing a wave of water from the pool above to douse the fire. Without hesitation, I turned the corner and began to sprint towards Seraphina's palace.

I could see the large spires in the distance, looming high in the night. Small flickers of light from tower windows looked like floating lanterns in the gloom. Three palaces stood between me and my destination which was more than a mile's run. It immediately became clear that if I was going to follow Tristin's plan, I would need to find a way to get there first. With renewed anxiety, I quickened my pace, sprinting as fast as my legs would carry me.

As I sprinted, the cobblestones beneath me began to tremble, and my feet slipped on the shifting stones. The unnatural movements were familiar, and I was prepared for them. Leaping into the air, I twisted back around and held my left hand towards Isar. The geomancer's large hammer struck the ground, and a series of cracks began branching out in all directions. He heaved his mighty hammer again and slammed it into the stones once more. A section of the road beneath me shot into the air and struck my side. Gasping, I dropped to one knee.

My eyes swam and blinking away the pain, I took a deep breath to focus. Burning the trunks of the leafless trees beside the gate to fuel my fire, I cast a lance of flame at the geomancer. Water rose from the ground, forming a wall between my fire and Isar, drowning out my fire lance. Steam drifted up as the water evaporated from the heat. While my attack was thwarted by the hydromancy, the ground had stopped shaking, allowing me to gain my footing and continue towards Seraphina's Palace.

Keeping my eyes focused on the path ahead, I used my other senses to detect the sorcerer's inevitable pursuit. A sharp whistling sounded in my ears and a hundred paces ahead, a small cloaked figure dropped from the sky. Malin drifted down to the ground like a diving hawk. When she was a few feet from the ground, her movement slowed to a near stop, the edges of her cloak billowing around her as the wind buffeted the fabric. Landing lightly upon her feet, the aeromancer held out both arms and clapped. The sound from the clap deafening me to the other sounds of the night. With ringing in my ears, I took a hesitant step forward. Malin reacted quickly, thrusting forward her hand. The moment after I saw her movements, a strong gust of wind blasted against me. Bracing myself against the wind, I took a few steps forward and felt like I was trying to walk through a stone wall.

Malin waved her arms again and another wall of air crashed against me like a wave, knocking me to the ground. Landing hard on my back, a cobblestone jabbed my side and knocked the air from my lungs. Gasping for air, I rolled onto my side and pushed myself up onto my elbows. Another gust of wind struck me and I rolled with the air, using the new momentum to get back onto my feet. Slightly disoriented, I flailed my arms for balance and choked in a breath.

Igniting a flame on just the tips of my fingers, I took a stance facing the city so my right side was facing Malin and my left was facing Isar and Nels. I forced out my breath and waited for the span of three heartbeats. Malin raised her hands and a large gust of wind nearly tore the trees on either side of her to the ground, leaves blasting into the sky. Then, the leaves and debris shot towards me. Smiling, I flared the fire burning on my fingers, burning the shredded leaves and twigs as they soared towards me. When the enormous gust of wind slammed into me, the debris had turned to ash and the fire swirling around me was like a forgefire. The wind acted like bellows, strengthening and growing the fire as they floated around me like ribbons. Putting all the energy within me into the flames, I released them to the wind and watched as they soared backwards towards Isar and Nels.

The two men leapt to the side as the swirling ribbons of fire shot towards them. My fire was carried from Malin's wind engulfed the two sorcerers as they rolled on the ground. Taking in a deep breath, I drew the fire back towards me, burning the dozen trees which lined the cliff side of the street. The well of fire within me swelled as the trees disintegrated to ash forming a dark cloud all around. Paired with the near darkness of twilight, the ash provided perfect cover and I sprinted across the road towards the edge of the ridge.

Diving over the small stone wall which lined the cliffside, I braced myself as I landed upon the foliage. Branches snapped as I tumbled past, landing hard upon the rocky ground. I rolled for a hundred feet, tumbling down the steep slopes. My foot caught on a root and twisted hard. Yelping out in pain, I twisted around just before my body slammed into the base of a tree. Fire erupted from my mouth as the air rushed from my lungs. A sharp hot pain in my back made it difficult to breathe and I sucked in a shallow breath. Involuntary tears slipped from my eyes and my vision blurred. Controlling the pain, I embraced the fire within and forced myself to my feet.

Beneath the canopy of trees the night sky was completely shrouded from view. I heard cursing from above as the sorcerers gathered beside the stone wall which lined the cliffside above. Remaining still, I watched and waited. Having fallen far enough that only their shapes were visible, I hoped that I would be similarly shrouded by the darkness. My heart pounded and I took slow breaths as I waited. Once they made their move, I would be forced to flee again. Running through my options in my mind, I debated if it would be possible to return to Seraphina's palace for my weapons and armor. The most likely outcome was that I would need to flee down the ridge to the city. From there I had a few options of places to hide. No matter what choice I made, I had a limited chance of success. If I returned for my sword, I would be gambling my freedom with the possibility to better defend myself.

Realization struck me which seemed as strange as it was sudden. I did not want to kill these sorcerors. Not yet. Doing so would delay my capture for a time, but the vengeance of the Malketh King would be swift. I would not let my actions lead to more death and destruction. For the briefest moment, I considered surender. It was the only option which had the highest chance of saving life. All but my own.

No, I thought. *Nothing is ever so simple.*

At that moment, my decision was made. It was time for me to set a trap of my own. With as much silence as I could manage, I began to crawl down the slopes towards the city.

"There he is!" Malin's voice shouted from above.

Shit, I thought, growling.

Climbing back to my feet, I began to rush down the mountain, falling as much as I was running. The sound of shifting dirt on the slopes from above was followed by shouting voices. Glancing over my shoulder, I saw Isar's bald head gleam as he barreled down after me. The ground began to shake and I tumbled forward, slamming against another tree.

"Here goes nothing," I muttered, drawing out the remaining fire I held within. Placing my hand against the trunk of a tree, my handprint left a mark of flame. Breathing, I willed the fire to burn deep into the tree and within a moment, the aspen was ablaze.

Throwing a few stray flames onto the ground as I ran, I left a fire blazing in my wake. Catching quickly on the mulch which littered the ground, a large wall of fire rose into the air, separating me from my pursuers. Through the flames I could see Isar's angry face. He lifted his arms and large clumps of rock and soil lifted into the air. He threw the earth over the flames, dousing a small section.

With a wave of my hand, I caused the flames to spread further and higher, reblocking his path. In a matter of seconds, the fire was out of control and burning all around. The flames leapt from tree to tree as they climbed the slopes of the ridge towards the palaces. I looked at the fire for only a moment, a sinking feeling filling my gut.

The wiser part of my mind urged me onward. Leaving the flames to run their course, I hurried to the bottom of the ridge, sliding down major portions of the ridge until I reached the road which zig zagged up the slopes. The cobblestones were a welcome change and my dirty boots dragged large clumps of soil for the first dozen feet as I ran. I didn't look back until I reached the bottom of the ridge where the road merged with the main street that split the city in twine. When I looked back up, all I saw was large plumes of smoke glowing orange atop the ridge. The fire was contained to a small section, but part of me feared what would happen if I let it spread.

My eyes scanned the darkness, unable to see much of anything else on the road which led up the steep mountain slopes. Closing my eyes, I reached my hand outwards and felt for the fire. Taking hold of the Empyrean, I reached for the small lights just beyond my normal vision. Finding a spark in that well of power, I opened my eyes and focused on the flames. Immediately, I felt the fire as if it were an extension of my being. I closed my fingers in a fist and willed the flames to subside. Suffocating the wildfire took my entire will power, and I concentrated hard on preventing the flames from consuming any more trees.

In an instant, the flames vanished. It was like a candle snuffer had been used to extinguish the flame. The orange glow vanished, plunging the ridge into darkness. As the smoke cleared, the lights of Shandrice Palace began to show. Relieved, I turned and stalked into the night, prowling for a den to hide in.

CHAPTER SIX

VANISH

The market square before Ravens Cross was full of people. Though night had set, the whole city was in an uproar. White flowers littered the streets and most were mid celebration. Many were still clambering with speculation, pointing towards the ridge. No one seemed to pay me any mind as I hurried past, but my anxiety kept me on high alert as I walked through the crowd. Most ignored me, but the closer I came to Ravens Cross, the more the strangers began to recognize me. Looking down at my clothes, which were too fine for a mercenary, I began to think seeking refuge at Ravens Cross was a mistake.

Desperation to get out of the open pushed me forward. It might not have been the best choice, but the longer I stayed out in the open, the greater chance I had of Malin discovering me. Passing the fountain in the middle of the square, I looked up at the large three story tavern and paused. Music and laughter still echoed from within, but clustered around the porch were well armored men that all had shaven heads and bright polished armor. Painted on their breastplates was a familiar black eagle.

Stopping dead in my tracks, I froze, an old half forgotten fear rushing through my body. The shiver which rushed through me caused me to grit my teeth. Taking a step back, I bumped into several people, knocking them to the ground. The man, who was a little older and had shoulder length gray hair cursed at me.

"Watch where you're going!"

"Valon save us, it's him!" The man's companion said, climbing to his feet. "It's the pyromancer."

Their voices carried over the crowd and people started to look at us. My attention snapped to the front porch of Ravens Cross where the Malketh soldiers were still laughing. Relieved they had not taken notice, I turned back to the men and snarled.

"Mind your business and get out of my way."

Their faces went white and the two men stepped back several paces. Stalking past them, I walked away as fast as I could manage without drawing attention to myself. Eyes followed and fingers pointed, the whispering crowd growing louder and bolder. Realizing my discovery was inevitable, I sprinted forward.

"Stop that man!"

The cry came from the middle of the square and I looked over my shoulder. The man who had called out was not who I would have expected. A mercenary, wearing the pin of the crow atop a ram skull on his lapel, who was standing beside the fountain.

This time, the Malketh Soldiers looked at me. They dropped their drinks and drew their swords. Cursing under my breath, I turned and sprinted away. The people who were entering the square from the street gave me bewildered expressions as I passed them. From behind, I could hear screams which were followed by the slapping of boots on cobblestones. Glancing over my shoulder once more, I saw that both mercenaries and Malketh Soldiers were rushing after me, pushing people in the crowd back. Several fell to the cobblestones while others stumbled into one another in a desperate attempt to back away. All shouted their anger at the rushing mercenaries, some cursing and others making obscene gestures.

I seriously underestimated them, I thought as I continued running away.

My mind raced through my options and I decided that perhaps the best course of action would be to take a stand and fight. While there was a chance I would lose them while running through the city, I did not want to give any clues to where Isar and the others could search for me.

Reaching the edge of the city square, I raced to the front door of a shop where two lit lanterns hung. Swiping my right hand through the air, I drew out the flames and pulled them into my body. The energy flowed through my veins, chasing my blood like venom. Connecting the fire to the wooden roof tiles of the same shop, I took in a deep breath and flared the fire within me. The energy formed a well which grew until it was almost too much to contain. The sound of the tiles breaking apart above was followed by the sound of crackling flame. Holding out my hands, I conjured two balls of flame the size of pumpkins and threw them at the Malketh Soldiers and mercenaries who pursued me.

With raised shields, the front two men swatted away the fire. The firelight caused their shaven heads to gleam and their bared teeth to glisten. Drawing out more fire from within, I brought my hands together and thrust both palms together. A thin blade of fire blasted forward and struck the frontmost soldier in the center of his head. He dropped like a sack of flour and landed with a loud clang. His body went still and a burning hole in the back of his head smoked. Through the wound I saw a seared brain and broken skull.

He was trampled over by the soldiers who continued to rush forward. They were closing in fast and readying myself, I burned more roofing from a nearby building and caused my entire body to erupt into flames. This made the soldiers hesitate, giving me another opportunity to strike. Drawing out all of the fire from within my body, I waved my arms and cast spiraling wheels of flame towards the soldiers. Once again, they raised their shields, but the spiraling flames whipped around the sides. Each of the men screamed as the flames engulfed their bodies. The men dropped to the ground and began to roll around in a desperate attempt to douse their burning clothes.

These too fell victim to their friends who trampled over them. The first man that reached me, raised his sword and prepared to attack. I took in a controlled breath and stepped back, readying myself. He swung, his blade angled to cut my neck. Ducking, I stepped towards the man and placed my hand on his neck. Fire erupted from my hand, burning his flesh. The Malketh Soldier screamed as smoke billowed up around his face. Dropping his weapon, the soldier fell to his knees. I retrieved his weapon, and raised it in time to deflect a blade from a black clad mercenary. Snarling, the mercenary shook his head, tossing long strands of greasy black hair over his shoulder.

"What do you know? I guess the Valon are smiling down on me today," he said, jumping away. "I can't wait to collect the reward for taking you down."

His brandished rapier had a black loop-guard and he swiped it through the air with astonishing speed. Deflecting several more attacks, I stepped back and swung my newly acquired broadsword towards his leg. The tip clipped the mercenary's leg, causing him to leap back and howl with rage.

"How much are they offering for my head?" I asked.

The mercenary didn't answer. Instead, he began attacking again and was joined by several soldiers. Drawing fire from another lantern, I connected the flames to the cloth of the mercenary's shirt. The cheap cotton crumbled away and I threw a ball of fire at his bare chest. It struck him in the sternum with enough force that he tumbled back several feet. As the mercenary landed on the ground, his head smacked against a stone, a loud crack sounding in the night. Blood pooled around the man's head before he was stepped on by more foes.

Four mercenaries lined up before me and I held up the broadsword, preparing for their attacks. The mercenary in front of me and the one to my left attacked at once. I dropped to a crouch, rolled forward, and spinning, thrust the broadsword upwards. The tip lodged into the front man's armpit. He cried out in pain, pulling back. The second mercenary spun around while the other two attacked me together. Leaping backwards, I moved with long controlled swings to deflect their attacks.

This placed me between the increasing number of soldiers and mercenaries who had continued to gather. Raising the broadsword, I prepared myself for one final attack. Half closing my eyes, I reached out and touched the Empyrean. Every flame in the square was immediately visible in my mind. Drawing them all out at once, I linked their energy to a row of wooden market stands and tables which had been closed for the night. The wood went from polished to charred in the blink of an eye. Another moment passed and each of the tables crumbled to ash. The fire within me swelled and I released the power all at once.

Fire blasted in all directions, creating a large circle of flame which knocked down all of my adversaries. The flames continued to burn in the air above them and I willed them to remain in place. They hovered just high enough to not burn the soldiers, but the heat kept them from getting back up. I connected the flames to another row of tables which quickly began to turn to ash. I held the circle of fire in place for another second before slamming it down upon the fallen men.

Screams of anguish were cut short and those who remained alive groaned softly. Taking a moment to look at the scorched armor and charred skin, I saw that the crowd of people who'd been in the square were all looking at me with wide eyes and gaping mouths. Silence dawned on the crowd and I felt frozen as I beheld what I had done. Almost thirty men had fallen to my fire and I realized I was still the monster I had always been. Desperation had caused me to bring more harm than was necessary to these men and I felt guilty. Though I had thought I was no longer the demon of the north, it was clear to me now that I had buried my past in a shallow grave. It had taken very little to draw that monster out and that terrified me.

Averting my eyes, I ran away from the market square, turning down an unoccupied sidestreet. I clung to the stolen sword awkwardly. I did not want to surrender the weapon but holding it would be strange and draw unwanted attention. Deciding that keeping the weapon was better than improved stealth, I held it upside down, keeping the cross guard placed against my side. Hopefully it would at least look sheathed, though I doubted it.

I made several twists and turns as I rushed through the city, being careful to cling to the shadows. No one followed me and my eyes stayed alert, watching the rooftops. I did not see Malin stalking me from above. My anxiety began to increase with every passing minute and I was starting to feel exhaustion overtake me from the running. Slowing so I could catch my breath, I walked quickly through the semi-empty streets. Those I passed did not look my way, hurried about on their own business. Though it was slightly comforting to be ignored, it didn't dispel the aura of dread which hung over me.

The silence of night increased my agitation and my fingers twitched as I turned the final corner and began to walk towards the alchemy shop. The sign had been taken down and boards had been placed over the windows. It had been months since I had set foot in the shop and as I drew closer, I felt the pit in my stomach grow heavy. Memories of my dead friends filled my mind and when I reached the porch, I froze.

The shop looked hollow which seemed fitting. Through the small gaps in the boards that covered the windows, I could see only darkness behind the glass. My eyes looked at the door as I pulled a small ring of keys from my pocket. I thumbed through them until I found the key to the shop. The worn brass was scratched and starting to tarnish. Rubbing the cold metal, I forced myself up the stairs to the porch and placed the key in the hole. The lock stuck and it took a moment of jostling before it turned.

As I pushed open the door, a soft creaking sounded from within. Lifting my sword, I watched as the door swung in and stepped back. The sound of groaning floorboards was followed by a soft click and moving shadow. My heart leapt into my throat and I leapt back and to the side. Something shot at me from within and grazed passed my ear. Sharp pain stung my earlobe and blood began to drip down my neck.

I leapt from the porch to the street. Landing softly upon the cobblestones, I backed away until I reached the middle of the street. A large figure, cloaked in a thick hickory cloth, emerged from the alchemy shop. He held a black crossbow which was already cocked and the bolt was tipped with a serrated point. The hood of the cloak shifted back, revealing a brutal scarred face. The man smiled and clamped his hand down on the lever. The bolt shot at me with alarming speed and struck me in the shoulder as I twisted away to dodge it. Pain shot across my shoulder and up my neck.

Growling with pain, I looked at the small cut the bolt had made as it had grazed my shoulder. Though the wound wasn't deep it was bleeding quite a bit, staining my shirt and causing it to cling to my arm. Growling, I turned to face my new enemy. He'd reloaded his crossbow and was once again taking aim. My reaction came instinctively and I reached towards the lantern which hung from the building across from the alchemy shop. The light flickered as I linked the flame to the string of his cross-bow. The fibers of the bowstring burned quickly and the crossbow snapped, the tension being released unnaturally. The bolt fired but only traveled a few feet, falling to the cobblestones.

Cursing as he tossed the crossbow to the ground, the large man flung back his cloak and drew a longsword. As the hickory material fell to the ground, my foe's full body armor was revealed, the polished metal gleaming in the moonlight. The sharp serrated edges of the armor were accented with blades and spikes. My mind recalled the armies of Chezek soldiers I had defeated so many years ago.

So, your people joined the empire, I thought, taking a tentative step back.

The man marched towards me and I fully realized his massive size. The Chezek Amok was a head and shoulders taller than me, with a wide torso and massive hands. Being taller than average, I was not accustomed to people being larger than me and it was strange to face someone who loomed over me. Despite this, my intimidation was short-lived.

The Chezek soldier had caught me by surprise, but now that we were out in the open, he was exposed and had lost his advantage. Drawing upon the power of all the nearby street and home lanterns, I pulled them all towards me. The fire consumed the lamp oil from their original sources quickly and the twisting ribbons of flame which shot through the street grew larger by the moment. Coalescing before me, I formed a large ball of flame which I hurled at the Amok. He turned away from the blast, and raised his hand to cover the gap in his visor. The ball of fire engulfed the man, but as it faded, he stood tall, his large sword raised.

Lifting my broadsword, I deflected the blade, and found myself on the defensive. The Chezek Amok swung his longsword with quick controlled motions. His long arms and longer sword gave him more reach which made it difficult for me to do anything besides block and parry. His skill with the sword was on par with my own and it quickly became clear as we traded blows that he lived up to his military designation. The Amok truly were brutal fighters who went hard and heavy. But the man lacked the discipline required to maintain stamina over a long fight. With a focus on brutality and overwhelming their enemies, the Amok's greatest weakness was longevity. All I had to do was hold my ground while he wore himself out.

Weary as I was from the fighting and running, I soon found myself outpacing my foe, fighting with reserved strength. It took less than ten minutes for the Chezek Amok to wear himself out. As his long sword swings slowed, I found an opportunity and struck the man in the inner side of the elbow on his dominant arm. The sharp steel of my broadsword broke through the leather and cloth, slicing the tendons. Groaning, the Chezek's arm went limp and he lost grip on his sword.

Twisting the hilt of my blade, I turned the steel to the side and swiped wide. The edge sliced across the man's throat with a spray of blood. Choking, the man fell to his knees then back, grumbling and sputtering, blood spraying out with every beat of his heart. Instead of allowing further suffering, I made another swift strike with my sword, and ended the man's life.

Several people had emerged from their homes and were looking at me. Two ran away screaming for help, and I wondered how long it would take for the city guard to arrive. Knowing that my time was limited, I decided I would risk a few more minutes to take what I could from the corpse. Kneeling beside the body, I quickly unclasped his belt and pulled it free. Strapping the belt over my own, I picked up the Chezek longsword and sheathed it. The belt had a dagger which I quickly inspected. The fallen soldier had a small pouch of coins which I also pocketed. I wondered if I had time to strip the man of his armor but decided it would not be worth the risk. Tugging off one of the man's bladed gauntlets, I put it on my left hand. Leaving the body, I rushed to the fallen cloak, pulled it on, and hurried through the street.

Those that had gathered called after me, but no one gave chase. I raced through the streets towards the River Earn. The places I could turn to hide were growing limited and if the alchemy shop was compromised, that meant any place I had frequented was not safe. That ruled out the Crooked Inn, which was perhaps the only other refuge in the city where I might have had friends. Isar was smart and had prepared well before making his move. He had anticipated every step I would take. Though, as I began to think, I realized there was another option.

The underground was the final hiding place where I knew I would be safe. Even after all these months of fighting the slush trade, I had only a small inkling of the maze which existed below the city. Even if they did try to look for me there, there are plenty of places to hide and it would be almost impossible for them to find me. I doubted anyone but Sheyor would have the skill required. I muttered a silent prayer to the Valon that they wouldn't find out about the young girl.

Even with that thought, worry still filled me. I began to think through what would happen should I be discovered in the confined and restrictive tunnels of the underground. Many tunnels had water and while that had played to my advantage against the necromancer, it would be a death sentence against a hydromancer. The tunnels were also a prime place for a geomancer to trap me and collapse the tunnel around me. I also considered what resources I would have at my disposal. Without fuel to burn, my pyromancy would be limited.

As I raced towards the River Earn, I could hear the rushing of the water and the knocking of docked ships against the board-walk. I thought through all of the benefits and potential catastrophes of the choice I was about to make. Ultimately, I recognized that there were no other options. Hiding in the underground was my only recourse, so I shut away all of my fear and doubts, and my decision was made.

Reaching the end of the street, I slowed my pace and crept down the boardwalk. Sleeping or drunken sailors sat on crates beside their boats. My mind made every shadow look like a hiding place and my eyes remained alert for anyone lurking within. It felt like I had been wandering forever before I finally found the old boat house which hid an entrance to the tunnels below. Since Vivienne and I had emerged, the locks had been changed and additional chains had been added to the door. Removing a lantern from a nearby dock, I walked up to the door and inspected the new chains. Tugging on them, I saw that the wood of the door bowed from the strain. Pulling on the chains, I tore them free from the old wood which splintered. The sound of breaking doors was loud in the night and several dogs began to bark in response.

Hurrying inside, I closed the doors behind me, but damaged as they were, the left door would not stay closed. It swung open, groaning on old hinges. Leaving the door open, I turned my attention to the tangle of nets and fishing equipment which had been piled in the shack. The dinghy which had originally blocked the entrance had been moved, this time covering the underground entrance completely. Shoving the small boat to the side, I watched it tumble off and onto the floor. It landed with a loud thump and smacked against the far wall causing the entire structure to shake. The barking dogs were growing louder and ignoring them, I knelt down beside the trap door and pulled it open. Looking inside, I saw nothing but darkness.

Holding onto the lantern, I climbed one handed down the ladder and into the darkness. Closing the trap door behind me, I felt my tension release. Entering the darkness was comforting and my pounding heart began to slow. Taking in a deep breath, I found that my body was no longer trembling. Sliding down the ladder to the bottom, I landed softly upon the damp stones of the tunnel. Closing my eyes, I searched my memory, trying to remember which path would lead me safely through towards the Raha. If I had to make this my hiding place, I might as well remain with the others who called these tunnels home.

Taking in a deep breath, I pulled the fire from the lantern and let it warm me from within. Concentrating on the flame, I felt my worry melt away, replaced with resolve. Returning the flame to the lantern, I looked down the long tunnel. No matter what I had to move forward and find a way to defeat Isar. I would not let him take everything from me. I did not give up all those years ago and I was not going to give up now. It was with these encouraging thoughts that I set out into the darkness and began to think up a plan for what I would do next.

CHAPTER SEVEN
VILE DELIGHTS

Time passed strangely in the tunnels. I wandered for hours, searching my way through the dark passages, doing my best to follow the markings on the walls. When the lantern burned out leaving me to the darkness of the tunnel, I was surprised to find I could still make out the lines and shapes of the walls and ceiling above. My eyes had never before been so sharp and I was glad not to be left to wander the underground without any form of sight.

The labyrinth of tunnels was confusing to navigate and the symbols written at each intersection still did not make sense to me. I longed to have Vivienne with me, but was also glad she did not have to join me in these tunnels. With any luck, she and the rest of the Syndicate had been left out of the conflict. My mind began to wonder what Isar would do and every path led to the same destination. Complete and utter retaliation. My heart sank but still I forced myself not to go any further with my imaginations. It would do me no good at all to preoccupy my mind with needless worry. There were enough problems before me that would be a better focus for my time and mental efforts.

Exhaustion began to set in and stumbling down a long

slanting tunnel, I found a small narrow cavity in the wall. Squatting down, I peered inside and saw a narrow tunnel that led downward at an angle. The tunnel didn't go far before opening up again. Getting onto my hands and knees, I crawled through the opening and found myself in a small stone cellar. It was musty and filled with wooden barrels. The wooden stairs on the far wall were rotted and they did not lead to any door or exit. The stones dripped with mortar which looked to have been hastily applied when the original exit had been sealed off.

I checked the nearest barrel and unsheathing my dagger, used the tip to pry open the top. The loud popping sound echoed in the cellar and a putrid stench filled the air. Gagging, I covered my mouth and shut the lid, pounding it shut with the pommel of the dagger. Sheathing the small blade, I uncovered my mouth and was for once glad to only smell the usual dampness of the underground tunnels.

"I bet they're all spoiled," I thought aloud. It was strange to hear my own voice as it echoed in the silence. It reminded me of how quiet it had been since I'd entered the tunnels.

My heart suddenly beat loud in my ears and every sound seemed intensified. Though I could see vague outlines in the shadows, I was still blind to most of the small critters and bugs which crawled along the walls or hid in nasty corners. The thought of such things made my skin prickle. Shivering, I shoved away the thoughts as the back of my neck began to prickle. Feeling as though a spider were slowly crawling up my back and across my shoulders, I shrugged and reached over my shoulder to scratch the nape of my neck.

"This was a terrible idea," I muttered, grabbing ahold of the same barrel I'd foolishly opened. Rocking the heavy thing back and forth, I shimmied it over to the small tunnel I had crawled through and placed it before the entrance. It blocked most of the entrance but still left a sizable hole a child could slip through.

Walking to another barrel, I performed the same slow rocking back and forth as I moved it across the floor to join the other one.

Perhaps it was unwise to block my only means of escape, but if I had to, I was certain I could knock the heavy barrels aside. Taking a step back, I found myself unsatisfied by the fortification. So I took another barrel and, like I had the first two, moved it into place between them. Together, I was confident that anyone who tried to enter would have insufficient leverage to displace the blockage or at the very least would have a difficult enough time that I would be roused from sleep.

I quickly searched through the rest of the cellar and found no occupant, animal, insect, or otherwise. Taking a seat in the furthest corner from the blocked tunnel, I removed the Chezek cloak, rolled it up, and used it for a pillow. Sleep came quickly but my rest was disturbed by nightmares. The shapes and impressions of these dark imaginings burrowed deep into my mind, making my sleep fitful. I awoke several times, each time slightly disoriented. Eventually, once I jolted awake from a strikingly unpleasant nightmare of Isar torturing Vivienne by slamming his hammer repeatedly onto her hands and feet, I decided not to try to fall back asleep.

The darkness began to make me feel claustrophobic and the desperate need to get fresh air increased my agitation. My fingers began to twitch and after a few moments I began to bounce my right leg up and down. Controlling my breath became difficult and my body ached to find fire. The desire which overwhelmed me made my pulse race and the space behind my eyes began to hurt. An overwhelming nausea flowed from my bowels and into my stomach. Rushing to an empty barrel, I vomited slick vomit into it. The horrid and sour bile rushed from my lips and my diaphragm contracted repeatedly. Dry heaving for several minutes, I eventually fell back onto the stones and gasped for breath. My head pounded and eventually what vision I had in the black cellar returned. Slowly, my vision turned crisp and I could see more than just the vague outlines of the shapes. Everything came into focus as if lit by a small candle. The sudden contrast was like night to day.

I laid on the cold stones for hours, having no desire to move. Hunger eventually forced me to my feet, though I knew there would be nothing here that would satiate me. Despite this, I looked around, examining the barrels, crates, and piles of rubbish which had been left in the cellar. In some of the crates, I found spoiled food. There were a few turnips and potatoes which might have been edible, but were so shriveled that I decided not to risk it. To my surprise I found a small cask of cider in the back corner among the rubbish.

I tapped the cider cask and took a long drink, washing away the residual bile taste which still filled my mouth.The cider was exceptionally dry and was almost like drinking vinegar. I only managed to force myself to down three gulps before I set it down. Letting out a groan, I retrieved the Chezek cloak and put it back on. Deciding there was nothing of value to bring with me, I removed the barrels I'd used to block the tunnel entrance and crawled my way back into the underneath.

Making my way deeper into the maze, I began to listen for movement in hopes it would lead me to the others who dwelt within the darkness. Perhaps there I could barter for something to eat. My eyes continued to pierce the darkness which made it easier to navigate the twisting jagged tunnels which connected sewers, caves, and old buildings together. It was strange to be able to see so well in the dark, but I didn't dwell on how. For the time being, I was simply happy to have the power.

Turning the corner, I began to walk along a small underground river which rushed past with alarming speed. Water from the river continuously splashed up onto the side making the walkway slippery. Taking each step with care, I moved forward, recognizing a small bridge up ahead. I was getting close to the underground sections beneath the Raha. Despite the pervasive criminal element I knew I would find, it would be the safest place to hide.

When I reached the bridge, I heard something in the tunnel behind me. The sound of scratching claws raking the ground sent chills down my spine. Remembering the claw marks outside the gate the last time Vivienne and I passed through this place, I drew my sword and prepared myself.

The scratching sounds grew closer as the creature in the darkness increased its speed. I waited and watched, tightening my hands around the grip of my longsword. The Ghoul emerged from the tunnel, its ravenous mouth open wide. It leapt at me and I cut it down mid-air. The soft pale flesh of the creature cut easily as the sharp steel sliced it in twine. Blood splashed onto the bridge as the two halves of the creature bounced and then flopped into the water.

Chirping barks from the tunnel came in response and the scratching of more claws echoed from all directions.

"Shit!" I cursed, fleeing across the bridge and down the tunnel which led to the gate.

The sounds of screaming Ghouls were loud in my ears as they echoed down the tunnel. I sprinted forward and raced against the creatures who were pursuing me. Glancing over my shoulder, I saw a group of five Ghouls who were within reach. Twisting around, I swiped with my sword and sliced off several limbs as well as a head. As the Ghouls fell to the ground they were trampled by more. The feral screams filled the tunnel and I was left with no choice but to stand my ground and fight them.

Placing my back up against the wall, I began to cut and slice, matching their ferocity with my own. Blood sprayed with every strike and bloodlust filled me. My mind went blank and I released my rage, killing these creatures as fast as they could come. The killing felt good and I snarled.

My bloodsoaked cloak dripped as I walked down the tunnel. I held my sword aloft, resting the dirty blade on my shoulder. With nothing to clean it, I hadn't wanted to ruin the scabbard by sheathing it. I had found my way to familiar ground and made my way back to the homeless encampment Vivienne and I had discovered a few weeks ago. The light from the camp illuminated the long tunnel and I felt a renewed sense of determination to press forward fill me. When I reached the gate which blocked the tunnel I found that the chains had been secured with a new lock. Though along with a new lock there was an additional chain and lock looped around the first. There was fire burning on the other side and reaching my hand through the metal bars, I drew a small portion into me.

The fire shot through the air, entering my hand through my index finger. The fire rushed through my blood and I immediately felt calm. Warmth spread to every fiber of my body and I sighed with relief.

In the piles of trash just to the left of the gate was a sleeping man. His hand was resting beside an empty bowl, the fingerless gloves showing red-stained fingers. His chest rose and fell slowly as he slept.

"Osbert," I called, reaching through the gate with my sword to prod at his boot. "Osbert!"

It took a few minutes to rouse the man who grumbled awake before shouting in surprise. He crawled across the ground, his screaming cut short as he looked at me. His drug-addled mind seemed to recognize that I was on the other side of the gate instead of a Ghoul. Osbert calmed down and brushed the wild strands of greasy hair from his eyes.

"You!" Osbert cried. "You're back."

"Yes, now can you let me in?"

Osbert's eyes looked past me into the tunnel. He then looked back at me and seemed to see my blood covered cloak for the first time. "You killed them?"

"Not all, but I killed a lot of them."

"Give me a moment."

Osbert returned to the rubbish pile he called a bed and began to search through the fabrics and papers. It took him several minutes but he found a brass ring with three keys. Tossing the keys to me, I caught them. Unlocking the gate, I unwrapped the chains before pulling it open. As before, the gate scraped across the stones and got stuck after a few feet. It took effort to squeeze myself through. Relocking the gate, I tossed the keys back to Osbert.

"Thanks," I said. "Do you mind?" I pointed to a stray piece of cloth on the ground.

Osbert shook his head. Retrieving the cloth, I wiped the fresh blood from the longsword and sheathed it.

"What were you doin' in there?"

"Hiding."

"Not a good place to hide. Not at all."

"You're right about that."

"But you killed em' which is good."

"I suppose." I looked at Osbert who had settled down upon his bed, his head dropping. "Don't have any food, do you?"

He looked up at me and shook his head, mouthing the word *no*.

"Where can I get some?"

Osbert pointed towards the exit.

Nodding, I left the man alone and wandered through the camp. Most people ignored me and those who looked did not do so for long. The stench of unwashed bodies and excrement was masked somewhat by the Ghoul blood on my cloak. Regardless, I felt disgusted. The squalor and filth that covered the entire camp was hard to look at and the prospect of making it my new home was somewhat humbling. I'd been living with decadence for so long, I had forgotten that life was often more cruel than kind. These people deserved better than this and now I was among them, needing what they had.

Reaching into my pocket, I felt at the coin pouch I'd stolen from the Chezek Soldier. I fished out a coin and concealing it in my hand, I looked at it. It was a golden crown, marked by the King's symbol. I wasn't surprised to see that it was a Kings Keep coin, but the newness of the mint was surprising. The coin looked as clean as the day it had been made.

Interesting, I thought, placing the coin back into my pocket.

The tunnel which led up and out emerged on the Raha canal. I looked up at the sky, my eyes taking a long time to adjust to the light. The sun was low in the sky and the buildings which lined the canal cast long shadows. Despite the foul water below, the scent of semi-fresh air was a welcome relief.

Pulling the hood of my cloak as far over my face as it would go, I walked down the side of the canal towards the nearest street. The scents of baking bread and roasting onions filled the air. My stomach grumbled and I quickened my pace, eager to eat. When I reached the bridge which spanned the canal, I stepped up from the ravine and onto a busy street. The Raha was bustling with life as people rushed about. The dirtiness of my clothing made me shrink back, but after a moment, I realized there was no need. Everything was wet from a recent rain and most of those who wandered about were as dirty with mud and grime as I was. Stepping out into the street, I began to make my way to a bakery on the corner. The small building had a line out the door and I joined the back of the line.

My anxiety returned and my eyes darted to the rooftops. There was no one above watching me though I began to feel foolish. Keeping my head down, I watched my boots, trying to draw as little attention to myself as possible. I waited until everyone in line had made their purchase and the bakery was empty before entering. Closing the door behind me, I took stock of the small counter. The shelves in the back were covered in bread loaves and I was greeted by a rotund man with red cheeks and thin wispy hair.

"What can I get you?"

"How much for a loaf?"

"A silver bit."

I slid the golden coin from my pocket and doubted he would have enough to break the large coin. Not in a place like this.

"Can I pay you for a week's worth of bread for two in advance?"

The baker's eyes narrowed and he took a step back. "I suppose so. Why?"

"I only have this," I showed him the coin and his eyes went wide.

"Of course lad," he said, reaching down his hand. I passed him the coin and it disappeared into his apron quickly.

"Also, discretion would be greatly appreciated."

"Of course, of course." The baker began to rub his hands together. "What loaves would you like?"

"Two mixed grains will be fine. Do you sell drink?"

"No, but the brewery across the way is open." The baker fished in his pocket and handed me a silver half. "Here's a bit of change so you can buy something there. I'll keep a tab for the rest and let you know when you run out. But that is quite a bit of an advance."

I took the coin and thanked the man. He wrapped the loaves in thick brown paper and handed them to me.

"Can I ask another favor?"

"Of course," the baker said, dusting his hands on the dirty apron. Flour dust coated his hands and drifted down to the food.

"Will you have the loaves ready and set aside for me to pick up every morning at dawn?"

"Joan!" the baker called. A short stout woman emerged from the back. She had gray hair and her face had flour dust on it.

"Yes, Gabe."

"This gentleman has purchased bread in advance and has requested that we have it ready for him by dawn. Could you see that it is ready?"

"Of course," she said, looking at me.

"I'll be outside at dawn."

"We will have those ready for you." As Joan spoke another patron entered the small bakery.

I gave the two bakers a nod before turning to leave. The youth who had entered the small bakery did not look at me as I passed. Exiting into the muddy street, I hurried to the brewery where I purchased a keg of ale and two clay tankards. With some confidence I left the Raha Street and went back down to the canal. The closer I got to the underground entrance, the more my heart beat. It felt like I was racing against time and at any moment I would be discovered.

The strange emotion and anxiety was bothersome and my rational mind agreed that every moment I remained outside, the more I put myself at risk. Malin, if it had been her, had first shown herself to me here in the Raha. Reaching the entrance to the underground, I pulled it open and passing into the darkness, I felt a sense of relief flood over me. The tunnel sloped downward and then turned sharply at an angle. I walked with careful steps so I would not drop either the ale or bread.

This time when I passed several hungry eyes looked up at me but none seemed bothered enough to try and fight me for it. One woman, her eyes and cheeks sunken, did sit up as I walked past. Instead of reaching for me, the woman reached for a small pot. Removing the lid, she scooped a glob of slush and placed it on her tongue. The red crystalline drug melted in her mouth and soaked into her tongue. She fell back to the pile of fabric she'd been laying on and began to groan with pleasure. Leaving her and the others to their vile delights, I returned to Osbert who was rocking back and forth in his pile of worn blankets and cloth.

"Mind if I take a seat?"

He looked up at me with surprise before nodding.

"Thanks for helping me," I said, passing him a loaf of bread.

Osbert took the bread with tentative fingers. "Thanks."

He took a small bite at first, chewed, then began to scarf down the loaf like a starving child. Taking a bite of my own bread, I sighed in relief. Eating in silence, I poured us each a mug of ale and we washed down the meal with several tankards full. With food in my belly, my head began to clear and I felt the tension melt away. The alcohol didn't last long in my stomach, burning away quickly, but what small soothing I got from the drink had helped me relax.

"So, Osbert. I have a question for you."

"What is that?"

"Do you know your way around down here?"

The man nodded, flashed me a smile, which showed off his rotten teeth. "Ay. These tunnels are my home."

"Good. Can you teach me how to navigate them?"

Osbert paused, his head tilting back and forth. His eyes glanced toward the gate and his smile turned sour.

"I will pay you." Though I didn't want to provide the man more opportunity to drug himself, I needed to know my way around more. Still, I felt guilty knowing I would be enabling the man by giving him money.

"How much."

"A golden crown."

"How often?"

"Every week."

"Done."

Osbert smiled, reached out his hand and we shook.

"I want to start tonight."

"Of course, of course." Osbert climbed to his feet. "Follow me."

CHAPTER EIGHT
BURROW

Resting atop a new collection of blankets all my own, I watched a small cluster of homeless that had formed in the center of the camp. A man dressed in thick leather armor painted with a large Red Hook had emerged from a tunnel at the southern end of the camp, a fresh batch of slush in toe. The small hand wagon had several barrels of the awful stuff which he was selling to the crowd. I watched as Osbert joined the rest, clutching the golden coin I had given him for his first week's work.

Two things about the man continued to surprise me. His kniving determination to acquire as much slush as possible and his generosity at distributing it. Now that I had given him more than enough money to acquire the vile drug, I wondered how much he would buy. To my surprise, he handed the entire coin to the Red Hook goon and began to distribute the drug to the others. The gang member didn't even seem to care how Osbert had come across his coin and pocketed it with glee. Almost everyone from the camp seemed to cluster around, hands reaching out for their share. I was among a handful of people who did not go for slush, instead sitting back, content to watch. I wondered if we would attract attention but the Red Hook goon did not even glance my way.

He probably only cares that they have the money to buy.

Fresh disdain for Red Hook and the other gangs who made and distributed the vile drug flooded me. I wanted nothing more than to walk over and drown the man in the vile shit he was selling. But knowing that would change nothing and that another would come in his stead, I remained in place. Pulling out my new dagger, I began to twist it back and forth out of boredom.

When Osbert returned he was carrying a large clay jar of fresh slush in his hand. His red stained fingers were already working the lid and the moment he sat down, he plunged them deep into the red crystalline substance. A small portion sloshed out and fell onto his trousers. Small wisps of smoke rose from his fingers and Osbert sighed with relief.

I felt a pit form in my stomach and I looked away. Pretending to sleep, I watched the Red Hook goon drag his hand wagon back the way he had come, a wide smile on his face. This brute had a long scar on his cleft chin which looked like a small cross. His face was covered with grime and his shoulder length hair was stringy from oil and grease. The man wasn't observant and walked with single minded determination. He whistled as he walked past the small shacks and tents where my homeless companions slept.

My eyes followed him until he disappeared down the tunnel. It was the one place Osbert had not allowed me to go, clear in his direction that there were places in the tunnels too dangerous to ever venture. Glancing over at my friend, I saw that his eyes were glazed over, drool spilling down his mouth. With a sigh, I climbed to my feet and followed after the goon.

When I reached the end of the homeless camp, I waved my hand over a fire and pulled a small flame with me. Connecting the fire to the small sack of coal which now hung from my belt, I left the flame within my body. Its power rushed through my chest, pulsing with every beat of my heart. My eyes adjusted to the darkness of the cave and I followed behind the goon who moved with a slow steady pace through the tunnels. The wheels on his wagon grinded slightly on the axle causing a soft squealing noise. The noise echoed down the tunnels and masked my footsteps.

The lantern the man carried cast long dancing shadows which shifted up and down the walls. Remaining constantly out of reach of the light, I stalked him for over an hour. Despite the relaxed and rather uninterested demeanor of the man, he seemed to keep a sharp eye on the tunnels as he navigated through the twisting and turning pathways.

Eventually we crossed the main sewer line which I knew rested under the central street of Kings Keep. The street was crooked but ran from the north gate to the south gate. Making a mark on my mental map of the intersection, I began to picture the city above as we walked. It was still difficult to tell where I was exactly, but we were close to the end of the sewer where it merged with the River Earn just beyond the city wall.

I followed the man along a ledge which lined the filthy water that flowed below. Though I was beginning to grow used to the stench, there was a sharp bitter scent in the air which was worse than normal. The smell continued to grow worse as we continued. When I thought I could no longer withstand the stench, the goon finally stopped. He was still several hundred paces ahead, and though I could see him from the shadows where I lurked, when he turned to look back, he did not see me.

Watching as he placed his hand on the wall, I heard the sound of stones scraping together. The Red Hook goon pushed on the wall and then stepped forward. After a moment, the sound of grinding stones filled the sewer and the orange glow of his lantern disappeared completely. My eyes adjusted seamlessly to the dark and I kept my attention on the sewer walls.

I waited for several minutes before I followed. Walking with more speed than before, I quickly reached the section of wall where the goon had disappeared. The wheels of his wagon left marks on the stones which turned and led directly under the wall. The wall was made from stones poorly mortared together. Sections of the walls had large claw marks and scrapes which did a great job of masking the edges of the entrance. After a few moments of careful study, I saw where jagged sections had a seam that was darker than the rest of the stones. Running my fingers along the edge, I felt the stones and the texture was smooth on my skin. Pulling my hand away, I rubbed my thumb and index finger together and a small amount of mortar dust fell from my fingers.

Taking a step back, I felt my foot slip. Flailing my arms, I reached forward and placed my hand against the wall. Catching myself before I could tumble back into the river of sewage, I bit back a curse. With more care, I steadied myself and tried to recall the exact position the goon had been standing in when he'd triggered the mechanism which would unlock the passage.

Looking down at the ground, I placed my feet beside the wagon tracks, using them to gauge where he had been standing. It took me several minutes before I spotted a small stone in the wall which was almost completely covered in gray mortar. Reaching out, I pressed on the stone and it clicked into the wall. The grinding of stone followed and the wall shifted back. Pushing it open, I readied myself for whatever was inside.

No guard stood at the entrance but there was a stool and small table directly to my left. The lantern which sat on the edge of the table was burning and the front glass panel had a broken corner. The tunnel ran down at an angle and the end glowed with red and orange firelight. I hesitated for a moment before stepping back into the sewer and pulling the door closed behind me.

Don't do anything foolish Caden, I thought, scolding myself. *You're supposed to be hiding.*

Making another note on my mental map, I left the secret entrance behind and began to make my way to the camp. Walking slowly through the darkness, I took extra care to memorize the notable markings and passageways. My eyes were seeing through the dark more clearly every day. A skill that both excited and worried me. But it, like so many other worries, would have to wait. When I arrived back at the homeless camp, most were unconscious and Osbert was still sleeping.

The jar of slush had tipped over and spilled onto the dirt. The strange red liquid crystals shimmered in the firelight. Turning the jar upright, I put the lid back on and tucked the jar away. Kicking dirt onto the spilled slush, I turned my attention to the camp. Nearly two hundred souls all around were in similar drug addled states. I wanted so badly to return to the Red Hook hideout and destroy whatever I found there to cut off the slush supply at the source.

But as I looked at everyone, for the first time, I considered what that would do to these people? That thought kept me seated, reluctant to make a move. I made a list of all the things that I would need to do to be successful and finding a way to truly help these people off their dependence on the drug was first on that list. Glancing over at Osbert, I watched him twitch fitfully as he slept. His eyes moved back and forth rapidly beneath his eyelids and soft grumbles escaped from his lips.

Just help one, I thought as I closed my eyes and laid down to rest. *Just help one.*

~

The days all began to feel like an eternity but the weeks seemed to pass in a flash. Now that it was the beginning of my third week living in the tunnels, I was beginning to feel comfortable creeping through the dark shadows. With only drug-addled companions for company, I was beginning to feel like I was going mad.

Stuffing the remaining morsel of barely bread into my mouth, I chewed quickly. It was still early, just after dawn, though it would have been impossible to know down in the tunnels. Without my daily surfacing for bread, I would have been left entirely without a sense of time. Though I would have liked to stay on the surface a bit longer, many still spoke of me and I could tolerate only a few minutes out in the open before I felt like I was going to be captured. Even with these daily surfacings, my sense of time had been distorted which caused me to sleep at odd intervals. My anxiety kept me awake and I used fire to keep me stimulated. Despite this, I was still able to find rest often enough that I wasn't in danger of growing weak from exhaustion, as that would be the worst thing I could let happen to myself.

Osbert groaned and rolled over. His eyes opened and he looked at the small brown loaf I had placed on a plate beside him. My friend sat up, picked up the bread, then began to eat without a word.

Finally, I thought. *Hurry up so we can get going.*

"Always early, always ready," he mumbled, dusting crumbs off his lap.

"I figured that while I am paying you, I should get my money's worth."

Osbert snorted. "Of course my *liege,* I forget myself."

I didn't like how Osbert had taken to calling me liege. The man found it funny and I almost corrected him. This time, I decided to take another approach and play along. "Now, when shall I expect my faithful squire to have the preparations made for today's expedition?"

"Let me see," Osbert reached into his pocket and produced a broken pocket watch. He pressed down on the latch and the top flipped open. It was broken, and the glass had two long cracks in it. "Whenever it swiving pleases me."

I chuckled. "Well, don't keep me waiting too long."

Osbert grinned, showing off his cavity riddled teeth. Behind the dirty face, long hair, and scraggly beard, there was a respectable face with keen eyes. It seemed that more of his old self had been returning these last few days. His consumption of slush hadn't lessened, but it hadn't increased either. It seemed too early to call that progress. But perhaps I was expecting too much.

"My liege, can I ask you something?"

"Sure. What is it?"

"It's just, I am trying to understand. Why did you come down here?"

"That's a good question. Why does anyone come down here?"

"People come down here," Osbert paused, looking to the nearest cluster of canvas tents and wadded blankets. "They come because they're running away from something or they're hiding from something. So, which of the two brought you down here?"

"Perhaps a bit of both," I added.

"So, what are you running from?"

"Something really bad, Osbert. Worse than I think you could imagine."

"I don't believe you. Nothing is so terrible that I couldn't imagine it. I've seen dark things, darker than these tunnels."

"Trust me, you've never seen anything like these people."

"Are they like you?"

"What do you mean, like me?"

"You know, mystics."

I paused, unsure how to respond. Osbert was indeed more observant than I had given him credit for. It was a reminder that I needed to be more careful with my magic and how I used it. Even small things didn't seem to go as unnoticed as I'd thought. Perhaps my time of taking refuge here was coming to an end.

"Well, Osbert. To answer your question, yes, they are like me. But not like me. It's complicated."

"What are you going to do?"

"I am trying to figure that out." I paused, looking at my new friend. He was scratching the back of his neck. "What are you running away from?"

Osbert didn't answer, only shrugging. I waited in silence, allowing for it to grow uncomfortable. I was in no rush and he'd been courteous enough to ask me.

"I suppose I am running from myself. I don't have anywhere else to turn."

"What do you mean by running from yourself?"

"I am running from, from all the bad things I did."

I nodded. "We are more alike than it would appear."

"Oh, how so?"

"Well, I suppose everyone has a past and has done things they are not proud of. But I understand running from a past of mistakes. I too have done my fair share of that."

"Ah, I see." Osbert leaned forward and rubbed his knees. "It doesn't work."

"No," I agreed. "I don't suppose it does."

"I'm ready if you are," Osbert said, climbing to his feet.

Getting up from the blankets, I snagged a small lantern and ignited the wick with a pinch of my fingers. The fire which burned within was small, but the sack of coal which hung from my belt would provide any needed fuel that would be required during today's journey through the tunnels. The Chezek sword and dagger so far had been more than enough to fend off the Ghouls and I was determined only to use my magic to fight as a last resort.

"Let's hope we don't find anything nasty today," Osbert said with a wry smile.

Wordlessly, I followed him through the gate and down the

main tunnel which led back into the city below. It was becoming clearer to me that it was more than just a series of tunnels and caves which filled the underground network below the city. It was a sprawling labyrinth built atop a city which had been submerged long ago. Some of the tunnels we had stumbled upon led deep into the ground, connecting us to older buildings. Osbert never let us stray too far and if we did venture into the older sections, our explorations were always short. He was more comfortable with the new tunnels and I was in agreement.

We walked first to the central sewer tunnel which ran down Gate Street. The same sewer which if we turned south would lead us to the secret Red Hook tunnel. My eyes only glanced down for a moment. Osbert turned left, taking us north.

"Where are we going today?" I asked.

"We've explored the tunnels beneath the Raha well. I was thinking we could venture into the tunnels below the northern part of Kings Keep. Is there anywhere specific you like to go?"

I thought for a minute, considering what would be the most beneficial. "Do you know how to get to the warehouse district?"

Osbert nodded.

"Let's start with that."

"Is there a specific part of the district you want to find?"

"Are you familiar with The Crooked Inn?"

"No."

"It's a set of buildings just behind the lumber mills."

"Ah, I know the mills." Osbert reached out his hand, gesturing for the lantern. I passed it to him and he began to stalk forward.

We walked in silence, following the sewer line for miles. As we walked, I found myself glancing down into the river of excrement below and realized that I no longer noticed the stench. Somehow, the realization resurfaced my senses and I caught a whiff of putrid stench. Gagging, I rubbed my nose on my sleeve only to realize I didn't smell any better. Sighing, I refocused my attention on the walls.

Each intersection was marked with several symbols. Though they had been confusing to me at first, I was starting to make sense of them. The system was clever and used a system of roughly drawn characters to denote street corners, or other landmarks above. By using my knowledge of the city above, I was able to solidify the mental map of the underground much better. We turned sharply, entering a small narrow tunnel that appeared to have been cut from an existing crack in the stone. Small veins of metal marred by pickaxe marks lined the right wall. The mine tunnel joined with a more natural cave opening. This cave had a floor of strange cobblestones which were worn down by carts. The cobblestones were exceedingly out of place with the more natural looking walls.

"What is this?"

"Not sure. But those stones are part of the old city."

"How deep does the old city go?"

"I don't know. Not too many people go down there. Those who go too far never return. Dark things dwell below. Best not to think of it."

We continued on and entered another tunnel which was more of a more familiar brick and mortar. The scents of lumber began to fill the air as we climbed down a set of steps carved into the rock. While the stench of the underneath was unpleasant, I was growing accustomed to the usual smells and had learned to ignore them. A sudden change in this was strangely pleasant. It did make me take a deeper breath than normal which I immediately regretted. Gaging, I covered my mouth and nose with my cloak.

Making our way up, we entered a narrow passage that merged with a drainage pipe. The water slicked the sides which were covered with green moss and glittered in the lantern light. Small holes in the roof showed the street where water drains were positioned on street corners. We followed the drain to the river where a grid of metal bars blocked our passage. Just beyond was the water of the River Earn. It rushed past quickly, the fresh scents of lumber and of factory air a sweet bouquet in comparison. This time when I took a deep breath, the air was fresh and I let out a sigh of relief. Placing my hand on the metal bars, I looked out over the river.

"Osbert, how do we get out?"

"I am not sure. All I know is that the lumber mill should be directly above us. If the Crooked Inn is located behind the mill, it should be rather close."

Turning my attention back to the thick metal grate, I examined it for weakness. The criss crossing metal bars were woven together and sealed with a metal band. The metal band, which was near perfectly fit to the inside of the circular tunnel exit, was bolted in four places. The iron had corroded from the water and the bottom bolts were rusted. Placing my hands on the bars beside the bolt, I pushed hard. The metal groaned slightly as it flexed, but it did not give way.

"Here, help me with this."

Osbert joined me and together we pushed. The metal bars bowed outward from the pressure, then the bottom bolt snapped. The sound was loud, echoing back down the tunnel from where we had come.

I froze, waiting and listening. There was no sound from either within or without. A few minutes passed in silence and my throbbing heart slowed.

"Again," I said, this time pressing my entire body against the metal grate.

Together we pushed, bowing the metal and bending several of the bars. The second bolt broke free of the stone and we lurched forward. Catching myself before slamming my head against the metal bars, I let out a grunt. My hand stung from the small cuts in my palms. Osbert growled and shook his head, letting out a string of foul curses under his breath.

"Are you alright?"

"Yes. I'm fine."

"Good, because I am going to need a favor."

"What do you need?"

"I have a friend who runs the establishment above. Her name is Madam Acacia. I want you to go discreetly to see if she is available. I need her to get a message to my friends, but I need to know it is safe."

"So what do I need to do?"

"Simple, I want you to ask her how Tristin is doing. Tell her that a mutual friend was inquiring after her well being. Do not say any more than this unless you are in private."

"And if she says no."

"Then return and make sure you are not followed."

Osbert shook his head. "I don't want to go out there."

"I know. But I can't. If someone recognizes me, then I will be in danger. If you've never been there before, chances are you won't be recognized. Please Osbert."

My friend paused, seeming to mull it over.

"Here," I pulled out a few silver coins from my purse. "Buy a few drinks while you are up there."

Osbert took the coins without hesitation, then getting onto the ground, crawled underneath the grate. His waist caught on the bars and I rushed over, lifting them up so he could wriggle the rest of the way out. Standing up, Osbert glanced over his shoulder, gave me a single nod, and then began to climb up and out of the pipe. He disappeared from view and his footsteps faded, replaced by the sound of rushing water.

As I waited for Osbert to return, the minutes stretched into hours. Sitting beside the broken grate, my eyes traced the river, watching as the small swells and waves glittered bright from the sunlight. Tapping my fingers on the metal bars, I listened for any sounds or movements from above. My heart pounded in my chest and my breathing was shallow and staggered. Slowly, the sunlight faded, and the afternoon became dark and cloudy. My eyes grew heavy and I struggled to remain awake. Getting to my feet, I stood, which helped, though I still felt drowsy.

When the sound of footsteps finally came from above, I scooted back into the darkness, placing my hand on my sword. A pair of old boots dangled from above and I relaxed. Osbert dropped down and stepped to the side. He reached up and a second pair of boots fell into view. Drawing the sword a few inches, I readied myself. The second person was much smaller, with a face painted in white with dark fox-like eye lines. It was strange how relieved I was at seeing Omaria. We were still little more than acquaintances, but seeing someone I knew I could trust after weeks of isolation was a relief I needed.

"Caden?" the woman asked, stepping up to the bars.

"I'm here, Omaria," I said, emerging from the tunnel into the light. "I was expecting Acacia."

"She is otherwise occupied. But rest assured that whatever you need, I will relay your message to my mistress." The woman lifted her hands and gave me a soft smile.

"Of course. Did anyone follow you?"

"No."

"Good." I let out a deep breath and relaxed. "I was hoping you would be able to get in contact with Tristin."

"I am sure that can be arranged. But it might take a few days in order to remain discreet."

"How are things going?"

"Things in the city have been quite chaotic. To be honest, you are the talk of the city."

"Are they watching the inn?"

"Who's *they*?"

"The Malkethians."

"No. They might have a few people watching the place, but the new Sorcerers are honored guests of the city. The Queen has them staying at the Castle."

"What about their soldiers?"

"Most of them are being housed with the Queen's guard. I've seen a few of them about, but we haven't had any come to the inn."

I paused, taking in the information. "So you are certain you can get a message to Tristin."

"I already said I could. What do you want me to tell her?"

"Just that I am alive. I'm more interested in any information she can provide me about the state of affairs. She should also have something of mine that I need and we need to arrange a way that I can acquire it undetected."

"Can you be any more specific?"

"No."

"Fine. I will see your message is delivered."

"Thank you." I felt a sense of relief come over me. For the first time in weeks, I finally felt like I had a chance. With my weapons and armor, I would stand a much better chance at a head on confrontation with Isar.

"Caden, do you need anything?"

"Perhaps a change of clothes, a new cloak, and food."

"Wait here. I'll go get that for you."

"I will go with Omaria for the supplies." Osbert said. "I still need to buy that drink."

"Just be sure to bring one back for me," I said.

"Of course," he said.

As the two of them climbed out of the tunnel, I sat back down and found that I could actually relax. For the first time in a long time, it felt like there was something more to do than wait for an inevitable tragedy. Closing my eyes, I began to drift off to sleep. As my mind slipped into dreams, I heard the soft echoes of distant laughter.

CHAPTER NINE
WRETCHEDNESS

T he end of the tunnel glowed a bright red and acrid smoke filled the air, swirling at the top of the tunnel. Osbert rushed ahead, light from the swinging lantern causing strange shadows and shapes on the walls. The walls were slick with blood and long pawprints covered the ground.

Shit! I thought, drawing my sword and rushing forward.

When I reached the gate, I barreled into Osbert, knocking him to the floor. He said nothing as he rolled over and got back to his feet. Both of us examined the absolute butchery which had taken place in the camp.

Blood covered the ground, dismembered body parts littering the ground. Each corpse had been torn apart into almost unrecognizable pieces. A severed head resting on the ground was missing its face, the skin a bloodied mess. The eyes were still intact and it almost felt as though they were looking up at me. My eyes scanned the ground quickly, searching for movement, searching for survivors.

The tents had been torn down and set alight, the cloth still burning, sending black smoke into the air. Several large jars of slush had spilled out and were burning with bright pink flames.

Holding out my hand, I pulled the fire towards me. Flames shot through the air, twisting and spinning like ribbons caught in a wind, and coalesced into a single sphere of fire which hovered over my left hand. I shrunk the ball to a size just larger than my fist, turning the flames a brilliant white. As everything stopped burning, the last plumes of smoke floated up to the ceiling where it slowly began to filter up and out through the tunnels which lead to the canal exit.

"Osbert, stay put," I commanded, stalking forward.

I walked through the butchery, careful not to tread on any body parts, which proved to be rather difficult the further I went in. An unnatural rage swelled within me, enhanced by my magic, and prodded at me to unleash it. Forcing myself to remain in control of my power, I bridled the rage within, and focused only on my search.

Reaching the edge of the camp, I climbed up the stone steps towards the tunnels which led out of the underground. There was no blood on the steps and when I reached the top, there was no sign that anyone had come or gone. Wanting to be certain, I followed the tunnels up and around the corner to the door which led out onto the canal path. It was still secured with the chain and there were no signs of blood or other markings. Smoke continued to flow past me, moving with ease through the gaps of the door. I paused, wondering if the smoke would attract attention.

I placed my hand on the stake which held the door in place and tugged on it. The door jostled slightly. Opening the door, I peeked out, the dark cloudy sky slightly orange from the setting sun. The smoke rose up but mingled with the other smokestacks rising from nearby chimneys. The canal was as abandoned as it always was. I took a few breaths of fresh air before closing the door and turning around to go back to the camp.

Walking back down the tunnel, I took a moment to pause at the bottom of the stairs. I tossed the ball of flame towards the center of the cave and once it reached the center, held it in place. The floating fire cast brilliant white light upon the entire camp and from my vantage, I could see everything. There was a pattern in the carnage. Both human and Ghoul footprints covered the ground, blood leaving clear marks where they had gone. The handmarks of Ghouls were prevalent and I could see where they had torn and rent the cloth tents.

I counted the bodies, and it soon became clear that the pieces had been scattered in an attempt to conceal the numbers. Less than half of the people who had been living in this cave seem to be accounted for.

Did they flee into the caves or were they taken?

Following the trail of bloody prints with my eyes, I saw they led towards the southern end of the cavern where the Red Hook gang member would come and go with his wagon of slush. The blood which covered this section was smeared and trod upon by such a significant enough number of feet that I couldn't tell how many people had been forced through. The gate which blocked this entrance off was broken into pieces and a body had been nailed to the wall with long spikes. The bald head had a gash in the side and blood covered most of the upper torso. A small hand wagon lay broken at his feet, the empty jars of slush piled at his feet.

That rules the slush trader out, I thought, examining the body.

Over the next hour, Osbert and I carefully looked through all of the half burned tents and bodies. There was nothing left behind that gave me a clue as to who was responsible. Joining Osbert by the burned pile of rubbish that had been his bed, I placed my hand on my friend's shoulder. "We should go."

"No. We cannot leave them like this."

"I wasn't planning to."

"But how can we bury them?"

"That wasn't the idea I had in mind."

"You mean to burn them?" Osbert asked, more to himself. He shook his head for a moment before grunting in agreement. "Do it."

I reached up and called the sphere of fire down. It fell slowly, and I let it land among the mess of ruined tents and rubbish. As the flames caught alight, I waved my hand and each of the piles of cloth which surrounded the bodies burst into flames.

"Go back down the tunnel and wait for me."

Osbert picked up the pack of supplies Omaria had given us and stalked back down the tunnel from where we had come. As soon as I could no longer hear his footsteps, I stepped forward and raised my hands. Fire flared from the ground to the ceiling, burning everything at once. I felt the fire as it ate at the cloth, at the flesh, and the refuse of the cave, cleansing it. The smoke which filled the cave created a cloud of darkness which hung over the brilliant light.

The flames swirled around me, but as I stepped forward, it parted for me like fog before a boat. As quickly as the fire had begun, it was snuffed out, leaving me in complete darkness. My eyes took a moment to adjust but I could see the ash covered ground of the cavern well. The smoke slowly descended from the cavern above, creating a cloud which swirled all around me.

A strange figure took shape from the cloud of darkness, appearing in the form of a man, the phantom slowly walked towards me. The first thing that came to mind was the shadowy figure of the Shantenbose and I drew my sword on instinct. The man of smoke held up his hand and stopped walking towards me.

"Caden."

Hearing my name spoken aloud was like listening to stones grind together. A shudder went down my spine and I grit my teeth against the sensation. The wave of cold which washed over me drove the fire from my blood and replaced it with a void of darkness. My breath caught in my chest and I dropped to my knees.

"Caden?"

Looking up, I saw the shadow cross the distance in a single step, coming to a step before me. The shape had shifted and was smaller, more fluid, and feminine. The face looked down at me with kindness, a smile parting curved lips.

"What are you?" I asked, my voice little more than a croak.

"Get onto your feet."

I obeyed the voice which seemed to have more substance, more surety. Once again, I asked my question again. "Who are you?"

"Come, find me." The voice was silky smooth and almost intimately familiar. *"I wait for you."*

The apparition vanished in the blink of an eye, leaving no trace in the air that it had ever been there. Standing in place, I found myself unable to move, unable to think. My mind swirled with strange unfamiliar images of a large cavern, the walls made of skulls. Clenching my fists, my entire body began to shake, and I fought back a wave of nausea that was filling me. A soft echo from behind stirred me back to my surroundings and I looked over my shoulder to see Osbert emerging once more from the tunnel. He pushed open the gate, his eyes looking around with alarm. The small lantern he held gave off only enough light to illuminate the sharp lines and edges of the cave.

"Caden."

Hearing Osbert speak my name banished the strange residual feelings the shadow had made upon my mind and I took in a deep breath, relaxing.

"Sorry, I didn't mean to take so long."

"What do we do now?"

"We should find a new place to camp. We can't stay here."

"I want to find the people who did this. I want to kill them."

"We're in agreement. But we have to find who did this first."

"It was Claudius."

"How do you know that?" I asked, walking over to join him beside the gate.

"This is not the first time a camp has been slaughtered. People disappear from time to time. Claudius takes them down to the city below. He does terrible things to them, feeds them to his beasts. That is why we built these gates. I thought that we would be safe here. That we would be better off together than alone."

"Do you know where this Claudius is?"

"Yes."

"Then let's find you a weapon."

Traveling through the tunnels seemed to take no time at all. I led Osbert through the tunnels to the central sewer line, following the side path until we arrived at the secret Red Hook door. It was the only place I could think of where we might find a weapon that was close. When I pressed the stone, unlocking the door, Osbert did not hesitate to push it open. As soon as I stepped into the room, I closed the secret door which groaned slightly. The sound of grating stone echoed down the tunnel which as before ended with orange light.

"How did you find this place?" Osbert asked.

"A few weeks ago, after you had purchased some of the slush, I followed the man here."

"That wasn't a good idea."

"We'll see."

Osbert grunted and with some confidence started down the tunnel. Though I was unsure what we would find, I strangely felt the same lack of apprehension. When we reached the bottom, I found that we were in a simple yet spacious rectangular room.

Rows upon rows of crates were stacked, all painted with the familiar Red Hook. Symbols had also been painted on the outsides, marking dates. These looked exactly like the crates I had found in Merek's cellar after he had disappeared.

In one corner, separated from the crates of slush by a short brick wall was a living space, furnished with a bed, table, and small kitchenette. The wood stove was burning and a small lantern was lit on the table. They were the only sources of light, but provided a good glow that lit the entire room.

"Check the rows, see if there is anything or anyone else here."

My voice fell on deaf ears.

Osbert had wandered to one of the crates of slush and was looking at it with wide eyes. He reached in and pulled out a giant jar of the foul stuff. He had the jar open before he seemed to realize what he was doing. His fingers hovered over the top, twitching as he contemplated plunging them deep within the drug.

"Osbert," I said, trying to make my voice steady. "We still need to find who killed the others. I need your help. Without you, we won't be able to avenge them."

He looked at me and his eyes were wild. Osbert bared his teeth and with a growl put the lid back on the jar. It took him several minutes before he placed it back into the crate. As soon as he took a step away, the hold the slush had over him seemed to break slightly. Osbert growled again and turned away, tears spilling down his eyes.

"This is not a good place for me. We should leave."

I nodded.

Taking the lantern from the table, I took a quick look through the kitchenette and was disappointed by the contents. The food was little better than what Omaria had provided us and mostly looked like it was on the verge of spoiling.

"Caden," Osbert said, his voice strangely desperate.

My eyes snapped to him and I saw that he was pointing to something on the far wall. Following the direction he pointed with my eyes, I scanned the far wall. In the corner a dark black slime was leaking from the walls. The strange substance reflected the light like tar but it didn't seem to omit any sort of smell. Though it was strange, I didn't seem to find it any cause for alarm.

"What is it?"

"We need to leave, now."

I didn't question my friend, following him up and out. When we reached the top, I pulled down on the inner mechanism which secured the false wall and it swung open. Osbert stepped out, wringing his hands. A fist emerged into view, connecting with Osberts jaw, and sending him toppling back over the edge of the walkway. He cried out as he fell backwards into the sewer and a large man with a studded jerkin stepped into view. The man lifted a large iron mace and swung it at me. Stepping back, I slammed my back against the wall and unable to draw my sword, I drew my dagger.

Swinging the mace again, he connected with my dagger close to the cross guard. One of the mace spikes struck my finger. Pain shot across my hand and I dropped the dagger. Ducking, I managed to dodge another attack as I backed into the tunnel. The man pursued and as he raised his mace to swing, I punched him in the face with my razor gauntlet. As the blades and spikes cut his skin, the man stepped back and knocked his shoulder into the door. Leaping out of his way, I moved down the tunnel and drew my sword. As the attacker regained his bearing, I did a quick step and thrust, cutting the man in the side of the neck. The steel of the longsword was sharp and it sliced through the skin easily. The man lifted his arm and used his metal vambrace to knock away the sword.

Two more goons stepped into view, entering the tunnel. The

three of them paused, looking at me with narrow eyes. Each wore the same metal studded armor and held a metal mace, but their appearance was vastly different. Of the two new goons, one was tall and thin, the other fat and balding. They stood on either side of the first man who's long beard was dripping with blood from the wound that I had made on his face with my gauntlet. While the tunnel entrance was large enough for the three men to stand together, the tunnel was too restrictive. This gave them pause and I raised my sword, ready to fight the first who was brave enough to attack.

"Is this him?" The pudgy goon in the middle asked. He wiped several strands of his long wispy hair from his face.

"No, it ain't him," the first man who I had attacked replied. "But we can't have any witnesses."

The three men smiled, their teeth as gnarly and rotten as Osberts.

"So you killed the others?" I asked.

The three men paused, the first furrowing his brow before saying, "Others, what others?"

"The camp below the canal."

"We don't have time for this," the third gangly man who hadn't yet spoken said. "Kill him Ike!"

The first man, Ike, growled and brandished his mace. Holding out my sword, ready to defend myself, I saw someone else creep out of the darkness behind. Osbert was sopping wet and was holding a dagger. Growling to draw additional attention to myself, I lunged forward and thrust the longsword towards Ike. The tip of my sword grazed his jawline before the man knocked aside my blade once again with his mace. Leaping back, I thrust again, this time catching the man in his knee. The blade glanced off the bone and Ike howled with pain, losing his balance and falling to the side. As Ike fell, one of his companions lunged forward, swinging a club at my head.

Blocking the blow with my longsword, I took several quick steps back, drawing the man deeper into the tunnel. My eyes glanced past him and I watched as Osbert crept up behind the third goon and plunged a dagger deep into his neck. Blood sprayed onto the wall as the man fell, landing with a thud on the ground. The man who challenged me was startled by the sound and as he turned back to look, I stabbed him in the side. My sword cut through the side of his leather jerkin, piercing deep into his stomach. Wordlessly, he fell to his knees, eyes wide and mouth open as he looked at the ground.

Pulling out the longsword, I quickly slashed down again, cutting off the wounded man's head. It toppled forward and rolled on to the ground, passing me by as it tumbled down the tunnel behind me. Osbert pulled his knife from the neck of the man he had killed and stalked over to Ike who was groaning with pain. Placing the knife against his neck, my friend looked up at me, anger in his eyes.

"Should I kill him!"

"No! Please, don't kill me," Ike blubbered.

"Give me a good reason why we should spare your life," I hissed.

"I will do anything, please."

"Tell us, why did you come here?"

"We followed you."

"Why?"

"The boss sent us to make sure there were no witnesses. When we saw you emerge from the tunnel, we knew you had seen what the boss had done."

"Who is your boss?"

"Claudius?" Osbert asked, pressing the knife closer to Ike's throat.

"No, Claudius is dead. He was killed several weeks ago when

the Red Hook Compound was raided. Several thieves broke in and set the Ghouls loose upon us."

I clenched my jaw and nodded. "So, who is in charge of Red Hook now?"

"No one. My boss took control of the eastern side of the Raha. We've just about lost control of the rest of our territories."

"You still didn't answer my question. Who is your boss?"

"His name is Dreth."

Why does that name sound so familiar?

"What does Dreth want?" Osbert asked. He was pressing the knife hard against Ike's skin, the blade drawing blood.

"He's trying to take over all of the slush trade in the city. Now that both leaders of Red Hook and Grinning Tombstone are dead, there is a void to fill and my boss intends to unify the trade under a new banner."

"Shit!" I growled and punched the wall. The razors on my gauntlet created sparks as they collided with the stones. I punched the wall again, this time, bending one of the spikes. "Dammit all!"

"Should we kill him now?" Osbert smiled as he said it.

"No, please! There is so much more I know. Don't kill me." Ike's pleading turned into a burble of sounds which were unintelligible.

"Where did he take the captives?"

"To the Sunken Foundry."

"And what does he intend to do with them?"

Ike went pale, his eyes dropping to the stone ground he knelt upon. "They will be killed, slowly."

"Why?"

"To collect blood to make more slush."

I froze, a chill rushing down my body. Osbert looked up at me with wild eyes. He slacked his grip on the knife and Ike bucked him off. Kicking the goon in the face, I pressed the tip of my sword against his throat.

"Move, and I will kill you."

Ike froze and whimpered.

Osbert shook his head, crawled to where the dagger had fallen, then got to his feet. "What now?"

"I need a moment to think. Go shut the door."

Nodding, Osbert stalked up to the entrance and shut the door. It closed with a loud grinding of stone. Plunging us into semi-dark, I waved my hand and produced a flame. Ike recoiled, closing his eyes.

"Get to your feet."

Ike obeyed and I marched him down the tunnel where I instructed him to sit beside the wall. Osbert stood over him, once again pressing my knife against the man's throat. Reaching into the supplies Omaria had given us, I removed some rope and went over and bound Ike's hands and feet. As soon as the goon was secure, I dropped the fire at his feet and watched as it burned on the stone. The goon's eyes grew wide as he looked at it which made me smile.

Walking over to the old bed, I sat down on it. Rubbing my eyes, I contemplated my next move. I had inadvertently taken out the leaders of the city's two most dangerous criminal organiza-tions and now an underground battle was raging for control. The right thing to do would be to end this once and for all. After months of working to eradicate the slush trade, it was clear my efforts had made things worse. Vivienne and I had been going about it the wrong way. But my frustration and guilt would get me nowhere. Hindsight however could perhaps provide me with a clear path forward.

Glancing at Ike who hadn't moved an inch, I noticed that his attention was still on the fire. I then looked to my left at Osbert who was rolling a jar of slush between his hands. He had a deep frown as he was looking at the stuff. Our eyes met for a brief moment and I could see both shame and pain in his eyes. Knowing a little more about how the foul drug was created seemed to give him enough strength to resist, but only just. The longer we stayed here, the longer I took to make up my mind, the harder it would become for my friend to resist temptation. Some fights cannot be won by willpower alone.

"What are you thinking?" I asked Osbert, hoping that a conversation would help us both make up our minds.

"That I am sitting next to enough slush to finally kill myself." Osbert's eyes seemed far away. "But I've never been so disgusted in my life."

Getting up off the bed, I walked over to Osbert and placed my hand on his shoulder. I had no words for him, but I felt his pain. More than that. I knew his pain, the urge that drove someone to do what they shouldn't. When he looked up at me, tears were streaming down his face. I gave his shoulder a gentle squeeze.

Osbert threw the vile of slush against the wall. "I can't fathom how many people have suffered because I kept using this swiving drug! Caden, I feel sick. My skin crawls at the thought of myself. Everything I have given up because of it."

"Then let's burn this place and go rescue the others."

"May the Valon guide us," Osbert said, wiping his eyes on his dirty sleeve.

I went up the tunnel and found the mace Ike had dropped on the ground. Picking it up, I returned and handed it to Osbert.

"Here's a proper weapon."

Osbert took the mace and ran his hand along the handle towards the metal spikes. He then glanced down at Ike who was looking at us, a defeated expression on his face. I used my sword to cut the bonds on Ike's feet.

"Get up. It's time you take us to the foundry." I commanded.

Struggling to his feet, Ike remained hunched over as he began walking towards the tunnel. Osbert followed after him, keeping the mace at the ready. I heard their footsteps echo until they reached the top. As soon as I heard the grinding of the stone wall, I walked over to the first row of slush crates and placed my hand upon the wood. Taking in a deep breath, I pulled the flame I had left burning on the ground, from the stove, and from the lantern into my body. The fire invigorated my blood and rushed down my arm and out my fingertips.

Pulling my hand away, I saw a handprint of flame on the box for a fraction of a second. The flame spread quickly and I willed the fire to burn hot. The flames leapt from the first crate to the second. Waving my hand, I pulled a portion of the fire away and formed it into a ball. Casting the ball at the second row of crates, I watched as they ignited. Jars of heated slush began to explode, the sound of breaking clay and glass was loud. The fire began to burn a strange pink color and dark smoke rose to the storeroom ceiling.

As the fire raged, I felt the urge deep within me. The subtle call that whispered for me to use magic. Since it was an ever present force, one which had plagued me for years, I had forgotten what it was like not to feel it. It connected me to the flames, whispered things to me, made my fingers tense with anticipation. But there was a renewed urge, something deep and primal which was unfamiliar. It pulled me to the darkness, whispered things in my mind. I could hear it laugh at me. Despite the fire, I felt a chill, as though ice were being pressed against the back of my neck. Something was terribly wrong and I fixated on the feeling, unable to move a muscle.

The flames continued to dance and spin, moving of their own accord as they spread. Quickly, every crate was touched by their orange and red hunger. Odd shapes moved in and out of the flames and I saw dark faces. The shadows were smiling at me and I took a tentative step back. These faces took on familiar shapes until standing before me in the fire was an older man with gray hair and criss crossing scars which covered his cheeks. My pulse quickened as I beheld my master, unsure if it was a vision or the beginnings of madness. Master Cairan smiled and then was gone, replaced by flickering flames. Blinking away the visions of the ghost, I let out a breath.

"Don't lose your mind," I said.

Turning from the fire, I retrieved the pack of supplies and hurried up the tunnel. Osbert and Ike were standing without. Closing the false wall behind me, I gave my friend a stiff nod and he pressed the tip of the mace into Ike's back.

"Get moving," Osbert growled. "Take us to the foundry."

CHAPTER TEN

THE SUNKEN FOUNDRY

Ike had led us deep below any section of the underground where I had ever ventured. The first set of tunnels were hewn from the rock and buttressed like the tunnels of a mine. Then the staircases descended through naturally occurring caves and cracks in the earth. It was a maze of tunnels which were not marked like the other more familiar passages above. When we reached the bottom, Ike began to grow nervous, wringing his hands and wiping sweat from his bow.

"Do you see these markings?" He nodded to the red symbols painted on the walls as we turned down a right passageway. "The sharp angular symbol will point the directions you are supposed to go. There is always an arrow pointing the right direction, you just need to know where to look."

"And the other symbols? What do they mean?"

"They don't mean anything. Just added to be a distraction."

I paid close attention to the markings and as we continued to go deeper and deeper. Each time we saw one, I picked out the arrow. Now that I knew what I was looking for, it was easy to find what I would have otherwise missed. As we passed another cross-roads, we turned left and began to descend a stone staircase which was carved from the stones of a narrow passage. With every step, I felt my unease grow. Notwithstanding, I felt confident that I could find my way back. At least I prayed to the Valon that I would be able to.

As we continued down the stairs, I could sense that Osbert was also getting nervous. He was twitching his fingers, constantly tapping on the mace which hung from his belt. Ike still took the lead but with his hands bound before him, he hadn't made any attempt to escape. I followed the two men, carefully watching.

"Why haven't we seen anyone?" Osbert asked.

"Do you want to?" Ike replied.

"No."

"There are many ways to get to where we are going. There is one in the sewer, another through the canal, but can only be entered from outside. There is also a final entrance just outside the northern wall. But seeing as how you wanted me to lead you there unnoticed, we are taking the tunnels."

"How many men should we be expecting?" I asked, taking in a deep breath and we reached the bottom of the stairs and entered a more natural cave formation.

"At any given time, a hundred. Perhaps more."

"How many captives?"

Ike was silent. "Many."

Osbert growled at the answer and I placed my hand on his shoulder.

"Keep calm my friend. We'll rescue them soon enough."

"And make them pay."

Ike didn't say another word as he led us through the maze for another hour. Making a few sharp turns we entered a rather sizable cave. There was a small opening up ahead at the base of a wall. To get through it, we would have to crawl on our bellies and slide under one at a time.

"It's just under there."

"Keep an eye on him, Osbert. I'm going to take a look."

Walking over to the wall, I got down on my belly and crawled slowly through the opening. It emerged into another small grotto which was partially shrouded by stalactites. Through the sharp hanging rocks, I could see down a hundred feet into the larger cavern below. Awestruck, I looked at the twenty or so stone buildings that had been erected on the floor of the cave, creating a strange underground village. Several of the buildings were built right next to the walls and windows had been carved from the walls. Lanterns lit the cobblestones streets and shone a dull orange light upon the buildings. Several people were walking about, carrying boxes or barrels. Sentries walked between the buildings, their worn leather armor stained a blood red.

On the far side of the village was a gate which was guarded by four sentries. Behind the gate was a tunnel and stairs which ascended. From my vantage point, I couldn't see more than twenty steps up before the top of the tunnel cut them from my view. Several other entryways and exits could be seen, these were also guarded similarly but they did not have gates.

In the middle of the cavern, a deep chasm split the village in two. My eyes followed the crack towards the back left corner. A bridge spanned the gap, leading to a five story building built into the wall. There was a large open door and through the opening I could see the light from a forge fire. The sounds of whips and screams permeated the air, echoing from the building. Through the shutterless windows I could see moving shadows. Leaning forward, I focused on the shadows and saw several human shapes pass before the upper windows.

I studied the small underground village, tracing the lines between buildings, trying to plot out different paths we could take so our passage would continue to remain unnoticed. Before we did anything, I wanted to know exactly how many captives needed to be rescued. If worse came to worse, I would fight my way through every soldier. For the last few months I had been fighting these gangs and I was certain that if they realized we were there to rescue the captives, that would put them in danger. I was not about to let my recklessness cause any more death.

The small village made a lot of noise and the more I observed, the more obvious their industrialization became. One of the buildings beside the foundry was blowing glass. I watched as they crafted glass bottles. The building beside it seemed to be a large storehouse and men were carrying crates inside. A whole operation had been built and was running like a well manned ship. Everyone seemed to have a task and was going about it quickly.

I observed a distinct difference between the two types of people. Those who guarded or managed the operations all wore dark red or black. Those who were laboring were dressed in rags and had iron collars and bracelets. Though no chains hung from them, there were single rings attached to each. As I watched the prisoner slaves work, I wondered by what misfortune they had come to this fate.

No matter, soon you will be free.

A shrill cry from the tunnel behind me made me jump. My skin erupted with gooseflesh as I waited to be noticed. After a few minutes, I realized that the sound had gone unnoticed and everyone below continued about their business. The screams from the foundry continued to echo around, a perfect mask. Crawling back through the tunnel, I found Osbert standing above the collapsed body of Ike. The tip of his mace dripped blood and a wound was dripping from a large gash on the side of Ike's head.

"What the hell Osbert!"

"He tried to attack me."

"His hands were tied. You didn't have to kill him."

"I'm sorry. I turned my back on him to look under the tunnel and he rammed me."

Stooping over, I placed my hand on Ike's neck and felt for a pulse. It was weak but present. The blood was still leaking from the head wound and I had nothing to stop the bleeding. In a few minutes he would be dead.

Muttering a string of curses under my breath, I began to think of what to do next. "Put on his armor."

Osbert balked at me.

"Do it."

He obeyed but grumbled the entire time. Somehow it looked rather fitting on my friend, the dirty metal studded leather making his grimy hands and face look less out of place. Osbert hung the mace on the belt and folded his arms.

"What now?"

"Follow me under. We need to find a way through and if you look like one of them, we may be able to convince them we belong."

"Not a terrible idea. But if they see us, how do we explain away your appearance? You don't look like one of them."

"We'll figure it out."

"That's not at all comforting."

"It's the best I can manage."

"Fine. I'll go first."

I watched Osbert as he got to the ground and crawled through the opening and into the cavern. I followed him through and remaining as silent as possible, I got to my feet, stepped up to my friend, and peered through the hanging stalactites.

"What is this place?" Osbert asked, shaking his head. The long greasy strands of his hair swayed back and forth, catching on his shoulders. "I can't believe this exists."

"It's quite astonishing."

"I am assuming the large building at the edge of the chasm is the foundry?"

"That makes the most sense."

"Then we should climb the chasm."

"What?" I asked, raising my eyebrows. Osbert looked at me then pointed.

"See down there."

I looked, following where my friend pointed. The crack which split the cave floor and ran between the buildings and the foundry was deep. There was a line in the stone, like a small pathway that started on the edge and worked its way towards the foundry. I almost lost sight of it in the darkness, but it eventually led to the stone wall just beneath the foundry. The wall was rough and climbable. My eyes retraced the pathway and where it would start. There were no guards and the two buildings below would hide us from the sight of their view. It was possible, though perhaps foolish.

Are there any better options? I wondered.

Letting out a sigh, I nodded. "Fine. We may be swiving fools, but it seems like the best option for us to remain unnoticed."

"Follow me."

Osbert proved to be a skilled climber and he moved with the grace of a man accustomed to the dark underground. It was almost like watching a spider at work, crawling down from the grotto and onto the odd cobblestone paved floor of the cave. Slinking between the buildings, we reached the edge of the chasm. It was much deeper than it had appeared from up above and the depth made me feel like I was looking into the abyss of perdition itself. Bracing myself, I watched Osbert carefully as he climbed down to a ledge more than a hundred feet below. Once his feet were firmly planted on the stone, he looked up and beckoned for me to follow.

With some reluctance, I swallowed the fear of falling into the chasm and began my descent. The stone was rough and broken, leaving a good number of firm handholds. Once my feet were resting on the small lip of rock, I felt a little more steady. Slowly shuffling to the side, we placed our backs against the wall and began to slowly move our way down the crack towards the foundry.

The walls were slick from water and keeping my hand pressed against it, I searched for handholds in the lumpy stone. Where possible, I gripped cracks and ridges which only momentarily made me feel more secure. My eyes kept glancing down into the darkness, each time it seemed to grow deeper and deeper. Cursing under my breath, I forced myself to continue making progress downward. After an hour of slowly creeping along, I found myself glancing into the chasm and this time I actually saw the bottom. The shapes on the ground were a blend of rounded and sharp. The color was distorted by the shadow, but parts of the ground appeared yellow-white while others were black as tar.

"Osbert," I whispered.

My friend turned to look back at me, glowering.

"What?" He hissed.

"Can you see the bottom?"

Osbert looked down and his scowl deepened. "What kind of swiving question is that? Of course I can't."

"I can," I admitted, looking back down.

"Please tell me that you see water down there."

"I'm afraid not."

"Well, that's unfortunate." Osbert said with a wry chuckle. "What do you see?"

"It looks like a pit filled with bones."

"How wonderful. That's even better than I'd hoped for."

I let out a laugh and shook my head. Osbert smiled and continued inching forward.

"Caden, if by some grace from the Valon we survive this, I plan on leaving these horrid tunnels for good."

"What will you do?"

"I don't know. But I can't stay here any longer. I'd rather die trying for a better life than to remain down here."

"Os, when we finish this, I promise to help you in any way I can. Whatever aid I can offer, is yours. Including the rest of my gold."

"You don't have to do that," Osbert said.

"It's not doing me any good. I've been hiding for too long anyway. It's about time I face my own problems head on as well."

"You've never told me why you came down here."

"Maybe when this is all over, I'll tell you."

We were silent for a while, moving along the ledge at a snail's pace. There were sections where we were forced to climb deeper and others where we climbed back up. Reaching a much bigger ledge which allowed for a better footing, we began to make better progress towards the foundry.

"Caden, do you see that?" Osbert pointed down below. "There's movement on the wall."

Stopping, I looked down and saw nothing. There were small cracks and crevices in the section of the wall that Osbert gestured to which made it difficult to see. I watched and waited. A howl sounded through the cave, breaking the silence. It was the shrill cry of wind as it tore through a tunnel rather than a cry from the lips of a beast. The sound made the hair on the back of my arms rise and the back of my neck began to prickle.

As silence once more returned to the cavern, I saw movement from the corner of my vision. My eyes snapped to the location of the movement and I saw that the wall was shimmering. The stones were sliding, oozing upwards. Fascinated by the strangeness, I leaned forward, squinting in an effort to get a better view of the creature. It had been a long time since I had seen a Flesh Eating Mire. The creatures lacked intelligence and moved about like living rot. With little interest for the living, the mire would keep to itself.

"Don't worry about it," I said, shuffling a few inches forward on the ledge. "It's just a Mire."

"A what?"

"It's a Mire. A flesh eating slime. Don't worry, it's on the other side of the chasm and they only are attracted to things that are already dead. Most of the time."

"And what about when they aren't?"

"Like I said. Don't let it touch you."

"Caden. Then what is that?"

Osbert motioned to the ledge about a hundred feet ahead. The wall was moving downward, the thin dark slime coating the entire pathway. It was moving slowly, like molasses being poured over griddle cakes. Looking back the way we had come, I saw that the walls of the crevice below were similarly moving. The thick Mire was crawling towards us and my skin began to crawl as the sharp scent of rot filled my nose.

Reaching out my hand, I sensed something in the air, like there was a thick invisible vapor that lingered around us that made my fingertips cold. The slime stopped moving, everything growing still. Taking in a deep breath, the scent of the rot had vanished, replaced by the cold dampness of the cave. Licking my lips, I found that they tasted like cold wet stones and iron. It was almost like an old rusty nail had been placed into my mouth. Resisting the urge to spit, I wiped my mouth on the back of my hand.

Looking back at the Mire, I watched as it slowly moved away, climbing back towards the cracks and crevices from which it had emerged. My nose felt warm and sniffling, I wiped my nose on my shoulder. Checking the walls for the Mire, I saw that they had disappeared. Looking at Osbert, I nodded to him, motioning for him to continue. Osbert looked at me with a perplexed expression and pointed to my face.

"Your nose is bleeding."

I felt my nose drip again, this time the warmth trailing down to the corner of my mouth. Wiping my nose again on my shirt, I sniffed, forcing the blood back up. I felt some of the blood travel up and then down the back of my throat. Unsure what to do, I leaned forward and let the blood continue to drip into the cavern rather than onto my clothes.

The droplets of blood fell into the darkness, invisible to my eyes as they disappeared below. The movement on the stone walls began again. Instead of crawling towards us, the Mire began to crawl down towards the floor of the chasm. After a few minutes, the blood from my nose stopped dripping. Leaning back against the wall, I pressed my sleeve against it, stopping the flow of blood. Turning my head to the side, I saw that the path ahead was now clear of the Mire. Osbert looked sick, his eyes wide.

"Os, I'm alright. Let's get moving."

"Sorry," Osbert said, shuffling a few feet further along the ledge.

It took us another half hour to get to the end of the crevice and reach the wall which sat just below the foundry. Placing my hands on several large jagged stones, I felt an immediate sense of security. Without the sense I was about to fall forward to my doom, I began to climb, clinging to the wall and staying in the shadows. Every few feet we climbed, I would check over my shoulder, looking to see if we had been spotted. My enhanced perception through the darkness made it seem as though every-thing were visible. Perhaps to the normal eye, we would be entirely shrouded in darkness. I hoped that was the case.

Osbert didn't seem to worry and climbed steadily upward. When we reached the top, we moved over to one of the foundry windows. The window was carved from the rock and narrow, not quite large enough for a person to fit through. Taking hold of the window sill, I pulled myself up and looked in. The room was large and carved from the stone. A wooden door had been fitted into an entryway, but there was a sizable gap in the bottom. Shadows flickered as someone walked in front of the light on the other side.

Lowering myself, I waited, listening for movement on the inside of the room.

When I heard nothing, I pulled myself back up and scanned the room once more. There were chains on the far wall and several hooks. Otherwise, the room was empty except for small pieces of straw which had been scattered about.

Climbing away from the prison cell window, I looked over at Osbert who was slowly climbing down to the ledge below. The windows there were much larger and with a grunt, he swung down and entered. The sound of his boots hitting the stone seemed loud in my ears, but the screams which constantly came from within the foundry quickly drowned out the sound.

With a little more caution than my friend, I climbed down the wall and set my feet on the stone lip of the window. Once I had my footing, I reached down and placed both hands on the sides of the window frame before lowering myself down. Perched on the window sill, I felt like a burglar about to enter a home. It made me think of Vivienne and a sad smile flitted across my lips. I missed her and hoped that she was doing alright.

Putting her and the rest of my worries aside, I entered the room and looked around. The room was similar to the one above, with a crudely made wooden door. However, there were no chains. Instead there were shelves which covered the walls. The calcinators, alembics, and lutes were all aligned neatly in rows. All were clean and new. Several boxes on the bottom shelves were sealed and there were no markings or labels. It almost felt like being back in Merek's Alchemy Shop.

Osbert was running his fingers on one of the alembics, tracing the curved top of the glass which turned into a tube that was angled downward, connecting with the cucurbit. He seemed transfixed by the objects, looking closely at them.

"What are these?"

"They're tools used for alchemy. The glass you are touching is called an alembic."

"What's it for?"

"Distilling liquid. I'm guessing these are used when creating slush."

Osbert grumbled and stepped away from the shelves. "They sure have a lot of these things."

"Seeing as how they are all glass, I would guess they might break frequently. Either that, or they are planning to increase production."

"What do we do now?"

"Ike said that they keep the prisoners here in the foundry. Let's split up and go looking for them."

"No. You should stay here. With this armor on, I should look like I belong which will help make it easier for me to wander the place and arouse less suspicion."

"Well, we're in the belly of the beast. If something happens, start making a lot of noise any way you can. If I hear anything irregular, I will come for you and we will abandon any type of stealth. We're either getting out of here with the captives or we aren't getting out."

"Agreed."

As Osbert opened the door, I held up my hand and motioned for him to wait. Walking over to the shelf, I pulled one of the unmarked boxes from the bottom shelves. It was lightweight and jostling it slightly, the contents tinkled together.

"Take this. If it looks like you are doing something, most people should leave you alone. If you are just lurking about, that will raise suspicion."

The advice had originally come from Vivienne and I knew that it would help.

"That's a good idea," Osbert said as took the box.

I opened the door for him and as he stepped outside, I

remained out of view. He looked both ways, gave me a nod, and I shut the door behind him. Standing on the left side of the door beside the hinges, I waited. Time passed so slowly it was grating. Taking a deep breath, I closed my eyes and began to clear my mind.

Each worry that bubbled to the forefront of my mind was fed to the fire which burned in my mind. Concentrating the magic within me, I pictured a single solitary fire which rotated like a giant wheel. The fire consumed all emotion, all worry, and all thoughts. It left me with both stillness and hunger. The fire called out to be fed, but in the void remained perfectly controlled. A color change shifted the normal yellow flame to one of ghost white. It began to flicker, creating shapes and images in the void. The images reminded me of death, of skulls, and of razor sharp fangs.

My eyes snapped open and I gasped for breath. My head throbbed and I felt faint. Catching myself on the shelf, I watched as one of the glass alembics bounced on the wood and rolled forward. The oddly shaped glass rolled forward then fell off the edge, moving in slow motion as it fell towards the floor. Reaching out, I tried to catch it. My fingers grazed the glass but they pushed it away. It shattered when it hit the floor, the sound of breaking glass echoing around the stone room. There was silence for the space of a minute. Just as I relaxed the screaming began.

CHAPTER ELEVEN

PRISONERS

The walls seemed to vibrate from the sound and my heart sank. The screaming stopped and the sudden silence which followed made me feel empty. Drawing my longsword, I walked to the door and flung it open. The lantern which had been hanging on the far wall had fallen and the pool of oil was alight. Waving my hand, I pulled the fire within me. As the flames spread throughout my body, chasing my blood like a venom, I felt strength rush through every muscle. Rushing down the hallway, I passed similar doors to my left as the one to the storage room I had come from. At the end of the hall, there was another hallway which turned right and a staircase which went down. Skidding to a halt, I looked down the hallway which was less than a dozen paces long and ended at a balcony.

Rushing to the balcony, I saw that it wrapped three of the four sides of the main foundry room. The far wall was filled with large furnaces which were alight, large piles of coal placed before them. Inside of each furnace were large quantities of heated glass. Shirtless men, wearing coal-stained trousers were shoveling more coal into the furnaces or adding sand to the molten glass. The foundry floor was three stories below and where molds would have been laid for casting metal, there were tables set out with alchemy instruments. Dozens of workers wearing leather gloves and aprons worked at the tables.

There were large barrels at the end of each table and I watched as one of the workers scooped out a deep red liquid. The liquid was thick, like syrup, and as it was poured into one of the glass alembics. The red syrup poured slowly and large clumps fell out. Another smaller barrel was then opened and a touch of silvery liquid was added to the mixture. Raising the alembic, the worker placed it over a flame. I watched the brewing of Slush for only a moment, another scream echoing through the large foundry. This scream was deeper, more guttural, and much closer. On the left wall, below the balcony, were shadowed cells. Dozens of people were crammed into each cell and I counted ten in total. The people within were huddling together, keeping as far away from the bars as possible. Just below the cells, the space was open, supported by rows of columns. Unable to get a clear view. I began to slowly creep along the balcony, staying as much in the shadows as possible.

No one seemed to be looking up at me and Osbert was nowhere to be seen. As I moved along the balcony, I turned back and looked in through the arched openings to the single large room below all of the cells.

Three people hung from hooks in the ceiling. Each of them were bleeding out into large stone bowls. Their bodies were badly bruised and long lacerations ran up and down their bodies. It looked like their skin had been racked by claws over and over again, creating dangling ribbons of flesh. A memory surfaced, and I pictured the flayed corpses at Renor Keep. The bodies which Hevron had tortured in the highest tower had looked much like these.

One of the bodies started to move and opening his eyes, he let out a scream of terror. The sound was one of pure agony blended with desperation. My heart sank further in my body as I watched him writhe back and forth, swinging from the hooks which were lodged deep in his shoulders. A man, his face covered in a black shroud, lifted a three bladed paddle and struck the man in his back. The blades cut into the hanging man's skin, cutting deep. More blood flowed from the body, dripping into the stone bowl at his feet.

Disgust, rage, and hatred overwhelmed me.

Without thinking, I sprinted back down the balcony to the stairs. Racing down the steps three at a time, I reached the second landing in seconds. Turning sharply, I descended the second set of stone steps and leapt to the bottom, landing hard on the foundry floor. The man closest to me, working at one of the slush tables, looked up. Snarling, I lifted my hand and pushed the flames burning before him outward. The fire erupted as I caused it to burn the wooden table. The boiling liquid within the glass instruments exploded, coating the man. He screamed, falling to his knees as he frantically wiped at his melting face.

This sudden explosion drew everyone's attention. Holding out my hand, I reached forward toward the large furnaces and pulled the fire out. It was like watching a fountain of pure fire erupt from the mouth of the giant furnace. The flames washed over the nearest tables, consuming them and the workers who stood there. Letting go of the flames, I lowered my sword and turned towards the arched entryway where the poor tortured bodies hung.

As I entered, thugs and goons began to rush into the room. I paid them no mind, instead focusing my attention on the black hodded man who was holding his instrument of torture as a club. He had backed up to the far wall and through the slits in the hood which showed his eyes, I saw fear.

Good, I thought, lifting my sword, *I am fear.*

Rushing forward, I attacked the man, thrusting with my longsword. He met my attack, but his instrument was awkward and did little more than push my blade slightly to the side. Instead of striking directly in his heart, my blade went into his left lung. He grunted, dropping his weapon as I drove the blade deep. Twisting, I pushed my blade to the side and then pulled. The blade cut through his body, erupting out of his side as I pulled it back. Blood sprayed as he fell to the ground. The torturer shuddered once then fell still, dead.

"Get him!" The cry came from behind me.

Turning, I lifted my sword and deflected a wild sword swing. The man, dressed in black leather armor studded with iron spikes, snarled at me. He attacked again, just as wild as the first. Parrying my enemies strike, I stepped forward and kicked his left ankle. His leg buckled and as he lost his balance, I slashed him across the back of his other knee.

Falling forward, the thug lost grip of his sword which tumbled away, the metal scraping the stones as it clattered to the ground. He looked up at me with wild eyes just as I slashed my sword across his neck. His head tumbled to the ground, rolling several feet before the man's body collapsed. Blood spilled from the neck stump, running down the stone floor towards the stone bowl where one of the tortured men still hung.

Of the three half naked men who hung from hooks, only the one on the right still moved. He swayed slowly back and forth, but the blood which had been dripping from his body had stopped. The man's head now hung forward and his chest no longer expanded from labored breaths. He, like the others, had succumbed to his wounds.

On the other side of the bodies, a dozen thugs had gathered, their swords raised. They stood between me and the raging fire which burned across the entire ground floor of the foundry. Almost all of the tables had been consumed, the workers rolling on the ground as they screamed in pain. Raising my hands, I pulled the flames towards me. The fire slammed into the backs of the thugs, knocking them to the ground as they singed their hair. Each man screamed as his hair ignited. I watched as they flailed around, trying in vein to douse the flames.

Connecting the fire to the coal which hung on my belt, I willed them to burn faster and hotter. Within moments, their scalps were charred black and their faces were a deep red. The skin on some of their faces had begun to melt from the heat, drooping down over their eyes and mouths. The screams only lasted a few more moments before the guards stopped moving and fell to the ground. Stepping over to the corpses, I waved my hands over their bodies and pulled the flames inside of me.

The raging inferno within me grew, the flames joining the wealth of power which already flowed within me. Walking forward, I took a stance at the archway and looked out over the burning foundry. The plumes of smoke which rose to the ceiling was a mix of black, pink, and purple.

Prisoners, still trapped in the cells above, began to groan or scream, the sounds echoing around the foundry. Reaching out, I sent the flames back into the furnace, leaving behind charred tables and ruined glassware. The bodies of the workers were still, all of them charred black. The final traces of smoke floated up towards the ceiling, joining the small cloud of swirling multi-colored smoke which obscured the ceiling.

Looking up the second floor, all of the prisoners were pressing up against the bars, their eyes wide with alarm. No one made a sound as they looked down at me. My eyes lingered on them for only a moment before I darted towards the stairs to free them. Leaping up the steps, I reached the first landing and turned. From around the corner, another man emerged and I almost ran him through with my sword. Pushing the figure to the side, I knocked him to the ground. He yelped and held up his hands in protest.

"Caden, it's me!"

"What the hell, Os? Where have you been?"

Osbert brushed his hair away from his face and he looked up with shame in his eyes. Offering a hand, I helped pull Osbert to his feet. His right fingers were stained with a deep red and he was swaying slightly on his feet. He had a laceration on the side of his head and another cut on his arm.

"I didn't mean to. I found their storeroom on the other side and I got into a fight." Osbert seemed to struggle for more words, his eyes looking at me with a pleading expression. "It was an accident. By the Valon, I swear it."

"What's done is done. We need to focus on getting these people out of here."

My friend nodded and we hurried around the corner and turned down the balcony which lined the cells. The people crammed into the first cell yelped in surprise and pressed themselves against the far wall. The bars were thick and were connected by metal strips which were woven between them and riveted together. The door was secured with a large lock that was encased in a metal box leaving nothing to cut.

Sheathing my sword, I reached out and produced small flames in both hands. Burning coal from my pouch, I increased the temperature of the flames, turning them a bright blue. Holding them close to the metal, I heated the lock. The fire that burned between my hands was small which helped concentrate the flame's temperature. The flame became a cone shape, with a darker blue shifting around a lighter blue cone. Moving closer, I concentrated the flame on the lock for a minute and watched as the iron turned to slag.

As the locking mechanism began to melt, the metal looked like it was beginning to blister. Cracks broke free as the iron turned first to a deep red then to a bright yellow. I pulled away the flame and took a hold of the bars. Pulling the door, I broke it free from the lock and let it swing open. The prisoners within looked at me with stunned faces. Each regarded me for only a moment before rushing forward to the door. They squirmed their way free, trying to exit as quickly as possible, and getting stuck in the process.

"Calm yourselves!" I shouted, raising my hand and flaring the fire. This got their attention and all of them paused. "Line up along the wall. We will lead you out together."

The prisoners obeyed, cowed by my words and by my magic. I felt bad yelling at them, but I wasn't about to have this rescue attempt thwarted by fear. I would not let them rush to their deaths.

I proceeded to unlock each of the five other cells the same way I had the first. It was quick work and everyone remained quiet. When I pulled the last cell door open, I watched as each one of them exited single file. Just as I was about to turn and leave, I saw a shadow move in the corner of the cell. Pausing, I held up my hand and flared the flame, creating a bright blue ball the size of my fist. The fire light revealed a small frail woman huddled in the corner. Her face was gaunt, her hair gray, and her lips dry and cracked. She looked up at me with sunken eyes, yellowed from malnutrition. Her fingers were stained dark, the fingernails missing. The woman reached out towards me and whimpered.

Entering the cell, I walked over to her and knelt down beside her. She was missing her left foot and the other did not have toes. The skin around each was black and small cuts showed recent signs of bleeding. Old dry blood which was a rusty brown covered the skirts of her dress.

"I can carry you," I said, quenching the flame I had been holding and showing her my hand. "I will not be leaving anyone behind."

Tears formed in the corners of her eyes. She did not speak, but she nodded. Placing my arm around her waist. I hoisted her into the air and carried her from the cell. Though she had no strength, the woman clung to me, her long boney fingers wrapping around the upper part of my forearm. When I left the cell, I could see the final few people turning the corner to the stairwell which would lead down. I walked as quickly as I could, being careful not to knock the woman's severed leg against the railing.

Reaching the stairwell, I heard the echoes of shouting. Hurrying down, I reached the bottom and saw the prisoners as they crowded around the entrance to the foundry. People were shouting and the prisoners were once again crowding together, all in a hurry to get out. A middle aged man, who stood in the back, holding his hands together at his belt, looked over at me.

"Will you take her?" I asked, glancing down to the woman in my arms.

The man nodded and walked over to me, extending his hands. Gently, he lifted the woman from my arms and held her close. She looked up at him, then at me, then down at the ground. Leaving her in the stranger's care, I raised my hands and conjured another flame.

"Silence!" I shouted.

Those closest to me dropped to the ground in a crouch, covering their faces from the sudden light. The prisoners all fell silent again. Osbert turned from the door and looked at me.

"They are coming. A group of about fifty men are gathering on the bridge."

Drawing my sword, I strode forward. The group of prisoners parted before me and walking past them, I could see sheer terror in their eyes. We had given them a small glimpse of freedom, but I could see the hope dwindling. The desperation that came off of them seemed tangible and I was left unable to comfort them.

"Osbert. Keep everyone back. I will handle this."

My friend looked at me with consternation. But with a frown, he stepped aside as I reached the door. Through one of the looking holes, I could see the Red Hook mercenaries gathering. They seemed confused and disorganized.

Good, I thought. *It's time to give these men some well deserved punishment.*

Lifting the crossbeam, I let the large wooden crossbeam drop to the ground before pushing the doors open. The mercenaries turned to look at me and immediately raised their weapons. As I emerged alone, they began to scoff.

Snarling, I raised my left hand and produced a flame the size of a lance. It burned bright blue and cast ghostly light upon the bridge which spanned the chasm. The mercenaries backed away, their amused expressions replaced with panic. I threw the lance of flame at them, striking the first guard in the chest. The fire was not strong enough to break through his armor, but it created a large charred spot and he caught fire. The leather burned quickly, sending black smoke up to engulf his face. His beard caught fire and as he screamed, the mercenary began to choke on the smoke. Thrashing about, he tripped on the stones and fell off the side of the bridge and into the chasm. His screams could be heard for a few seconds before they were silenced. The sound of his body as he struck the ground echoed within the chasm.

Before the others could react, I dashed forward, brandishing my longsword. My anger overwhelmed me, and screaming, I breathed fire. Feeding the fire with more coal from my belt, I cast it forward and watched as it engulfed the men. Raising their hands to shield their faces, the gang members turned sharply away from me.

Taking advantage of the opportunity, I struck the first two men in quick succession, slicing through their jugulars. As they dropped to the ground, I lunged towards a third and stabbed my longsword into his thigh. The blade emerged through the far end, bringing with it a few shards of bone. Twisting the blade, I pushed down and cut through the back of the mans leg. The mercenary fell to the ground, blood gushing out rapidly from his obliterated thigh.

Recovered from the fire and from my attacks, two of the mercenaries who still stood lashed out at me in tandem. I deflected their blades, the sound of steel ringing out. Stepping forward, I retaliated and lunged. The tip of my blade struck the nose of one of the mercenaries, cutting it deep. As blood poured down the man's face, he stepped back and tripped over one of his dead companions.

Not missing a moment, the other mercenary swung his sword at me again, telegraphing his strike with a loud shout. I parried the blade easily and with a quick twist of my longsword, I disarmed the man by cutting his wrist.

"Get back!" one of the gang members shouted. "Do you not know who this is?"

The dozen men who remained all took steps back, the shock of sudden attack being replaced by reason.

"We must kill him!" another responded. The man had a bald scalp and red beard. His longsword was similar to mine, but was more tarnished and the edge showed traces of rust. He rushed forward, not giving his companions time to respond, and I raised my sword to defend myself.

Fighting this man was easy. He moved with long, exaggerated motions, lacking the grace of a true swordsman. With each swing, he telegraphed his attacks and didn't balance his body weight against his large swords. Letting him swing, I ducked beneath the blade. As the man temporarily lost his balance. I jumped forward and punched him in his pelvis. My spiked gauntlet punctured the armor and drew blood. The man grunted, doubling over and cursing. As he tried to raise his sword to strike, I kicked him in the chest. Tumbling back, the man fell over the edge of the bridge, joining the first of his fallen comrades.

The rest of the gang members stood frozen. They were still holding their weapons aloft, but their stances were uncertain.

Some tapered back and forth on the balls of their feet, looking like they were about to run. I was not about to allow that.

"None of you are getting out of here alive."

∽

Breathing hard, I cleaned my sword on the shirt of one of the dead goons, and sheathed it. The final man had fled before I'd killed him. He'd reached the far gate, but without the key, he had been unable to escape. His blood had sprayed across the cave walls just beyond the gate and the torch which hung in a sconce on the wall cast a brilliant light upon it. The blood glistened, making it look a deep black. Turning away from the body, I looked at the small town. Bodies littered the streets, showing a path of my violence back to the foundry.

Walking slowly back through the buildings, I took a few minutes to look for anyone who might have hidden themselves to avoid my wrath. Finding no one, I quickly returned to the foundry door. It was closed once again and when I pulled on the handle, the door didn't budge. Knocking on the door, I took a step back so I could be seen through one of the metal view slots.

As the slot slid back, I saw a pair of dark eyes look out at me. The sound of scraping followed and a moment later, the doors swung open. Osbert smiled wide at me before he leaned over to look at the fallen bodies of the dead mercenaries. He walked forward and with hesitant steps the prisoners began to make their way out of the foundry.

The bravest of the prisoners hurried up to the dead men and one of them stomped on the corpse. I took a step back and watched them as they filed out. The man who had taken the crippled woman was the last to emerge. She was no longer moving and her eyes were glassy. Cradling the body softly, the man sniffed, a few tears dripping from his eyes.

"She didn't make it." His voice was deep and gravelly.

"You can set her down," I said. I was surprised at the lack of emotion in my voice. Though my heart felt heavy, I knew that these people needed any strength I could give them.

"No. She doesn't deserve to be left down here."

"You're right."

The man nodded.

"What's your name?"

"Jael."

"Will you take her up to the surface, Jael?"

"Yes."

"Let's get everyone out of here."

Jael followed me as I began to make my way through the crowd of prisoners. There were several hundred of them and they all looked lost. As I passed them, they all looked at me and a few of them smiled.

"Follow me. It's time to get out of here."

Passing a few prisoners, I saw three men who were more muscled. Though they looked badly beaten, they were not gaunt from starvation. Pointing at them, I got their attention.

"You three, take those swords. We may have another fight waiting for us at the top."

Everyone obeyed as I led them over the bridge towards the gate which blocked off the large stairwell. If Ike had been honest, the tunnel should lead to the surface. Holding out my hand, I blasted the locked gate with a column of fire. The metal lock turned a bright yellow and I swiped it with my sword. The steel of my blade sliced through the weakened metal and the lock drooped to the floor. Pulling open the gate, I beckoned to Osbert.

"Get them out." I reached down to my belt and pulled off the coin purse. I held it out to Osbert. My friend did not take it.

"You're not coming with us?"

"No. I have to stay."

Osbert frowned, looking at the coin purse. "I don't need that."

"Take it Os. Start a new life. Do something better. Help these people. I know you can."

"How?" My friend looked at me, his eyes wide with frustration. For a moment it seemed like I was looking in the mirror. "What if I can't do it? What if I fail?"

"Then you just have to try again. Don't give up. No matter what."

Osbert let out a sigh and snatched the coinpurse.

"Everyone, follow me."

Leading the charge, Osbert drew his mace and walked through the gate. The prisoners followed him up the stairs and I watched them until they disappeared from view. For a long while I looked up at the darkness of the tunnel and felt as though I had been swallowed by a gigantic beast. In the silence of the cave, I realized how terribly alone I now was. The hollowness inside slowly began to fade and was replaced by a worry. The anxiety was similar to a hot coal in my stomach.

"That's right Caden," I muttered to myself. "Don't give up."

Walking away from the tunnel, I strode past the first two buildings, one was a carpentry workshop where crates had been assembled and the other was a storehouse. When I came around the corner, I saw movement from the corner of my eye. Drawing my sword, I turned towards the foundry. Standing on the bridge, looking down at the bodies of the dead mercenaries was Merek.

CHAPTER TWELVE
A SHADOW FROM THE PAST

"What the hell are you?" I asked, my voice little more than a whisper..

"Don't you recognize me, Caden?" Merek smiled and he laughed. "It's been too long my friend."

Tightening my jaw, I raised my sword and took a few tentative steps forward.

"Come now Caden. Put that away. You can't kill someone who is already dead."

I lowered my sword and took a moment to study Merek's face. His goatee was well trimmed and matched the dark curls of his hair. His eyes were a deep shade of green, full of life and joy. He smiled again, and folded his arms.

"How are you here?"

"Does it matter?"

"I suppose no. Then again, I am talking to a ghost." I sheathed my sword but kept my palm on the pommel, my fingers curled forward so my fingertips touched the sword handle. "My mind could also be addled from the slush smoke or perhaps I'm just swiving crazy."

"You are not crazy my friend. Or at least, no more than you ever were."

"If you won't tell me how it is you are here, can you tell me why?"

"Of course. I wanted to check in on you. Make sure that you are doing well."

I paused, unsure how to answer, debating whether I should answer. Whatever this was, I doubted it was real. *What does it hurt to talk with an old friend?*

"No, I'm not doing well, Merek. Everything is falling apart. I know I have to move forward, but I just can't see the way."

"But you always do. That's one of the reasons I always followed you. It's what made you a good leader."

"Ha! Some good leader I turned out to be. Everyone who used to call me their leader is now dead. I'm sorry, Merek. I couldn't save her. I failed."

"I know. I don't blame you. You know that right?"

"Absolution from a ghost doesn't make me feel better."

"You don't believe it's me?"

"No"

"Then what am I?"

"A phantom, a devious apparition wishing to trick me. There is almost no end to the terrible things you could be."

"I can assure you, I am none of those things."

"So what are you?"

"Your friend, back to offer you aid." Merek sighed, and reached out to place his hand on my shoulder. Where his fingers touched, there was no sensation. But his flesh did not pass through. It appeared as though he truly were touching me.

Strange, I thought. I reached up and placed my hand over his fingers. My hand felt nothing, but my fingers did not pass through his. Intrigued, I reached out and placed my hand on his arm. My hand did not fall through. It was remarkably odd to have my hand floating in the air, resting on some non-tangible entity.

I pulled my hand away and shifted a few inches away from my friend. His presence disturbed me. Taking a seat on the edge of the bridge, I leaned forward and looked into the darkness. It took a few minutes, but my eyes adjusted and I was able to see the bottom. As before, I could just make out the bones which littered the floor. There were several new bodies down there, their dark shapes easy to spot amongst the yellowed shapes. The Mire were there as well, swelling and bubbling as they consumed the flesh. It was faint, but I could hear the hissing noise as the oozing creatures consumed the flesh.

"What is troubling you my friend?"

"I am trying to decide what I should do."

"Why is that giving you so much trouble?"

"What the hell, you might be a ghost, but I doubt you'll be telling anyone."

Merek smiled.

"I can't decide if I should just leave. If I do that, I can at least have my fight with the Malkethian's without causing collateral damage."

"But is that not what you want?"

"Yes, and no. I don't want anyone else to get hurt on my behalf, but I don't want to run. I promised myself that I would stand my ground. If I was going to run, I should have done it long ago."

"I think there is something deeper going on here. It's the same reason you didn't run in the first place. The reason you have stayed in Kings Keep since my death."

I paused, taking a moment to reflect on his words. "You're right."

"So, tell me then. Why do you want to stay?"

"I have spent years making Kings Keep my home. I never

intended to become so attached. I'm not going to let them take everything away from me again."

"That was always your biggest problem Caden. You always tried not to show it, but deep down, you care about your home. But more than that, you care about the people who live here."

"Only some people," I corrected.

"Sure. No one cares about everyone. But you discredit yourself. If you didn't care about people, then you would not have helped those prisoners tonight. Are they not strangers to you?"

"That's different."

"How so."

"They were in need of help. I couldn't stand by and do nothing."

"Why not? You stand by every day while thousands in this city suffer or come to harm."

"I can't be everywhere at once. I can't help everyone."

"But you can help some."

"Yes."

"Why?"

"I already told you."

"You said you couldn't stand by and do nothing. Why couldn't you? What made these people different from all the others?"

"I don't know." I let out a long breath, searching desperately for an answer. "I felt like I had to. No one else could have come for them."

"Do better than that. Think, why did you help Osbert? Why go through any of this at all?"

"Because he is what I could have become. I see so much of myself in him. He deserved a chance at a better life. I wanted to try and give him that."

"That's exactly what I am trying to show you. Caden, you care about people. You can't help it. That's why you took Kori and I under your wing. It's why Evand joined our mercenary band and why Jash so stubbornly followed you into that forest. That is something that comes naturally to you. Something I don't think you can help but do."

"Then why do I feel so conflicted? Everything feels so much harder than it should be. It should be easy for me to make the right choice. To leave. Though I might suffer as a result, it would prevent the suffering of others."

"Are you so certain it will?"

I paused, looking at my friend in his dark green eyes. He was studying me, his eyes boring into my very soul. The more I thought, the more I was beginning to question my assumptions. "Perhaps I am assuming too much. You might be right. There is no guarantee that if I do leave that they will not retaliate. Isar did say he wanted more than just to bring me in. He wants vengeance for my desertion of the Malketh army."

"So, what are you going to do about it?"

Merek's question sent a chill through my body. It was a question I realized that I had been unintentionally avoiding.

"If he wants to try and see me destroyed, I will show him why they should have never come after me in the first place. But I will surrender if that means it prevents bloodshed."

"Perhaps if you are interested, I can give you another piece of unsolicited advice."

"Of course."

"Tell the people you care about how you feel. They should never have to doubt how you feel about them. Trust me, it goes much further than you would think."

"I want so badly to believe this isn't just in my head." My eyes began to sting as I fought back tears. "I missed getting your advice."

Merek smiled, saying nothing.

We sat alone in the darkness for a time, looking down into the crevice which divided the cavern in two. My eyes looked up from the chasm and I didn't feel as terrible as I had before.

"Merek?"

As I spoke I turned and my friend was no longer sitting beside me. I leapt up to my feet, spinning around as I searched for him only to find nothing. The cave was silent and sitting back down, I let myself think.

Hours passed slowly as I remained in contemplation. There was so much that needed to be done, but was I willing to do it? The path ahead would require me to make several hard choices. Several hours ago, I might not have been able to make them. I realized I had been holding onto a hope that I could find a way to return to how things were. I had been foolish, trying to think up an option where I would remain in Kings Keep and continue living my life as part of Seraphina's Syndicate. But that life had come to an end. It was time that I accepted that. Sooner or later the time would come for me to leave this place. My goal was to ensure I did not leave it as a captive or a slave.

My eyes turned and looked once more at the foundry. Light from the burning furnaces within made several windows glow. The building, built into the stone wall of the cave, looked almost like a large beast, with a dozen eyes and a snarling mouth. The atrocities which had been committed within made my gut tighten.

It was time to make this place burn. Walking through the doors, I hurried passed the charred bodies and tables of the slush makers, and walked up to the large furnaces. They were still burning, but the flames were withering. The molten glass was beginning to cool, turning from a brilliant orange to a dull red. Like all fire, it would survive only as long as it had something to consume. If left alone, it would eventually burn out, leaving behind dust and ash. Walking up to the furnace entrance, which stood twice as high as I was tall, I waded into the flames. They flickered around me, but I willed them to remain just out of reach. The fire did not eat at my clothes, my boots, or my flesh. Instead, it parted for me, like it was afraid.

Deep within the furnace, I closed my eyes and reached out with my mind to feel the fire. The burning coal below my feet pulsed with energy, feeding into the inferno. Taking in a deep breath, I began to absorb the fire. Slowly, the fire which burned all around me flowed into my hands. Every fiber of my being absorbed the energy, growing warm from the power as it flowed like blood under my skin. I continued to pull in the fire until my entire body felt like it was about to burst.

When I opened my eyes, I was standing in a cold furnace, but light shone from cracks in my skin. Looking down at my hands, I held them up and marveled at the charcoal-like color. Flames flickered between my fingers. Smiling, I strode forward and out of the furnace, leaving footprints of flame in my wake. Stepping outside of the furnace, I looked at the large piles of coal on either side. Lifting up my hands, I conjured two balls of red flame and cast them upon the coal. Each pile ignited, blasting apart into chunks which cast embers into the corners of the foundry. Raising my hands high, I willed the piles of coal to burn, channeling the flames high until they touched the ceiling.

Exhaling, I closed my fists and then thrust both hands forward. Releasing the torment of flames within, I blasted a large column of flame through the front walls and door of the foundry. The rubble, the bodies, the instruments of alchemy all ignited once more. Pieces of glass melted, falling with a hiss to the stones. As the column of flame dissipated, I formed two balls of fire, one above each fist, and cast them at the walls. Where each ball of flame struck, stone exploded, breaking into thousands of small pieces.

I threw balls of fire indiscriminately as I walked through the foundry. The destruction felt good and brought a sense of satisfaction that relieved some of the pain caused by the horrors of this building. Though I wished I could undo the tragedy which had taken place in these caves, the most I could do was cleanse it with fire. It wasn't much, but it was better than nothing.

Emerging through the hole which had been the doors to the foundry, I turned around and continued to cast balls of flame through the stone wall. It didn't take long before the dozens of holes caused the face of the building which jutted out from the walls of the cave to collapse, leaving behind nothing but rubble. Crossing the bridge, I reached down and let fire drip like burning oil from my hands. When I reached the other side, I raised both hands above my head and produced a ball of flame the size of a boulder. Bringing the fire down upon the bridge, I blasted a large hole in the middle of the stone structure. The bridge crumbled, the stones falling into the abyss below.

The sound of rock striking the bottom of the chasm echoed around the cavern. It was an echo that came with the force of thunder. Watching the walls, I saw the high stalactites shake from above. Forming another ball of flame, I threw it upward at an incredible speed. The fire struck the roof and the large hanging stone stalactites broke free and fell. A smile spread across my lips as I watched the stone rain down upon the buildings of the small slush town. The buildings crumbled to rubble, falling to pieces as they were bombarded with the falling stone. Dust filled the cavern for a moment, reflecting the glow of my fire, creating a deep burnt orange haze.

When the dust settled, I strode forward and blasted apart the walls which still remained upright. It seemed no time at all before everything was destroyed and I was standing atop piles of shattered stone. There would be nothing for the members of Red Hook or Grinning Tombstone to come back to. With any luck, this would see an end to their misdeeds here.

Muttering a soft prayer to the Valon, I made my way back to

the cave and entered the labyrinth of tunnels which would lead me back to the surface. In three days time Osbert and I had agreed to meet up with Omaria. I could bide my time in the underneath until then. It was time for a new hunt to begin, and this time I didn't intend to let myself play the part of the prey.

CHAPTER THIRTEEN
CONSPIRE

Waiting in the darkness of the tunnel below the Crooked Inn, I looked out at the river and watched the flowing water as it shimmered in the moonlight. The scent of lumber was heavy in the muggy air and the loud chirping of crickets echoed down the tunnel from the grate. The cacophony of insects outside was joined by a lone cricket within. The solitary chirp seemed off balance, isolated from the others. It was strangely easy to relate. Still, I found the sound to be grating and it made me grit my teeth in annoyance. I felt a strange and unpleasant longing for the peace and quiet of the tunnels below. Something about their dark quiet depths attracted me. This was an odd feeling, but one that should have been expected. After a month of hiding, I had become quite used to the new environment.

My longing for the world outside still remained. I pressed myself against the grate and took in a deep breath, inhaling the scents of the river. Closing my eyes, I tried to ignore the chirping crickets and focus on the burbling of the river. Only a few minutes passed before I began once more to feel restless. My mind began to wander, thinking through different plans of attack. But each mental exercise ended up at the same frustrating intersection. When I next confronted the sorcerers, it was going to be violent. The question was not if such a conflict would take place but where. Collateral damage was unacceptable.

I began to picture the map of Kings Keep as a game board. Each stone a potential enemy. But I did not know the placement of the enemy pieces. Without that knowledge, I was playing blind. A growl slipped past my lips as I forced myself to think more positively. It would not be productive to run through plans in my head that would be ineffective.

Omaria, what the hell is taking you so long?

As I continued to wait, I drew my dagger and began to twirl it about my hands. The curved blade was sharp and chipped slightly at the tip. Lifting my left index finger, I produced a flame and held it out. Placing the tip of the dagger into the flame, I watched, waiting for the metal to heat up. After some time, the tip turned a deep shade of red before slowly brightening to a yellow. Snuffing out the flame, I held out the dagger and studied the yellow metal. It gave off a small amount of heat as I moved it towards the palm of my left hand. When the heated dagger's tip struck my skin, the heat flared across my palm and up my fingers. The sensation was calming as I drew out the energy trapped within the metal. Within seconds, the metal of the dagger cooled, returning to the simple gray.

It was an odd way to pass the time, but I repeated the process, playing the game I had once used to occupy my mind years ago. After the fifth repetition, I heard footsteps approaching the tunnel entrance. Closing my hand around the heated blade, I absorbed the heat into my hand, snuffing out the light. My body tensed as I waited and I retreated several feet back into the darkness. A small form dropped down from outside the tunnel, splashing in the small stream of water which poured out.

"Caden?"

"I'm here," I said, my voice carrying down the tunnel. Getting to my feet, I walked out of the shadows and into the moonlight. The metal grate which stood between me and Omaria was slick. I placed my hands on the metal bars as I leaned in close. "You're late."

"For that you will have to forgive me. Things have been a little tense these last few days. It's hard to find ways to avoid watchful eyes."

"And tonight. Are you sure you were not followed?"

"I circled the district twice. No one followed me."

I sighted, relaxing my grip on the grate. "Did you deliver my message?"

"I did. They're waiting for us. That is, if you are willing to come."

"Oh, trust me, I'm willing."

Getting onto the ground, I crawled underneath the grate, my clothes soaking in the water from the pipe. The ground smelled strongly of shit and I held my breath until I was on the other side standing.

Omaria looked me up and down, her painted lips turning down into a frown. In the darkness, she looked like a fox, ready to hunt.

"What?"

"Those can't be the same clothes we just gave you."

I looked down at myself. I was stained from head to toe with ash, slime, or blood. "It's hard to stay clean down here."

"And your friend. Is he going to come along?"

"No. Os is gone. Hopefully making good use of the money I gave him."

Omaria nodded, and didn't ask me any follow up questions. Her posture relaxed and she turned back to the river. "Will you hoist me up?"

Interlocking my fingers, I let Omaria place her boot in them.

Lifting her upward, I watched as she took hold of the top and pulled herself up. She reached down her hand and I took it. She lifted me just enough for me to get a good grip on the ledge which hung above the sewer pipe. Pulling myself up, I dusted my hands on my pants which only smeared more grime on my palms. Shrugging, I followed Omaria away from the river.

The lumber mill was to my right and I could see the leaning silhouette of the Crooked Inn just behind it. There were several large warehouses in front and a small port dock to the left. Omaria led me towards the warehouses and I saw a lone man standing guard at one of the back entrances.

"Where are we going?"

"Not far. But we wanted to keep things private."

"And who is that?"

"Not to worry. Wes is one of us."

I looked at Wes as we approached with suspicious eyes but said nothing. Once we reached the back entrance of the warehouse, I saw his face a little better in the lantern light. Wes had a salt and pepper beard, with shoulder length black hair that was gray at the temples. He was wearing a dark brown tunic and a sword hung at his waste. His expression did not change as he regarded us. Omaria gave him a stiff nod and Wes opened the door.

Beckoning us to enter, Wes stepped aside. Passing him by, I entered the large brick building and found myself in a large open space. Five columns of wooden posts ran down the large open room, supporting the vaulted ceiling. The cross-beams connecting the posts ran horizontally, connecting the pillars together, which ran down to where the roof met the walls. The warehouse was packed with crates and barrels; all were organized by size and stacked carefully. There were large double doors on the other side of the warehouse, closed and locked with two large crossbeams.

There was a single lantern on the wall which provided dim light and I saw no movement. When the door closed behind us, I looked over at Omaria. She gestured forward and began to walk down the center row of the warehouse. About halfway down, she turned left, and following her, I saw a staircase at the far end leading to the foreman's office. There was a small amount of light on the stairs coming from under the door at the top.

The bottom step creaked when Omaria stepped on it. In the silence of the night, the groaning wood sounded like the grunt of an ox. Cringing, I placed my foot carefully on the wooden step. Groaning loud under my weight, I clenched my teeth and felt my muscles tense. Though I knew there was no reason to have such a drastic reaction, the sound made me feel uncomfortable. Omaria didn't seem to notice and reached the top of the wooden staircase while I was still lingering on the bottom step. My heart was beginning to pound and my breath caught in my chest.

A knock on the door drew my attention and brought me out of my stupor. I shook my head and hurried up the steps. I reached the top just as the inside bolt was drawn back and the door was pulled open. The light within was bright and I found myself squinting. Omaria entered, stepping past the small slender figure who stood in the doorway.

My vision cleared and I saw Vivienne standing before me, a wide smile on her face. Before I had time to react, she threw her arms around me and pressed her face to my chest. Wrapping both of my arms around her, I pulled her tight.

"It's good to see you," I whispered.

"You stink," Vivienne said, pulling away. "But I'm glad to see you too."

Smiling, I looked at her face, studying the soft curve of her cheek where a lone tear had fallen. Reaching up, I wiped it away, taking a moment to study her eyes. There was a storm within those eyes but for the moment, everything seemed to grow still.

Relaxing, I took in a deep breath, then looked up at the others who were standing around a small wooden table.

Seraphina looked at me with a grave expression. Her lips were pulled down into a frown and her blond hair was braided up and wrapped around the back of her head, forming a bun. Tristin stood beside her. She had a dark bruise on her cheek and the white of her left eye was darkened with red. She too wore a frown.

Acacia stood across from them, her dark hair flowing down to her shoulders. She wore a deep purple shawl which hung around her bare shoulders. Nero stood beside Acacia and he was not wearing a mask. Nero, who's missing lips were surrounded by jagged and scared flesh, showed off his sharp silver teeth. He looked more vicious than I had ever seen him.

"Where's Nila?" I asked.

"She's watching over the palace," Seraphina replied. "Keeping an eye on our guest."

I raised my eyebrow, and Tristin looked up to answer my unspoken question.

"Malin has been staying with us by order of the Queen. It wasn't easy to sneak out of the palace to see you tonight."

"Thanks for coming." It was all I could say. "I know it must be a lot to ask."

"Nonsense. We are not going to just abandon you," Seraphina said. Her voice was strained, but there was conviction in her words. Her eyes looked tired and a sad smile crept to her lips. "Not yet anyway."

"Let's take a seat," Acacia prodded, pulling back on her own chair. "And I am all certain we could do with some wine."

Omaria, who had been silently standing beside the door, quickly darted down the stairs, obeying her mistresses command.

Following Vivienne over to the table, I took a seat on the far end. Vivienne sat beside me, pulling her chair over so she was positioned right in front of the corner. As everyone settled down into their chairs, I found myself studying each of their faces. I had never seen fear in Seraphina's eyes quite like I did tonight. Not when we were attacked by Wendigo's. Not when we confronted the Deathmonger. Not even when the Queen was slain by the Shantenbose.

"What have you been doing this last month?" Tristin asked.

"Hiding mostly." I answered with a shrug. "And I killed some monsters."

"What do you mean, monsters?" Vivienne asked.

"Well, aside from the Ghouls, I found where Red Hook makes their slush. Let's just say they're all dead now."

"Well damn," Acacia whispered. "I should have guessed that was you."

Everyone around the table paused and looked at Acacia. I found myself smirking a bit.

"Do you want to fill us in, Acacia?" Tristin asked tersley.

"Just outside the northern part of the city, there was a group of slaves who emerged from an underground tunnel. They over-whelmed a sizable estate and killed most of the guards who were staying there. The estate is a Red Hook stronghold. One of the wall guards, a man named Moran, is a contact of mine. He tends to frequent the Inn and he was rather talkative two nights ago. How did you manage that?"

"The underground is a much larger place than most of us real-ize. There is a labyrinth of sunken tunnels and buildings below the city. Perhaps it was luck or perhaps by the will of the Valon, but I was led to their stronghold after some of them decided to attack the camp I had taken refuge in. I'm glad to know that they were successful in their escape. Do you know where they are now?"

"I don't know. Some may still be here in the city, some may

have fled north. The stronghold is currently under guard by the Northern Brigade. I am not sure what Prcilla plans to do, or if she will do anything at all."

I nodded, content that at least they had all made it out. Part of me realized I should have gone with them to make sure they didn't run into trouble. But I had been too concerned with my own needs. I felt a small twinge of guilt in my stomach and clenched my jaw.

"Do we even want to know what you found down there," Nero asked.

He looked me in the eyes and I shook my head. "Probably not, but if you wish to know the details, I will tell you."

"From the look on your face, I can only imagine how bad it was," Tristin said.

"I'd like to know," Seraphina said.

"So would I," Nero said, reaching up and placing a finger alongside his jaw. As he tilted his head, the lantern light caught on his silver teeth, causing them to shine.

Just as I was about to start recounting what had happened, Omaria returned, carrying two large bottles of wine and a set of cups. We were silent as she poured drinks. I took mine and muttered a word of thanks to her. Taking a sip, I suddenly felt parched. Forcing myself not to gulp down the wine, I set the drink down on the table.

It took a little more than an hour for me to recant what had happened to me in the tunnels over the last month. I was loose on most of the details, giving brief explanations of how Osbert had helped teach me how to navigate the tunnels below. I did provide details regarding the way slush was made. As I described the method of torture, each one of my companions began to look sick. When I finished, everyone was silent. It was a good ten minutes before any of them even lifted a cup of wine to take a drink.

"I suppose you've had it much worse than the rest of us," Nero said. "I'm glad you killed those bastards. They deserved it."

Nodding in agreement, I refilled my cup of wine and took a long drink. The wine felt good on my parched throat and the refreshment seemed better than normal. The simple floral fragrance of the wine seemed sweeter to me than any wine I had before tasted. Tsking my tongue on the roof of my mouth, I finished the wine in my cup before setting it back down. Running my hand across the smooth surface of the table, I mustered the courage to speak.

"Give it to me bluntly. How bad have things been up here?" I asked.

Everyone looked at Seraphina who only let out a sigh.

"They've been tearing this city apart looking for you. To be honest, I am actually surprised they haven't discovered the underground yet, though they have been searching the sewers. "

"Where do they suspect I fled to?"

"I suppose they still think we are hiding you away somewhere, though, I have been trying to suggest that you may have fled south on one of my ships," Seraphina said with a smile. It was fortunate that one of the shipments departed the day after you disappeared. Isar didn't take the bait. I don't know how, but he knows you're still here."

"We have a history. He knows that I didn't leave. Just like I know he's not going to give up looking for me."

"What kind of history do you have with him?" Vivienne asked.

"We fought together for years. In the Malketh Army, they have sorcerers fight in pairs of two. My first companion, a geomancer named Graham, was Isar's mentor. The details don't matter, but when Graham was killed, I was paired with Isar. I have seen first hand how good Isar is at killing and he's one of the best."

"Were you friends?" Tristin asked.

"We weren't friends, but we looked after each other. We never

AUSTIN COLTON

truly saw things eye to eye. Isar and I only fought as companions for three battles. It wasn't too long after that, perhaps six months, I left and fled south. Of course, a lot can change in nine years, and he sees me as a traitor."

"From what we've seen, Isar is not a patient man," Tristin said, glancing down. "Nor are any of the men he brought with him."

"How many soldiers?"

"A hundred. Perhaps a little more. They are stationed around the city, along with the Queen's guard." Seraphina picked up her cup of wine and took a long drink. "Isar is staying with the Queen and Nels is at Raven's Cross. Since Malin is staying with us, that places them strategically enough that should you be found, one of them can easily get to you."

"I am surprised they are not staying together."

"Oh, they are not alone. Each has a few subordinates. Three each." Tristin added.

"What do you mean, subordinates?"

"Each has a small squad of armored soldiers. Their armor is covered in razors and spikes. Each seems like their own personal death squad."

I took in a deep breath and relaxed. "Thank the Valon, I was worried for a moment."

Seraphina eye'd me, conveying an unspoken question, *why?*

"It almost sounded like they brought along a few seekers. But Chezek are much more manageable. What else has been going on?"

"Pricilla has issued a warrant for your arrest and there is a sizable bounty for your capture." Tristin reached into her cloak and produced a folded up piece of parchment. She placed it on the table and slid it over.

Reaching out, I picked up the paper and unfolded it. The drawing was a decent likeness of me, but the eyes were not quite right. I doubted that would make a difference. My reputation had been growing and many people knew my face. Every mercenary guild member at Ravens Cross would know me. The entire Castle guard would know me. And most of all, the great houses on the ridge knew me. It didn't matter that the drawing was wrong.

My eyes found their way to the bottom of the page where the bounty for my capture was posted. Cursing under my breath, I looked up at Seraphina who was studying me with her emerald eyes. "By the Valon, there is no way the Queen would offer that much."

"It's not the Queen who offered to pay it," Seraphina said. "Your northern friends are offering it."

"There is no way they brought enough money with them to offer a reward of twenty thousand gold pieces."

"Caden, I've seen the money." Tristin gave me a grave look. "So has everyone else."

"They announced it to the city a week ago," Acacia said. I looked at the woman and saw concern in her eyes. She almost looked like a mother who was preparing to defend her child. It was a strange expression, one that I didn't understand. "Everyone has seen the gold."

"Well, that might complicate things a bit," I said, placing my hand flat against the table. I took in a deep breath to calm myself, letting out a deep sigh. Smoke streamed from my mouth, drifting up towards the ceiling. The fire burning within me still raged and I pushed it down, quenching it. Blowing another stream of smoke, I felt the tension ease from my body. Without the power, I felt tired, but my mind also seemed to clear. All of the aches and pains of my body seemed to become more prevalent and I slumped forward. Placing both of my hands on the table, I forced myself to look up at everyone. "I assume that makes our list of allies non existent."

"Outside of the people in this room, I wouldn't count on more than a dozen people who will help you." Seraphina said, her voice matter of fact. "Aside from our palace guard, of course. But even then, we are hopelessly outnumbered."

"So be it," I said, forcing myself to smile. "There's nothing about that. I have a question for you all."

Everyone sitting around the table nodded in unison.

"Why not turn me in? I'm certain that idea has crossed your minds."

"Caden, you're not for sale." Vivienne said fiercely. She placed her hand on my arm and gave it a gentle squeeze.

"We are among the only few who see it that way," Seraphina added. "But we are in agreement. You are worth more to this city, more to us, than twenty thousand pieces of Malkethian gold."

"Why?"

"Because without you, we would all be dead." Nero's voice sounded strange, as though he were having trouble speaking. I looked over at my friend and saw a bit of blood leak out of his mouth. He shifted his head and I saw bruises beneath his shirt. Nero coughed, then wiped the scarred skin around his exposed teeth. "We owe you our lives. I would gladly pay that debt with my blood. My honor is not for sale."

"I would say we are in agreement." Seraphina added.

"What about you two?" I waved my hand at Omaria and Acacia. "I apologize for my bluntness, but you owe me no allegiance, nor debt. We have worked together out of a mutual benefit. How does this benefit you now?"

Acacia looked down and Omaria's face looked angry.

"I don't mean to offend. But I don't want you to put your lives on the line for me."

"Caden, I have a deep seeded hatred for your kind." Acacia paused, drumming her fingernails on the table. "But I look at you and at what you have done, and I do not see a monster. But when I look at these new foes, this Isar and his pack of dogs, it makes me feel like I am facing my doom. They will destroy this city and I do not believe they will honor their word should we hand you over to them."

I was silent for a long while, mulling over what Acacia had said. My friends all seemed content to let me think for which I was grateful. "I think they will honor their word. They came back to take me back alive, nothing more. Though if we do stand and fight, they will retaliate."

"I don't see how we can move forward," Seraphina said. "How do you see this ending, Caden?"

"In my heart I know that the only way to ensure all of you survive is to hand myself over. I would happily give my life for yours."

"No," Vivienne said. Her hand was still placed on my arm and I felt her fingers tighten. "You can't hand yourself over to them."

"You're right. One of you must do it. I've been thinking through our options and the best way to fight them without innocent people getting killed is to take this fight out of the city. They won't be lured into a trap and they know how much I care about all of you. The best way to get them out of the city for a fight is to trick them into it. That means you will have to hand me over and make it look like you decided to betray me."

I looked at Seraphina whose face was a blank mask. We locked eyes and as I stared into her green irises I could see the cold calculating mind going through the options of my proposal. She understood what I was asking of her.

"I see. If this was your plan from the start, why wait until now."

"This was not my intent. I had some help coming to this realization over the last few days." My thoughts turned to Merek's Ghost and a sad smile flashed across my lips. "But if we are to do this, then it needs to look like I am going against my will."

"Bold suggestion, but how do you intend to pull this off?" Tristin asked.

"The best way will be for you to give them the location of my hiding place. You could tell them you discovered where I was hiding and get them to set up an ambush."

"Why don't you just hand yourself over to them?" Nero asked.

"If they are offering that reward, it would be a shame for that to go to waste."

"Then what?" Nero asked.

"We set up an ambush of our own." As I looked at everyone, I couldn't help but smile. The somber mood had vanished and it felt like a regular Syndicate meeting."

"Are you certain that this will work?" Seraphina asked.

"No. But I think it's the best option available."

"Then I agree. Let's finish this."

CHAPTER FOURTEEN
TREPIDATION

For the first night in a month, I slept peacefully and comfortably. When I awoke, I was surprised to see rays of sun streaming in through the warehouse window. Yawning, I sat up and looked through the foggy glass. The blue sky was cloudless and bright, the sun sitting halfway to its zenith. It was nice to look up at the sky after what felt like an eternity of darkness. My stomach rumbled, compelling me to climb out of the small cot.

Walking over to the table where the Syndicate had met the night before, I saw a small brown package with my name scrawled across the top. Tearing open the paper, I was relieved to find dried meat, cheese, and flatbread within. I ate slowly, savoring the meal as I washed it down with the remnants of last night's wine. Once my meal was finished, I looked back out of the window and continued to watch the sky. It was going to be a long uneventful day, and I was looking forward to relaxing.

Returning to the cot, I laid back down and rested, my eyes trained on the window so I could continue looking at the sky. There was silence in the warehouse, not a single person coming or going. I could hear the shouting of men as they toiled about nearby, calling from ships on the river or as they entered the nearby buildings. Once, it seemed as though someone was trying to enter the warehouse below, the knocking at the door causing me to sit up in bed, but in the end, no one entered.

I spent the entire day in and out of sleep, climbing out of the cot a few times to stretch my legs. It wasn't until the sun was setting that company arrived. Soft footsteps on the stairs was the first indication that I was not alone. Crawling from the bed, I drew my longsword and moved as silently as possible to the far corner of the room. A month of creeping through the underground had improved my talent for sneaking considerably and I hardly made a sound as I snuck to the far corner beside the door. When the door did open, it would hide me, giving me an advantage over my enemy. Though it was almost certain whoever was climbing the stairs was a friend, I was too paranoid not to be careful.

Remaining still, I waited, watching the brass doorknob turn before the door was pushed open. Creaking on the hinges, the wooden door hid me as expected as a small figure entered the room. Removing the hood of her cloak, I saw the long flowing black hair. I lowered my sword and cleared my throat. Vivienne spun around, a dagger appearing in her hand.

"Dammit Caden," she cursed. "Are you trying to give me a heart attack?"

"For a spy, I was expecting you to be a bit more prepared," I jested. "I wasn't sure who it would be. I was just being careful."

Vivienne sheathed her dagger and closed the door. I set the sword down, tip on the ground, and leaned it against the corner of the wall. It wasn't worth walking across the room to sheath it. I had hardly done so when Vivienn threw her arms around me.

"Today felt like an eternity," she said, pulling back just enough so she could look up at my face. I smiled down at her and nodded.

"I've had worse."

"I'm sure you have."

We held each other for a while before moving to the table. Vivienne set her bag on the table and began to pull out food similar to what was left for me in the morning as well as a fresh bottle of wine.

"I know that it isn't much."

"Trust me Viv, this is better than I've had for a long while." Tearing a piece off the dried meat, I popped it into my mouth and chewed quickly. "I've mostly been surviving off barley bread and beer."

"Sounds better than eating rat meat."

"Oh, believe me, I was tempted."

Vivienne laughed and tore off a small piece of the bread. She ate it and she glanced at the window, the final rays of the sunset bathing her face and accentuating her beauty. I couldn't help but smile. When she looked back at me, I smiled wider.

"I missed you," I said, reaching out and placing my hand on hers.

"I missed you too." Vivienne smiled. "It was smart of you to do what you did. I'm glad to hear you were able to do something to help those people while you were down there."

"Os is a good person. You met him, remember?"

"The man with the gatekey?"

"That's the one. I hope he is doing well."

"I'm certain he will do fine."

As we ate, my eyes looked at her bag. There was still a large lump inside. "Did you bring it?"

"Of course." Vivienne dug into her bag and pulled out the small black box. She set it on the table and slid it over.

I reached out and touched the polished wooden box. The silver lock was free from scratches and there were no other signs of damage or tampering. *Good.*

"How did today go?" I asked, my voice a little too eager.

"According to plan. Seraphina met with Isar and the Queen and from what Tristin said, made a rather impressive show of her betrayal of you. Though it will be hard to say if they believe it."

"Well, we have to sell it, no matter what it takes."

"Chances are, they will. Seraphina has a way with people. She's been bonding with Malin which may play to our benefit."

"If anyone can sell a ruse like this, it will be Seraphina."

"I think we should extend the timetable. Give it at least two weeks before we bring you out. It would be strange if you suddenly appear the day after Seraphina decides to give you up."

"One week will be sufficient. Two will be too long. Tomorrow you need to start showing them the underground tunnels."

"The plan is to take them down there early in the morning." Vivienne smiled. "Tristin has made all of the arrangements for you to leave here tomorrow. Seraphina's ship arrived a little over an hour ago. Once it has been checked by the palace, it will dock here for the night. In the morning, you should be able to slip into the ship while they load the cargo and no one will be any the wiser. After all, I plan on keeping them down in those tunnels all day."

"Good."

"One week outside of the city should be a nice reprieve after what you've just gone through."

"Indeed. Though I wish you could come with me."

"The feeling is mutual. I still can't believe we're just going to hand you over to them. I understand the plan, it just was the last thing I thought we would be doing."

"Trust me, I am just as surprised as you are. I have had a lot of time to think recently. I was also reminded that I needed to tell those I care about how I feel." The words caught in my throat and I paused to take a drink of wine. Setting the cup down, I looked at Vivienne's eyes, then down to the table, then back again. "We've been through a lot together. I told myself I would never open myself to anyone again. But since the first time we met, I just haven't been able to help myself."

Vivienne smiled and batted her eyes which made it even more difficult for me to put into words what I was trying to say. So I decided to just keep it simple.

"I love you. Whatever happens, I didn't want to go through with this without telling you how I feel."

"And I love you," Vivienne said, shifting forward.

I leaned forward and kissed her, breathing in the scent of her perfumed hair. The feel of her lips against mine was velvet petals. The kiss lasted for what felt like only a moment and when we pulled away, I paused, catching my breath. *At least now she will know.*

"We didn't really have much time to catch up last night. How have you been through all of this?"

"Mostly unscathed. The majority of my time has been spent assisting Malin. Not like she needs any help." Vivienne's mouth tightened as she looked at her fists.

"What is your impression of her?"

"She's intolerably sweet, level headed, and generally pleasant company. I absolutely hate her."

"That seems a little contradictory."

"I don't know how to explain it. There is an aura about her that makes my skin crawl. Like a flower with poisonous thorns. She is also very talkative and will chat about anything so long as the subject never touches on her. Malin also hates questions about the Malketh. The only times she's ever been short with me was when I asked her about them."

"Has she told you what her attitude is towards me?"

"No. If the topic ever strays to something of substance, she is quick to change it. Strangely, the only times she is quiet is when

Isar is around. I think that's more to do with avoiding his wrath than anything else."

"Is that what happened to Tristin, why she has a bruised face?"

Vivienne nodded.

"Swiving bastard."

"He broke a pillar, the stone flew out and struck her in the face. Nero jumped in front of a larger section of rock, cracked his shoulder and bruised most of his chest. Let's just say, Pricilla was very unhappy when that happened. Still, the bitch didn't do anything. They basically have free reign in this city. I think the Queen is afraid of them, afraid of what they might do if she doesn't bend to their will."

"She's right to be afraid. So should you."

"Trust me, I am rightly terrified. It still angers me how spineless the Queen is. Aveza would never have stood for this."

"I think Pricilla is wise to remain guarded. Aveza is dead because she put her trust in a sorcerer to protect her."

"Caden, what happened wasn't your fault."

"Yes it was, and I am tired of pretending it wasn't. I gave the talisman to Kori. I prolonged her life, pushed her to learn magic, and let her into the palace. Aveza is dead because I was selfish. It's time I start thinking about what is best for others for a change."

"You know that we don't see it like that. I don't even think Pricilla sees it that way."

"I know you are trying to be kind, and I am not being too hard on myself. Viv, I'm just trying to be realistic. Knowing what I have done, whether it was intentional or not, I have to accept the consequences. All of what is happening now is a consequence of what I have chosen to do with my life."

"You didn't choose for the Malkethian's to come. You didn't choose any of this. Sometimes things just happen. There are some things in this life which are out of our own control. Only the Valon knows why some things happen the way they do."

"I don't necessarily disagree. But there is accountability. I did not choose where I was born. I did not want to become a pyromancer. But my freedom was granted. Since that day, everything I have decided to do was of my own will and of my own accord. I cannot discount the ramifications of my actions, both good and bad. Nor do I regret any of them. What I chose to do, at least at the time, was what I thought to be right. Hindsight has shown me what a fool I have been, but that will not change the past. My hope is that I can use my experience and mistakes to change what happens next."

"Do you expect the plan to fail?"

"I didn't say that."

"Then what?" Vivienne raised her voice as she stood up. "What Caden? What do you think is going to happen?"

"I think there is a strong possibility I will fail. That terrifies me."

Vivienne let out a breath and sat back down. "What makes you think you will fail?"

"Because when everything is all said and done, I will surrender before letting anyone else die. There is enough blood on my hands. I cannot stand to see them painted any darker."

The next morning, I arose early, dressed and ate, then prepared myself for my departure. Removing the key from around my neck, I unlocked the black box and looked inside. The bone white talisman bracelet sat next to the small idol of Nirlos. The silver had tarnished slightly, turning black around some of the edges. The idol vibrated softly and placing my thumb atop it's smooth surface, I felt a pulsing energy within. The darkness of the room grew more intense, shoving away the pre-dawn light, and my vision magnified. For a moment, it looked like I was observing the talisman through a lens. Dropping the talisman back into the box, I took a step back. Now that I was no longer touching the talisman, my vision returned to normal.

Locking the box, I placed it into a small sack. Taking a moment, I tidied the room, making the bed and pushing in all of the chairs. I took one final look around the small room before opening the door. The stairs creaked as I walked down to the bottom where I found a place to sit among the crates. I didn't mind waiting, though it proved difficult to keep my mind at ease.

When the doors opened and the first two dock workers entered, I got to my feet to greet them. The dock workers seemed surprised to see me, but the third man who entered raised his hand and waved at me. He had a short brown beard and his hair was long and messy. He wore a blue coat with a captain's pin on the left shoulder.

"It's alright men, Tristin said we would have a guest today."

"How can I help, Captain?"

"No no, please, call me Gil. Just follow Nathan here to the ship. You are welcome to my personal cabin for the time being."

"That is very kind of you."

Nathan, a thin man with dark brown skin and a wide smile waved me over. Picking up my pack, I hurried over to the three men. Nathan nodded to his captain before turning around. I walked side by side with the man as we left the warehouse and it didn't take us long to walk up the path towards and reach the dock. A river boat that was wide and long with a cabin in both the front and the back leaving the middle almost entirely flat. The gang plank which led to the boat was only wide enough for a single person.

Following Nathan up the plank, I looked over the side into the water. My eyes lingered on the small sewer pipe which barely hung over the water. When I stepped onto the boat, I felt my tension rise. Several men were preparing ropes which were threaded through brass rings nailed to the wooden planks of the deck. The sailors only glanced up at me, none of them seeming all that interested. Nathan didn't hesitate and walked to the back of the ship, stopping at the cabin door. He folded his arms and narrowed his eyes as he looked at me.

I hurried over to him and gave him a sheepish smile. "It's been a while since I've been on a ship. I apologize for being distracted."

"Just keep to the cabin and out of the way of my men." Nathan gave me a sharp look, his eyes narrowing. "We intend to load the cargo and get through the southern gate before noon."

"Understood."

"And I am certain the captain wouldn't mind if you helped yourself to a bottle of rum. Though I am certain there are other liquors if you prefer."

"Thank you."

Nathan left without another word and I opened the door to the captain's quarters. Inside was small and the furnishings simple. A table was bolted to the center of the room, a large high back chair sitting behind it. In the corner was a bed built into the wall. Beside the bed was a cabinet filled with liquor bottles. The doors to the cabinet were partially made of glass which seemed a bit out of place for such a ship.

On the opposite side of the room were shelves filled with ledgers and a few maps. Walking over to one of the maps I examined it. The map was a detailed rendering of the River Earn south of Kings Keep. The three road crossings were clearly defined as well as the two major towns, Daven Ride and Rock Port. Part of me mused at what life would be like if I stayed on the ship until it reached its destination.

Perhaps when this is all over, I will get to explore again.

Setting my pack down in the corner, I unstrapped my sword

and placed it on top. If none of the sailors were armed, it seemed like a good idea to keep myself unburdened. Taking a bottle of rum from the cabinet, I took a seat in the captain's chair and began to drink. Though it was a little early to start drinking, I was certain that the sailors wouldn't care. Not that I would get drunk anyway.

The rum was slightly cool, well aged, but rather dry. I silently wished for a glass and a bit of water to cut the drink. Regardless, the alcohol helped calm my nerves and since I wasn't burning any fire, it didn't burn away too quickly. Still, every few minutes I found myself taking another small sip to keep up its effects.

Hours passed and I sat with nothing but my thoughts for entertainment. I ran through the plan over and over in my mind, examining it for flaws. In one week I would return to the city and would return to Gresh Manor. There I would be discovered by Vivienne who would inform Isar and the other sorcerers of my presence. The place should be abandoned so that should allow me to fight without risk of injuring someone. Once I allowed the Malkethian's to overwhelm me, I would be taken from the city. Once we were far enough north, Seraphina's palace guard would ambush my convoy, free me, and I would be able to attack.

That's where things would go wrong. But in order to do what I must, I needed to get out of the city and lead them into a trap without them knowing. They would not go willingly should I flee. They had too much leverage. My mind began to comb through the hundreds of possibilities, of how all of my friends might end up dead. It seemed that the more I thought, the more worried I became.

Lifting the bottle, I raised it to my lips and drained the final few swallows of rum. Clicking my tongue on the roof of my mouth, I grimaced. My head was swimming and taking in a deep breath, I felt a wave of nausea overcome me. Leaning forward, I rested my forehead on the table and looked down at my boots. There were small traces of mud on the edges and the creases in the leather were starting to crack. The nausea vanished as suddenly as it had come, leaving me feeling cool. The inebriation dissipated and the swimming in my head stopped.

Odd, I thought, sitting up. I heard creaking outside the cabin and I looked up at the door as it was pulled open. Captain Gil stepped inside, a stern expression on his face. His expression turned to bemusement as he looked at the empty bottle in front of me. I shrugged and tried my best not to chuckle.

"We're setting off. From what I understand, we are to let you off after we get through the gates?"

"That is correct."

"Well, that shouldn't be too hard to arrange. Though you will need to hide when we pass through inspection."

I nodded. "And where will that be?"

Gil smiled. He walked over to the liquor cabinet and opened one of the glass cupboard doors. He reached in and pushed down on a wine bottle. A distinct pop sounded and the lower section of the cabinet slid into the wall. Beneath the cabinet was a small coffin-like hiding hole. Though it was large enough to hide a man, I could tell that it was going to be a tight fit.

"I hope you are not afraid of confined spaces."

"Not going to say that I am all too fond of them." I shook my head. "But I think I will manage."

"Well, no need to worry about getting in until we reach the inspection docks. Who knows, perhaps the guards won't board us at all." Gil's face grew grim. "Well, they might."

"Thanks for doing this."

"Not a problem Caden."

I felt my muscles tense and my jaw locked. Though I hadn't known for sure if Captain Gil knew who I was, hearing him speak my name banished all doubt. What little trust I had suddenly vanished. Gil smiled and raised both hands, making a placating gesture.

"You don't remember me, do you?"

I looked at the man, studying his face. There was something familiar about him, but beneath his mop of messy hair and beard, I couldn't place where I had seen his face before. "I apologize. I'm not usually one who forgets a face."

"I don't blame you. You were preoccupied at the time. It was my caravan that you and Tristin came to rescue. If you remember, you helped us onto a ship much like this one before chasing off after those bloody buggers."

"Ah, I remember you now. My apologies for not recognizing you."

"Well, let's say that after that I was not keen on caravanning any more for Lady Seraphina; but she offered me a position as captain of this boat. I figured I would take it and repay your kindness when I could."

"So, your men. Do they know who I am?"

"No. I am going to keep that to myself."

"You are aware that there is a reward out for my capture?"

"Indeed. Which is why those men out there should not know who you are."

"Do you think any of them are suspicious?"

"No. Most of these lads have worked on this ship for years. They are loyal and by the Valon they are good men who mind their own business."

"I am putting my trust in you." As I said the words, I knew that I didn't have much of a choice in the matter. I could always try to sneak out of the city again or go back down into the tunnels. But I wanted to get out of the city. *You're just going to have to run the risk.*

"I owe you my life. Suffice it to say, that is worth more than any reward." Gil smiled and pulled out the bottle. The cabinet popped back into place and I found myself trying to find any mark on the floor where the cubby was. The floor was seamless.

"When do we depart?"

"The mates are just tying down the inventory now. We should push off within the hour and by noon we will be out of this swiving city."

"Do you not like Kings Keep?"

"Does anyone?" Gil asked with a shrug. "I would rather be out in the woods, free of people and the messes of city life."

"Then why not leave?"

"It's not so easy when you have a family. The wife has family here and this is the only place the kids know. But one day we will all get onto this boat and leave this place."

"I hope you get that chance."

The boat glided on the water, moving through the city quickly as the crew rowed our way towards the southern gate. We rode with the current, which seemed to make it easier and faster. I watched the river through the window, keeping an eye on every guard we passed. No one seemed to take much notice of us until we approached the southern gate.

Kings Keep's southern wall loomed high, running between the eastern and western mountains where they naturally drew together. Due to the oval shape between the mountain ranges, Kings Keep was perfectly positioned with natural fortifications. Atop the wall were hundreds of soldiers, almost standing shoulder to shoulder. It was more than twice the normal amount and I felt my heart rate increase.

If I get out of this city, how in the hell will I sneak back in?

I didn't have much time to consider the question before Gil entered the small captains cabin.

"You should hide now. It looks like they are inspecting every boat today."

Without a word, I walked over to the cabinet and opened the door by pressing in the wine bottle third from the bottom left. Hearing the pop, I watched as the underside of the cabinet slid in, revealing the coffin-like cubby. Taking in a deep breath, I climbed in and situated myself so I was laying on my back with my arms crossed.

"Comfortable?" Gil asked, smirking.

"Piss off."

Gil pulled on the wine bottle and the cabinet closed above me. There was no light in the cubby but within a few seconds my eyes adjusted to the darkness. My breathing slowed and I relaxed all of my muscles. Listening, I could hear the water lap against the side of the ship followed by the soft splash of the oars as they were lifted from the water. The wooden handles of the oars made a grinding sound as they were slid forward and placed back into the water. Everything was rhythmic and had a motion I could visualize. In my mind, I pictured the boat moving towards the large opening of the wall.

The words were muffled, but it was clear when we reached the gate that we were being boarded for inspection. The heavy footsteps of men in full armor walking across the deck was louder than it should have been.

One misstep and they would go tumbling into the water.

At first the idea of the armored guards slipping and falling into the water brought amusement. But after a moment, the thought of the water made me shiver. I could picture Nels standing on the dock, hands raised, a wide smile on his face. I was trapped near his domain in a wooden coffin. How easy it would be for the river to swallow us, drowning me while I could do nothing to change it. As these thoughts went through my head, my breathing grew heavy. Gasping for air, I reached up and placed my hand on the underside of the cabinet above me. Fighting the sudden overwhelming claustrophobia, I forced myself to take deep breaths as I studied the groves in the wood above me.

The cabin door squeaked as it opened and two sets of footsteps followed.

"I can assure you, we're just running a simple operation," Gil's voice was calm and confident.

"We're just doing our due diligence." The second voice was high pitched and nasally. "I don't see any problems here."

The floorboards of the cabin creaked as one of the men walked closer to me. Holding my breath, I tensed my entire body and tried to remain as still as possible.

"Say, Captain. Do you have a license for transporting liquor?"

"That is my private collection. Not for sale."

"Still, it could be considered contraband."

"Well, if her majesty is worried about the contents of my liquor cabinet, her representative is welcome to *inspect* a bottle or two."

My heart beat in my throat as I heard the doors to the cabinet open. It seemed like every moment dragged on for an hour as the man who stood above me searched through the liquor cabinet. It felt like any moment he would find the wine bottle and trigger the mechanism that would uncover my hiding hole. The sound of chinking glass made my hands balled into fists, but it was followed by the creaking of floorboards as the man stepped away. My pounding heart slowed and I allowed myself to let out the breath I'd been holding.

"I hope that they are to her majesty's liking," Gil said.

The other man muttered something unintelligible as the door to the cabin swung shut, slamming hard against the doorframe. My body relaxed and I began to breathe in a more regular cadence, not as concerned about making sound. The pounding in my head and chest subsided as I caught my breath.

"Son of a bitch," I muttered.

Soon I felt the boat lurch forward and we were moving again. It felt like an eternity before I heard Gil enter the cabin again. When the top of the cabinet above slid above me, I was blinded by the sudden light. Squinting, I climbed out of the cubby and stretched.

"You had me worried there for a minute."

Gil shrugged. "That was a little closer than I would have preferred."

"At least we are out of the city."

"True."

I looked out the cabin windows and saw the tall trees which lined the river. The mountain still loomed above and as we rounded a bend in the river, I caught a glimpse of the southern wall. Rubbing the back of my neck, I looked back at Captin Gil who had taken a seat at his desk.

"Where should we let you off?"

"The same place I originally picked you up last autumn."

"Of course. It should take about an hour before we get there."

"If you wouldn't mind, I'd like to get another drink."

"Please, help yourself."

Opening the liquor cabinet, I took a bottle at random and biting off the cork I took a deep swig. The rum was better than the first bottle, sweeter but not smooth. The liquor burned as it passed over my tongue and ran down my throat. The burning felt soothing. Placing the bottle on the desk, I walked over to the corner where I had set down my pack and sword. As I strapped on my sword, I could feel Gil's eyes on my back.

"What?" I asked, my tone a little harsher than I'd intended.

"I was just wondering. Why are you getting off so close? Aren't you trying to escape the city?"

"I am not trying to escape. But I needed to get out of the city for a bit. Besides, I have something that needs to be attended to."

CHAPTER FIFTEEN
VISION

Weeds grew rampant on the sides of the road, long thorns and purple thistles looking violent and angry. Drawing my sword, I cut them down as I made my way up from the banks of the river. Once I was on the road, I looked back over my shoulder at the riverboat which was already on its way. I followed the boat with my eyes until it disappeared around the next bend. It was almost a relief to see it go and to be alone once more.

Crossing the road, I cut down more weeds as I made my way onto the field which sat at the base of a tree covered mountainside. I looked up at the sharp green tops of the pines which were occasionally broken by the white barked aspens. Reaching the base of the slope, I sheathed my sword and began the steep climb to the plateau. The journey was much easier than the previous two I had made during the winter. With no snow to deal with, it almost seemed easy.

Regardless of the ease of the climb, I took my time. I still had a week before I needed to be back in the city. Though I had come to say one final goodbye, I found myself reluctant to do so. The thought of never returning saddened me.

You've said so many goodbye's. Why should this one be any different?

When I got closer to the top of the slope where it plateaued, I could see the massive Dryad tree. A few branches snapped to my left and in an instant, my sword was in hand. Lowering the tip so it was perpendicular to my chest, I slowly scanned the foliage. One of the trees shifted slightly and a youthful face emerged a few inches from the bark. The face smiled at me, its soft green eyes glowing like the back of a firefly.

Several more faces emerged from neighboring trees, and they all looked at me with child-like fascination. Relaxing, I sheathed my sword and continued on. When I was a hundred paces from the top, a tree bent over, blocking my path. The white and gray bark of the aspen moved a thin Dryad formed from the tree. Standing at half my height, the Dryad looked like a young girl. Thin branches hung from her head, almost like hair, dangling past her shoulders. The branches were covered with small heart-shaped leaves which had serrated edges. The Dryad looked up at me and tilted her head.

"Do I look strange to you?"

The Dryad giggled and nodded.

"Can I get past?" I asked, trying to make my voice as pleasant as possible. The Dryad's eyes widened and she looked over her shoulder. I could see the large trunk of the main tree. The branches had grown so wide that the canopy of leaves shaded hundreds of yards past the top of the plateau. Even where I now stood, I was under its sheltering canopy.

"Da' said you can pass." The Dryad reached up her small hand.

Taking her hand, I let the small wilder-spirit lead me the rest of the way. She moved with the eagerness of a child wanting to show a sibling something they had found in the woods. It was a strangely familiar thing that caused me to smile. It had been such a long time since I had been reminded of my childhood. Though the negative memories seemed so prevalent, I was overwhelmed by an uncommon nostalgia for the days I had been allowed to run wild through the woods. The scents of the trees, the sharp pine and musty earth suddenly filling my nostrils, enriching the memories and sense of familiarity.

When we reached the top, I was surprised by the bright and colorful plants and flowers which now covered the plateau. Instead of the white ghost flowers, thousands of sky blue daisies, pink azaleas, and yellow tulips covered the ground. It was more beautiful than anything I'd ever seen. The scene even made the extravagant gardens the Queen kept look drab in comparison. Finding myself overwhelmed by the beauty, I smiled, muttering a prayer of thanks to the Valon.

The central tree groaned, the bark splitting and cracking as a gigantic figure formed. The Dryad I had come to know smiled wide as his face formed. He pulled himself from the tree, shaking his head. The leaves which covered the back of his head rustled which made him look like a dog shaking wet fur.

"My friend. It is good to see you again. I see you have met some of the saplings."

The small Dryad who had been holding my hand pulled away and skipped over to her father. He reached down and took hold of her in his massive hand. Lifting her, he placed her on his shoulder. Standing almost fifty feet tall, the sapling girl looked exceedingly small on the Dryad's shoulder.

"It is good to see you as well. I didn't know saplings would grow so quickly."

This seemed to make the Dryad happy for his smile widened so far I half expected his face to break in two. "It is wonderful. Come spring next year, there will be hundreds of us. We will once again thrive in these lands. All because of you."

"I did little more than plant you."

"Don't underestimate the importance of such an act. You have brought much magic to this place and so has your friend."

At the mention of Kori, I felt my heart break, an old wound reopened. I was not prepared for the overwhelming sorrow to strike me and my breath suddenly caught in my throat.

"Do not be sad. The death of this place has birthed new life. Like a forest after a fire, new seedlings have sprouted from the ashes."

"It is good to know their deaths have brought forth life." I had a hard time saying the words.

Though what the Dryad said was true, it didn't make the loss any easier to hear. As I looked past him at the flower covered mounds where my friends were buried, I realized the grief was still as large as it ever was. But I was surprised to find that I had grown strong enough that the heavy burden was more manageable to bear.

"What troubles you my friend?"

"I am just sad. I came to say goodbye to my friends. I am afraid this will be the last time I will be able to do so."

"Then I will not keep you from them." The Dryad motioned forward. "Mind the flowers."

"Of course."

I placed each step carefully as I made my way through the flower beds to the small mounds on the far side of the plateau. Shrugging off my pack, I set it on the ground as I unbuttoned the flap. Sitting on top was the small wooden box. Gingerly, I removed the box and opened the lid. Sitting inside was the bone white talisman bracelet and the small silver idol of Nirlos. Reaching into the box, I removed both objects, and a wave of cold washed over me.

The plateau darkened, as though a cloud had passed over the sun, and the warmth of the day vanished. Letting out a breath, I watched as it froze and misted. The unnatural cold which hung in the air made me feel as though I'd been running naked through a snowstorm. Still, I did not shiver. Instead I remained still as the chill ran deep through my body and into my heart.

An amused laugh sounded to my right. Looking up I saw two individuals standing together beside the mounds. Kori and Merek were holding hands, both smiled wide, then laughed again. Unable to move, let alone speak, I looked at them awestruck. My heart leapt with joy, but part of me almost felt repulsed by the phantoms who stood before me. Something about their too pale skin, hollow eyes, and overjoyed expressions seemed off. It was almost like I was looking at a facsimile of my friends who no longer had their souls.

"We're glad you came to see us, Caden," Merek said.

"Why do you look so unhappy?" Kori asked. Her head tilted to the side and her smile widened.

Taking a tentative step back, I pulled my hand from the talisman box and snapped it closed. The light returned to normal and the surrounding flowers seemed more vibrant than before. Along with the color, the warmth returned and I felt my body shiver at the sudden change. However, the ghosts of my friends still remained. They were no longer smiling.

"Why are you here?" I asked.

"Do you not want us to be?" Kori's voice was a mix of hurt and anger.

"Of course I want that. But you are dead."

"But we aren't completely gone," Merek said.

"Then how are you here? Why remain as a ghost?"

"Caden, is it not obvious to you yet?" Merek's brow furrowed as he spoke. "Please my friend, think for a moment."

I looked back down at the box. "You are not real then. Only a vision from my mind."

"Almost. We are trapped, Caden. You need to release us.

Destroy the box. Destroy the talismans and our souls can finally find their peace."

Opening the lid of the box again, I reached in and touched the bracelet of white bones. It was cool to the touch, but I felt no strange sensation. Moving my hand over to the idol, the moment my finger touched the silver the light dimmed again and the cold returned. Jerking my hand free, I accidentally dropped the box. Falling to the ground, the box toppled over and both talisman's tumbled out. Where the bracelet landed, the flowers remained unaffected. But everything the idol touched withered and died.

Crouching down, I scooped up the idol and held it tightly in my fist. The withering of the flowers continued and to my alarm, began to spread quickly. Whirling around, I watched as the ripple of rot reached the central tree. The Dryad, standing fifty feet tall, had his hand stretched towards the sky. He was not moving. Nothing was moving except for the rot.

When the rot reached the tree, the leaves began to fall, turning brown and then black before hitting the ground. Withering to a husk, the tree died and the Dryad crumbled, breaking apart piece by piece. The rot continued to expand until I was standing atop a plateau overlooking a valley of dead trees. The sky had turned a dark gray and ash began to rain down from the sky. The temperature decreased until my entire body felt like it was about to freeze solid.

Everything was dead and for a brief moment, I wondered if this was what was waiting for me on the other side. Letting out a frosted breath, I turned around and saw my two friends standing side by side, but they were no longer recognizable. The skin on their faces was withered and cracked, with sunken cheeks and shriveled lips. Their eyes were gone, replaced by empty rotten sockets. The clothing which hung around emaciated bodies was shredded and torn, leaving large sections of rotten skin and cracked bone exposed.

The corpse which had once been Merek opened its mouth, but instead of words, he only groaned. Kori did the same, groaning with a little more effort as she raised her hand and pointed with a long bony finger. Following the direction she pointed, I turned my head and saw a tall figure wreathed in shadow emerge from the forest of dead trees. He moved with long flowing strides, gliding forward as if being carried by the wind. The shadow which wreathed his face pulled back, revealing a bone white skull. Reaching into his robes of shadow, he pulled forth a long dark blade.

What stood before me was no necromancer, no Shantenbose, nor any other monster with which I was familiar. It seemed as though I were standing before Nirlos, the Valon of death, himself.

"Come to me, my child. Save this world from wretched death."

The voice was a thin rasp which made my skin crawl.

"Save me, save them."

The entity smiled, then, like smoke in the wind, vanished.

Color returned to the world, and in the blink of an eye, everything was as it should be. The large tree at the center of the plateau was healthy, the large canopy of leaves above intact. My eyes lingered on the Dryad who was now looking at me with his large glowing amber eyes. Taking in a deep breath, I inhaled the rich fragrance of the flowers and my shoulders relaxed. My left hand was still so tightly clenched in a fist that my palm was beginning to hurt. Relaxing my fingers, I looked down at the idol and saw where the hard edges had left an imprint on my hand. The silver was no longer tarnished and it shimmered in the small beams of sunlight which broke through the canopy of leaves above.

Turning back to the ghosts of my friends, I saw solemn expressions on their faces. When I looked into Kori's eyes, I saw deep hollowness. When I looked into Merek's, I saw profound sorrow. Neither of them said another word before they vanished, their images breaking apart like smoke. A gentle breeze rustled the flowers around my feet and carried away the smoke of their image, leaving no trace they had ever been.

A stillness descended upon me as something reawakened in my mind. The realization that I had been hunting down the wrong monsters was accompanied by clarity. There was still a more sinister evil lurking in the shadows of Kings Keep. One which had compelled a necromancer to commit extreme evil or at the least, guided him to it.

Picking up the broken talisman bracelet, I put it around my wrist and pocketed the idol. They would not be buried here. Not today. Not while there was work to be done.

"So, it seems as though you too have been touched by the darkness." The voice came from above and made me jump.

Looking up, I met the eyes of the giant Dryad. "I suppose I did not make it out unscathed."

"Few who fight evil ever do."

"Tell me, if death is a natural part of life, why do we consider those who walk in its wake evil?"

"It is not death which lends power but the fear of it. Fear and pain lead many good things down evil paths. Even among my kind, there are those who would rather blight the land than see it flourish. Perhaps they are afraid of your kind, afraid of what will become of the wild in your presence. I have seen many of the wilder spirits destroy the very land they claim to love to spite your kind."

"And what do you think?"

"I am a tree. It does not take much effort for me to fulfill my purpose. I have cultivated a wonderful garden and my roots run deep. My purpose is to spread life, not to take it." The Dryad waved his hand over a small patch of flowers and they grew new blossoms. A strong fragrance filled the air, one which was sweet and soothing. "But tree's do not live forever, and thus death comes. But the fungus and rot also thrive upon my death, returning me to the soil from whence I came. We are all part of a natural order. Your kind and mine."

"And the evil dark things?"

"Also exist with a purpose. Perhaps they exist as opposition to good or are a natural cause of life. But destruction is as necessary as creation. Just because you are a destroyer lad, doesn't mean that you are not required."

"Quite honestly, I am not accustomed to receiving wisdom from a tree." I said with a smile.

"How often do you listen?" The Dryad smiled. "The trees are always talking, but they do not like to speak above a whisper. Easy to miss if you aren't paying attention."

I paused and listened. The soft breeze that came through the trees, ruffled the leaves and swayed the branches. Still, I heard no voices, if the trees were speaking, it was still too subtle for me to hear.

"What are they saying now?" I asked.

The Dryad hummed and smiled. "You must learn to listen. If you cannot hear what they have to say, you are not yet ready to hear."

Nodding, I felt a little cheated by the Dryad's answer.

"The evil isn't gone yet," he said, reaching down and placing his finger beside a large tulip.

"No, I don't think so." I patted my pocket, feeling the talisman. "I am uncertain if it ever will be."

"You need to return to the place we first met."

"Why? Is there something wrong with the place?"

The Dryad frowned, kneeling down beside and leaning forward so his face was level with my own. "You did not have the eyes to see before. Now that I have seen the change in you, I think you will find some of the answers you seek."

"You speak like you know more than you should. How do you know what I seek?"

The Dryad shook his head and waved to the trees. "We talk. There are few secrets in the forest. We are the casual observers of the world. Most of my brothers and sisters live their entire lives in the same place. After years of seeing only the same things, you tend to ask what others see. I know these lands better than most."

"So, can you tell me, are there many things in these woods I should be wary of?"

"Of course. There is something coming from far distant lands. It seems all dark and dangerous things are being attracted to this land. They stay away from here, but we are little more than a small refuge in the darkness."

The light grew dim and looking up through the gaps in the leaves, I could see the swirling dark clouds. The floral scent of the plateau was now joined by the scent of rain. Distant thunder rumbled and it made me feel like the forest was grumbling.

"Take refuge under my leaves until the storm passes. Then you must go. You must see."

As the Dryad spoke, rain began to fall, smacking the leaves above. Only a few droplets made their way down through the canopy. Following the Dryad over to the base of his tree, I took a seat and rested my back against the thick trunk.

Only a few minutes passed before rain began to fall in earnest. With my head resting against the back of the trunk, I watched as rain dripped through the canopy and showered the trees and flowers. Though I could not hear what the trees had to say, I patiently listened. For the first time in months, I felt truly calm and the worries of my mind were set aside. As the rain continued to fall, my eyes grew heavy and slowly I drifted off to sleep.

When I awoke, the brilliant rays of a setting sun bathed my face. My right arm was outstretched before me, partially hidden between the stems of tall tulips. Sitting up, I stretched and groaned. I felt neither groggy nor sluggish as I got to my feet. The rest had made me feel better than I had in ages. Taking in a deep breath of fresh air, I turned around and looked at the large Dryad tree. The dark brown bark was rough and reaching out I placed my hand upon it.

"Thank you," I muttered. Picking up my pack, I slung it over my shoulder and began to make my way to the edge of the grove. Though I knew I would not be coming back, I was not sad to say goodbye. The trees would carry word back to the Dryad for me. Anything I ever wished to tell him.

Reaching the edge of the flowers, I heard the rustling of leaves and turned to look back. The Dryad had emerged from his tree again, his large amber eyes looking at me. He raised his hand, waved farewell, before motioning to his right. Following the gesture, I saw the same sapling who had escorted me wander over.

"Father has asked that I join you," she whispered.

"If that is what you wish, you are welcome to keep me company."

"He says that you may need help listening to the trees."

"Indeed I will." I paused. "Do you have a name?"

"Arelaurel."

"What a beautiful name.

The sapling smiled, then looked over her shoulders at her father.

"Be well," he said. "And may the wrath of the just strengthen you."

CHAPTER SIXTEEN

NECROMANTIC BLIGHT

I t took three days of hiking through the mountains before we crossed the final peak and began our descent into the valley where I had almost a year before discovered the Wendigo Caves. Arelaurel had remained silent for most of the journey, content to walk beside me. Every attempt I had made to begin a conversation had been met with single word answers or short phrases. Whatever interest the Dryad had in accompanying me did not seem tied to communication.

The descent down the slope was laborious, the wild plants that grew on the steep ground gnarled and tangled together. The Dryad moved beside me, shifting from tree to tree with absolute ease. Though I had not expected myself to be with a companion, it was a comfort not to be alone.

When I finally reached the bottom, I searched for the small river which cut through the valley. I found it easily, the sound of splashing water loud as it permeated the forest. As before, I observed the strangeness of the wood. It was devoid of the humming of insects, the chirping of birds, or the movements of animals. Save for the rushing of the nearby river, there was no sound at all.

Walking alongside the banks of the river, we quickly made our way through the valley towards the caves. The closer we got the more foul the air became. The scent of rotten plants was strong in the air, and clusters of mushrooms grew at the base of diseased trees. Each mushroom was topped with a white powder and was as large as a dinner plate.

Arelaurel sauntered up to one of the trees and reached down towards the Grave Duster.

"Don't touch those," I warned, placing my hand on my sword. "They're nasty buggers."

The Dryad took a few steps back and nodded.

"Rotten?" She seemed both perplexed and fascinated. She looked down at the mushroom top like a child discovering something new that was just on the edge of their comprehension.

"Yes."

Arelaurel's eyes widened and she walked back over to where I stood. She only stood as tall as my chest and her bark covered limbs were thin. She reached out and placed her hand on my sword.

"What is this?"

"A sword."

"What does it do?"

"It's a tool that cuts. We use it to fight and to defend ourselves."

Arelaurel raised her hand and each of the long twig-like fingers grew sharp thorns. The Dryad smiled and then continued forward.

"I can feel it. The rot and the danger." Arelaurel's voice sounded haunted. "There are others here. But not like me."

Drawing my sword, I walked with caution, ready to be attacked at any moment. We hiked beside the stream for another half hour before reaching the section where a path had been carved from the uncountable crossings of the Wendigo's. Though some small plants had grown over the path, it was as easy to follow as any other man-made trail. Unlike the first time I had come here, the trees which lined either side had deep black splotches, their leaves an unsavory yellow. Several were leaking a deep black sap, almost like a wound leaking pus. The stench was worse than the sewers and I found myself gagging. Covering my nose with my wrist, I held my breath until the nausea abated.

Taking in short shallow breaths, I found that I could taste the stench. The queasiness returned and I took a few steps back until I was standing in the stream. The cool water flowed over my boots but did not seep in. The smooth river stones made me feel uneasy and the current was quick, pushing strongly on my ankles.

"Get ahold of yourself," I said, muttering aloud my personal chastisement. "Swiving coward."

Tightening my fingers around the hilt of my longsword, I stepped out of the river and proceeded up the hill towards the caves. More Grave Dusters sat at the base of the infected trees, some small as a snail, others as large and round as a pumpkin. Careful not to disturb them, I gave them as much space as possible. When I reached the top, I realized I was alone. Looking over my shoulder, I saw Arelaurel standing at the base beside the river. She was looking at me, her glowing green eyes fixated on something above me.

My pulse quickened and I snapped my attention back around and saw the large black tree in the middle of the clearing. The branches had withered and what remained were only a few feet long, all sticking out at odd angles. The trunk was black as coal and oozing with infection. At the tree's base sat a pool of the ooze which covered the ground in all directions for several feet.

The ground was rotten like it had been before, but the rot had turned a deep black and had a more withered look. Stepping forward, my foot crunched on the hardened black soil. Pausing, I looked around at the circle of dead trees which enveloped the clearing before the cave. Each was infected with black splotches, their leaves yellow. As I looked upon them, I noticed that the branches were swaying despite there being no wind. This realization caused the hair on the back of my neck to rise and a chill to rush down my spine. Preparing myself, I walked forward, sword held at the ready.

The branches of the trees still swayed, but there was no other movement. The Grave Dusters which formed small circles in the clearing did not move either. Once I reached the edge of the pool of ooze that circled the black tree trunk, several sounds erupted from the woods. It was like a dozen trees had been cut down all at once. The sharp cracking of splintering wood was followed by strange growling.

Four trees which had lined the clearing had collapsed into mangled piles of splintered wood and branches. Then the first one rose. Unlike the Dryad, this creature had no grace as it formed itself from the ruined tree. Each of the limbs were twisted, mangled, and lacking correct proportion. As the first rose, the left arm hung almost to the ground while the right hung to its hip and was thick as a stump. The face was formed from splintered wood and broken branches. The mouth looked like the maw of a wild beast with sharp wooden teeth coated in black sap. When it met my eyes, I saw red eyes that glowed like those of a Wendigo.

"Shit!" I cursed, as the other three piles began to form like the first. Within moments I was surrounded by four of the foul beasts.

Is this what you meant? I wondered.

Reaching into my pocket, I pulled out a box of matches. Taking one out, I flicked the top with my nail and the match flared to life. The flame flickered on the match for a moment before entering my skin through my thumb and index finger. As the fire traveled up my hand, I felt my skin prickle and both my arms erupted into gooseflesh. Each of the creatures sank to the ground and prostrated themselves before me.

Pausing, I took a moment to look at each of the creatures and remembered seeing a drawing with their likeness in Hevron's Grimoire. I searched my memory to try and recall their name, and as I looked upon the rot which covered the ground, I remembered. The Wood Blights continued to remain still as I regarded them. However, despite being prostrate upon the ground, their red eyes were all looking up at me.

Unsure why these creatures were behaving so strangely, I turned to the cave and saw that it was filled with a dark vapor. Like a black fog, the vapor leaked from the mouth of the cave and drifted a few inches above the ground towards me. Swirling images and shadows formed from the fog and a dark cloaked man emerged. He wore a silver mask under a large black hood. The man reached out his hand and upon his wrist was the same bone white talisman which hung from mine.

"Hevron!"

"Calm, these beasts will not hurt you."

"How are you alive?" I lowered my sword and produced a ball of fire in my left hand. "You're dead!"

Hevron pulled back his hood and the silver mask which covered his face vanished. His face was marred by splattered blood, his lips a dark blue, and his eyes absent of color. The milky iris's had flecks of black within them. When he opened his mouth to speak, his tongue was black and swollen. "I am dead."

"Why am I seeing the dead? First my friends, now you."

"You are one of us now. My mind is foggy, almost like this is a dream of a dream. But my master had required it and so here I am."

"Your master? You wrote of him before. Who is he?"

"Nirlos, the Valon of Death, harbinger of a new age. *One where he will have power and dominion over this world.*" As Hevron spoke, his voice shifted, as though two beings were speaking at once. His speech changed, no longer in the common tongue. The words were ancient, sounding soft as velvet and powerful as thunder. There was a small pause, and his language changed back. "*I have come to claim your allegiance. You must awaken me, release me from my bonds. Once I am free, you shall have all my power.*"

"I have no intention of setting you free, you bastard! I will destroy you."

Hevron laughed, and the sound was like a cackling demon.

"He has chosen you." Hevron's voice was once again his own. "You are one of many he has called. When I failed him, he chose you to do what I could not. He even sent me back to kill your friend. She was not who he wanted."

"You were the Shantenbose?"

"In part. My power still remains in that bracelet around your wrist." Hevron lifted his own hand and showed off the phantom copy which hung on his own arm. As he jostled the talisman, it disappeared. "You do not understand the power you now possess. Embrace it Caden. Go, find him and you will have the power to change the world."

"I never wanted that power."

"Don't lie Caden. The power to keep those you love from death? To bring back those you have lost? Nirlos has dominion over all those things."

"I will not become a monster. I would rather die!"

Hevron shook his head. "You will not be a monster. There is still so much you cannot see. Give it time. The power will show you that death and pain are as natural as the fire which burns within you. He wants you to become the great destroyer. You can cleanse this world in a way I never could."

"Shut up!" I raised my sword. "I will never use your power."

"You already have. You already are. Why not use it to spite

your enemies? Caden, this power will change everything. Go back to the city, destroy your enemies. Save those you love."

"I can't."

I lowered my sword and looked away from Hevron. I felt ashamed. His offer was tempting. More than I wanted to admit. Everything I wanted was at my fingertips.

He's lying, I told myself.

Growling, I raised my sword and rushed forward. Thrusting, I drove my longsword through Hevron's chest. The phantom image only shimmered as the blade passed through him. Turning, I slashed through his form over and over again. Unaffected by my blows, Hevron laughed.

"Stop, you're wasting your energy."

Growling, I slashed my sword through his face one final time before stalking away. "Leave me be."

"So be it. But until it is done, I will be here. All you must do is call for my aid and I will guide you."

Hevron walked back to the swirled black vapor of the cave. Just before he stepped in, I raised my hand and called out. "Wait."

Pausing, Hevron looked back over his shoulder and smiled. "Yes?"

"Why?"

"I do not understand your question."

"Why did you sell yourself to Nirlos?"

"I didn't. He chose me. Just like he chose you."

"That doesn't make sense. Why would a Valon need anything from a mortal? Or is he not as powerful as we are led to believe?"

Hevron smiled. "I think it would make more sense for you to figure that out for yourself. The answers are all in my book. You just didn't look close enough."

Without another word, Hevron entered the darkness and vanished. The darkness within the cave dissipated and I was able to see partially into the dark hole. The four Wood Blights stood up but remained where their trees had been. Each looked down at me with their glowing red eyes and it made me feel like I was looking down a charging bull.

Sheathing my sword, I held out my hand and produced another ball of flame as I approached the cave. The slanting entrance was coated with dried blood and at the bottom sat the skeletal remains of the hundreds of beasts the Wendigo's had dragged into their lair. Entering the cave, I carefully climbed down the sloping entrance and stopped before the pile of bones. The inside of the cave was partially lit from the large crack which went up through the mountain. The small beams of sunlight looked strange next to the flickering of my fire which caused the skeletal remains to cast wicked shadows upon the walls.

Inscribed upon the walls were symbols that had not been present on my last visit. Written as if with blood, the symbols were of a pictographic language I could not read. Looking upon the writing caused my heart to sink and my throat to tighten. The longer I looked, the more my mind began to make sense of the images. They were written with the same power which had obscured the writing of the Grimoire, the writing which Kori had been able to translate.

Closing my eyes I took in a deep breath and opened them again, focusing on the writing. Each marking had changed, written in plain familiar characters, though the meaning was still lost. None of the letters formed intelligible words and I first tried to read them left to right, then the reverse, then from top to bottom. Regardless of the direction, I could make no sense of the writing.

Stepping around the pile of bones, I made my way to the far wall where I could look at the writing from a greater distance. Once I was on the other side, I reduced the focus of my eyes and just let myself gaze upon the wall. Within the writing, I saw an image take shape. Depicted in the space between words was a map in a similar shape and size as Kings Keep. The River Earn still snaked through and there was a large gap where the Kings Castle still stood. The buildings and roads were different, and several large landmarks were placed where the north and south gates stood.

I stayed and gazed at the map for some time, trying to memorize the pathways. The longer I looked, the more my mind began to form connections. A strange marking stood on the left, just beyond the marker which noted the northern gate. Its path was familiar and my mind made a connection.

"The foundry," I whispered. The lines all started to make sense and two mental maps merged together. The one I had been keeping of the landmarks in the underground began to align with the map I saw on the wall. "The underground."

How long were you mapping this? I wondered, thinking about Hevron.

Something stirred in the back of my mind and my vision went fuzzy. Shaking my head, I pushed away any thoughts of the man and my vision cleared. I studied the map until it was memorized, then I turned my attention back to the cave where I examined the bones. The remains were of different animals and beasts taken from the forest. All human remains had been removed on our previous visit to be buried in the city. Still, it felt wrong to be amongst so much death, but I did not want to miss anything else which had been left behind.

The cave in the back connected with a large crack that went up through the mountain above. Small beams of light illuminated the passage which was just narrow enough for me to climb through if I wanted to crawl. While too small for a Wendigo, I considered if Hevron had ever bothered to climb it. Taking off my pack, I set it against the wall and decided to see where the narrow passage led.

Getting down onto my hands and knees, I crawled forward

and up the small passageway and after a hundred feet found it opened up into a much more spacious cavern. Standing, I lifted my hand causing my small ball of fire to float so it would illuminate the cave. The cave was empty, but the floor was covered in strange scratches, almost like metal spikes had been dragged across it multiple times. As I walked closer, I saw that the far side of the cave, which had originally looked like a pile of fallen rocks, hid a small corridor. With caution, I proceeded across the cave towards the narrow opening. With my back pressed against the stones, I shuffled down the passageway and into the silent darkness.

Emerging into another cave, I raised my hand and saw a hundred glimmering soldiers. The steel helmets were dirty and tarnished, some with scratches and dents. Each soldier wore loose chain mail which hung around their wilted frames. Holding swords or spears, each of the soldiers were at attention, remaining still as statues. Flaring the fire which hung over my hand, I shed more light upon the company and saw dead faces staring back at me. The dead men had withered flesh that looked hard. Bones showed through, oftentimes showing slashes or the wounds which had caused their deaths. These dead men were not unlike those Hevron had used to attack the ridge the night I killed him.

But why did these not collapse?

Each of the deadmen I had faced before had fallen the moment I had killed the Deathmonger. Drawing my sword, I approached the first deadman and thrust my blade through his chest. My steel longsword cut through the rusted chainmail with ease, cutting through the withered flesh and breaking the bone of his ribcage. The deadman did not react, but the body leaned backwards from the force of being run through with my sword. Pulling out my blade, I took a step back. The body collapsed turning into a pile of rotten flesh, bone, metal, and cloth.

A terrible idea came to mind, and I looked at the bone talisman which hung on my wrist. Though several of the pieces were cracked, I wondered what I could do with the power that remained. Holding out my hand, I let the fire ascend high above before reaching out towards the deadmen. Waving my hand, I tried to reach out and connect with the empyrean. The small flecks of light shimmered in the air all around and a warm sensation traveled up my arm to my shoulder, like it had been plunged into bathwater.

The stars of the empyrean vanished and nothing happened. My fire continued to hover above the company of deadmen as I finished examining them. Near the back of the cave, there was another tunnel which curved to the left. There was just dim light streaming in, and small shadows flickered on the wall. Walking between the rows of the standing dead, I left the cave and followed the tunnel around the corner to where it opened up into a small clearing. Like the clearing below, the ground was black and rotten, but it only spanned about twenty feet from the entrance. The trees growing on the edge of the clearing were sick, with black splotches, but these were not half as infected as those from the other entrance. There was a path on the right which led back down the slope and ended at a cliff. Walking down to the edge, I looked down and saw where the path connected with the clearing below. The Twig Blights were still standing in their places, not having moved since I had entered the cave.

From the higher vantage point, I could see over the line of trees and caught a glimpse of Kings Keep. The small river below ran down the slope towards the Raha. The buildings had begun to climb higher as more people continued to build up the slope. The southern wall was plainly visible and the shimmering of armor denoted the guards that patrolled above. Looking down upon the city, I felt an overwhelming sense of dread. The words Hevron had spoken echoed in my mind.

Go back to the city, destroy your enemies. Save those you love.

Balling my fists, I returned to the entrance of the cave and drew my sword. Passing through the opening, I walked down the short tunnel and entered the large cavern. Taking one final look at the small army of deadmen, I began to dispatch them. I stabbed each, one at a time, through the chest. Each collapsed into a pile and the faster I went, the more they began to knock each other over. Still, I took the time to see that each was little more than pieces before moving on. I would not use this new power to destroy my enemies. Not when it would make me a monster in the process. I had come too far to fall back into old ways.

I was just going to have to deal with two problems: defeat the sorcerers, then hunt down Nirlos. As I cut down the final deadman I let out a sigh. It was folly, but somehow I would need to kill the Valon of death. If he needed me to be set free, then he wasn't all powerful. That glimmer of hope was small, but I latched onto it. It would have to do.

CHAPTER SEVENTEEN
DARK ENTITY

Seraphina's palace was dark save for a few windows in the uppermost towers. From the edge of the garden, I watched and waited, wondering if sneaking into the palace was worth the risk. Though I was certain that our plan would work, I was growing restless waiting in the woods and desperately needed something to distract me and prevent me from overthinking. It was long past the middle of the night and only a few hours from dawn when I was confident enough to make my move. Sneaking around the garden turned battle ground, I noticed that the grass had grown back and all of the catapults had been cleared away.

Looks like no one's been training, I thought with a grumble.

My eyes glanced at the building which had been erected in the back of Seraphina's palace grounds and I wondered if they had all departed. Our ambush's success was dependent on their participation. I hoped that they would be ready.

Once I reached the edge of the forest that was closest to the palace, I took a moment to check that no one was looking before darting forward. Concealing myself in the bushes which lined the walls, I crept forward until I was standing right below Vivienne's window. Searching the dirt below the bushes, I dug several pebbles from the ground and placed them in my cupped palm. Looking up, I took one of the stones in my hand, then took a few steps into the open where I would have a better angle.

Tossing a stone up at the second floor window, I cringed as the loud clack rang out in the silence of the night. I waited impatiently, my eyes darting back and forth, searching for anyone to notice me. Throwing another stone, I darted back to the bushes where I hid myself. Listening, I looked up towards the window and was disappointed when no one came. Rolling a third stone between my fingers, I prepared to toss it at the window when I heard the sound of the latch.

Smiling, I watched as the window was pushed open and a familiar face looked out. Vivienne was scowling as she scanned the grounds. I cleared my throat and she looked down at me. Her expression instantly changed to joy and a wide smile blossomed on her face.

"What are you doing?" she chided.

"Come on. I need to talk to you."

"Go. I'll meet you at the edge of the woods. Quick, before someone sees."

I nodded and Vivienne closed the window. I waited for a few moments before creeping through the bushes to the edge of the palace. I took a moment to scan the garden and palace rooftops. Seeing no guards, I dashed back to the line of trees. Once I was safely hidden in the shadows of the forest, I walked through the woods to a familiar cluster of trees. Taking a seat at their base, I began to run my thumb over the talisman bracelet.

Though it was difficult to gauge time in the dead of a moonless night, it was a half an hour before I heard footsteps. Looking up, I saw Vivienne making her way through the woods, still a hundred yards away. I remained calm and still as I watched her approach. She held a small lantern which had a tinted lens in the front. This focused the firelight and guided her path. I shifted my weight onto my left hand as I climbed to my feet. A small twig snapped under my weight and Vivienne stopped.

"Caden?" She whispered.

"I'm right here."

Vivienne's posture relaxed and she continued forward. Making her way around the last row of trees, she finally saw me. The light from her lantern dimmed as I took in a deep breath. A small wisp of flame spun through the air to my hand where I fed it using the dead leaves that littered the ground. As the leaves turned to ash, the fire became a large apple sized ball which hovered above my hand.

Without hesitation, she leapt towards me and we embraced. Planting her chin on my chest, she looked up into my eyes. Her smile faded somewhat as she examined my face.

"What?"

"You don't look healthy."

"I feel fine Viv."

"Are you eating?"

"Well enough. But I didn't come here to talk to you about my eating habits."

"I know that. But I'm still concerned for your wellbeing."

"Sorry," I said with a shrug. "I've been eating plenty."

"Good. So, what are you doing here?"

"Since we are going to let the sorcerors capture me tomorrow night, this was the last opportunity I had to make sure there is a contingency in place."

"Caden, you worry too much. Trust me, everything has been in place for days. Nila is already out with the soldiers. The ambush will be ready. We even smuggled out your sword and armor. Everything has been done as you requested. And we got quite a bit more help than we were expecting."

"Help?"

"There are a lot of people, some of the great houses included, that are not at all happy to have the Malkethian's here. It is starting to feel like they are in charge. Pricilla is not winning people over to her side by allowing them free reign to *investigate* as they please."

"Is Malin still staying at the palace?"

"Yes, but she still hasn't returned from the banquet at the Castle. Seraphina and Tristin went with her. You picked a good night to come by."

"Do you think Malin suspects anything?"

"I don't know. It doesn't seem so. She was more than happy when the Queen told Seraphina she would be using the palace guards as reinforcements to help search for you. The Malkethians have been spending a lot of time at the palace which has made our jobs a little easier."

"I am sure that was a complete coincidence," I said with a laugh. "And I am certain Seraphina made it seem like it was the Queen's idea in the first place."

Vivienne shook her head. "Now that is something that we've truly missed."

"What? My cynicism."

"No one can quite pull it off like you do. Our meetings of late have lacked a certain *charm* because of your absence."

"Well, I am glad to know I contributed something in the past."

"I really want this to be over with," Vivienne said. We were still holding on to one another and her arms tightened around me. "I want these swiving sorcerors gone."

"You and me both."

"Caden, I wanted to ask you something else, if you don't mind?"

"Of course Viv. Anything."

"Was that the only reason you came here tonight?"

I frowned and let go of Vivienne. The fire still floated to the right of my shoulder and the forest floor where we had been standing had now turned completely to ash. I reduced the fire to the size of a thimble, and connected it to the single remaining piece of coal in my pouch. Looking absentmindedly at the trees which surrounded us, I thought about what I should share. Even with a few days of mulling things over in my mind, I had not been able to determine if what I had seen was real or if it was all in my head.

"I came to warn you, and to prepare you for what is coming."

"What do you mean?"

"I, I've been seeing things. Ghosts of old friends, old enemies. I am afraid that the evil I thought we had destroyed has been safely nesting right below our noses."

"Caden, don't mince words. What exactly have you seen?"

"I saw him, the monster behind the voice. The entity Hevron was communicating with. He calls himself Nirlos, though I do not believe that to be true. If so, then the Valon of death is entombed below the city and he's trying to get free."

Vivienne was silent, her eyes growing distant as she processed what I had said. When she looked at me, she didn't have fear in her eyes like I had suspected. Instead, there was a calm determination in them. "I see. Then it looks like it is up to us to stop him. We were trying to rid the city of evil. It looks like we've finally found the true source."

"That's not what I expected you would say."

"And what did you expect?"

"For you to think I am as crazy as I feel."

"Oh, I still think that," Vivienne smiled, "but that is not new."

"Of course. I am beginning to wonder if it would be better for me to be crazy."

"Well, tell me everything that's been going on with these visions."

It took me the better part of an hour to explain what I had experienced when I spoke to Merek at the Sunken Foundry, then again when I ran into him and Kori at the plateau. I relayed to her with as much detail everything I saw when the entity revealed itself to me in the vision of the burned world. Finally, I told her of the dead men and the map of the underground which I had seen in the Wendigo caves.

Vivienne looked down at her hands, flexing her fingers back and forth. "What if it is Nirlos? Do you think we have a chance at stopping him?"

"Stopping him? No. Preventing him from escaping, hopefully. One thing I keep coming back to is why he needs someone to help free him. He tried using Hevron and was unsuccessful. I don't know if he tried to use Kori, but he for sure is trying to use me. Part of me doesn't believe that the ruler of death needs help. And if he does, then that means he can be stopped."

"How?"

"I don't know. I can't figure it out. Not on my own. Not while Isar and his lackeys keep hunting me. I have to stop them first."

Vivienne shook her head and bit her lower lip. "Do you think they would help?"

Scoffing, I let out a snort.

"Come now, I know that Isar is not a kind man, but he doesn't seem unreasonable."

"He won't believe me and I have no means of proving it to him. Isar has always been single minded and will do everything in his power to do what he came here for. I need to put him in the ground."

"Why does he hate you so much?"

"The Malkethians teach their soldiers to use hatred of their enemies as power. He probably hates me because he thinks I betrayed Malketh. Though it is possible he thinks he is getting retribution for Graham's death."

"I have to be honest, I think there is more to it than that. I haven't seen the type of hatred Isar has for you in very many people."

"Well, I can't claim to know exactly what drives him. We were never close, but he's a jealous man. Maybe he's seen the life I have built for myself and envies me. It's a life he could never have. That could explain why he is so damned determined to destroy every piece of it before bringing me in. A task he has done a wonderful job at completing."

"He hasn't done that good of a job," Vivienne said. "Once this is all over, you'll still have a place with us. Seraphina would never cast you out."

"Viv, we need to be pragmatic. When this is over, when I am certain this dark entity is no longer a threat, I will leave. The damage has been done. Isar saw to it that the Queen will not allow a sorcerer like me to live here peacefully ever again."

"But Pricilla can rescind the decree. Make it as if this never happened."

"And then what? She has made me her enemy. I cannot trust her and so long as I remain, Seraphina will not be able to prosper."

"Caden, we can't do this without you."

"You can and you will. Just as you did before I came along."

Vivienne turned away, her head falling. She crossed her arms and as I watched her, I saw her shoulders tremble.

"I would ask you to come with me. That is if you want to."

She looked at me and her frown deepened. "Do you even want that?"

"Of course I do. I just wasn't sure if you did."

Vivienne shook her head and snorted.

"But," I started, pausing for a breath, "I wouldn't blame you if you wanted to stay."

"Caden, my heart is yours and where you go, I will follow. But, would you do the same?"

"Without question."

We looked each other in the eyes for a moment and I saw relief in Vivienne's dark eyes. "Promise me something. That you won't leave before we have at least tried to find a way to stay."

It was a fair compromise, one that I didn't have a difficult time accepting. Though I was certain of the outcome, Vivienne deserved to feel the same. "I agree. If we can find a way that makes it possible for us to stay, I will. So long as we are together, that is the only thing I care about."

"Well, if we do manage to kill three sorcerers and this dark entity, we may find convincing the Queen to let you stay is an easy task."

Do I want to stay?

I smiled, but refrained from sharing my thoughts. It was possible the last month had clouded my judgment. But Vivienne was right. It was a little early to be thinking of leaving when there was still too much to do. So much could still happen. I paused, swiping the floating fire from the air. Holding it in the palm of my hand, I formed a flower from the flames and let it spiral around in a slow circle. Allowing the fire to take a more regular shape, I let it hover between us again.

"Viv, is Sheyor still staying with Acacia at the Crooked Inn?"

"Yes. Why?"

"I was curious, I've learned a lot about the tunnels, but the map I saw was so extensive. There are layers to the underground city, layers which will be difficult to navigate alone. I thought perhaps if we talked to her, we could create a map of our own."

Reaching back into my pack, I pulled out a small plank of wood. Burned into the surface was a facsimile of the map I had seen in the Wendigo cave. I had added a few markings of notable landmarks, but it was far from creating a detailed map.

"I'll talk to Sheyor. Have her take a look at the map and see what she can tell us." Vivienne took the map, biting her lip. "Where did you get this?"

"It's the map. I don't want to go in blind."

"Did you find this in the cave?"

"No, I copied it from the wall. Hevron had scrawled it using symbols. I didn't see them before."

"There weren't symbols before," Vivienne said, her eyes narrowing. "How did you see them now?"

"I have reason to believe that I have started to use necromancy. I am not sure why or how, but if the power could be passed from Hevron to Kori, then it's possible it has been passed to me. I held onto the talismans instead of burying them. They help connect me to the power. I think that is why I have been seeing these phantoms."

Vivienne went silent, her face growing pale. She took in a deep breath and shuddered. "Are you sure?"

"It's the only explanation that makes sense."

"I don't think it is wise for you to use Hevron's power. It did such terrible things...I don't want that to happen to you."

"No, I don't want that either. But I don't think I have a choice. Whether I use it or not, if I have the power within me, there isn't going back." I reached into my pack and removed the wooden box which contained the two talismans. "Will you take these? I need you to find a safe place for them until this is all over with. I can't let them fall into the wrong hands. No matter what."

Vivienne took them, holding the box gingerly.

"Promise me Caden, don't do anything too stupid."

"Not too stupid," I laughed. "Not this time."

"Remember, the same way you feel about us, we feel about you."

"That's all I can ask for." *And all I ever wanted.*

The gates to the Gresh Estate were chained closed. The stone wall which wrapped itself around the property was as pristine as ever though the stone gargoyles atop their pillars on either side of the gate had been broken. The head from one of the gargoyles was laying at the base of the pillar with one of the fangs chipped. No one was on the street and the loud sound of chirping crickets filled the air. It was getting close to dawn, at the moment before even the earliest of risers would be about their day's work. The stillness that prevailed over the street was soothing. It made me feel like I had found a moment secluded from time, a brief reprieve from what I was about to do.

Walking up to the gate, I pulled off my pack and threw it over. It landed softly on the other side, but the gravel still crunched slightly beneath its weight. The cast iron gate was connected to the stone wall in three places, each long spike the perfect foothold. Climbing up the side of the gate, I slipped over the wall and leapt down to the ground on the other side. Landing in a crouch, I took a moment to scan the overgrown trees which lined the path leading up to the lone Manor. Nothing which might have been hiding beneath the canopy of leaves moved. Standing, I walked back over to the drive and retrieved my pack. Slinging it over my shoulder, I walked alongside the path, not wanting the sound of my boots on the gravel to attract any attention.

When I reached the end of the drive, I found a broken down wagon beside ruined bits of furniture. I remembered the wagon full of furniture and the bodies of the looters I had killed. Whatever fate had befallen the bodies and the loot did not interest me, though I was curious why they hadn't bothered to take the cart. Walking up to it, I kicked one of the wooden wheels. The spoke splintered and the cart groaned and the axle snapped. As the cart collapsed to the ground, I leapt back to avoid the splintering wood. The sound of the collapsing cart was loud and I felt myself cringe.

"Dammit. There goes my stealth," I whispered. "Not like it matters."

Walking away from the ruined cart, I made my way up to the front of the ruined Manor, pausing at the open doorway. The splintered remains of the door were as I had left them. Peeking inside, I saw that the bodies which had littered the inside of the Gresh Manor had also been cleared away. Entering, I took a moment to look around. What little furniture had remained was gone and everything was bare. Scrapes on the walls and blood stains on the floor still showed where each body had lain.

Just beyond the front entrance was the staircase which led to the second floor. Almost without thinking, I started up it, each stair creaking under my weight. The wooden banister felt cool against my skin, and I paused to feel the sword marks which had cut large gouges into the otherwise smooth polished wood. Moving past the damaged section, I hurried up the remaining stairs and turned right when I reached the first landing. Absent-mindedly, I walked down the hallways until I reached the door of my old room. The door was ajar and badly damaged. The markings of fire had ruined the paint and a section towards the bottom hinge was charred.

When I pushed open the door, it stopped after a few inches. The ground was littered with bits of stone and the night sky was visible through the holes in the roof. Ramming the door with my shoulder, I managed to push enough of the debris away that I could enter. Standing among the ruined room, I looked out through the broken wall and ceiling. I was able to see the mountains off in the distance, their dark outlines just visible to my enhanced eyes. I looked out for a few minutes before turning my attention back to the rest of the room

My old bed was still there, though it was covered in rock dust and smelled of mildew. Pulling off the blanket, I shook it free before placing it back over the mattress. Taking a seat on the edge of the bed, I looked out through the broken wall and watched the mountains. Darkness slowly began to fade as the dawn approached. The black faded to deep blue, then to brilliant pink just before the sun rose. There were clouds in the sky which seemed to catch fire as dawn broke. I took in a deep breath as I began to prepare myself. The day had finally arrived and I was ready.

CHAPTER EIGHTEEN

THE HAMMER FALLS

T he city was on fire, the burning mountainside illuminating the night. Running along the edge of the Raha, I waved my hands, pulling the flames inside of me. The trees which had been set ablaze were burning wild and the fire had spread to the surrounding buildings. Dark smoke rose into the night air, creating a haze that obscured my vision. There were other fires burning all across the city, all of which had sprung up simultaneously an hour ago. Whatever was happening was not going according to plan. The sorcerers were supposed to come and ambush me where I would be isolated, where no one could get hurt. Though I knew this was a trap, I refused to stand idly by and watch the city burn.

Malkethian bastards!

People were running through the streets screaming. Mothers clutched infants to their chests as they hurried into the throng. Some men and boys were rushing about with buckets of water, desperately trying to douse the flames. A vain effort, but one that was commendable.

Screaming came from within a nearby building and shadows darkened the windows of the second story. Rushing up to the burning home, I leapt through the front door and took in a deep breath. The flames were quenched in an instant, leaving the room dark and smoky. Apart from the smoldering remains of a kitchen table and chairs, there were no bodies. Screaming once again sounded from above. Rushing to the stairs, I leapt up them two at a time. Upon reaching the second landing, I was greeted by more fire. Drawing the fire into my body, I felt both invigorated and overwhelmed by the energy. Gritting my teeth, I cursed under my breath.

Four people were huddled in the corner, small burns on their hands and faces. Their clothing, though partially burned, was no longer on fire. Each was looking at me like rabbits caught in a snare. There was so much desperation in their eyes that they looked on the verge of popping out of their skulls.

"Come with me! You need to get out of here."

The woman, who was holding a toddler in her half burned arms, backed into the corner.

"Now!" I shouted.

The family jumped at my voice and they seemed to comprehend that they were free. Together, they rushed past me and down the stairs. As they fled their half burned home, fire leapt from the nearby buildings again, reigniting the roof. Walking over to the wall, I placed my hand upon the wooden support beams. I could feel the fire as it ate away at the surrounding buildings. These homes, made from an amalgamation of poor quality materials burned quickly. Drawing the fire into me, I began to growl from the strain.

Walking to the window, I leapt from it, not bothering to walk down the stairs. Landing in a crouch on the ground, I looked at several bystanders who were still holding buckets of water. I had pulled the fire which had been consuming the buildings into myself, though they continued to smolder. Each of the men blow were looking around in confusion, seeming at a loss for what to do. Each looked similar to the family I had just saved. Not everyone managed themselves well in high stress situations.

"Go!" I shouted to them. "Save whoever you can!"

The men dropped their buckets and ran. As the people fled, I watched and waited as fire came back down from the mountain, reigniting the homes on the street. The sudden return of the fire caused those fleeing to scream louder, adding to the chaos of the night. Leaving the building, I entered the street and threw up my hands. The fire flowed like water from off the homes, drawn into my hands and arms. The flames licked at my clothes, singeing my sleeves which turned to ash and crumbled down around me. As I drew the fire into my body, I began to feel as though I would burst from the pressure. The more I drew in, the harder it became to keep moving. The fire had to go somewhere and I had no talisman to channel the energy into. Reaching up with both hands, I blasted a column of fire into the sky. The fire burned white hot as it blasted through the smoke to the clouds. In an instant, all of the power was released from my body and the strain of holding so much energy vanished.

Shit, I thought. *There's no way they didn't see that.*

A building to my right collapsed, sending ash and crimson embers into the air. Reaching out my hands, I waved, pulling the fire into me. The fire which consumed the five closest buildings, all swelled, soaring towards me like ribbons caught in a windstorm. The fire was drawn into my hands and I took in as much as I could before I felt like I would burst. Then I released another column of white fire into the sky. It was like lightning had struck, quick and gone in an instant. The sound of roaring flame faded, the air around me turning hot and dry.

Looking up at the forest mountainside which led up the mountain, I watched with dismay as the fire continued to travel upward and away from the city. As the wildfire illuminated the entire mountain, I worried how far the fire would spread. Gritting my teeth, I forced myself to leave the fire to travel up the mountain, so I could focus on keeping the city from burning. Saving the city was my first priority, though I couldn't help but worry for the trees and the Dryad.

Directing my attention back to the burning buildings of the Raha, I sprinted through the streets, drawing in fire as I went. I didn't stop to think about where I was going, but I ran towards where the fire burned brightest. With every passing moment, I knew that they would come for me. Whichever of the three sorcerers had set this fire would not be far off. As I cast another column of white flame into the air, I couldn't help but realize how it was like a beacon, drawing attention to myself. But it didn't matter. They had made a gamble by setting these fires and had won. It was as simple as that.

I doused burning buildings as I ran past, pulling in as much fire as I could hold. When I reached the end of a large cluster of buildings, I raised my hands and prepared to cast another pillar of fire into the sky. Just as I was about to produce a column of fire, I stumbled, lost my footing, and tumbled forward. Landing on my hands and knees, I looked at my fingers as they struck the stones. Small flickering white flames danced between each of my fingers and caused the stones beneath my hands to grow warm.

Something large and heavy struck me in the back which caused me to roll forward. My body turned over once before something stopped me. I let out a grunt and fire erupted from my lips. Pain continued to shoot down my spine and across my belly. Looking down, I saw the point of a javelin sticking out from my shirt. Blood trickled down the weapon and drizzled to the ground. Rolling onto my side, I craned my neck to look at who had attacked me. On a nearby rooftop stood a short blond woman. Her cloak billowed in the wind and she raised another javelin, pulling back to throw.

Reaching out my hand, I let out a deep breath and released all of the energy I had been holding within. The ball of fire which erupted from my hand was larger than a cart. It soared towards the rooftop, its massive size growing as it soared through the air towards Malin. The ball of flame struck the roof, blasting apart the top floor. Roofing titles exploded, their shards spraying into the air.

As the fire vanished, a plume of smoke followed. Something tore through the smoke, moving with such speed that I perceived only a blur. I moved as quickly as I could to my right and the javelin grazed my shoulder, cutting a wide gash. My shoulder jerked back in response to the pain which caused me to ram the butt of the javelin which had speared me into the stones, driving it further through my body. The pain intensified and I let out a scream.

Getting onto my knees, I reached around back and tried desperately to pull the javelin from my back. Managing only to pull it out a few inches, I lost my grip as blood from my wounds squirted out and slicked the wood of the javelin. With one final groan, I placed my hands back upon the javelin and drawing upon the fire still within my body, I ignited the wooden shaft. Willing the fire to burn the wood, I caused the fire to consume it in an instant. The flare of fire burned a large hole in the front of my clothes and I watched as the steel javelin tip fell to the ground.

Touching the burned wound, I was satisfied that it was no longer bleeding. Struggling to my feet, I drew my sword and turned back to the building I had blasted with fire. The roof was smoldering, the broken tiles and bricks littering the street. Malin was standing upon the ground, her third and final javelin in her hand. She was looking at me with cold eyes. Raising my sword, I prepared to defend against her next attack.

Malin took a step back just as the ground around my feet began to rumble. Leaping into the air, I watched as the cobblestones I had been standing upon erupted, breaking into small shards. The rocks pelted my legs, striking with such force that they tore through my trousers and dug into my skin. When I landed on the ground, the dirt shifted and I fell forward.

Landing hard on my left arm, I was just able to retain my grip on the longsword. The ground below me shifted again and I rolled onto my back. Looking up, I saw Isar looming above me. He heaved his large war hammer up and then swung it down towards my face. Lifting my sword, I swatted away the hammer as I rolled to the side. The massive weapon struck the ground beside my head, the reverberation from the impact making the ground vibrate. On my back, I was not positioned to strike and my feeble attempt to hit Isar did little but make the man laugh.

"Pathetic," he said, grunting as he lifted his hammer again.

Closing my eyes, I drew out the remaining fire and conjured a bubble of fire. The flames erupted in all directions and Isar got caught in them. He leapt back, patting his clothes to douse the flames. Springing to my feet, I felt the wound in my side tear, hot blood once again flowing down to my belt. Raising my sword, I slashed at Isar. As my blade was about to strike his chest, a violent gust of wind knocked me aside, sending me sliding a dozen feet to the left. My blade swiped nothing but air and I flailed my free arm to balance myself.

Glancing at Malin, I watched her throw her final javelin at me. It soared through the air faster than I thought possible, a gust of wind in its wake. Dropping to the ground, I avoided the strike and the javelin soared over my head. The gust of wind which Malin had cast to propel the weapon forced me back. The wind caused me to slide across the cobblestones until my back slammed into the brick walls of a half burned building.

The force of the impact expelled all of the air from my lungs. Gasping for breath, I choked, blood dribbling from my lips. My eyes swam and my vision blurred. Blinking away the tears, I watched as Isar approached, hammer in hand.

"When did you start to care about random people?" Isar mocked. "I remember a man who would burn down a city without a second thought. You've grown soft, just like your friends."

Sucking in a breath, I coughed and blinked to clear my eyes. Looking up at Isar, I forced a smile to my lips. "Well, we can't all be bastards."

Isar laughed, ignoring my insult. "This was remarkably easy. We should have done this a month ago."

"You truly are as evil as I remember. I should have known better than to think you would not murder innocents to draw me out."

"We didn't murder them. We did what was necessary to draw out a dangerous criminal. Their blood is on your hands."

"Spoken like a true coward. I should have expected as much."

Isar growled and lifted his hammer, swung it down towards my head. The hammer head struck the wall beside my face, sending small chips of brick in all directions. Fragments struck my face, cutting the skin of my cheek and neck. I didn't flinch, instead glaring up at the geomancer. This made his frown deepen.

"I thought this would give me more pleasure. You put up a poor fight."

"You want a true challenge?" I said, between breaths. "Catch."

Isar's eyes opened wide, then I reached up and thrust my hands forward. A column of white fire blasted him in the chest, sending him sprawling across the street. His body tumbled, arms and legs flailing, until he struck the building on the far side. Malin reacted quickly, leaping high into the air. Once the aeromancer was at the peak of her jump and began her descent, I reached out and cast a beam of fire at her.

Malin was struck by the fire and fell quickly towards the ground. She wrestled with her cloak as she fell and cast it off, letting it plummet to the ground. Malin recovered, flipping over so her feet were once more pointed to the ground. She glided down, drifting like a feather until her feet settled softly down upon the cobblestones.

Climbing to my feet, I raised my longsword and prepared myself for retaliation. Malin made no move to attack, instead standing in the middle of the street, her arms folded. I looked her up and down. Without her cloak to hide it, I saw that she was wearing light leather armor which was covered in so many daggers, it almost looked like it was made from steel feathers. Each dagger was designed for throwing and I knew how deadly she could be.

Why is she just standing there?

From the corner of my eye, I saw Isar struggle to his feet. He used his war hammer for support and his armor was scorched along the front breastplate. When I looked at him, I saw that the ends of his beard had been singed from the fire. There was nothing but hatred in his eyes as Isar bared his teeth at me. My eyes flicked between the two sorcerers as I began to analyze my options. My mind quickly ran through the different ways I could attack. Backed into a corner like this, there were few places I could go. No matter what, I needed to avoid the river.

As we stood across from each other, I felt a stirring in the back of my mind. The darkness around was calling out to me, whispering a warning. My senses intensified, first my vision, then my hearing, and finally my sense of smell. Hundreds of new sensations struck me at once. I could see the sweat on Isar's brow, hear the thudding of his heart, and smell the stench of fire on his clothes. My attention was drawn to the street, where the scents of woodsmoke mingled with burned flesh and oil. Cries from the wounded were sharp and desperate.

Then I heard footsteps. Hundreds of sabatons and thick leather boots stomping on the ground. They came from both directions and turning my head, I looked to my right. My vision cut through the darkness, piercing its veil like a knife. At the far end of the street were soldiers and mercenaries painted with the black eagles of Malketh on their breastplates.

When I looked back to Isar and Malin, I found they were both smiling. They had set their trap well, and I was out of options. Taking a moment to look at my longsword, I beheld the Chezek blade. It was sharp, the cool steel smeared slightly with ash. The weapon was not truly mine, though it had served me for a time. I longed for my true sword, for Burnfinger, who would have delivered me from my foes with ease. Still, the weapon had served me well.

Casting the sword onto the ground, I watched it slide across the cobblestones towards my foes. Malin stopped the blade with her foot, her smile fading. Tilting her head to one side, she took a moment to examine me, then stooped down to pick up my weapon.

"Do you recognize the blade?" I asked. "You can trust that your friend did his best to kill me."

"We should have prepared better that night." Isar said. "You can rest assured that all has been accounted for."

"I am wise enough to know when I am defeated." I held up my hands and let out a sigh. Though things had not gone according to plan, my intent was for them to capture me and at least that part had been accomplished. As I looked upon the ruined street, I felt my heart sink and hoped that most had escaped the fires.

"We should put out the rest of the fires," Malin said. "Do you want me to send the signal?"

Isar frowned, looking towards the burning hillside. The trees created a wall of flame that was now a quarter of the way up the mountain. Isar looked back at me and then turned to Malin. "Do it."

Malin reached into a pouch and drew forth what looked to be a candle wrapped in red parchment. The wax-like substance sticking out from the top of the paper was chalky and a deep green speckled with black. The long wick which curled out of the end was black and three times as thick as what should be in a candle. It took me a moment before I realized what it was. It had been a long time since I had seen a battle flair. Almost without thought, I reached out my hand and produced a small fire. The flame flickered above my right index finger.

Isar reflexively lifted his hammer, then lowered it again. "Light it."

The flame flickered from my finger to the wick. As it began to burn, the wick began to throw off sparks. Malin threw the flare into the sky and pushed upwards with her hand. The flare shot through the air, soaring high above us when it exploded like a firework. A large cloud of green smoke filled the sky above just as the crackle from the explosion reached us.

Seconds after the flare had gone off, lightning streaked across the sky. Then came the rain. I watched in silence as the thick rain-drops doused the fire which burned on the hillside. Within moments, I was soaked, water streaming off my hair and down my face. The soldiers continued to close in around us, almost an entire company on either side. Isar moved over to me and pulled small obsidian shackles from his belt.

Holding out my arms, I winced as he put them around my wrists. The sharp glass like stones were chipped to make them jagged on the inside. Isar smirked at me and I clenched my fists. The shackles dug into my wrist and I had to force myself to relax. It wouldn't take long for them to shred my skin raw. It had been a long time since I had been in a pair of these, but the memory came back as if it had just happened. Closing my eyes, I imagined standing in the commander's tent beside Lyla who was pleading for my life. A shudder ran down my spine and I cast the memories from my mind.

It sank in how prepared they had been for this attack.

Suddenly I felt overwhelmed and took a deep breath to calm my emotions. As the rain continued to stream down my face, another burst of lightning fractured the sky. The crackling thunder followed and the rain grew in intensity. The glow from the burning forest and buildings had begun to lessen as it was quenched by the rain.

"Surround him," Isar said, motioning to a group of Chezek warriors.

Ten soldiers formed a circle around me and Isar began to lead us down the street. Without protest, I walked, careful to hold my hands aloft before me so the shackles would not jostle or rub against my skin. Malin took her place behind us, just beyond the ring of guards. When I looked over my shoulder at her she glared at me.

Returning my attention to the front, I focused on my steps and prepared for a long night. As we marched I found myself thinking of the evil which rested in the deep caverns below the city. Whatever evil rested here must be stopped. A pit began to form in my stomach as uncertainty about how to best defeat my captors filled the forefront of my mind.

Nothing has changed, I told myself. Not in the grand scheme.

I trusted that Seraphina and the syndicate would have everything prepared regardless. As soon as I was out of the city on the northern road, the true trap would be sprung. These thoughts did little to sooth my worry. Instead, I found myself contemplating my fate should I fail. It was in these thoughts that I stumbled upon a realization. I would rather die than allow myself to go back. What was more terrifying was that I was prepared to see myself to that end sooner than I'd expected.

We marched through the Raha and when we crossed the bridge which spanned the River Earn, I found a prison wagon waiting for me. Nels stood beside the wagon, completely dry despite the rain. He gave Isar a firm nod as he opened the back door of the wagon. The soldiers who had been my escort parted to allow me through.

"Get in," Isar said.

As I climbed into the tumbleweed wagon I took a seat upon the ground. The floor was wet from the rain. Resting my shackled hands on my legs I gently twisted them. The sharp obsidian scratched my skin and an intense pain traveled up my arms. Looking up, I glared through the still open door at my captors. The three sorcerers were standing side by side as they looked at me. Isar looked pleased, while Malin and Nels looked pensive. The door slammed shut and one of the soldiers locked it. As the wagon pulled forward, I closed my eyes and a small voice in the back of my mind laughed.

CHAPTER NINETEEN
OUBLIETTE

Hunger came first, then an overwhelming thirst. Since being pushed into the pit, I had received no visitors, no food, no water. I had lost track of time. The small oubliette was just large enough for me to lay down, with little space between me and the walls. Up above was the hole, the criss crossing metal bars barely visible in the darkness. The obsidian shackles enveloped my wrists and they had cut them deep when I had fallen. Now, the blood had dried and they remained firmly in place. Not that I moved more than the occasional twitch.

I had long since grown bored of wondering why they had chosen this method to punish me. Perhaps it was the only way they felt they could safely contain me. They were right. But as the hours stretched on, I began to grow curious about what they were waiting for. Certainly they were eager to get me out of the city. If that was not the case, I could hardly fathom the reason why.

As time stretched on, it was starting to become hard to keep my mind focused. Reflexively, my throat tried to swallow and my tongue slid across the dry roof of my mouth. Taking in shallow breaths, I found myself daydreaming of water. This continued for hours until I began to forget what it was like to have a drink. Just as the thirst became almost too unbearable, it subsided, leaving me feeling dry and withered.

An insurmountable itch began to cover my feet, then crawl up my legs, until it covered my entire body. It felt like my entire skin was trying to separate from my body. Remaining still, I tried to focus my mind on anything else. My mind settled on the darkness. As the agony of the present continued to grow, I began to turn my mind to the void. Letting out a deep breath, I separated my mind from my physical body and reached for the Empyrean. As I reached for the power just beyond the veil of the natural world, my mind slammed against a wall. It was an unnatural repulsion that I had never before experienced. Pushing up against the barrier, I opened my eyes and growled. A deep and passionate rage filled me and my heart began to beat faster in my chest. Yelling, I held out my hand and continued to push. The barrier gave way, shattering like glass, and on the other side was a strange sickly warmth. My stomach constricted further, not from hunger, but with the urge to vomit. The wave of nausea which overcame me made me break out in a sweat. My breathing started to become harder and through short labored breaths, I was able to stave off the urge to vomit. Not that there was anything in my stomach to expel.

The small lights of the Empyrean began to appear, but they were much smaller and far and few between. It was like looking at small motes of dust falling through a beam of light. Small black specks in a world of white. Again, the Empyrean was the complete opposite of what I had ever before experienced. The longer I looked, the more difficult it became to keep myself focused. My head started spinning. Relaxing, I released the power and let my mind return to my body where I was greeted with an overwhelming itch.

Groaning, I rolled over onto my side and opened my eyes. Looking at the wall, I found I was able to see every detail despite the darkness. I began to count the stones, starting in the bottom corner and working my way across. I counted all of the stones in the oubliette and then began again. Sometime during the third counting, I drifted into a calm sleep where there were no dreams, only darkness.

~

I awoke to the sound of metal hinges squealing and a heavy wooden door scraping across stone. Heavy footsteps echoed in the stone room above and was followed by the grunting of two men. Opening my eyes, I saw the glow of torchlight reflect on the ceiling above the grate which covered the hole to the oubliette.

"Get the rope," the voice cut through the silence of the dungeon, reverberating down into the hole.

Watching and waiting, I remained absolutely still as the grate above me was removed and a long rope was extended downward. The bottom of the rope was tied in a loop and landed on my stomach. I looked at the coarse rope but did nothing. It was not that I was too weak to move, I just could not will myself to do so.

"Oi. Swine! Get your swiving carcass moving. We don't have all day."

I do, I thought, a small defiant smile creeping across my lips.

I didn't move, instead fixating my eyes upon the hole. One of the guards poked his face over the edge, tilting his head to the side.

"Is he alive?" the out of sight guard asked. I heard him step up beside his companion before seeing his face appear over the hole. He held the torch of the hole and the first guard slapped it away.

"Careful. We can't let him get too close to the fire. Don't you know who that is?"

I found myself chuckling, the raw dry sound slightly grating to my ears. The guards above jumped back, cursing.

"Water," I croaked. "Before I do anything, I want a drink of water."

"You're in no place to make demands of us, you piece of shit." The first guard poked his head over the hole again. Unlike the first time, when I looked upon him I took in the details of his face. He had pockmarked cheeks, long greasy hair, and a mole on the side of his nose. He was not a palace guard I recognized, which made me wonder how many new guards Pricilla had hired. I doubted anyone friendly to me remained.

Not like they would be able to help, I thought. *Nor would I want them to.*

"Now hurry up and wrap the rope around your waist."

"No." Though my voice was a whisper, it carried up the oubliette.

There was an edge to the sound of my voice which made the silence that followed all the more harsh. The silence lasted a moment longer than I expected and when the guard did respond, it was little more than a sputter. As the two guards stepped away from the hole above me, I saw the torchlight dim, casting two long silhouettes onto the ceiling.

"Just get him the water."

"No! We were not instructed to give him anything."

"Well, are you going to go down and get him?" The second guard let out a wry laugh. "I'm not. Her majesty can send me out on my ass for all I care."

"More like to the gallows." The pockmarked guard stepped back over and looked down at me. After a moment, he wrinkled his nose, then shook his head. "Get the bucket. He can drink the cleaning water."

The guard pulled up the rope and disappeared for a few moments. I listened while they rummaged around, but they did not leave the dungeon. When the guards returned, they held a bucket over the hole and began to lower it down with the rope.

For the first time since I had been placed in the pit, I sat up and moved so my back was against the wall of the hole. The bucket landed on the ground and I reached out and took it.

The water was dirty, but I didn't care. Gulping it down, I swallowed almost as much air as water. Burping, I wiped my mouth and ignored the taste. Setting down the bucket, I looked up at the guards and glared at them. The two palace guards glared down at me in disgust. I might as well have been a rat that scampered before them at the dinner table.

"Now, place the rope around your waist so we can haul you up. They're ready for your sentencing."

Getting to my feet was a greater challenge than I had expected. My legs were numb and I felt all of the pain in my back and shoulders from laying upon the rough stone floor. Moving my arms to work out a few of the knots in my muscles, I stepped through the loop in the rope and situated myself so I could be hoisted up.

"Ready?" The second guard called down.

"Yes," I grumbled.

They hoisted me up, which proved to be more difficult than either had imagined. When I got to the top, I had to reach up and guide myself up. Shackled, I found it difficult to provide any true assistance. As soon as I was able, I forced my arms out and placed my elbows upon the edge of the hole. The guards reached down, each taking hold of one shoulder, and lifted me out of the oubliette.

Without hesitation, they half carried, half marched me through the dungeon. My eyes looked around and I saw the large gash in the stone from where I had fought the Shantenbose. My eyes flickered to the corner where the remains of a bloody cot still remained. A shiver ran down my spine and I did my best to walk despite my weakness. My legs felt rubbery and each step took a concerted effort. When we reached the stairs, I found myself utterly helpless to climb them.

"Come on, we ain't going to carry you the entire way," the pockmarked guard grumbled.

"He's been down there for three days. I doubt he can walk."

"Fine. Let's just drag him."

I looked up at the second guard and saw consternation on his face. He had short hair, a sharp nose, and a scar on his cheek. The man completely avoided eye contact with me and seemed as though the act of touching me was more than he could manage.

"Set him down, Tobias," the second guard said.

"Don't say my name!" Tobias shouted.

"Like it matters."

The guards dropped me and I landed hard on the ground before the stairs which led out of the dungeon. Tobias and his companion took a few steps away and began to exchange heated whispers that I couldn't understand. They bickered for a few minutes and with a groan Tobias smacked his hand against the wall.

"Enough. Let's get moving. We're already late."

"Give me a few moments gentleman," I croaked. "As soon as I am able, I will get to my feet and walk myself out of here."

"We didn't give you permission to speak, disgusting rat."

Sighing, I closed my eyes and tried to gather my strength. The fire from the torchlight flickered and I was unable to draw it in. Looking down at the shackles, I let out a groan. The two guards leaned down and pulled me to my feet.

Raising my arms before me, I held them steady so the obsidian shackles wouldn't cut through the scabs on my wrists. Looking down at my hands, I saw deep black lines running up my wrists from the cuts on my wrists. The infection was turning my veins black and blotches of my skin were beginning to turn a deep shade of blue.

The self pity I had been feeling faded. I had to move forward, and taking the first step, I looked at the two guards who had rushed to my side. They reached out to take hold of my shoulders, but I shook my head.

"I'm not going anywhere."

Nodding, I was allowed to walk up the stairs unaided. When we reached the top, I found a squad of Malkethian soldiers standing at the top. Each had their armor painted with the black eagle and these had maroon capes.

An execution squad, I thought as I looked at their helmets. *This complicates things.*

Each of the execution squad members' helmets completely covered their faces, but left a rectangular gap where their eyes were perfectly visible. Each looked at me with the cool calculating gaze of men who were trained to kill.

The guards who had fetched me from the dungeon remained at the door while the execution squad formed a circle around me. Without a word, they began to march forward and I followed, keeping pace. As we made our way through the castle, I saw a pair of guards posted at every hallway intersection. They all saluted the squad as we passed, then returned to their stations, standing at attention. It made me feel like I was once again in a Malkethian palace. Pricilla had unwittingly let in a lion to catch a mouse. Slowly, she would lose control and would find that this city had fallen to the Malketh Empire without them so much as lifting a finger. Part of me almost wanted to let it happen.

In my mind, I pictured all of the spires of the castle flying the black eagle flags of Malketh. Kings Keep had become my home and just picturing such a thing filled me with indignation. I was not going to allow them to take this city. They would all have to die. Then I could turn my attention to saving the city from the true threat burrowed deep below the city.

One problem at a time.

Remaining as upright as possible, I cleared my mind and put on a blank expression. When we reached the main atrium which had the brass bowl in the center, I found that no fire burned. Each of the statues of the previous rulers of Kings Keep had been shifted and a new statue had been erected. Queen Aveza's likeness had been captured almost perfectly. The face was stern and lacked all kindness which, in my opinion, was the only flaw. The marble crown of the dragon horns was as intricate as the crown had been in life. Now immortalized in stone, here she would stand with those who came before. It was a strange feeling to look at it, one I didn't quite understand how to put into words.

As I looked upon the statue, I hesitated and the Malkethian soldier who had been walking behind me shoved me forward.

"Keep it moving," he grunted.

Nodding, I was careful to keep pace as we marched from the main atrium, down the hall, and into the throne room. The large doors were open, and a long purple carpet led down the center of the room towards the throne. Guards lined either side of the carpet, their helmets covering their faces, long purple capes hanging off their right shoulders. Each guard held a pike, had a short sword strapped to their waist, and a bowed rectangular shield. These men were fit for the battlefield and stood at attention like they were hardened soldiers.

The throne was the same as it had been before, perfectly aligned at the center of the dais before the large windows. The woman who sat upon it was hardly recognizable. Dressed in a black gown that was accented with deep green, Queen Pricilla lounged rather than sat. Her auburn hair was pulled up and woven into a new golden crown that was a mirrored set of four descending spikes. Each spike had a large emerald embedded in the base which caught the light as it streamed in through the windows. The sky outside was dark with clouds and the haze of rain could be seen over the mountains. All of the trees in the gardens were blowing in a fierce wind and I could hear the howls through the windows. It was the only sound which permeated the room.

Turning my attention back to the Queen, I saw the three sorcerers standing to her right. Isar, Malin, and Nels stood shoulder to shoulder, their hands folded before them. They dressed in matching deep green robes. Isar smiled, his beard freshly trimmed, the burned sections cut away. A small red blotch of skin on his neck ran down into the robe, a mark showing I had burned him more than I thought. Malin's blond hair was pulled back into a braid and she scowled at me. Nels looked indifferent, his square jawline tense, the muscles on the sides bulging. I met his cool gray eyes and they seemed to stare through me and into my soul. Uncomfortable, I looked away.

On the left side of the Queen stood three people I hadn't expected to see. Seraphina, blond hair hanging loosely about her shoulders, stood with her arms crossed. Next to her stood Tristin. Both women wore matching green dresses. Madam Acacia was the final woman who stood an awkward distance from her sister. Each woman masked any emotion with dignified expressions, but as I looked at Seraphina, I found that she was unwilling to meet my gaze.

A pinprick in my chest made me clear my throat and turn my attention to Tristin who likewise avoided looking at me. When I looked at Acacia, she stared at me and I saw deep sorrow within them. It was all the warning I needed. Something had gone terribly wrong. I silently hoped that whatever it was, the blame could be laid entirely at my feet. If the Queen had learned of my friend's involvement and of our plot against the Malkethian visitors, she would retaliate with the full power her throne granted her.

There were more than a hundred people gathered on either side of the large dais which held the throne. It seemed every noble family and their attendants were here to witness the affair. Though there were fewer people here than there had been a few months prior when I had fought the duel to defend Aveza's throne, I found myself recognizing many familiar faces.

How long have you planned this? I wondered, glancing back to Isar. The man's smile widened.

We arrived before the throne and the guards who had been my escorts stepped away, joining the line of soldiers where they drew their swords and stood at the ready. Glancing down at myself, I shifted my feet and twisted my arms. The sharp inner edges of the obsidian shackles tore through the scabs and I felt warm blood slowly ooze out and ran down my wrists. Looking at my hands, I saw the dark veins of infection had spread across my palms and down several fingers. As I noted the lines of infection, I watched as blood trickled down to my left index finger and began to drip to the ground.

Forcing a smile to my face, I lifted my head high and looked at Queen Pricilla. Her eyes narrowed and she raised her hand and pointed at the line of guards. I kept my eyes fixated on the Queen as one of the guards stepped out of line and moved into position behind me. I braced myself for what he would do and when he kicked me in the back of the knee I was prepared. Dropping to the ground, I landed on my knees, the carpet doing little to cushion the fall. Pain shot up my legs to my hips but I retained my smile and kept myself from making a sound. Now kneeling before the Queen I kept my head held high.

"My Queen, the traitor and vagabond, is brought to you for judgment. May we proceed?" Isar said, his voice loud and confident.

"Silence. I have suffered you and yours, but I will not suffer further disrespect of my authority." Queen Pricilla's voice was harsh but unsteady.

Isar nodded. His smug expression did not fade. He looked at me and then stepped back, clasping his hands before him.

"Caden, you have been brought before this court to be judged for your crimes against Kings Keep, this throne, and my people." Pricialla's voice was softer and more regal as she spoke to me. "You will be presented with an opportunity to speak in defense of yourself before you are sentenced. Should you refuse to present a defense, sentencing will proceed. Do you understand that this is only a formality to demonstrate our obedience to the laws of the land, and for this reason alone you have not already been placed into the custody of your countrymen?"

"I understand," I said, my voice sounding more confident than I felt. Clearing my throat, I added, "my Queen."

"In this case, we will proceed." Pricilla leaned forward and waved her hand to her master servant Ervin, who had been waiting in the periphery. Evand's green robes matched the Queen's dress and they swayed as he rushed forward, a rolled parchment in his hands. "Evand, will you read the charges against this man?"

"Yes, my Queen." Evand cleared his throat and unrolled the parchment in his hands. He took a moment to look over the writing, glancing up at me several times before starting. "The pyromancer Caden stands accused of the following crimes: public endangerment, fleeing from and resisting arrest, damage to public and private property, murder, arson, and for the unauthorized use of magic within the lands of her majesty. Does the accused wish to refute any of these crimes?"

Ervin raised his eyebrow when he looked at me. I had committed each of those crimes, though I was certain they were being rather unfair by charging me with murder. Though I had killed enough mercenaries and Malketh soldiers that it wouldn't be difficult to see why that charge had been added. No matter what I said, this was not a true trial, it was a formality. My fate had been decided more than a month ago. I just needed to go through the motions.

"No," I said with a gentle shake of my head.

Evand looked back to his parchment and began to read once more.

"Since the accused does not refute any of the charges, does he wish to plead guilty to the crimes in which he stands accused?"

"Yes."

"Then, as decreed by law, the crimes in which you have plead guilty carry a sentence of death, the manner of which our valiant Queen shall declare. Your majesty," Evand turned and bowed to the Queen. "That is all."

"Thank you. Please, rejoin the others." Pricilla's voice was cold, and her eyes did not glance away from me. "Do you have anything you wish to say?"

"No."

"Then you are hereby banished from Kings Keep. Though you would otherwise be sentenced to death, your fate will be left in the hands of Isar who assured me that you will face punishment back in your homeland."

Isar's smug grin widened.

"So be it," I growled.

"Then may the Valon have mercy upon your soul."

CHAPTER TWENTY

HEAR

T he hot sun bore down upon the metal prison wagon as I sat waiting to be carted through the streets and out the northern gate. Resting my head against the back of the wagon, I felt the heat of the metal seep through my hair and into my scalp. The sensation was soothing and were it not for the noise of the Malkethian soldiers all around, I might have drifted off to sleep.

"Keep alert!"

The voice was followed by the clanging of the metal bars. Opening a single eye, I looked at the wagon driver who was clutching his baton like it was a club. He slammed the wooden baton against the bars again, causing them to ring at an unpleasant pitch. I scowled at him, then closed my eyes. The driver slammed the baton against the bars one final time before huffing and turning away. I listened to his footsteps as he walked away, his boots clopping against the cobblestone drive before the castle.

I impatiently waited through the morning until mid day when the doors to the castle opened and the rest of my captors emerged. Sitting up, I turned my head and watched as Queen Pricilla, Isar, Nels, and Malin emerged down the steps. Behind them, two squads of Malkethian Deathguards followed, their black armor looking like glistening tar in the sunlight. After a few moments they all looked at me. While the sorcerers all had expressions of satisfaction, I was surprised to find Pricilla's brow furrowed. Her lips were pressed tight, the corners turned down in a frown. Her eyes only met mine for a moment before she looked away.

"Please, take your time. I want him paraded through the city so all can see him." Pricilla's voice was cool and she looked back at me, this time keeping her eyes fixed on my face. When she smiled at me, the expression never touched her eyes. "Alas, I bid you all farewell and safe travels back to your homeland."

"It has been an honor. We all wish to thank you for your hospitality, the Queenly accommodations, and for the cooperation in apprehending this criminal." Isar bowed with the formal Malkethian flair of his hand. "Malin, would you please retrieve our parting gift for the Queen?"

Malin didn't hesitate, striding gracefully to the foremost of the row of wagons ahead of mine where she removed a small wooden box. Keeping her back straight as an arrow, Malin walked forward, arms extended. When she reached the Queen, she knelt on the ground and opened the box. Isar reached down and placed his head into the box. Slowly, he lifted out the contents. His back was turned to me and I was unable to get a good look at what he held in his hand.

Isar presented the gift to the Queen who lifted her chin. Isar stepped forward and brought his hands around the back of her neck. After a few moments he stepped back and to the side which allowed me to see the gift. The necklace was bright silver, the pendant an eagle in mid-flight, with one wing arching upward and the other angling down. My eyes widened and I couldn't help but grimace. Even after all this time, the symbol enacted a fear in me that I had almost forgotten about.

"You and your Kingdom are recognized as friends to the Malketh. We wish to bestow upon you this highest of honors and recognize you as we would any ruler under our empire." Isar bowed again, this time in the formal and less ostentatious manner that was common in Kings Keep. Malin and Nels bowed as well, keeping their backs stiff and frozen for the span of ten seconds before the three sorcerers straightened in unison.

"My many thanks," Queen Pricilla said. "May the Valon bless your journey and see to it that your task is finished."

There were no more words exchanged as the Queen returned to the castle, the large doors closing behind her and her guards. Alone with the Malkethian soldiers and sorcerers, I began to feel like a large stone was hovering above my head and at any moment it would fall and kill me. Isar looked at me, his smile turning to a scowl. He said nothing, marching to the front of the line of wagons with Malin. A few members of the black armored death squad followed them.

Nels approached my prison wagon and placed his hands on the bars. His fingers glistened and I saw that a thin layer of water covered his hand like a glove. He examined me for a moment before calling for the attention of the baton wielding wagon driver.

"Let him out, but leave the shackles on." Nels looked at me through the bars, watching me closely as the wagon driver unfastened a ring of keys from his belt and waddled around back to obey his command. "Don't try to do anything foolish or mark my words, you will remain in that wagon the entire duration of our trip."

I nodded to him as the door to the prison wagon opened.

There was a single step down to the bottom which creaked as I put my weight on it. When my bare feet touched the cobblestones I found them to be much cooler than the metal floor of the wagon had been.

"Bring me the chain."

An armor clad man strode up to us, a long chain with a collar in his hands. Without words he stepped up to me, placed the metal collar around my neck, and locked it. Then he placed the chain through a metal ring in the back of the wagon and locked the chain together.

Do they intend to make me walk as they parade me through the streets?

Growling, I pulled back my shoulders and looked towards the sky. There were no clouds in sight and the bright sun sat near its zenith. Within ten minutes everyone was ready and the first wagon, where Isar and Malin sat, pulled forward. I watched and waited as the line began to move. As soon as the prison wagon before me pulled forward I began to walk. Slowly, we made our way down the drive from the castle to the gates.

Soldiers lined the path as we went, and once we reached the gates, I looked up and saw dozens of guards on either side. Tilting my head I looked past the procession of carts and wagons before me and caught a glance of what stood on the other side. Hundreds of people had gathered before the castle gate, crowding the sides of the street. Some had even climbed to the rooftops of nearby buildings to get a better view. The citizens of Kings Keep had come to watch my humiliation.

When my wagon finally reached the gate, I glanced over at the Queen's Soldiers and saw the hatred in their eyes. None made any aggressive movements towards me, but a few did spit on me as I passed. The captain did not mutter a word at them for doing so. Instead, he took a step forward just as I was about to step through the gate and slammed his gauntleted fist against the side of my face.

Staggering to the side I almost stumbled, but the chain connected to the metal collar around my neck kept me upright. Regaining my footing, I jumped forward as the wagon pulled on me. No matter what, I had to remain on my feet. As I walked, I kept my back straight and chin high. When we reached the crowd, the murmuring changed to screaming. The clothing these people wore was exceptionally meager and many had burn marks. Those who had survived the fire in the Raha were the first to come and see me. Stones were hurled from dozens of hands, but only a fraction of them hit me. Still, after having traveled a single block, I had been struck by over a hundred stones. My head throbbed from the pain and the cuts on my face and scalp were bleeding.

The crowd continued to shout at me, their curses and threats muffled together. I did not pay close enough attention to discern any insult, instead keeping my eyes trained on the back of the wagon. As every new stone struck my body, I forced myself not to react, not to show pain, not to grow angry. In a way, I almost admired the work that Isar and his subordinates had done. To turn people I had never met against me, to get them to violently hate me, all while I had been hiding was impressive. I couldn't help but wonder how they had managed it and I finally understood what Isar had meant when he had threatened me. They had succeeded in turning Kings Keep into a place I could never come back to. A place I would never again call home.

Sorry Viv, I thought.

We proceeded slowly through the streets, but the further we got from the Castle, the less hostile the crowd had become. Stones were no longer thrown at me, replaced with bits of rotten food or rubbish. The clothing was a little finer and the people looked cleaner than those from the Raha who had been the most vitriolic.

I presumed that those who had recently lost their homes and possibly their loved ones would have greater grievances than those from other, more prosperous parts of the city.

Reaching the main road that ran along the River Earn from the northern to the southern gates, I found a group of people waiting I had not expected. Accompanied by several guards, each of the leaders from the nine great houses stood to watch. Seraphina was with Tristin and five of the palace guards. She stood at the end and next to her stood Arvid and Akai who were accompanied by two guards of their own. Their dark faces did not attempt to hide their sorrow. Arvid muttered something and made a sign with his hand that I did not understand.

My eyes darted back to Seraphina who looked at me with a blank expression. I made no effort to communicate with her, to signal anything. Instead, I tried to look as defeated as possible, and for the first time since leaving the palace I began to slouch. Keeping my head down as we passed the rest of the nobles, I focused on just placing one foot in front of the other. Walking barefoot was beginning to hurt and the rough stone street had cut the soles of my feet.

When we reached the northern gates there was no crowd, no gathering of soldiers. The way had been cleared and prepared for our departure. Passing through the open gates, I took a moment to look at the countryside. It had been more than eight years since I had set foot north of the wall. The cool breeze which came down off the mountain slopes tore at my clothes and brought with it the scent of pine. At that moment, I felt more trapped than ever. Looking up at the sun I saw that we were now past mid-afternoon. We wouldn't reach the ambush point for two more days if we continued at this pace. That was good. I needed to rest.

We continued for only a mile past the gate before Isar called for everyone to stop. As the prison wagon before me slowed I felt immense relief. The wagon driver got down and made his way around to the back. He unlocked the chain which tied me to the back and let it fall to the ground. Nels did not move a muscle. When I looked at him, it seemed as though he challenged me to try and run. I didn't.

The back of the metal wagon opened and the driver stepped aside.

"Get into the wagon," Nels commanded.

I obeyed, and stepping onto the first step, my foot felt hot on the metal. Almost falling forward onto my face, I took hold of the bars to steady myself. With a deep breath I climbed into the wagon and took a seat in the middle of the floor as the door was locked behind me. The chain that hung around my neck rattled on the metal floor of the wagon as we pulled forward. After a few minutes, the sound began to annoy me, so I picked up the chain and coiled it in my lap. Remaining as still as possible, I closed my eyes and gave my mind over to the exhaustion. Though I did not sleep, my mind was still for the space of a time and remained so until the wagon jostled me violently to the side.

My arms jerked apart as I tried to catch myself and the skin in my wrists tore as the obsidian shackles prevented it. Landing on my side I smacked my head against the side bars. Grumbling, I remained on my side as the cart pulled off the road into a clearing beside the river. The wagon driver unhitched the team of horses that had been pulling the prison wagon. Nels remained in place, though his back was turned. I watched and waited as the others began to set camp. My eyes wandered first to the trees and then to the sky where I watched the setting sun drop below the western mountain peaks. The sky remained a bright orange, broken only by the silhouettes of black birds.

"Let's get you cleaned up." Nels said. "You stink."

Nels climbed down from the wagon and ran his hand along the bars as he made his way around back. His hands were still covered in the water gloves. Taking the brass key from his belt, he unlocked the door and pulled it open.

"Again, let me remind you not to do anything stupid."

I didn't have the strength to speak. Nodding, I crawled across the wagon floor and swung my legs over the edge. The wagon was tall, but sitting on the end, my legs were long enough that my feet touched the ground. The touch of the grass below my bare bloody feet felt nice. I followed Nels forward towards the River Earn where he pointed for me to sit beside a tree. Obeying, I took a seat and rested my hands on my knees. The blood which had dripped down my wrists onto my hands had dried, staining them red and hiding the black veins which traveled through my fingers. Shifting my hands, fresh cuts opened old wounds. As the fresh blood flowed over the old, what little of my hands were clean were covered. Groaning, I held my arms close as I stood up.

"Come with me." Nels motioned for me to step up beside him. Together we walked towards the river. When we reached the banks, Nels placed his hand on my shoulder and pushed me to my knees. The water from his hands flowed down my shoulder, washing away a small part of the grime and dirt. "Remain still."

Nels raised his hands and water flowed from the banks like a serpent. Flowing through the air, the water collected above my head and began to fall around me like rain. The water was cool as it rushed down my face. Blood, dirt, and grime dripped to the ground and soon I was clean. When the water stopped pouring down upon me, I took a moment to let the water drip away before getting to my feet.

"What are you doing?" Isar's voice demanded from over my shoulder.

Turning, I looked at him as he stalked towards me, his war hammer held aloft in both hands.

"I am just washing him off."

"Did I tell you to do that?" Isar demanded, his lips pulling back in a snarl. "This man shall remain in his filth until I say otherwise."

"My apologies." Nels bowed his head. "I didn't want his wounds to get infected. We have to keep him alive. I was just doing what I thought was best."

Isar growled but did not say anything more to Nels. He directed his anger at me and reaching out, placed his hand on the metal band which wrapped around my neck. Pulling down hard on the metal collar, Isar forced me down to the ground.

"You are a tremendous pain in the ass and by the time we make it back home, you are going to regret that you were ever born."

I laughed.

"You think this is funny?"

"Remember, you're a monster, just like me. Unwanted, unloved, and abandoned. The first thing our mothers did was regret we were ever born. There is nothing you can do to me that I haven't already endured."

Isar kicked me in the chest. Landing on a rock, my back spasmed and I yelped in pain. Rolling onto my side, I curled slightly, pulling my hands close to my chest. Glancing up at Isar, I watched him raise his war hammer high.

"Don't!" Nels' cry came too late.

The hammer fell and struck my leg. The sound of breaking bone preceded the pain. Gritting my teeth through the agony, I watched as Isar lifted his war hammer again. My eyes locked onto the square block of steel and waited for it to fall. It didn't. As I watched the weapon lower, I looked back to Isar and saw Nels standing behind him. His hand was wrapped around Isar's wrist, keeping him from striking.

"Enough. You've proved your point."

Nels looked down on me with pity, an expression that disgusted me. I did not want pity from the swiving bastard. My anger helped mute the pain in my leg until it was a distant ache.

"Fine, he will be your responsibility," Isar spat on the ground beside me before pulling his arm free of Nels grasp. Stalking away, Isar disappeared into the throng of tents, joining the soldiers who had set camp.

Alone beside the river, I watched Nels closely. The pity on his face remained and he gave me a sad smile. When he knelt down beside me, I reflexively pulled back. The man placed a firm hand on my knee and hot blinding pain shot down my leg. Groaning, I closed my eyes, every thought absorbed by agony.

"Brace yourself Caden. This is going to hurt."

Taking a deep breath, I watched as Nels twisted my leg to the side. The cracking of bone was once again loud in my ears. The pain which followed was more excruciating than ever and it was some time before I became coherent. Looking down at my leg, I saw that it was in place and wrapped with a splint and bandage. The top part of my foot was exposed and my toes were red and swollen. Nels was sitting a few feet away, next to the river. He was waving his hand through the air, twisting his fingers in an odd way. A small stream of water, like a ribbon caught in the wind, waved back and forth before him.

Shifting my weight, I scooted across the ground to the base of a tree where I leaned against it to rest. Placing my ear against the trunk I took a moment to listen. As expected, the tree said nothing.

I looked back at the camp and saw that all of the soldiers were sitting around campfires. The scents of stew drifted in the air and my stomach rumbled. I scanned the groups until I saw Isar. He was sitting on a log beside Malin, a mug in his hand. He laughed and drank, the other soldiers near them joining in the laughter. I could only stand to look at them for a few moments before I turned my attention back to the river.

"I used to hear stories about you," Nels said. "The way the others used to speak of you, I was amazed that someone like you could have ever existed. A demon of fire on the battlefield who killed all in his path. I remember wishing to have seen it."

I grunted, but said nothing.

"You're nothing like I expected."

I raised my eyebrow. "No? So what did you expect?"

"I expected to find the greatest warrior Malketh has ever produced. Instead we found a cowardly, weak, and sentimental man who is unfit to clean a latrine, let alone fight alongside the Empire's great army."

"Sorry to disappoint."

"Do you know what bothers me more than that? I still think you are capable of the same ferocity that I heard about in the stories."

"What gives you that idea?"

Nels lowered his hands and the ribbon of water which had been flowing through the air splashed back down into the river. "We had a lot of time to learn about you during the last month. Isar thinks you are this pathetic coward of a man who deserted his post. He thinks you have grown weak since fleeing to Kings Keep. But from everything I heard, you have faced several incredible foes in the last year. I think you were holding back when you fought us the other night. But I don't understand why."

I laughed, a dry mirthless sound that was followed by silence. Nels looked from me to the nearby soldiers, then back. Everyone's attention was on me and I forced a smile to my lips. "I am not surprised that you do not understand. You, Isar, the whole swiving Malkethian army would never understand. Tell me, if I was holding back, what would you do about it that you haven't already done?"

Nels crossed his arms and remained silent.

"Exactly. I figured Isar broke my leg for a reason. I'm not

running anywhere on a broken leg. If I was holding back, I must have had a good reason. Perhaps I did surrender myself to you. But you might have been smarter than I and captured me fair and square. Does it matter?"

"Yes!" Nels growled.

"Why?"

"Because I need to know if retrieving you was worth what we sacrificed."

"It wasn't."

Nels shook his head and turned back to the river where he sat back down on the banks. We remained beside the river for another hour before Nels got back to his feet. He waved for me to follow and I found that it took considerable effort to get to my feet. My broken leg smarted and I was forced to put all of my weight on my good leg.

"Vince," Nels called, waving his hand to the wagon driver who was sitting beside the nearest campfire. "Will you get him back to the wagon?"

The wagon driver bumbled over and taking hold of the chain he pulled at it. Struggling to step forward, I balanced on one foot, keeping the other aloft. Vince's eyes widened and he looked with desperation to Nels. The sorcerer drew a dagger and walking up to me placed it against my ribs.

"Try anything and I will stab you," Vince said.

"Ya, I got the swiving message. You all don't have to keep repeating the same threat."

With Vince's help, I managed my way back to the wagon where I crawled in. When the door slammed shut I took a moment to look Vince in the eyes. He met them for only a moment before he glanced down at the ground. I watched as he locked the wagon and put the key into his pocket. Vince patted the baton which hung from his belt and then stalked away, joining the other soldiers at the campfire. The line of tents was well organized and they formed a circle with the other carts and wagons. Nels had found a seat at the edge of the camp, sitting so he could keep an eye on me while still enjoying the company of his friends.

Crawling to the edge of my cage, I watched the fire and was tempted to draw some of it in. I knew it would be impossible with the shackles on, so I forced myself to roll over and closed my eyes. Tuning out the sound of the chatting Malkethians, I focused on the burbling of the water and the rustling of the leaves. The wind was soft and carried with it the rich scents of a summer forest. The chirping and humming of insects accented the sound, creating a cacophony that was distraction enough.

The longer I listened, the more my aches and pains began to dull. For the span of an hour, I listened to the trees, trying to follow the Dryad's advice and see what they had to tell me. Again, I heard nothing. My mind began to work over the idea behind that advice and I had a realization. Taking in several dozen consecutive deep breaths, I began to feel a rich tingling in my fingers and toes. As I continued the deep breathing, my nose and face began to prickle, rich with renewed breath. Expelling all of the air from my lungs, I held my breath and waited for the sensation of prickling to intensify. The pain returned, but it was separate. It was as if everything I was feeling was on the other side of a window. Though I knew with perfect clarity what was on the other side, I was separated from it. As my lungs began to tighten and ache for breath, I felt my pulse quicken. Still, I continued to hold my breath until I felt the pressure build in my head. When I did take in a deep breath, the pressure dissipated all at once and the tingling stopped. My body relaxed further and a wave of calm rushed over me.

Opening my eyes, I looked out over the river and the tree lined banks on the other side. Small things stirred in the shadows beneath the trees. Listening to the darkness, I began to hear the whispers. The darkness spoke to me, not with words, but with feelings. The closer attention I paid, the more I learned. I was almost surprised at how many things crawled beneath the canopy of night, and they were hungry.

Smiling, I rolled onto my back and sighed. *Soon it will all be over.*

CHAPTER TWENTY-ONE
THE NORTHERN ROAD

W e were on the road before dawn making slow progress northward. Within the first hour, several carts and merchant caravans passed us heading south towards Kings Keep. The tension which filled the air as they passed was tangible. The Malkethian's remained calm, but I could see the way they grabbed their weapons that they would be ready to attack at a moment's notice. I couldn't help but wonder if they suspected an ambush. Left with nothing to do but wait, I found my patience wearing thin. I was in pain, tired, and hungry. I was beginning to worry I would not be strong enough to fight when the time came. I wasn't going to be able to walk.

My foul mood worsened as the day dragged on. When we finally pulled off to the side of the road, it was well past noon. The soldiers dismounted from their horses, wagons, or carts, and gathered near the front where rations were handed out. Vince leapt down from the prison cart, looked at me over his shoulder and shook his head, then joined the others to get his food.

The four guards who had been riding their horses behind my prison wagon dismounted, then impatiently paced back and forth. Looking at them I saw irritation in their eyes. Fortunately, it didn't take long before four new soldiers came and relieved them. Each was still munching on their lunch and they kept a casual eye on me. Most ate quickly and they spoke among themselves between mouthfuls. I didn't ask for food and none was offered. My stomach grumbled and I did my best to ignore everything and everyone.

This is going to be a long day, I thought as I began to tap my foot on the hot metal floor of my wagon. The chain rattled as the tapping continued.

"Quiet!" One of the soldiers yelled.

"Stupid son of a bitch." Another called out. This soldier had a hooked nose and black beady eyes which made him look like a hawk.

I stopped tapping my foot and instead lifted the chain up and dropped it onto the metal floor. The clanging of the chain on metal made the soldiers growl and I repeated the process. From the corner of my eye, I watched the nearest soldier, the one with the black eyes and the hooked nose, draw his sword. He slammed the pommel against the bars which rang out like a bell.

I looked at him, lifted the chain, and let it fall on the ground again.

"Stop antagonizing him," a soft feminine voice sounded from behind me.

Turning, I looked at Malin who was walking with a small loaf of bread and a wine skin.

"Apologies ma'am," the soldier said, bowing his head so far his chin was tucked to his chest. It made him look even more like a bird getting ready to roost. That made me smile.

"None needed," Malin said, with a gentle wave of her hand. "We are all just going to have to learn to ignore Caden and his antics. We must refrain from stooping to his level."

"Of course."

"You four can go join the others. I'll keep an eye on him until we leave."

The soldiers bowed, thanked Malin, then left, all too eager to join the group and get away from me. I didn't blame them and I made a note not to antagonize them again. When the time came to fight, they would be caught between me and my true enemy. They deserved mercy, at least as much as I could give them.

"Take this." Malin held the small loaf of bread up to the bars. "We aren't going to let you starve."

Tentatively, I reached through and took the bread. Carefully, I tore off a small piece and put it in my mouth. The bread was sweet, the hints of honey pleasant. Eating slowly, I savored every small bite until the loaf was gone. Though I was still hungry, I was grateful for the food and for the small relief it brought.

"Thanks," I muttered.

"Here, drink this."

Malin passed me a wineskin through the bars. Unstopping the top, I smelled the wine and though it was cut, it smelled fresh. Taking a sip, I found the watered down wine soothing on my parched tongue. Drinking as slowly as possible, I savored the experience. Once the skin was empty, I wiped my mouth and replaced the stopper. Scooting over to the bars, I took the skin and held it out beyond the bars for Malin to take.

The sorceress took the wine skin and finally reached into her pocket to retrieve something small and wrapped in a leaf. Unwrapping it, she produced a small white glob that was textured like sap and honey.

"This will help with the pain."

Holding out my hand, she placed the glob of white sap into my palm. Despite its appearance, the object wasn't sticky but was hard as a stone. Placing it into my mouth, I grimaced from the taste. It was strong and bitter, making my tongue go numb.

"Don't keep it in your mouth."

Swallowing, I took a deep breath and scraped my tongue on my front teeth, trying to mitigate the bitter taste. The effects of the drug were quick and for the first time in days the constant pain vanished.

"How long will it last?" I asked.

"It will take away the pain for a few hours, but by nightfall the effects will have worn off completely. Should make the ride a little easier to endure."

"I suppose another thank you is in order. Though I get the feeling you aren't doing this because you want to. Can't let the prize starve and die on the road."

"Self pity is unbecoming of a sorcerer."

"Are you saying I should be ashamed of who I have become? Or are you going to lecture me about unmet expectations? I think I got enough of that from your friend last night."

"Caden, you are as poor an actor as you are a liar. We both know that you are here because you want to be. Everyone knows this and because it serves Isar's purpose, we are all going along with it. But when you decide that you are tired of playing this game, I want you to know that we are prepared."

"If I did give up and surrender, why would I have waited so long? I failed, simple as that. I am honest enough to admit that."

Malin raised an eyebrow at me.

"What? Did you truly expect me to destroy everything to save my own life? If so, I am not sorry to disappoint you."

"Then you really do care about those people."

I found myself nodding in response. "Did you think I was a heartless monster?"

"Caden, do you not remember what you were?"

"Trust me, I have not forgotten."

"I refuse to believe you changed. I do remember you though it is clear you do not remember me. Unlike Nels, I've seen you in battle. When Isar said he had been tasked with bringing you home, I was the first to volunteer for the task."

"I didn't realize I was so hated."

"That's not what I meant."

"What then?"

"Why do you pretend to be different from who you are?"

I looked at the sorceress and her eyes looked earnest. Like she was trying to understand me. Pausing for a moment, I reached down and picked up the chain, running the links through my fingers. Malin remained silent and when I looked back at her, she had folded her arms.

"Do you really want to know?"

"Yes."

"Malin, you met my friends. You saw a glimpse into the life I had found for myself. When you have something like that, it changes you. I didn't set out to find friends, to make a home for myself. Despite my best efforts, I found both. I'm not pretending, Malin. I am not who I once was. I would not destroy my home, not even to save my own life."

"How? How is that possible?" Malin seemed genuinely frustrated. "They are weak and you were following their command. You could rule over them but have chosen not to. Subservience is not the Malkethian way."

"And I left Malketh behind. Do you not grow tired of the killing? You fight for people who don't give a damn if you live or die. I chose to fight for people who did care. It doesn't matter to me who is stronger or who has the largest army. There is more honor to fight and die for my friends than to fight and die for some wretched King who couldn't give a damn about me. I might always be someone else's pawn, but at least I got to choose a side. If you are so hell bent on castigating me for being weak, so be it. I don't care for your approval nor do I care if you don't understand my actions. But you are one of the Valon's fools if you believe I will ever fight beneath the Malkethian banner again."

"There's the fire I've been looking for." Malin smiled. "Lyla was right. You're still you, even after all this time."

The mention of my old friend's name filled me with more rage than it should have. I clenched my hands and my swollen wrists pressed against the sharp inside edge of my shackles. Even with the drug, I could feel the pressure my clenched fists caused. Forcing myself to relax, I looked down at my hands and watched as a trickle of blood ran down my wrist and into my palm. Allowing the blood to collect in my hand for a moment, I turned over my hand and let the blood drip onto the metal floor.

"She said you were loyal. It was your most admirable characteristic, but your biggest flaw. In the end, I suppose we should be grateful for that loyalty. It's what led you to us."

"Are you done?"

"Almost. I have just one final question for you. Was it worth it?"

"It was."

Malin nodded, then waved to my guards who had been lounging over at the next wagon. They marched over, standing at attention as they took their place. The sorceress took a moment to look at me. Her cold blue eyes for the first time seemed uncertain. She placed her hand against the bar and leaned forward and whispered. "Never let anyone know. They will hate you more for that than anything else."

Without another word she walked away. Sitting back, I placed my head on the bars and smiled.

As the sun set on the third day, I began to grow anxious. We were close to reaching the end of the canyon where the vast northern plains began. I forced myself to trust that the others had made the preparations and would follow through. I was confident they wouldn't let me down. Vivienne would not let me down.

Still, it was difficult to remain positive with the constant strain the pain and soreness of my body had been putting on my mind. It was getting difficult to ignore and the strange drug Malin had given on the first day had terrible side effects. The vomit and nausea it induced when the effects wore off was not worth the relief; so I had refused it when she'd offered it to me again this morning. Part of me was regretting that decision.

The wagon made the familiar jostle as we found a clearing large enough to pull off. The trees were thicker now than they had been and though I could hear the River Earn, it was still separated by a hundred feet of woods. Not having the river so close put me at ease. Though Nels hadn't attacked me, knowing that I was within arms reach of everything he needed to drown me was one more worry I didn't want to deal with.

My eyes glanced over at Nels and Vince who sat at the front of the wagon. The bars that separated us were narrow and with my hands shackled, I could not reach forward to touch them if I wanted to. The overwhelming urge to do just that almost over-took me. Growling with anger, hunger, and general frustration, I layed back down and did my best to get comfortable as the Malkethian's began to set camp.

"You've been rather quiet today," Nels said, as he stepped down from the wagon.

"Well, when I'm surrounded by such stunning conversation-alists, what am I to do but lay back and listen."

"Vince is quite the talker," Nels admitted, looking at the man who scoffed. "Hand me the keys, I need to check his wounds."

Vince handed Nels his ring of brass keys. The door unlocked with a loud click and squealed as it turned on rusting hinges. Nels beckoned for me to exit and I slowly scooted my way across the floor to the edge. Placing my feet on the ground, I took in a deep breath then stood. My broken leg smarted and I put most of my weight on my good leg. Despite the pain, standing felt good. Stretching my back, I pulled my shoulders back and leaned from side to side. Careful to keep my hands close together, I found it difficult to close my fingers into fists.

Looking down at my hands, I grimaced. My wrists were swollen and my hands were covered in dried blood and black infected veins. The necromantic infection was worsening and I was growing concerned at its rapid progression. What worried me more was that I didn't understand why it was happening to me in the first place. Unlike Kori, I hadn't been wounded by a beast. My thoughts turned to the Shantenbose and the shadow blade which had pierced my body. If that had been the cause, why had it taken so long for me to manifest symptoms? As I contemplated the answer, Nels began to mutter and curse under his breath.

"Dammit. I was afraid of this." Nels ran his hand along the dark black veins which ran up my arms from wrist to elbow. "I told Isar we shouldn't leave these on for so long."

"Then take them off."

"Not my decision. You're still too dangerous, even shackled."

"Regardless, my wrists are so swollen now that they aren't cutting new wounds. Not since yesterday."

"I will see if we can have them removed long enough for me to dress the wounds. I will not have you succumb to sepsis on our journey because of negligence. Besides, if you do anything foolish, I will personally break your other leg and both arms."

"Promise?" I asked with a smirk.

Nels grumbled and took hold of the chain which still hung from my neck; he then placed his arm around me and helped me walk. Keeping my broken leg off the ground took a lot of effort and the throbbing had started again. The tents were already up and several small fires had been lit and cooking pots were hung above them. As we reached the camp, several soldiers returned from the river with buckets of fresh water which they poured into the pots.

As we passed by one of the fires, I felt an overwhelming urge to breathe in the fire. I felt my muscles tighten as I resisted the feeling and my pulse quickened. Clicking my tongue on the roof of my mouth, I stepped away from the fire. Nels pulled slightly on the chain and led me away from the cook fires towards the front wagon where Isar and Malin were searching through the bundles and crates.

"Isar, I need you to remove the shackles."

Looking up from the wagon, Isar scowled when he saw me.

"Hell no. You know the rule. He's too dangerous otherwise."

"We need to clean the wound," Nels protested. "Stop being a bloody fool and look at his arms. He's infected."

"I said no, and that is final. I don't want him free for a moment."

Isar placed his hand on my wrist and squeezed. The scabs and dried blood which glued my wrist to the shackles broke and fresh blood began to pour down my hand. Gritting my teeth through the pain, I growled and looked Isar in his dark brown eyes.

"I wonder, who between us is the better fighter." I mused. "You or me?"

"Are you trying to goad me into a fight?"

"Not at all. I just wonder if you are more than your magic. From where I am standing, it doesn't look like it. All I see is a man who is nothing without his power. I'm curious, when you look into my eyes, do you see the same?"

Isar glared at me, his lips pulling back into a snarl. "I see a mad man who has lost both his sanity and pride."

"Isar," Nels said. "I just have to release one shackle at a time.

So long as he has one on, he won't have enough strength to use magic."

He removed a small black key from his pocket and held it up. "Fine, Nels. Take the key. Just don't take too long."

Nels took the key and Isar stalked off. Malin glanced back and forth between us and Isar, not seeming to know what to do.

"Why must you antagonize him?" Malin asked.

"I didn't." Nels growled

"I was talking to Caden."

I didn't answer.

"He's going to kill you before we ever make it back to Malketh." Malin sighed and the underbrush blasted to the side as if struck by a strong gale. She glared at me before stalking off to join Isar by the fire.

"Come with me. We'll clean and dress your wound by the river and then you will go back to your wagon."

Keeping a firm grasp on my shoulder, Nels helped me walk to the river where he forced me to kneel like I had the first night. He reached down and unlocked the left shackle. As the clasp was undone and pulled away, the scabs which had formed over my cut wrist were pulled off. Warm blood began to flow down my hand and for the first time I was truly able to see how swollen my wrists were. The skin had been cut in multiple places and what wasn't bleeding was rubbed raw.

Placing my left hand in the water, I let the cold flow of the river wash away the blood. After a few minutes my hand went numb and I was tempted to plunge my entire body into the water. With Nels standing over my shoulder, I thought better of it. He seemed to be the only person not hell bent on killing me, but even being this close to the water was taking a much bigger risk than I was normally willing to take.

Taking a moment to clean the shackle, I rubbed away the dried blood and skin before allowing Nels to place it back around my wrist. Then, he unshackled the right side and again the scabs were torn free. This time was much worse and I let out a grunt. I left my right hand in the water until it too was numb from the cold water. Pulling out my hand, I looked at my swollen wrist and the black veins.

"Let me see your hand."

I held it out, palm facing upward. Nels took hold of my hand and turned it over. The bleeding had stopped and though the swelling was reduced, I had limited flexibility. I watched his expression change from disgust to concern as he ran his fingers along the cuts.

"Strange. You have lines of infection running up your arms, but the skin around the wound is not black. I've never seen this before."

"Perhaps it's a side effect of the shackles preventing my magic. When was the last time you used them on a pyromancer?" I knew it was a lie, but I hoped he would consider it.

"I doubt that is the problem. But still, I have never seen this before." Nels let go of my hand and pointed to the water. "Finish washing that off."

Cleaning off the right shackle, I took longer than I needed to. I found the water soothing and did my best to prolong the process. Nels caught on to what I was doing, but seemed content enough to stand beside the river. I glanced over at him from time to time, examining the way he looked at the water. His lips moved as though he were whispering. I recognized the expression in his eyes. It was the same look I had whenever I found myself beside a fire. He was feeling the allure, drawn in by the flowing of the water. For a moment I wondered how it felt. Water and fire were so different, but there had to be similarities.

"You keep glancing at me. Why?"

Unsure how to respond, I removed my clean shackles from the water and shook them to dislodge the largest of the droplets which clung to them. It felt odd to have them clasped around a single wrist. The sensation made me feel slightly off balance. With as much care as I could, I placed the right shackle back around my wrist. Holding them out to Nels, I winced as he pressed down and locked them. Gritting my teeth through the pain, I took in a sharp breath and whistled. After a moment, the pain dissipated and I relaxed. Nels was looking back at the water, the same glazed expression in his eyes.

"Nels, can I ask you something?"

"I suppose."

"I just noticed that you look at water the same way I look at fire. It made me wonder, what does hydromancy feel like?"

"You've never asked anyone this question before?"

"I never really cared."

"To be fair, you are the first pyromancer to ever ask me about how hydromancy feels. I don't think I've ever explained that to anyone who wasn't a hydromancer. People only ever seem to be interested in what I can do."

"I know the feeling."

"Well, how about a trade? You tell me what it is like to use fire magic and I will tell you what it is like to use water."

"I've always found fire to be alluring, the warmth, the light, the colors all draw me in like an intoxicating vapor. As a pyromancer, I can draw the fire into my body, keep it just below the surface of my skin. It often feels like venom coursing through my blood." I continued describing my magic to him without holding anything back. I spoke of the rage the fire fueled and how strong emotions often intensified my power.

"That isn't quite what I expected." Nels paused, reaching out his hands and drawing a small bead of water from the stream. It floated in the air like an oversized raindrop, hovering before us. "Water is similar, but it's a flow, a natural movement that soothes rather than invigorates. Like the blood rushing through my body,

I can feel each drop of water, no matter how small. It surrounds us in the air, thrives in the plants, and moves within your body. But the more polluted the water, the more difficult it is to bend to my will. Much to the dismay of many hydromancers, we are often ill equipped to control the living. It seems Ahnir didn't want us playing with life."

"Do you believe in them?"

"The Valon? Of course. How can I not? We have tasted their power, and drank of it from the palms of their hands. Do you deny this?"

"I question it."

"What is there to question?" Nels asked, his voice sharp.

"The nature of what they are. How we, if we are but mortals, can share in that power. It makes me wonder if they need us as much as we need them. Or if we need each other at all"

"It seems years away have done more to you than we expected."

"Are you saying I speak blasphemy?"

"No. Our creed claims only that the Valon'kesure are the children of the Valon. It does not claim that they do or do not need us. While I do not subscribe to your belief that they need us, I cannot outright deny such a thing. However, if you are to suggest that the Valon are not what we claim them to be, than what are they?"

"I don't know."

"Caden, you don't strike me as the type who questions the nature of things without reason. What led you to this thought?"

I only looked at Nels and shrugged. There was no way I could tell him without exposing my plot to escape. He didn't need to know, but part of me wished I could ask him. It had been so long since I had gathered with other sorcerers. *If only they would help*.

"Is this because of the necromancer you killed last year?"

"It is." I lied.

"I see. While it was surprising for us to learn that such a being had existed, it is not all that surprising. You were not properly brought up in the order, so there is much you do not know about the history of this world. Talon'Var used to be ruled by such monsters. Death seems to choose its bearers differently than the other Valon. But much of that is destroyed, a distant memory. What was not destroyed was sealed away. Still, fragments emerge back into the world, but that is inevitable. Life and death compliment each other. Each Valon is part of a whole. You cannot hope to destroy one any more than you hope to destroy another."

"But what if they are not in balance? Who is to say that just because one power exists it must be in exact proportion to another. If death used to rule, then certainly we could claim life's power has taken death's place. Ahnir and Nirlos may complement each other, but that does not make them equals."

Nels nodded. "Ah, I see your point. But what cause do you have to suppose Nirlos or Ahnir are responsible? Could it not be that in ages past more sorcerers chose death over life. Chose to use their gifts for evil than for good?"

"Are we so different now? Do more sorcerers in the Order choose life over death?" I scoffed. "Please. Don't kid yourself."

"The Order does more to bring harmony to this world than any other nation, kingdom, or people who dwells on the land. Do not think to insinuate that we fight our wars for anything but the continued peace and prosperity of Talon'Var."

"The way I see it, you're all just a bunch of evil tyrants trying to bend the world to your will; no different than anyone else. Malketh feigns to be virtuous and its deeds are evil. One cannot be good and evil simultaneously."

"I should not be surprised that one such as yourself is so jaded and short sighted. You've only seen the war, never the peace."

"Oh, I've seen peace, but only where the foul touch of Malketh has not spread."

"I see that it is pointless arguing with you. I might as well try to pluck the moon from the sky then try to change your mind with words."

"In that, we are in agreement."

We did not speak as we walked back through the trees to the camp. We stayed away from the others, walking along the edge to the back where my wagon had been left. The prison on wheels was deliberately positioned apart from the others and the box of metal bars looked like a cage in the moonlight. Nels helped me walk up to the prison wagon, offering his assistance with tremendous patience. It was difficult to maneuver with my broken foot, but I was getting used to the hopping.

Nels helped me into the wagon, and sitting down, I rested my shackled hands in my lap. The door swung shut and I watched Nels lock the door. He left me without a word. Laying down upon the metal floor, I rested my head upon my arm and watched the woods. The shifting of the trees in the wind was soft and soothing. The cool blue moonlight bounced off the leaves, casting nighttime shadows. My body ached and soon I drifted off into the place between wakefulness and sleep. A place where my mind began to turn like the wheel of a windmill. The thoughts were far from pleasant and flashes of death filled my mind. Echoes and memories from battles long past filled my mind and the deeper I drifted into sleep, these thoughts began to turn into nightmares.

The roaring crackle of falling trees was as loud as thunder. The sound startling me awake, I sat up just as another tree fell. The two sounds had come from opposite directions, one from the road south, the other from the north. As the Malkethian soldiers roused from their tents and shouted their alarm, dozens of men rushed out of the woods, weapons held high. Then the forest erupted into flames.

CHAPTER TWENTY-TWO

CYCLONE OF FIRE

T he heat of the fire bathed my face and I breathed in deeply. I could feel the flames despite my inability to draw them in. My fists tightened, my swollen wrists pressing against the sharp edges of my shackles, and I desperately wished to be free of them. As my eyes continued to gaze upon the inferno, I forced away all emotion and remained completely still as chaos erupted in the camp.

Shouting came from the ovaline shape of the Malkethian camp. The sentries were calling for help as dozens of black clad warriors emerged from the northern woods. Armed with swords, lances, and bows, they rushed the camp and killed the sentries. A loud battle cry rang out in the night, chased by the clashing of steel. As the surprised Malkethian's fell to the black-clad warriors' swords, they cried out shrill screams of pain. The ambush had begun and trapped in my cage, there was nothing I could do but watch.

The northernmost tent burst apart, blasting small pieces of canvas in all directions. Isar and Nels emerged from the ruined tend and within a moment were fending off the attackers. The ground began to split apart, large spider web cracks reaching the charging warriors. Once the warriors stepped upon the cracked earth, the ground began to rend itself, twisting and shaking. I watched as boots sunk into the ground before it shifted violently to the side. Legs and ankles snapped with such force that shards of bone burst from their legs. Screaming filled the air and Isar roared with pleasure.

More warriors poured in from the north as another war cry sounded from the opposite side of the road. Flaming arrows took to the sky and began to fall down upon the carts and tents. The tents caught fire and the Malkethian's who were still within began to emerge. Each wore their full armor and brandished large swords and shields. A strong gale of wind followed and the remaining arrows were knocked from the sky, blown back towards the forest from where they had come. As they rained down upon the woods, additional trees began to catch fire, their branches igniting with wild flames. Each fire sprung to life quickly and the rich scents of woodsmoke and burning pine needles filled the air.

Crawling to the door of my cage, I pressed myself against the metal bars and watched as more soldiers emerged from the burning trees across the road. Dozens of soldiers, garbed in dark black and brown clothes, seemed to spawn from the darkness as they emerged into the light of the burning trees. They shouted cries of war as they charged to meet the Malkethian's head on. The warriors outnumbered the Malkethian's three to one, but they were cut down with alarming speed. Malin leapt onto the road and began to fight the forces, blasting them back into the trees. The only chance my rescuers had against them were their numbers. Numbers that wouldn't be enough.

With desperation, I slammed my shackles against the metal ground of my cage. Pain shot up my arms and my wrists began to bleed. However, the shackles didn't so much as crack from the force. Slamming them down again and again, I managed only to create new deep lacerations on my wrists. Blood began to pour from my wounds, dripping down onto the wagon floor. Growling with anger, I placed my face against the metal bars and watched the flames. All the power I needed to turn the tide of this fight was right in front of me but I couldn't so much as touch it.

Shrill beastial cries began to sound out in the night causing my blood to run chill. For a moment, my heart seemed to be lodged in my throat. I stilled my mind and took in a deep breath to help settle my nerves. Closing my eyes, I listened for a moment and the night almost seemed to speak to me. Flashes of trees into the moonlight filled my mind and a cool sweat broke out over my skin. Seeing through strange eyes, I saw a short three-eyed ape leap onto the branch before me. The Night Howler continued and I followed. Pulling myself out of the creature's mind, I shook my head and grunted. Opening my eyes, I turned my attention back to the battle. Soon, we would have company, a new dangerous enemy which could foil our plans in an instant. Growling with anger, I took a hold of the bars to the door of my cage and desperately tried to get free. Though I knew it was useless, I couldn't keep myself from trying. As I struggled I saw something else move towards me from the south.

Twenty warriors emerged from the southern woods, preceded by a familiar figure dressed in black assassin's garb. As I saw Vivienne, my dread diminished and I smiled. The group ran to my wagon and when Vivienne reached the door to my cage the others continued to run past. Glancing over my shoulder as they went, I saw that the Malkethian's were focused on the fight to the north and west. Not a single eye had concerned themselves with the south. I couldn't help but smile.

"Why aren't you doing anything?" Vivienne demanded as she thrust two metal picks into the lock of my cage.

"I can't," I replied, lifting my bloody hands. "Not until I can get these swiving shackles off."

Vivienne nodded, and continued to work her lock picks.

"Viv, we need to hurry."

"I know. We got this. Trust me."

Letting out a deep breath, I nodded.

Each moment was agonizing and my eyes darted back to the battle. The soldiers who had come from the south charged the fray and began to attack the Malkethian's. Shouts of anger and surprise sounded and I watched as Isar turned. His face, illuminated by the raging fire, filled with rage as he regarded the new soldiers who had joined the battle. He shouted something that was unintelligible from where I sat and Nels, who continued to fight beside him, only nodded. A large wave of water rushed from the river and slammed into a cluster of warriors. As they fell to the ground, they were dragged back towards the river. Their screams were muffled by water which forced its way into their mouths. By the time they hit the river they were not moving, drowned by the magic.

More black-garbed soldiers rushed down from the north, taking the place of their fallen comrades. They loosed arrows into the group of Malkethian's who had gathered in a circle. They fought without fear though they were struck down by Isar and Nels with ease.

A large chunk of the ground erupted, spraying a cluster of men who raised their shields in defense. Several were knocked to the ground, but each sprung up and continued fighting. Standing together, Isar and Nels fought like wild beasts, cutting down all who approached. Rocks were thrown into the air, waves of water erupting from the river and splashing down upon the road. The ground was beginning to turn to mud as small streams continued to run uphill from the river. To my horror, I watched as one of my rescuers stepped into the mud and was pulled down. He landed face first and within seconds his body was sucked into the ground. Flailing, the soldier struggled to get back up but soon was covered by the flowing mud. After a few seconds, the ground went still and there was almost no sign anything had happened at all.

Looking up, I saw Isar glare at me from across the battlefield. He pointed at me and shouted another inaudible command. He left the fight and began to stalk towards me. With his war hammer, he continued to strike dark-clad warriors as he walked. The hatred the geomancer had for me seemed to radiate through the air hotter than the raging forest fire. Turning my attention back to Vivienne, I watched as she continued to work the lock. She bit her lip as she focused and then finally twisted her picks to the side. The lock clicked and the door swung open.

Rolling out of the cage, I landed hard on my shoulder. Pain shot up my arms from my bleeding wrists and my leg began to ache. Crawling forward, I rolled onto my back and looked up at Vivienne.

"We need to get these off, quick," I said, holding my hands towards her.

As I spoke, a strong gale of wind blasted me from above, knocking Vivienne and I to the ground. The wind continued to bear down upon me, driving my body down into the dirt. The horses which had been hitched nearby continued to scream and several broke free from their reigns. As the horses fled towards the south, I watched as more soldiers began to rush towards us.

"Caden, watch out!" Vivienne shouted.

I looked up into the sky and saw a small figure soaring down at us from above.

"Shit!" I cursed.

Pulling Vivienne to the side, I managed to get out of the way of Malin's dagger, and watched as it drove into the ground. Malin landed a few moments later and Vivienne sprung to her feet and kicked Malin in the side. The aeromancer moved with the blow and used the momentum to perform a kick of her own. Vivienne ducked, avoiding the first kick, but Malin twisted and drove her knee into Vivienne's chest. As Vivienne stumbled back, Malin lifted her hands and a strong gust of wind knocked Vivienne onto her back. Taking advantage of the distraction the fight caused, I reached out and wrapped my hands around Malin's foot. She kicked my face and my nose popped. Hot blood began to pour out and I choked slightly.

The black-clad soldiers who had been rushing in from the south cried out and lowered lances as they charged the sorceress. Lifting her hands, she blasted them with air, sending the first four rolling back which caused them to knock down those who followed behind. Vivienne sprang up and with a dagger in hand, leapt towards Malin. The women grappled for a moment before Vivienne was able to wrestle Malin to the ground. They fought fiercely over the dagger, both women getting cut as it passed from hand to hand.

Leaping to my feet, I felt the ground beneath me begin to tremble. Glancing over my shoulder, I watched as Isar lifted his hammer high. My warriors rushed him and Isar smiled as he prepared his strike. Once the first of the three warriors was within reach, Isar drove his hammer into the ground causing it to violently shift to the side. The warrior slid to the side and his attack met nothing but air. Unable to recover, the man stumbled forward and Isar slammed his war hammer into the back of his skull. His head exploded, blood spraying high as shards of skull and brain matter rained down upon the ground. Falling on his face, what was left of his brain bounced out of the skull, squishing as it landed upon the ground.

The two warriors who followed cried out in anger at the loss of their companion. They lashed out with their swords and attacked Isar. I watched for only a moment before my attention was drawn away by Malin who was now holding a knife above Vivienne's throat. Without hesitation, I leapt forward and tackled the aeromancer to the ground, using my shackled hands to wrestle the knife from hers. Wind struck me from all directions and Malin drove her knee into my gut. Grunting, I looked Malin in the face and smiled. She glared at me and as she raised her hands to call down another gale of wind, I drove the dagger into her side. Malin gasped and doubled over, dropping to the ground. Pulling out the dagger, I watched as blood began to pour onto the ground. Vivienne stepped up beside us and I gave her the dagger.

"Watch her and make sure she doesn't bleed out. I need to keep at least one of these bastards alive."

Vivienne nodded and kneeling down beside Malin, pressed the dagger to her throat. Malin stopped moving, her hand pressed firmly to her side. Blood seeped through her fingers and her face was contorted in pain. Turning from her, my eyes found Isar who was standing above the corpses of a dozen men. More warriors were pouring in from the west and two new attackers approached him. These men seemed wary, their eyes first looking to the fallen bodies of their allies before they trained them on Isar. Swords and shields at the ready, they approached the geomancer.

The first man rushed forward, blocking Isar's hammer with his shield as he thrust his sword towards the geomancer's chest. Isar side stepped, then swung his hammer again. His large blunt weapon slammed into the man's sword hand, breaking his fingers with loud pops. The warrior screamed, his sword dropping to the ground. Isar attacked again, this time his hammer slammed into the warriors side. Ribs cracked and the screaming stopped. Dropping like a sack of flour, the man struck the ground and spasmed for a moment as he made choking noises. He went still, blood dripped down from his mouth and Isar crushed his head with another strike from his hammer.

"Swiving bastard!" the remaining warrior shouted, raising his sword.

"Get back!" I shouted, but my cry sounded on deaf ears.

He attacked Isar who only laughed as he dropped his hammer

to the ground. Dirt and stone were thrown into the air, creating a ten foot wall around the geomancer. The earth blocked the attack and the wall of dirt and stone broke his sword. As the earth fell back down to the ground, Isar leapt over and slammed his hammer down upon the warrior's shoulder. The bone broke with a loud crack causing his arm to hang loosely. Stunned from the pain, the man staggered back and Isar slammed his hammer into the warrior's chest. He fell back, and landed on the ground, dead upon impact.

Stepping over the dead, Isar looked at me and smiled. "You and your fighters are fools."

Isar slammed his hammer into the ground. The earth trembled and cracked, breaking apart from the point of the hammer's impact to where I stood. The shifting earth twisted my broken leg and I lost my balance. Falling to my knees, I clenched my fists in pain as my eyes welled with tears.

"Shit," I muttered, watching the geomancer slowly approach.

He raised his hammer high and another warrior sprinted forward from the fray. Isar smiled down at me before spinning around and slamming his hammer into the side of his attacker's head. Blood sprayed in a wide arch, raining down upon the broken soil as the body fell.

"Pathetic," Isar spat. Turning his attention back to me, he rested his hammer against his shoulder and shook his head. "If I didn't need you alive, I would crush your skull. Alas, so long as you are alive, the condition of your body matters little."

Isar heaved his hammer upward with all of his might. Holding still, I half closed my eyes and flinched. As the hammer fell, I shifted to the side at the last moment, twisting my arms forward. The hammer struck my shackles and the obsidian exploded. Shards flew in all directions, several pieces cutting into my wrists and lodging themselves in my chest. Isar stumbled back, shards sticking out of his trousers. As pain rushed up my arms, I rolled over and looked up at Isar. I reached out my hand and the fire which burned all around rushed towards me. The trees all around turned to charcoal, crumbling to ash as they fell to the ground, consumed by the fire.

The pain from my wounds subsided as the energy poured into every fiber of my being. Broken pieces of bone in my leg fuzed back together, giving me the strength to stand. The well of fire within me swelled past my capacity to maintain it. Fire erupted from my hands and I pointed both palms towards Isar. Releasing all of the energy at once, I shot a column of fire at the man. Dirt erupted between us, forming a wall which absorbed the brunt of my attack. Some of the fire blasted through and struck Isar in the shoulder. He grunted and flung his opposing arm forward. The wall of dirt flung towards me and I was knocked off the ground by a wagonload of dirt.

Half buried, I shook my head to clear away my disorientation. The lower half of my body was buried beneath the dirt and I dug myself out with my hands as shrill cries once again sounded from the night. The howlers were close, but there was something else moving towards us. My stomach turned into knots and a strange sensation rushed through my body. As I reached within me to draw upon the fire, there was a separate and distinct power there that had not been present before. Like a ball of rotten flesh, the energy was repulsive to me, but I couldn't avoid taking hold of it while still accessing the fire. My vision changed and I was no longer on the battlefield, but crawling through the woods. My new eyes penetrated the darkness, drawn to the fire down below. The hundreds of small legs attached to my worm-like body clicked in rapid succession as I rushed forward.

Pulling myself from the mind of the terrible creature, I shivered and my stomach contracted. Falling to my knees, I vomited onto the dirt. The bile spewed out in a forceful burst, spraying the broken ground. Taking in a few consecutive deep breaths, I climbed to my feet and looked over at Isar who was crawling away, his right arm tucked in closely to his side. The geomancer was grimacing in pain and his eyes were wide, reflecting the burning trees.

Screaming ensued from the camp to my right and I looked at the battle still taking place. Nels stood in the middle of a circle of twelve soldiers who were fighting for their lives. Almost a hundred of my dark-clad soldiers were in a desperate battle with the Malkethian's who were successfully holding back their advances. The dead littered the ground, their blood soaking the ruined earth. One of the Malkethian soldiers, who was laying upon the ground, leapt to his feet and sprinted to the road. He rushed northward where another familiar figure stood. Nila was holding Burnfinger aloft. She raced towards the fleeing soldier and struck him with my blade. She sliced through his shoulder and severed his arm. Blood spurted from the wound and his arm dropped down to the ground.

With another quick strike, Nila separated the man's head from his shoulders. She waited until his body hit the ground before stalking forward. I looked from her to Isar who was now back on his feet. He growled, and then began to retreat to his allies.

"Caden!" Nila shouted as she rushed to me. "Here."

She held out my sword and once we were a few feet away from each other, she tossed it into the air. Reaching up, I caught it as it came down, my knuckles knocking against the curved back of the crossguard. Drawing in a deep breath, I pulled fire from the burning trees and channeled it into the sword. Burnfinger's blade shifted from the cool gray steel to a burnt orange. Heat radiated from the blade, causing the air above to shimmer.

Well, now you get to see what I am still capable of.

Willing the fire which rose from the trees all around to burn the trunks faster, I caused them all to crumble to ash. Pulling the fire from the trees, I fed them into my blade. Flames twisted through the air like ribbons, collecting together as they entered into the red gemstone set into the crossguard of my blade. The steel shifted from orange to white in a matter of seconds. I looked up at Isar who had rejoined his surviving allies. The battle had stalled as my forces surrounded the remaining Malkethian's. Though we still outnumbered the remaining fourteen Malkethian's four to one, I knew that the only way to keep the rest of my warriors alive, I would have to take them on myself.

"Stand down!" My command was followed by a shrill howling out in the night.

The sound was close, less than two miles away. I had minutes to finish this before we would lose our advantage. This wasn't a fight we could handle on two fronts and still win. The silence which followed the shrill howls was palpable. As my warriors backed away, the Malkethian's all looked at me. I only had eyes for Isar and Nels who were standing side by side. Each was ready to fight, Isar with his hammer and Nels with two whips made from water.

Holding up my sword, I watched as the air shimmered above the white hot blade. "Do you recognize Burnfinger?"

Isar clenched his jaw but said nothing. Nels' eyes opened wide and he looked to the geomancer. After a few moments both sorcerers were looking at me with loathing.

"What?" I asked, raising Burnfinger high. "Now that you aren't in control, you have nothing left to say?"

"Malin, now!" Isar commanded.

As he spoke wind began to blow down from all directions. Looking over my shoulder, I saw a smile on Malin's face, despite her having a knife pressed to her throat. Vivienne looked up into the sky as the trees began to break from the force of the sudden wind. Slamming the hilt of the dagger against Malin's head, Vivienne knocked the sorceress out cold. The wind did not abate and the pressure of the air all around shifted whirling around me in a circle. Lifting my sword a fraction of an inch felt like fighting to lift a boulder. The wind continued to twist and whip around me, lifting dirt, stone, and bits of underbrush into the air. The cyclone formed with me in the center, the sound of the wind deafening.

Fools, I thought, drawing in a deep breath.

I let the tip of my blade fall and once the burning white steel struck the ground, the trampled underbrush caught fire. Flexing my fingers, I willed the fire to burn and spread. Carried by the wind, the fire leapt to the nearby underbrush and yellow grass. The cyclone which had formed around me strengthened the flames, gave them air to breathe, and like a large billow caused the flames to erupt into the sky. The cyclone created a spinning column of fire which blasted several hundred feet into the air. Raising my hands, I looked to the sky and smiled.

Holding out both hands, I pushed the fire up and then outward. A large spiral of flame filled the sky above us, casting a red glow upon the battle. Everyone shied away from the light and the heat. I kept the flames spinning for a time, forcing them further up and further out. The furious wind went still and the flames sputtered and began to break apart like embers. As the fire vanished, I smiled and lifted my sword. As darkness descended, the white light from my blade bathed the Malkethian's faces. Each of them were looking at me, fear in their eyes. The time had come for me to end this.

"Surrender now or die."

CHAPTER TWENTY-THREE
NEVERENDING NIGHTMARE

My demand went unanswered for several moments. Every eye was trained on me and I felt my patience slipping. All of the wagons and tents were on fire, the blaze casting long flickering shadows which accentuated the Malkethian's angry stares. When no one answered my request for surrender, I took a step forward and raised Burnfinger, preparing one final attack.

"Final chance."

Instead of laying down their weapons, the Malkethian's took up battle stances and prepared themselves for a final stand. I took a moment to look at Isar. In his eyes I saw his undying hatred for me. It was clear he would never surrender to me. Hate that ran that deep would blind any rational mind and it was a hatred that I could relate to. Seeing my own eyes reflected back at me was a chilling spectacle that filled me with both regret and shame. I had looked like that once and after all these years, it was harrowing to be faced with a vision of what I could become.

"So be it."

Stepping forward, I raised my sword and swiped down with all my strength. An arc of flame formed with my strike and shot forward. One of the Malkethian's leapt towards me and, raising his shield, took the brunt of the attack. The flame broke through his shield and connected with his chest. Crumpling to the ground, his body smoldered, the clothing beneath his armor alight. The stench of his burning body joined the scents of other corpses that littered the camp.

Isar stepped past his men, and shifted into an attack position. Taking up stone battle stance, he held his hammer close to his chest. I mimicked his stance and from the look in Isar's eyes, I knew how offended he was by my actions. Graham had been a father to him, and he had taught us both to stand our ground. At that moment, I considered the toll Graham's death had on me, which made me realize it must have been just as terrible for Isar.

So, is that the reason you hate me? I wondered. *The reason we never got along.*

I frowned and met Isar's eyes. His hatred was like looking into a fire. I rose Burnfinger high into the air and then swiped down, releasing all of the power within my blade. A large arc of fire extended from my sword and then shot across the clearing to Isar. The geomancer sidestepped the attack and struck the ground with his hammer. A large clump of earth shot into the air, absorbing my attack and protecting the Malkethian's.

Shouts from my warriors sounded and arrows shot through the air. Together, my men and I rushed forward to attack. The Malkethian's did not hesitate and we met each other in battle. Nila led the charge from the west and met Nels on the battlefield as I raced towards Isar. Hammer and sword clashed, the sound ringing out over the fighting. Exchanging blows, Isar and I brutally slashed and lashed out at one another. He would swing his hammer and I would use my blade to deter the blow while trying to get him off balance. The man was a boulder, his feet digging into the ground. The stones beneath him kept him steady and I struggled to make any impact with my attacks.

Swinging with all my might, Burnfinger met Isar's hammer and rang out. The vibrations from the blow traveled up my hand to my elbow, and a wave of pain continued to my shoulder. My wounded wrists ached and gripping my weapon grew difficult. I could feel my fingers loosening and it was getting harder to fight.

Breathing in deeply, I pulled more fire from the burning wagons and using the wood to fuel the inferno, turning them all to ash and cinder. Reaching out with both hands, I pulled the flames from the wagons towards us and like a wave, they washed over the earth. Isar dropped to the ground and the dirt formed a cocoon over him. As the fire struck the mound of dirt which covered Isar, I redirected the energy and channeled it into Burnfinger. The red gemstone began to glow and then the cool steel of my blade once again turned a bright orange. Swiping the sword across the mound of dirt, I cut away a portion and scored the flesh of Isar's arm.

Dirt sprayed me and I leaped back, holding up my arms to keep it from pelting my face. When the ground settled, Isar was back on his feet, small pebbles and dirt hovering in the air around him. His beard was full of dirt as he opened his mouth, small bits fell down to the ground. His hammer rested on his shoulder and he spat to the side. His eyes looked at my sword, then back to my face.

"There's the warrior I was expecting," Isar said. Though he stood steady, his voice was chased by the sound of heavy breathing. "I have trained hundreds of men and none of them ever lived up to you. I never lived up to you. Not in her eyes."

"What are you talking about?" I said, taking a step back.

"I told her she didn't need you. But Lyla would rather sacrifice me for you."

"You can return. You can tell her that I am dead. That you killed me here and now. No one would be the wiser."

"No. If I do not return with you alive, I might as well let you kill me right now."

I let out a bitter laugh before clenching my teeth.

"There is so much more going on here, Isar. Lay down your weapons. This is your last chance to surrender and live."

I knew Isar's answer before he spoke. As his lips formed the word *no* I leapt forward and slashed with my sword. As my red hot steel clashed against his hammer. I reached forward with my left hand and cast a large ball of flame into his chest. Unable to move fast enough and dodge the attack, the fire slammed into his sternum and blasted Isar back. Doubling back, he struck the ground hard. His head bounced twice and his eyes glassed over, his shirt burning. Isar's chest rose and fell and lifting Burnfinger high, I turned the blade upside down and prepared to plunge it into his chest.

Crackling trees drew my attention and a burned trunk fell down, splinting apart as it struck the ground. On the opposite side of the road, something moved in the darkness. In my hesitation, Isar lifted his hands and a large chunk of dirt soared upwards and slammed into my side. Stumbling back, I swiped wildly with Burnfinger and missed Isar's face by inches. Crawling away, his eyes looked from me to the road as another half burned tree fell down to the road. The loud crashing drew the attention of the remaining fighters. Looking away from Isar, I watched in horror as a beast emerged from the darkness.

The massive creature burst from the woods and screeched. The sound was high pitched and disorienting. The Omukade looked like a centipede, but was the size of several wagons. The large pincers on either side of its wide arrow-like face snapped, dripping with venom. The two dark beady eyes set above a gaping mouth glimmered in the firelight. The Omukade's mouth opened wide and showed rows upon rows of needle-like teeth.

Moving with more speed than a beast of its size should be

able, the Omukade sped across the road and chomped down upon one of the black-clad warriors. The needle-like mouth wrapped around the head and sucked the man in. Sucking in the body, the creature ate him in seconds, blood dripping down from the beast's foul teeth to the ground.

"Dammit!" I shouted.

Raising Burnfinger, I drew in a deep breath and pulled on all of the remaining fire. Ribbons of fire soared through the air towards my blade. As Burnfinger began to glow a bright white, I used the energy of the blade to produce a fire. Linking the new flame to the line of trees on the opposite side of the road, I caused them to burst alight. The wall of fire bathed the Omukade in so much light, it might as well have been out in the noon day sun. As a creature designed to stalk the darkness, it shied away from the flames and rushed towards the river.

Nels and Nila, who were standing at arm's length from one another, glanced from the creature to me, and then back to each other. They raised their weapons and together they rushed towards the creature. Similarly, I looked at Isar who unhappily lowered his hammer.

"What the hell is that thing doing here?" Isar hissed.

"I don't know. Just help me kill it."

Reluctantly, Isar nodded and together we rushed after the beast. It moved faster than I could run and as it reached the woods which lined the river, large tentacle-like streams of water shot forth and began to pelt it. The stone-like armor of the creature's body was unaffected by the attack and it continued forwards towards the river. Swiping the air before me with Burnfinger, I sent a blade of flame towards the monster. Clipping one of the legs, my attack did nothing but encourage the creature to move faster.

Raising my hand, I produced a ball of fire. Separating the flame into a dozen pieces, I threw them into the air and watched as they soared towards the line of trees. Like shooting stars, they soared through the darkness and struck the line of trees. All of them burst to light. Waving my hand, I willed the fire to spread until a circle of trees all around us were alight. Surrounded on all sides by fire, the Omukade doubled back and began to lash out fiercely at several of the black-clad warriors.

Snapping with its oversized mandibles, the Omukade tore bodies in half with ease. Nels continued to strike the creature with a water whip but had the same result. Isar slammed his hammer into the ground and the earth began to rend, large cracks forming all around the massive creature. The hundred small sharp legs dug into the ground and turning its massive arrow-like head, the Omukade plunged its face into the earth. Digging and crawling, the legs propelled the creature into the ground, forming a tunnel which sealed itself as dirt was thrust out from the creature's continued movements.

All went quiet, the only sound was that of crackling fire. I looked first to Isar, then to Nels. Both sorcerers were standing at the ready. Nila was nursing her arm and blood was dripping from her elbow to the ground. Searching the battlefield, I found Vivienne crouching over the unconscious body of Malin beside the prison wagon. Standing guard beside her was Captain Terrowin, his haggard expression marred by blood which covered the left side of his face. Finally, I looked at the twenty or so faces of the survivors. Two were Malkethian's and the rest were Nila's black-clad warriors. Everyone began to gather in a circle, frantically looking about in anticipation of the creature emerging from the ground.

"Isar, do you feel it?" Nels asked.

"It's digging deep and moving fast."

"Caden, stop the fire!" Isar called. "We need to draw it back to us."

Holding out my hand, I pulled the fire into myself. Flooding through my body until every single fiber felt like it was about to burst, the fire made me groan in both pain and pleasure.

"It's moving."

Letting out a deep breath, I began to pour the energy within me into Burnfinger. The talisman sword ate the fire like a hungry beast, relieving the pressure the energy had been placing on my body. With renewed strength, I gripped my white hot sword. The blade glowed so brightly that it cast a strange glow upon the entire battlefield. The white hot blade made it look like I was holding a solid beam of moonlight.

Howling erupted from the woods, shattering the silence, and a shiver ran down my spine.

"What now?" Nels shouted, the frustration in his voice combined with desperation.

"Night Howlers." I answered.

As if in response to hearing their name, clusters of three yellow eyes began to appear from the trees. Remaining hidden in the foliage that was unburned, the Night Howlers began to call out to one another, creating a cacophony of howls and squeals. The cries of the ape-like creatures continued, growing in intensity. As I began to contemplate igniting the trees they climbed upon, the ground beneath my feet began to tremble.

"Caden!" Isar shouted.

The cry came too late. The ground beneath my feet began to shake and large sharp mandibles burst on either side of where I stood. Leaping forward, I narrowly avoided being snapped in half as the Omukade emerged from the ground. Thrashing, one of the long sharp legs scraped my arm, drawing blood. Flinging my arm back, my blood sprayed across the creatures' eyes and mouth. Suddenly, the world around me went cold and I froze in place.

The world drained of color and I was looking at myself, the white hot blade held aloft in my hand. My new body shifted and flexed, hundreds of feet tapping on the ground, propelling me from the dirt. Shaking my head from side to side, I snapped my mandibles and growled. The sound came from deep within my long twisting body. A single thought permeated my mind.

Eat.

Crawling forth, I moved towards the group of huddling soldiers, frantically scrambling across the dirt. The hunger inside was all consuming and opening my mouth, I secreted a thick liquid to coat the teeth which lined the inside of my mouth and esophagus. A strong force connected with my side and I reflexively recoiled. Turning my massive head, I looked over at a tall figure holding a metal hammer.

Isar, I thought, the name coming slowly to my mind.

The deeper I entered the mind of the Omukade, the more I seemed to lose control of my own. The experience was deeper, more primal than it had been when I'd been inside the mind of the Shantenbose. Unlike that wretched experience, I now seemed in partial control. Urging the creature to the side, I guided it away from Isar and away from the soldiers. Crawling in circles, the Omukade began to growl and the hunger became more intense. Frantic, the creature's growling intensified and it thrashed its head side to side.

My mind fractured and part of myself returned to my true body. The double vision I experienced was disorienting. Two images seemed layered on top of each other; what I saw and what the Omukade was seeing. Taking a step towards the creature, I raised my sword and willed the beast to turn its massive ugly head at me. The dark beady eyes reflected the sword. Shying away from me, the creature struggled back for control. Holding out my hand, I created a claw shape with my fingers and motioned downward. Following my command, the creature laid upon the ground, though it twitched.

"Isar, I need you to use the ground to hold the beast in place."

As I spoke, large chunks of earth shot up from the ground like pillars of stone. After a few moments, the creature was barely struggling though the hundreds of legs still tapped relentlessly upon the ground.

"What are you doing?" Nila's voice called from behind me.

"Stay back!" As I shouted the command, I lost control of the creature's mind and it broke free of the stones Isar had been using to hold it in place.

Moving with dangerous speed, it darted to the group of soldiers who scattered like roaches. One of the two remaining Malkethian's tripped and before he hit the ground, the Omukade's sharp mandibles skewered the man. Lifting the corpse into the air, the creature raised its head, then the mandibles retracted, dropping the man into its gaping mouth.

As it choked the body down, a group of dark-clad soldiers, led by Nila, rushed the beast. They thrust their swords into its pale white underbelly. The scales were not as hard and their steel pierced through, drawing plum colored blood. Screeching, the Omukade dropped and crushed one of the men beneath its massive head. One of the sharp single taloned legs struck Nila, cutting deep into the flesh of her arm. Blood sprayed the creature but before it could take my friend with its mandibles, I swiped down with my sword.

Burnfinger released its energy, creating a large arc of white flame that cut the ground as it traveled to the creature. Pulling away from the light, the Omukade turned its head just before the flame struck it. One of the long black mandibles was sliced clean off and dropped to the ground beside Nila. Isar leapt forward to my friend's side, pulling her away from the thrashing creature. Once they were clear of the beast, I raised my sword again and slashed down hard. This time, all the remaining power within Burnfinger shot out in a large blade of flame that was nearly ten feet tall and half a foot wide. The blade of fire struck the creature in the side of its neck, creating a deep wound which began to pour purple blood.

Shrieking, the Omukade looked down and began to dig into the dirt. Shoving its head into the ground, it dug, the long serpentine body thrashing back and forth. Closing my eyes, I felt the creature's presence still in the dark recesses of my mind. Much like entering the Empyrean, I found myself pressed up against a mental wall. Pushing through the barrier, I entered the creature's mind and issued a single command.

Still.

The creature stopped moving. I stopped moving. Pain in my underbelly and in the side of my neck had replaced the hunger. Remaining still was difficult and each of my hundred legs began to shake.

Splitting my focus, I retained as much conscious control of the Omukade as possible while my mind once again returned to my own body. The double layered vision was less disorienting this time, though it still took an enormous amount of focus to retain absolute control over the creature. Slowly I began to stalk around the creature until I was near its face. Half buried in the ground, the large scales which armored the Omukade's back were slightly parted. Between the gaps, I could see the soft flesh. Taking Burnfinger, I placed it between the scales, then thrust it deep into the creature's body.

I screamed with pain and yanking my sword free, I dropped to the ground. My vision went black and I released my control on the Omukade. Falling onto the dirt, I heard the creature thrash for a moment before it went still. My vision returned and I found myself laying on my back looking up at the stars. Taking in a few deep breaths, I found my relief fleeting as another chorus of howls started up again from the forest.

"Son of a bitch!" Nels cursed. "Will this nightmare never end."

Climbing to my feet, I looked at the survivors and gave them a smile of encouragement. "Get back to the wagon. I got this."

"Damned fool," Isar said. He was looking at me with both fear and admiration. "I will not stand by to let myself be saved by the likes of you."

Not bothering to argue with the man, I turned away from him and looked up the line of trees. The three yellow eyes of each Night Howler seemed like small candles up in the trees. Taking in a deep breath, I pulled the traces of fire from the ashes of the battlefield which still smoldered around me. Producing a small flame, I looked at the line of half burned trees and splitting the fire into a hundred small embers, I launched them towards the forest. Where each ember struck a tree, a fire ignited. The fire spread as if each tree had been soaking in oil for months. The sudden reappearance of the fire spooked the Night Howlers who began to shriek and howl in distress.

Pushing the inferno back, I caused them to leap into the untouched branches where the Howlers hung. The fire moved faster than the creatures could react and dozens of the creatures dropped to the ground, their immolated corpses smoldering. Most were dead before they struck the ground and those that survived only ran a few paces before dropping. Those who had been out of reach of the first burst of fire fled into the forest. I watched them disappear and after I could no longer see them, I listened. When the howling ceased, I reached out towards the fire and closed my fist. Quenching the flames, they winked out in a moment.

The cool moonlight shone down upon the battlefield, high-lighting the smoke as it drifted up to a cloudless sky. Turning away from the smoldering ashes of the first, I turned my attention to Isar who was looking at me in dumbfoundment.

"On your knees," I said, motioning to the geomancer with my sword.

Isar dropped his hammer and obeyed. Once he was on his knees, I took a moment to examine his half burned face. Most of his newly trimmed beard had been singed away and new parts of his cheeks and neck were red from the burns. Screaming, I raised my sword high and Isar closed his eyes. Slamming my sword into the dirt beside him, the steel rang out as it struck a stone. Isar slowly opened his eyes, looked to my blade then back to me in bewilderment.

"You earned mercy by saving my friend." I looked up at the twenty remaining warriors. Nels and the single Malkethian soldier stood among them, their eyes trained on me. "Bind them all and throw them into the wagon."

My command was followed by silence and I turned to look at the soldiers who stood dumbfounded. I growled and they all snapped into action. As they set about finding rope to bind the survivors, two warriors rushed to Isar and took hold of him. He did not resist, instead consigning himself to their commands. As they marched him towards the prison wagon, Nila staggered over to me. She was clenching her arm which was still dripping blood. Rushing to her side, I took hold of her arm and examined the gash. Producing a flame above my finger, I looked into the woman's dark brown eyes.

"Do it," she said.

Pressing the fire into her wound, I listened as her skin hissed and popped. After a moment the blood stopped and I pulled my hand away. The fire winked out and once again the only light which shone down upon us came from the moon.

We paused and watched as the three sorcerers were bound with thick ropes and cast into the prison wagon. The sole Malkethian soldier entered of his own volition and sat in the corner, as far away from the sorcerers as possible. The prison wagon door's hinges squealed as it was closed. When the lock was put back into place, the sound of metal striking the bars seemed loud in the quiet of the night.

Vivienne, wrapped in blood soaked assassin's garb, joined Nila and I on the side of the road. Her expression was grave and her lips were pursed. Folding her arms, she looked up at me and for a long moment we stared into each other's eyes.

"Are you okay?" I asked, looking at her bloodsoaked clothing.

"I'm fine. Just a few shallow cuts. Nothing that can't be mended."

"Good."

"We should not spare them, Caden." Nila said. "If you don't kill them, I will."

"No!" My voice took on a strange tone, as though several people had shouted at once. The sound made Nila flinch and she stepped back. Feeling guilty, I smiled sheepishly at her.

"Nila's right Caden. We can't let them live."

"I'm sorry. You both helped save me. But trust me, if I am to save you all, they have to live. At least for a little while."

"You said you only needed one alive," Vivienne argued.

"I know. I changed my mind."

I turned to look at the battlefield. Close to two hundred bodies littered the ground. Most were bent and broken, missing limbs or with deep cuts. Their blood stained the soil, running through the cracks caused by Isar's geomancy. It was a battlefield straight from my past, from the nightmare which had been my life.

My soul ached for their loss, for the lives and blood that had been given on my account. Muttering a soft prayer to the Valon, I found myself wondering if Nirlos would indeed welcome them into the great beyond. Or was he the foul creature entombed below the city of Kings Keep. A disgusted feeling overtook me, filling my stomach with a sharp heavy pain that made me want to vomit. The adrenaline from the fight was beginning to wear off and now that I wasn't using magic, the aches and pains began to return. I looked down at my sword and ran my thumb atop the gemstone. I had been right. This battle would have been devastating had it taken place in the city. Shaking my head, I turned my attention back to my friends.

"So what do we do next?" Vivienne asked. "It's not like we can just roll on back to Kings Keep."

"Who says he has to," Nila said. "We can go back through the front gate, but Caden simply has to go around."

"That could work." I paused, swaying slightly on my feet. Vivienne caught my arm and held me steady. When I looked at her, her face was pale and her eyes were wide.

"Steady," she whispered.

"Thanks. I've got this. Let's gather the dead so I can burn them. After that, let's get the hell out of here."

CHAPTER TWENTY-FOUR
A SILENT REMINDER

Climbing into the back of a wagon, I laid down and slept. It was the deep dreamless sleep of post battle exhaustion with which I was intimately familiar. The occasional bump in the road and jostling of the cart would wake me, but within moments I was fast asleep once more. Still, in the back of my mind, I could hear the moving of the carts and wagons as we made our way to Kings Keep. The sounds seemed distant, just on the edge of perception, and then all went silent.

When I did fully wake, it was dark and the symphony of crickets was loud in the muggy forest air. I took a moment and gazed up at the stars, though the tall trees blocked part of my view. The scent of pine was rich in the air, but I could still smell smoke and blood on my clothes. Wrinkling my nose, I sat up and looked around.

The wagon I had been sleeping in was surrounded only by trees, the road and river were nowhere in sight. The horses were hitched to a nearby tree and grazing silently on the forest underbrush. Besides the animals, I was completely alone. Though I wanted to call out, I restrained myself from doing so. The previous day's events came flooding back to me and I figured my companions had left me behind to go on without them.

"Look who's awake," the voice that spoke was familiar, but I couldn't place who it belonged to.

Turning, I saw two familiar faces emerge from the woods. The first one, a man, was dressed in deep brown clothing which blended well with the surrounding trunks of the forest pines. His hair was recently cut and his cheeks were gaunt but had a bit more color than before. Osbert smiled and waved to me as Vivienne stepped up beside him. Vivienne was holding several rabbits and a few branches of sage.

"You look like hell my friend," Osbert said, flashing me a smile. The rotten teeth I was expecting were gone, replaced by a new set of dentures. In such a short amount of time, the man seemed so different.

"What are you doing here?" I asked, with a smile. "I'm glad to see you. Just surprised."

"Well, since you gave me all that money, I've been putting it to good use. Madam Acacia has been helping me and everyone we found has either found their way home or is being looked after. She told me what had happened and when I offered to help, she put me in touch with Seraphina's people. That was yesterday."

"Osbert found us on the road yesterday and has been keeping me company while we waited for you to recover."

"How long have I been asleep?"

"Not long. Two days."

"And when did the others leave us behind?"

"This morning. They should have arrived at Kings Keep by sunset. No doubt they are having one hell of a time explaining why we took the Malkethian's captive."

I nodded and clumsily climbed out of the cart. My body was stiff and sore and I took a moment to stretch. "So, what is our plan?"

"That is up to you. We figured we would sneak into the city with you, though Osbert has offered to be our scout."

"I figure, not one of 'em knows me or that I know you. I can slip in and out without a problem."

"Good idea Osbert. What do you think is the best way into the city without hiking over the mountain?"

"We always have the tunnels."

I nodded, grimacing at the prospect. Now that I knew what was hiding down there, I felt aversion to going down there until I had to.

"From the look on your face, that doesn't seem to be something you want to do," Vivienne said. "Let's cook these up, have a meal, then we can talk about strategy."

"Yes please," Osbert said.

Creating a small campfire, the three of us sat and prepared our own rabbit. Using the sage as a dry rub to the meat, I skewered the dressed rabbits with a stick and began to slowly rotate it over the fire. As we sat and cooked, Osbert began to tell Vivienne more about the time we had spent together in the underground. He was a better storyteller than I was and the way he shared the experience at times felt like it stretched the truth. I had to remind myself he was telling it from his experience and Osbert was clearly fascinated and impressed with my ability to use magic; a fascination that I no longer possessed. Still, I found myself chuckling along at his descriptions and when Vivienne asked if Osbert's over exaggerated descriptions were true, I only smiled and nodded.

"So, Os, how have you been holding up?" I asked, taking the first bite of my roasted rabbit. The sage complimented the sweet meat and I chewed quickly, suddenly ravenous.

"I've been doing fine." Osbert pulled a small bottle from his pocket and held it out for me to see. The contents were a milky green and seemed as thick as molasses.

"What is that?"

"A potion Omaria gave me. Helps keep me from being sick, though I do still crave the foul stuff."

"I'm impressed. Slush is one hell of a drug."

"It was, but now all I see when I think about it is the flayed and tortured bodies of those people." Osbert set his half eaten rabbit on his lap and closing his eyes, he grimaced. Shivering, the man opened his eyes and placed the tonic back in his pocket.

"Perhaps we can talk of more pleasant things," Vivienne chimed in.

"No need to change the conversation on my behalf. We're just facing the reality of what happened. In fact, facing that reality is what is helping me change. I just regret that it has taken me so long."

"Well, I'm truly glad that you are doing so well," I said. "Have you decided what you are going to do now?"

"I was thinking perhaps I could return to stone masonry, but I think I might hang around the Crooked Inn. Acacia and Omaria are good people. Perhaps there is a way I can continue to help those who are like me and guide them into a better life."

"An admirable aspiration," Vivienne said. "One that I am certain you will find great success with."

"That is my hope." Osbert went back to eating and the three of us were silent for a time.

I let the small fire burn out and once it was only ash, I waved my hand over the coals and drew the remaining traces of fire into my body.

"You two should go on tomorrow, take the cart into the city, and meet up with the others. Os, I want you to go to the Crooked Inn and tell Acacia to be expecting me. Viv, will you go to Seraphina and see where we stand with the Queen and everything that has happened. I don't want to make a move until I know what we are facing."

Both of my friends nodded.

"I may not fully understand, but why go back to the city?" Osbert said. "If you get caught, the Queen will put you to death."

"I'm aware of that. There is something I still have to take care of."

"What?"

"A dark entity burrows below the city and I intend to see it destroyed. Then I will be leaving, this time for good." I looked up at the stars and blew out a long stream of smoke.

Let's just hope that the darkness can be defeated.

Having slept the entire two days before, I offered to keep watch while my friends slept. I kept myself alert by listening to the sounds of the forest. I could feel, though distant, the movements of many creatures that prowled the night. The thought of being inside the mind of the Omukade sent a chill down my spine. Clearing my mind of dark thoughts, I focused only on ensuring that we safely made it through the night. I didn't want to unwittingly draw dark creatures down upon us. Not again.

At dawn, we hitched the horses to the cart and made our way back to the road. Within an hour, we were well on our way towards Kings Keep, the sound of wagon wheels on the hard packed dirt road complementing the rushing flow of the River Earn. Several boats were already on the water, traveling north. The averageness of the activity was a casual but important reminder that things continued on. Despite my troubles and worries, it seemed that the world would move forward regardless. While a bit strange, the thought helped calm my nerves and made me reflect on what I was truly fighting to protect. I wanted Kings Keep to continue on and for those who lived within to prosper. There was so much more outside of myself that I realized I had been blinded to. The more I focused on myself, the less I truly ended up seeing. This was something I was determined to keep in mind.

After a time, Vivienne climbed over the front of the wagon and onto the bench beside me. She wrapped her arm around me and pulled herself close. Resting her head on my shoulder, she reached forward and placed her hand on my knee.

"Tell me, what's on your mind, Viv?"

"I've just been thinking about the battle."

"Oh? What about it?"

"You were right. We outnumbered them four to one and still most of those who came with us were killed. I'd hate to see what a battle would truly look like if all you sorcerer's fought together."

"Nila's soldiers did well. I feel undeserving of their sacrifice."

"They went in of their own accord. Remember that."

I nodded and let out a sigh.

"Is there something that is troubling you, Caden?"

"How long do you think it will take before people realize what I did?"

Vivienne was silent for a moment. Her hand moved from my knee to my wrist. The scabs which covered my wrists were a dark black and the veins which went up my arms to my elbows looked like they had been filled with ink. The softness of her touch felt good as she traced each vein for a prolonged moment.

"I think the only people who are going to figure it out are the Malkethian's. Nila and her soldiers all just seemed glad they survived. Had I not known, I don't think I would have realized."

"I don't know why I am so worried. It's not like I will have this power much longer. Once I kill the entity, my necromancy should vanish with it."

"Is necromancy forbidden?"

"I don't really know. The Valon'Kesure dedicate themselves to the elemental magics and to divination. Those who do study the sorceries of life and death often end up trying to prolong their life and in so doing deny nature. We have legends that speak of men and women who corrupted themselves in pursuit of immortality. I met men who, like Hevron, could control beasts and some who could animate the bodies of the dead, though not to the extent that he did."

"Do you think these people still exist?"

"I suppose as long as there are people who live in this world, there will be those who seek to live forever. It is not beyond reason to suppose that Hevron was one of many."

"When you kill this *creature* that is living below the city, will that stop them?"

"It might. That all depends on what we find."

"So, you are not convinced that Nirlos is the entity?"

"No. I am not convinced."

"Alright, now I've got to know," Osbert said, crawling up to the front of the cart. "Sorry, I wasn't trying to eavesdrop, but with all that talk of dark magic, I couldn't help myself."

"That's alright Os. It's not like we were trying to keep it from you."

"What's all this about Nirlos being trapped below the city?"

"A potential and dangerous reality."

"Well, shit. What are we going to do about it?"

"I'm sorry, we?" I glanced over my shoulder at Osbert. He looked me dead in the eye, a serious expression on his face. "I am not asking you to get involved with this Osbert. When I told you that I wanted you to go live a new life, I meant it."

"Hell, I can always get started with that after." Osbert flashed me a dentured smile and in the daylight, I could see the whiteness of the carved ivory. He'd paid a lot for a set of new teeth like that. I suspected that even Nero would be impressed.

"Well, I ain't going to stop you."

The conversation faded and we rode in silence for a time. Vivienne remained beside me and I was content to enjoy the moment. After an hour or so, I couldn't help but let my mind wander and I began to think through a plan.

"I just remembered, did you do what I asked with the map?"

"Of course I did," Vivienne said with a shake of her head. "When you do get to the Crooked Inn, make sure you take a moment and talk to Sheyor. She seemed rather excited about talking to you and said she wanted to give you something as well."

Picturing the thin, strange, blond haired girl and her pet pigeon, I couldn't help but wonder what she would want to give me. "Do you have any idea what it is?"

"Not a clue. But she was very helpful with the map. Who knows, she did quite a bit of work in the hour we were together. Now that it has been a few days, she might have finished it."

"That would be good news. I want to get this done as soon as possible." I looked down at my infected hands and my fingers clenched tighter on the reins.

The horses slowed and I relaxed my grip to let out more slack. The horses plodded along again at their normal pace and the cart lurched forward. Neither one of my friends said anything, though Vivienne did give my arm a gentle squeeze. We continued riding along the road, passing several other wagons as they went north. Aside from a polite wave and a nod, neither of them seemed to pay us any mind.

"We're getting close," Osbert said, pointing with his left index finger. "See that bend a span ahead?"

Following his finger, I saw a curve up ahead where the road forked. There was a small wooden sign as a marker but the lettering was too far away to read.

"That is where you'll get off. The road leads to a small village. I don't know if there are any guards there or not. The entrance to the underground tunnel is in the large square fort. It will be sealed off, though I doubt that will be a problem for you."

"Anything else I should know?"

"It's a long tunnel, but it leads straight down to the foundry. You know the rest."

"Os, I'll meet you at the Crooked Inn. Viv, if anything goes awry, send word to Acacia. If I am going to be walking into a fight, I want to be prepared."

I followed the road which led to the small village for a little more than three miles. The road was narrow, long, and it wound back and forth through the trees at an incline that was suitable for a single horse drawn cart, but only just. After the fourth switch-back, I grew impatient and began to cut through the woods. Though more difficult, I moved upward at a much better pace and soon found myself near the top. Emerging through the line of trees, I ended up back on the road which went up an additional hundred feet. At the end of the road were the two dozen buildings of the village.

A wall, a little more than four feet in height, circled the cluster of buildings. Each building was a simple rectangular shape, made from stone, with thin glass windows and a thatched roof. The eerie silence which covered the place made my skin crawl. Each building was locked, long nails driven into the wooden doors to keep them closed. As I passed the first building, I took a moment to look inside through the dirty window. Within there was only plain wooden furniture, with no decorations or wall hangings of any kind.

In a strange way, it seemed as though no one had ever lived here. The place seemed immaculate in the way that only a centuries old abandoned building could. With the sound of my boots for company, I continued onward through the village. I made my way towards the large square fort that Osbert had spoke about. The structure was smooth in places, though enough of the outer layer had chipped away that the stone blocks beneath were visible. In each corner sat a watch tower that had a flat wooden roof. Small slits in the walls showed where archers would be placed to defend each side and the massive door was guarded by a withered portcullis.

Examining the grooves that lined either side of the portcullis, I found there to be just enough space that I could fit my finger between the wood and stone. Looking up, I could see large chains used to lift the massive Portcullis, which would be far too heavy to lift on my own.

With a mental shrug, I removed a box of matches from my pocket and struck one against the wall of the fort. Flaring to life, I dropped the match into the dry yellow grass which lined the wall and watched as they burst into flames. Allowing the fire to grow for a moment, I drew Burnfinger and extended the cool gray steel towards the fort. Taking in a deep breath, I pulled the flames into my body before redirecting them into the gemstone set into the crossguard of my sword. As the red stone began to glow, the tip of my sword shifted from cool gray to a deep orange.

Holding my sword out before me, I stepped back up to the portcullis and threaded my blade through one of the large square holes. Pressing the tip firmly against the aged wood of the door, I waited for it to catch fire. The process didn't take long and as soon as the wood began to smoke, I drew back my sword and placed it against the portcullis. It too caught fire and stepping away I waited for the fire to spread. Within a matter of minutes, both the door and portcullis were burning, enhanced by the lacquers and oils that had been used to polish the door over the years.

Taking in another deep breath, I pulled the flames from the door into Burnfinger. With the added energy, the entire blade turned a dull orange. Continuing to feed more power into my weapon, I watched as the door began to turn into charcoal. It was like watching a fire burn without the presence of flame. Slowly, the door turned to pure charcoal, cracking under the weight. Once it was sufficiently weakened, both the door and portcullis fell to the ground. Splintering apart into a thousand pieces, I continued the invisible immolation until there was nothing left but white ash.

With nothing left to get in my way, I marched forward through the opening and over to the other side of the fort wall. Glancing for a moment at the winch, I saw that the chains had gone slack. Beside it was a body that had begun to decay from the exposure to the sun. Perhaps it has been a few weeks since he'd died. His was not the only body that littered the fort.

Dozens of corpses were strewn about the ground, most wearing armor, though there were a few in dresses or beggars clothing. The battle looked to have been swift and merciless. It seemed that Osbert and the other freed captives had made quick and efficient work of dispatching their captors. However, I was disturbed that the city guard had not properly disposed of the bodies during their time here. Growling, I forced myself to set aside my anger. I, unfortunately, had too many other things to worry about.

I walked past the corpses, following them, not to the large building at the center of the fort, but towards a squat stone building in the back left corner. The door to this building was broken and five dead bodies laid before it.

Careful not to trod on the dead, I entered the small stone building. Inside was a chair, table, and fireplace. The door on the other side had been nailed shut. Half of the long nails were bent and several split the wooden door, showing where they had been pounded into the stone wall. With Burnfinger in hand, I pressed the tip of the blade against the door. Catching fire like the first, it burned away in a matter of seconds, the flames absorbing into the hot steel.

On the other side of the door was a tunnel and stairs which led deep into the earth. I felt like I was looking down the throat of a beast, the light from my sword gobbled up by the darkness. Though I knew where the tunnel led, I felt immensely uncomfortable, more so than I should have. Before, when I had not known what was below, I had not felt the same fear. Now, I couldn't help but shudder at the thought.

"Pull yourself together," I said.

My voice carried into the tunnel, bouncing off the walls. I paused, my heart racing until the silence returned. Taking the first step was the hardest, but as I began to descend the fear settled and I proceeded with the calm certainty that I was prepared to meet what was down below. Even if that was only temporarily.

Osbert was right when he said the tunnel was long. It seemed to take an eternity as I descended down towards the foundry. On occasion, the stairs would end and I would walk forward on a gently descending path before the stairs would start again. With every twist and turn, I found myself examining the stones and parts of the wall which had been left rough. The tunnel seemed to connect with a naturally occurring cave system, connecting different parts together. Some parts of the cave would span out in both directions, the edges far beyond the reach of the light radiating from Burnfinger. Listening carefully, I remained alert for the small creeping and crawling things that lived in these depths. Though they were far away, I could feel them moving around down in the darkness. That made me wonder if they too could sense me which was far from a comforting thought.

When I saw the end of the stairs and the dirty stone floor of the Sunken Foundry, I felt strangely relieved. Tightening my grip on Burnfinger, I reached out and let the brilliant yellow light illuminate my path forward. Pushing the metal gate open, I took a moment to look around. Everything was as I had left it. All except for the corpses. Blood stains remained where the dead had been, the smears denoted where they had been dragged or moved. The first place my eyes looked was the chasm which separated the foundry from the now ruined village. There, on the bridge, stood a man dressed in black robes. He turned slowly and pulled back his hood revealing a silver mask.

"Hevron?" I muttered.

The figure said nothing, but began to walk towards me. Lifting my sword, I took a defensive position as the cloaked man approached. As he drew closer, I saw that he left no shadow. Looking at the mask, I saw two glowing red eyes through the holes.

"What are you?" I asked, this time making my voice as commanding as possible.

The figure laughed.

Raising my sword, I let out a growl. "Stop where you are or I will cut you down."

"Now now, Caden," Hevrons voice said from behind the mask. "Do not be impulsive. I did not come to harm you."

"Then what did you come for?"

"To warn you of course. That you shouldn't place your trust so blindly in those you hold closest to you. They will betray you."

It was my turn to laugh. "Is that all?"

"No. I came to extend to you a final invitation. Come to me. I have waited for you with great patience and long suffering."

"Trust me, I will come for you soon enough. With enough fire to destroy you once and for all."

The figure shook his head and turned away. "Do not fear the inevitable Caden. I await your arrival and I promise you, as soon as we are together, I will bring an end to all your sorrow."

CHAPTER TWENTY-FIVE
RAT

A brilliant red sky was fading to deep purple when I arrived at the Crooked Inn. The warped building leaned heavily to the side and a new door had been cut to accommodate the leaning shape of the door frame. The single lantern which hung above the door wasn't yet lit and as I passed under it, I waved my hand and the wick sparked to life. I didn't hesitate as I reached the door and pushed it open. I was greeted by the ruckus of a seedy tavern.

The scent of sweat, spiced meat, and ale were strong in the air. More than a hundred people were crammed into the room. Every seat was taken and the odd placement of tables only added to the clutter. Servers struggled as they moved through the crowd, delivering drinks and meals to the patrons. Aside from a few glances, no one acknowledged my presence. Pulling the door closed behind me, I casually started to make my way through the tavern towards the bar.

Sitting in the back corner, nursing a small glass of dark liquor was Acacia. She was chatting with a woman in a low cut black dress who was gesturing rudely with her hands. Seeing such a normal, or what I presumed as normal interaction, was oddly satisfying. I began to look around at the tavern once again to take in the average interactions, something I almost immediately regretted.

"Son of a bitch, it's him!" Someone shouted from the table just below the staircase. He jumped to his feet, knocking over a mug of ale onto the ground. The sound of shattering clay was followed by silence as everyone in the tavern went silent.

"Evening," I said with a nod.

Several men stood, drawing daggers, and moved towards me. They had barely made it a step when a loud wooden clack sounded from the back of the tavern. Everyone went silent and turned towards the noise.

"Go back to your drinks," Acacia said from the back corner where she sat. "Or I will sit back and let him kill you."

Although a bit dramatic, her words had their intended effect. Everyone remained quiet and most eyes remained on me as I started making my way towards Acacia. Patrons and servers parted before me. As I walked by, everyone made an effort to avoid touching me. For good measure, I pulled my lips back into a snarl and growled. An entire table of dirty faced men leapt back. Suppressing a smile, I made my way to the back where Acacia sat.

The woman in the low cut dress looked at me with curiosity rather than fear. Her eyes lingered on me for a prolonged moment and it wasn't until Madam Acacia cleared her throat that she looked away.

"If you don't mind Tala, may we finish our conversation later?"

"Of course, Madam." Tala said with a curtsey. She eyed me one last time before she turned and walked back into the crowd. I watched Tala find her way over to a table where she was met with wide smiles.

Taking a moment to look at everyone, I saw that most had gone back to their drinks and conversation was beginning again.

Still, nearly a quarter of the patrons still gave me wary glances and at least half a dozen were still holding knives. A man in a dark cloak slipped out the front door, glancing over his shoulder at me as he went before the door slammed shut behind him. With a mental shrug, I turned back to Acacia who took a deep drink from her glass. Omaria emerged from the kitchen door, holding a rather fancy looking bottle of wine. Her eyes widened when she saw me and I gave her a smile.

"Were you not expecting me?" I asked, turning my attention back to Acacia.

"No, we were expecting you. I just presumed you wouldn't be so bold as to walk in through the front door."

"What did you expect? For me to send a messenger?"

Acacia nodded, finishing her drink. "Consider yourself lucky that those who frequent this place would prefer to remain in my good graces. Still, I think we will have some trouble before long."

"I'm not looking to run from trouble. Not any longer."

"Clearly." Acacia sighed. "But I am."

"Sorry," I said. "I should have been more cautious."

"Well, there isn't anything to do about it now."

"Is Osbert here?"

"Let's say he is, preoccupied."

Nodding, I bit my lower lip. It wasn't like it was any of my business what Osbert chose to do with his time. Clearly, I was in a place where few made such judgments, at least openly.

"Since Osbert is indisposed, Vivienne said that Sheyor wanted to see me."

"Of course. She's been asking about you all day. Omaria, will you take Caden to see Sheyor?"

"Yes, I'll take him."

"Caden, when you're done, let's talk."

Omaria motioned for me to follow her. Making my way around the bar, I followed her down the hallway to the last door on the right. She opened the door and proceeded down the creaking wooden steps. Following her, I looked over the wooden railing at the strange cellar. It seemed like an odd place, though considering what Sheyor was like, it did make sense. Reaching the bottom, Omaria paused and pointed.

"She's through the door. When you're done, we'll be waiting for you at the bar."

"Omaria, is everything fine?"

The fox faced woman nodded, her darkly painted eyes narrowing. "Just don't let the rat out."

Rat? I wondered. *Did she make a new friend?*

As Omaria went back up the stairs, I walked over to the door and knocked. The sound of bare feet smacking stone came from the other side and within moments the door flung open.

"Caden!" Sheyor shouted as she flung her arms around me. She gave me a hug with as much strength as her little arms could muster and began to bob her head from side to side.

"How are you doing kid?"

"Good, good. Caden, I wanted to show you something." Excitedly, she spun around and hurried back into her small room.

There was a small bed, a small wood burning stove for heating, and a stack of books which were set along a single shelf which hung on her wall. The small girl twirled about as she leapt onto the bed and pulled a book from off the shelf. She held it with solemn reverence and as soon as it was in her hands, her movements became careful and slow.

"What's that?" I asked. I felt my smile grow wide and couldn't help but let out a little laugh.

"It's a book about plants and flowers and trees and bugs. It's Vasha's favorite." She looked at a small rat which sat on a small stool I hadn't noticed in the corner.

The rodent, who had been curled up in a ball, got onto its back paws and almost seemed to bob its head in response. Sheyor held the book out and the rat squeaked. Sheyor set the book down on the bed, knelt down, and started to leaf through it. Squatting beside her, I held the flame out to the side and shed more light onto the pages as she turned them. From the corner of my eye, I watched as the rat leaped from the stool, and scampered across the floor towards us. It crawled up the bed and sat at the base of the book, looking down over the pages. "See, Vasha, your book."

"It's very nice. Do you have a favorite?"

"Um," Sheyor drew out the word as she searched through the book and found a page close to the back "This one is my favorite." She put her finger on the page and I saw the sketch of a beautiful flower that almost looked like a dove.

"The White Egret Orchid," I read the name aloud. Sheyor nodded and repeated the name. "I don't think I have ever seen that one before."

"Me neither, but it looks a lot like Vasha does when he's outside. Don't you think so?"

"Ya, it does." I glanced over to the rat. "And he's also Vasha?"

"Of course he is, don't be silly. Vasha just doesn't like to be a bird all the time. It's much easier for him to be a rat when we are inside."

"I see," I felt my smile widen as I fought back the urge to chuckle. Perhaps there was something more to her strange relationship with the little rodent that sat on her bed than I'd expected. "Have you read them all yet?"

Sheyor looked up at the shelf of books and nodded her head enthusiastically. Her hair bounced as she did so and her hands clapped together with glee. "I have. Aren't they wonderful? I like them a lot."

"Good to see that you have been taking care of them."

Her face grew dark and serious. "Of course. Who wouldn't take care of books?" She almost looked like she would cry at the thought.

"Some people are just strange."

"Yup!"

Sheyor's smile returned and she closed the book, leapt onto her bed, and returned it to its place. As soon as she was satisfied that her books were all in their proper order, she sat back down on the bed and scooped up Vasha into her arms. She cuddled the rodent and gave it a kiss on the top of his head. Vasha squeaked and made little movements with his paws, almost like he was waving.

"Vivienne said that you were helping her with the map."

"Yes, I finished that ages ago." Sheyor bounded to the other side of the room where a stack of papers sat atop a wooden board. Taking them from off the shelf, she gingerly carried them back to her bed then began to lay them out. "I'm not as good with drawing maps as Vasha is. He's always had an eye for these sorts of things."

Once the papers were spread out, I was surprised at the detail. The city of Kings Keep had been drawn out on eight separate sheets of paper. The city depicted above was drawn in standard black ink while the tunnels and passageways of the underground were drawn in beetroot red. The map I had rendered on the wooden plank was set out on the side and glancing back and forth I saw it had been transferred with immaculate detail. I looked at Sheyor and found myself both amazed and baffled. It was easy to match the mental map to the drawings and suddenly everything came together. I knew exactly where to start our search through the tunnels.

Shaking my head, I let out a small laugh and Sheyor furrowed her brow at me.

"Sorry, I'm not laughing at you. This is amazing work. I couldn't be more impressed."

"Then why laugh?" Sheyor said, folding her arms and pouting.

"Now that I can see the map," I placed my finger on a section on the side of the paper which was just below the Castle, "I realized it was a little obvious where I should be looking."

"Oh," Sheyor unfolded her arms. "So you are going to the dark place?"

"That I am."

"Do you have the map memorized?" The girl spoke to the rat in a tone so serious I didn't dare laugh at the strangeness of it. To my surprise, the rat nodded, squeaked once, then turned its neck so it could look at me. "Can you take him?"

Vasha turned his attention back to Sheyor and nodded again. A wide smile once again split the girl's face and she held out the rat towards me. The rat's whiskers bounced slightly, his nose twitching.

"Why do you want me to take Vasha?" I asked.

"He wants to look after you, make sure you don't get lost." Sheyor looked so serious as she spoke I didn't dare refuse.

Gingerly, I took the rodent from the girl and holding Vasha in the palm of my hand, I felt his small feet tap several times. His black beady eyes looked into mine and I felt a strange sensation wash over me.

Am I really trusting a rat? I wondered.

With a little hesitation, I put Vasha in my pocket and felt him settle down at the bottom. "I'll make sure to take good care of him."

"I know you will."

Folding the map, I placed it into my other pocket. When she held out the board, I shook my head. "Keep that here. Just in case."

Sheyor nodded and bounding back across the room, placed the board back onto the shelf where it had been before.

"When I get back, I'll see about getting you a few more books."

Her smile grew so wide and her eyes went so big I was almost alarmed by the intense excitement on her face. "Really?"

"Absolutely."

Sheyor clapped her hands and twirled around. She leaped up onto her bed again and pulled another book from off her shelf, turning it open to the first page. As I left the small room, I heard her call, "Be safe Vasha!"

I felt the rat move in my pocket and I reached down to stroke the top of his head. Such a strange thing, but I was now convinced there was more to it than I'd first expected. Bidding farewell to Sheyor, I left her small room, closing the door behind me. When I returned upstairs Omaria and Acacia were both waiting for me at the far end of the bar. Walking up to them, I noticed that I got a new set of angry glances from the other patrons, but I paid them no mind.

"Everything go well with the girl?"

"Yes. She told me what I needed to know."

"Good. Then, come with me." Acacia stood, set down her empty glass, and smoothed her skirts. "Omaria, will you have food sent in to us?"

"Of course my lady," Omaria said.

She reached under the bar and drew out a large bottle of brandy which she proffered to me. Taking it, I swiped two glasses from off the bar and followed Acacia to a door in the backmost corner of the tavern. She held the door open for me and entering, I found myself in a rather ornate and highly decorated lounge. Silks and tapestries hung from the walls, all dark shades of red. Cushioned sofas lined two of the three walls and a small table was set in the center. Another door on the right wall was open and through it I could see an even more lavishly decorated bedchamber.

"Your private room?" I asked, raising my eyebrow

Acacia smiled. "Private, yes. But its intent is to serve our guests, not to simply satiate my own taste for luxury."

"I see," I said, eyeing the plush furnishings. Acacia took a seat beside the table and pausing for a moment, I took one opposite her. Pouring us a drink, I slid a full glass across the table to her waiting hand.

Raising my own glass, I took a small whiff of the brandy. It had a woody odor which complemented rather than over-whelmed the sweet. I took a sip and smiled, the sweet liquor pleasant on my tongue. Draining the glass quickly, I filled it again, this time forcing myself to take only a small sip before putting it down.

Acacia raised an eyebrow, but said nothing. She remained silent and I decided to do the same, giving her the space she needed to start the conversation. The longer I looked at her, the more difficult it was to read her. Before either one of us spoke, the door opened and Omaria entered, a bowl of stew in one hand and a small plate of bread in the other. She sat the food down before me, gave me a small one sided smile, then turned and left.

Tearing off a small piece of the dark brown bread, I dunked it into the creamy stew and took a bite. The rich taste of the potato and cheese stew was good, though with how poorly I'd been eating, I was certain that influenced my perception of the taste. I ate quickly, and ignored the bemused glances from Acacia. She was silent until I finished and when I did finally look up from my meal, she made a gesture for the dishes.

"Do you want me to send for more?"

"Thank you, but this was more than enough."

"Perhaps we can enjoy something a bit nicer. A desert perhaps?"

"I'm not really one for sweets," I said, lifting my glass of brandy. "This is all I need."

Acacia smiled at that, lifted her own glass, and we clinked

them together before drinking deeply. The woman let out a sigh, then she removed a small envelope from underneath her skirts and placed it upon the table.

"Vivienne said to give you this."

Reaching out, I placed my finger on the folded parchment and slid it towards me. I didn't open the letter, instead leaving it face up on the table. Picking up my drink, I took another sip while I continued to look at Acacia.

Why are you suddenly sizing me up?

The silence grew to become uncomfortable. Eventually Acacia lifted her glass and took a drink. She sat back against the cushions and hummed slightly.

"Every time I think I have figured you out, it turns out I am completely wrong."

"Oh? And what is it you thought you'd figured out?"

"I honestly thought that if you succeeded in your ambush, you would return to the city with the Malkethian's heads on spikes."

"Are you disappointed I didn't?"

"Disappointed is not the word I would use. Just surprised."

"We are in agreement then. Is that all you wanted to talk about?"

"Caden, I don't think you should go to Seraphina's."

My eyes glanced down at Vivienne's letter.

"I don't have to read that to know it's bad news."

"Did you really think I expected anything else?"

Acacia smiled. "I don't suppose I did."

"Then I guess I should read this," I said, finally lifting the letter.

Running my thumb below the wax seal, I opened the letter and unfolded the yellowed parchment. Written in neat cramped handwriting was a message from Tristin, not Vivienne.

> *Caden,*
>
> *The prisoners are safe, for now. Correspondence has been sent to the Queen and the entire ridge is currently under guard. Seraphina is not sure how the Queen will react, but she does believe Pricilla is afraid to act. Stay with Acacia until we send word. Don't do anything rash.*
>
> *Tristin*

Shaking my head, I tossed the letter into the table and scoffed. "Well, it looks like you were right about the bad news."

"May I?"

Reaching out, I pushed the paper across the table and was quiet as Acacia read. Her lips pressed to a line and when she finished she tossed the paper back onto the table. "Looks like you will be staying here for the evening."

"I can happily find other accommodations if my presence will be troublesome."

"Nonsense. I half expected as much. A cot has already been made up for you in the cellar."

"Oh, did this room become unavailable?"

"This room is for priority patrons and customers, not for down on their luck pyromancers who crawl in from off the streets."

Chuckling a bit, I finished my second glass of brandy. Unabashedly, I poured myself a third. As I leaned back on the sofa, the door opened, and Omaria poked her head in.

"Madam. We have a bit of a problem."

Shouting from the tavern floor followed, the sounds of over-lapping voices making it difficult to discern anything intelligible. Acacia rose to her feet, gave me a sideways look, then left the room. The door closed and the sound of the shouting was cut off.

Draining the brandy, I placed the glass upon the table and grabbed the paper. Holding it between two fingers, I produced a small spark between my fingers and the parchment burst into flames. Consumed as if it were flash paper, the note was gone in an instant. A haze of smoke hung in the air and small bits of ash fell onto the table.

Climbing to my feet, I walked to the door and pressed my ear against it. I could hear muffled shouting and the stomping of metal boots on the wooden floor. Deciding to ignore Acacia's warning look, I opened the door and was greeted by the sight of a dozen well armored soldiers standing with their swords drawn. Most of the patrons had fled and those who had not were the brutal looking men who had stood to attack me before. Every eye in the room turned to look at me and without hesitation I drew my sword.

"It's him!" one of the soldiers shouted.

Another soldier stepped forward. He had shoulder length black hair and a square face. Lifting his sword, he pointed it at Acacia. "You are under arrest for the crime of harboring a fugitive of the city."

One of the soldiers in the back lifted his torch and held it as if he were going to drop it.

What an idiot, I thought. Reaching out my hand. I pulled the fire from the torch and held it over my hand.

"You can't be serious," I said, forcing myself to laugh at the men. "Get out!"

As I shouted, I threw the fire at the square faced soldier. He screamed and ducked, avoiding the fire by an inch. The ball of flame struck the man standing behind him, knocking him to the ground. The rest of the soldiers stepped back, but they did not leave.

Drawing my sword, I charged their leader. The man barely had enough time to lift his sword in defense when I slashed at him. My blow knocked him off balance and I continued to swing my blade in quick swift motions. He blocked the next three strikes, but the fourth caused him to lose his grip on his own sword. As his weapon tumbled to the ground, I hit the man on the side of the face with the flat of my blade. The blow knocked him to the ground. Motionless, a small amount of blood trickled from a shallow cut on his cheek. His chest rose and fell, denoting he was only unconscious.

"Get out!"

This time, when I screamed, the rest of the soldiers rushed out of the Crooked Inn. Reaching down, I placed my fingers below the edge of the fallen soldier's breastplate and dragged him to the door. It took a significant amount of effort, but I managed to drag him to the porch and toss him down onto the dirt. I waited until the man regained consciousness. Once his eyes began to flutter, I placed the tip of my sword against his neck. Groaning, he looked first to the sword then to me.

"I want you to tell anyone that if they come for me, I will kill them. You will be the last life I spare. By the Valon, I swear this to you."

Sheathing my sword, I turned and walked back into the Crooked Inn. *So much for not doing anything rash,* I thought.

Acacia and Omaria stood at the bar. Both looked at me with grateful expressions but irritation was still evident in their eyes.

"Sorry about that. Perhaps I should leave after all."

"No. Let any of those bastards come if they dare." Acacia rubbed her palms on her skirts and let out a sigh. "Besides, it looks like we've lost our patrons for this evening anyway."

Nodding, I walked over to one of the fallen tables and helped set it right.

"Caden, don't worry about that," Omaria said, hurrying up to me. She placed her hand on my shoulder and I shrugged it off.

"Just let me help."

The woman nodded and together we straightened the tavern floor. Just as we finished, several men entered in through the door dressed as sailors, with dirty boots and tanned faces. They removed their hats and smiled. Acacia glided across the room, welcoming them and getting them seated. Others started to come back in, and within half an hour, the place was bustling as it had been before.

Finding a place in the back corner, I watched and drank, all the while thinking of what would become of tomorrow. I was lost in thought when the sudden movement of someone beside me dragged the stool out from under the bar. Osbert smiled at me as he took a seat.

"You missed all the action," I said.

"Sorry about that. It seems you had everything under control, as always."

"I guess."

"You look tired," Osbert said. "Go get some rest."

"Can I ask you something?"

"I suppose. What's on your mind?"

"Are you afraid of death?"

Osbert was quiet for a moment, then he shrugged. "For the past few years, I have been living in a state worse than death. No, I can't say that I fear death so much as I fear continuing not to truly live my life." He let out a deep sigh, and placed his hand on my shoulder. "I get the sense that you don't fear death. What is it that you do fear?"

"Failure."

CHAPTER TWENTY-SIX
ABOMINATION

A letter arrived at the Crooked Inn two days later and Acacia sent for a carriage. While I waited for the carriage to arrive, I looked down at the invitation written with scarlet ink. I couldn't help but smile to myself as I drank. The liquor was heavy in my stomach, but the fire that burned within removed the traces of inebriation which should have accompanied the strong drink. Setting down a half empty glass, I wiped my mouth on my sleeve and decided I would wait in front of the Inn.

There were only a few people drinking in the Inn, most of them nursing hangovers from the night before. It wasn't quite noon and when I stepped out onto the porch, I found myself looking at the morning sun. Half shrouded behind clouds, I could smell the scents of a storm on the wind. Pulling my cloak around myself, I stepped off the porch and onto the dirt, my boots crunching pleasantly.

Waiting in the cold wind for a few minutes, I found it to be relaxing. Turning to look at the Ridge, I studied the tall spires of the nine palaces which overlooked the city. On the southern end was Seraphina's palace and though I could only see the tops of the towers, I still found myself admiring their splendor. Once those magnificent buildings had been part of a world I had only fantasized about joining. Now, I felt as though I was about to return home. The sentiment brought a sadness I wasn't expecting.

"What the hell are you doing?"

The voice shouted from behind me. Turning to look, I saw Omaria standing at the doorstep.

"Just needed a bit of air," I replied. "We're still waiting for the coach."

Omaria let go of the door and the wind slammed it closed. She walked over to me, her arms folded around her. She was dressed in perhaps the nicest dress I'd ever seen her in. The gown was dark green and along each side bronze flowers had been embroidered. She wore her hair back in a braid which was pinned up with several wooden sticks and her face wasn't painted like it usually was. Her eyes were still outlined in black and were accented by shadows which covered her eyelids. She had freckles under her eyes and on her nose.

Unsure how she would take a compliment, I decided against saying anything. Omaria shifted back and forth, her fingers twitching. *Nervous,* I wondered.

"You don't have to wait out here on my account." As I spoke a strong gust of wind blew past us, ruffling my cloak and her dress. The hair on the back of my neck stood up and I looked over my shoulder half expecting to see Malin standing there with her javelins.

"Caden, do you think Os is going to get back in time?"

"I doubt it. When he left this morning for supplies, he said he wouldn't be back until late. No need to send someone for him. To be quite honest, I'd rather not get him involved with the Queen."

"That's good advice."

"So, why are you getting involved, Omaria?"

"Because I want to be there to watch the Queen get humiliated."

"That is not my intent. You may be disappointed."

"Don't be so sure that just because that is not something you intend, it will not happen. There is a reason she has chosen not to have you come to meet her at her Castle but to meet you in secret."

"If you don't mind me asking, why is it that you want to see Pricilla humiliated?"

"Because she deserves it. She chose the wrong side. You deserved better than what happened. Even now, you prove the kind of man you are. The kind of man that is far and few between."

"While I appreciate the compliment, I am not doing this for praise."

"And that is exactly my point. When I look at you, I see a man who chooses to do what his conscience dictates is right, no matter how hard that choice is to make."

When the carriage pulled up to Seraphina's palace, ten of the Queen's guards stood on either side of the gate. We rolled past them without interruption and through the window of the carriage I watched as heads turned, following us as we went. Acacia and Omaria sat on the bench opposite of me. The entire journey had passed in silence and the growing tension was putting me on edge. As the carriage rolled to a stop at the end of the drive, I immediately opened the door. My boots crunched on the gravel and holding the door open for the women as they stepped out, I looked up at the palace. Despite the cloudy sky behind and the distant rumblings of thunder, the large stone walls looked majestic.

Ten more guards were stationed on either side of the stone steps that led up to the front door. Captain Terrowin, in a new suit of polished armor and a green cape stood at the door. He waved us over, a grim expression on his face. Closing the carriage door, I joined Acacia and Omaria, walking with them side by side to the entrance. Terrowin said nothing as he opened the front door and beckoned for us to enter.

"Everything good?" I muttered as I passed him.

Terrowin's jaw tightened and he tilted his head back and forth. "Be careful," he whispered.

Stepping into the front atrium of Seraphina's palace, I was greeted by more guards who lined both sides and at the top of the staircase. My eyes flickered to the far wall where there was a large tile mosaic of the first great storm. In the dim light it seemed to lack its usual splendor. The door closed behind us and Terrowin motioned for us to follow him.

"They are waiting for you in the high tower." His voice was loud, devoid of all emotion, making the announcement feel like the recitements of a town herald. As we walked to the left staircase, two figures appeared at the top. Tristin and Nero were both wearing black and their faces were just as serious as Terrowin's had been.

Halting at the top of the stairs, Tristin gestured with her hands to Acacia and Omaria.

"You two will have to stay behind. The Queen has requested a private audience with Caden that only Lady Seraphina has been invited to."

"Do I need an escort, or may I go ahead?" I asked.

"No, we'll stay here. Go on, Caden. You know the way."

Nodding my farewell, I quickened my pace and took the shortest route through the palace to the high tower. When I reached the end of the hall and the spiral staircase, I paused, taking a moment to listen. Soft voices echoed down from above, though those who spoke did so in such hushed tones that I was unable to make out the words.

I did my best to make my footfalls loud as I climbed the stairs and almost immediately the voices from above went silent. Once I stepped onto the top landing, I wiped my palms on my cloak then pushed open the door to the high tower meeting room. The Queen and Seraphina occupied the two seats on the far side, Seraphina in the high backed chair always occupied by Tristin and the Queen in Seraphina's seat. Both women were dressed eloquently, and both looked unhappy.

My first instinct was to bow but I stopped myself before I'd moved more than a fraction of an inch. Instead, I turned and closed the door. Taking in a deep breath, I walked over and took my usual seat. The high backed chair was cool to my touch and lounging back, I turned to look at the Queen. Her displeasure was clear and she also seemed offended by my lack of decorum. But what the hell did I care? She'd banished me and handed me over to the Malkethians. She was no longer my Queen and she would receive no more respect than anyone else.

"Don't be so pompous," I said, my tone a little rougher than I'd intended.

"Caden," Seraphina said. "Careful."

"Let's not pretend I am not the most dangerous person in this city, let alone this swiving room." I sat up in my seat as I spoke and placed my hands on my knees. "I am here because I want to be. Are you going to try and arrest me again, or are you going to leave me be?"

Queen Pricilla remained silent, her lips pressing to a line. She looked from me, then to the ground, then spoke. "I see no point in arresting you. I have no way of controlling nor containing you."

"Then what was the purpose for this meeting?" I growled.

"Caden," Seraphina said, her voice calm and soothing, "be quiet and listen."

Swallowing my pride as best as I could, I sat back and met the Queen's eyes. There was a mix of emotions that went far beyond anger. In her haunted expression I saw embarrassment, fear, and genuine anguish.

"What was I supposed to do?" Pricilla asked.The pained look on her face deepened. "I have been Queen for less than a year and we have never been closer to being taken over by an enemy. Kings Keep has never fallen to an outside force. Because of you, this city was held hostage by Malkethian sorcerers."

"You chose to trust the wrong people."

"No, I chose to trust those who were not responsible for the death of my sister."

Clenching my jaw, I held back my retort.

"My Queen," Seraphina said. "Blame cannot be laid solely at his feet for Aveza's death."

"You're right. No amount of punishment of the guilty will ever bring her back. But when I was presented with the opportunity to see you brought to justice, I did not hesitate. Alas, my anger and grief blinded me and now it's too late to change anything."

For the first time since I'd arrived, Seraphina's mask slipped. True anger flashed across her face, though it vanished as quickly as it had come.

"I do not claim to be innocent, though I am not entirely responsible." I paused, trying to be careful about how I chose my next words. "I do hope that in some way I can atone for the mistakes I did make."

"In what way do you propose you atone? Nothing you do can bring my sister back." Pricilla's voice choked and anger once again broke through her calm expression. Before today, she had always played the part of a cold emotionless ruler well. But the woman who sat before me now was broken.

"First, I want to clarify what I came here to do. I am not doing it out of duty or out of penance for the death of your sister. To pretend otherwise would be a lie. Just like your admission of fault is not because of pure guilt but because you lost the dangerous game you thought only a few days ago to have won."

Pricilla's jaw clenched and her hands balled into fists. Hanging around her neck was the pendant Isar had given her of the Malkethian eagle.

No, not penitent at all.

"What have you returned to do?"

"I have good reason to believe that a true demon lives beneath the city of Kings Keep. Burrowed deep below, among the ruins of the underground, he has been imprisoned since the fall of the last age. He is responsible for guiding Hevron into power. He is responsible for the creation of the Shantenbose which killed your sister. Most importantly, this entity is on the brink of escape and he will keep infecting the minds of powerful people until he is free. It is my intent to kill him."

"How do you know this?" Pricilla asked, her eyes narrowing. "How can I be sure this is not some fabrication of your making?"

"Why would he lie?" Seraphina asked, once again taking on her soothing tone. "But I do second the Queen. How did you come across this information Caden?"

Taking a deep breath, I pulled off my gloves, and set them on the arm of my chair. The veins of black were clear, but my intent was to give a true demonstration of my affliction. Standing, I pulled off my cloak, I set it gently on the seat. My arms were left bare by my sleeveless shirt and showed off the long veins of black which ran from my hands to my shoulders.

"I too have been infected, as Kori and Hevron were before me, by the magic of this demon. It has shown itself unto me and has spoken in my mind its darkest and most vile desires."

Neither Seraphina nor Pricilla spoke. Both women looked aghast, their mouths hanging open as they beheld my infected flesh. Looking down at the black veins, I flexed my muscles and watched as they popped. My muscles ached and I could feel the infection below my skin as though it were a worm slowly sliding up through my skin.

"If this demon is down there, do you truly think you can defeat it?" Pricilla asked.

"I cannot be certain of any outcome. My hope is to defeat it, or at least see it trapped once more. But it could go wrong and there is a strong chance it defeats me."

"Can we afford that risk?" Seraphina's mouth pulled back in a grimace. "If it wants to get free, would we not be playing into its hands?"

"Another possibility. I either do nothing and let the evil remain, or I risk everything on the slight chance it can be defeated."

The three of us fell silent and I watched the Queen carefully. Her eyes were contemplative and she kept glancing at my arms, then to the window that overlooked Kings Keep. Lightning flashed outside, casting blue light across the cloud-dark sky. As the thunder rumbled, it began to rain. Starting slow, the rain drummed softly against the roof of the tower and beating on the windows.

"What happens after you defeat this monster?" Pricilla asked. Her eyes looked into mine, and in them I saw an inkling of courage.

"If I do succeed and kill the bastard, I am going to leave this city for good. It's past time for me to once again see new lands."

"Then I will lend my support and as many of my soldiers as are needed for this task."

I bowed deeply to the Queen. "Thank you."

As the sun set on what had been a long day, the Syndicate gathered together to eat. Dinner was served on the balcony overlooking the ballroom. The mood of the evening was somber and we began the meal in silence. I picked at my food, pushing bits of potato around with a fork between forced bites. Though I was hungry, I felt like a man in a sick bed forcing myself to eat. Lifting my glass of wine, I took a sip and found the flavor sour. Grimacing, I set down the glass and slid my chair back away from the table. The grinding of the chair legs on the polished floor was loud and everyone at the table looked up at me.

"Sorry," I muttered.

Vivienne gave me a soft smile and the others went back to their meals. I took a moment to look at each of them. Tristin and Seraphina looked slightly relieved, and Seraphina kept glancing over at me. Nila looked almost as sick as I was, her brow covered in sweat. Nero only took small bites and chewed quickly. Even among friends, he still seemed self conscious about the way he looked when he ate. Missing most of the skin around his mouth made him look like a snarling dog chopping down on table scraps, something he too realized.

"I know that I...that things have been difficult these last few weeks." As I spoke, the others all put down their forks. "I just wanted to thank you for standing with me and for everything you did on my behalf."

"Of course," Seraphina said, lifting her wine glass. "We were just returning the favor."

"You might be a bastard, Caden," Nero said, "but you're our bastard."

"What Nero means to say," Tristin said, a soft smile forming at the corners of her lips, "is that we look after our friends. Even the ones who are a bit rough around the edges."

"So, do you really think we can beat this thing?" Nero asked.

"I think he can," Nila said. Her voice was raspy and she

coughed for a few moments. "Vivienne and I saw him, saw what he is capable of now. It's terrifying, but brilliant. I do not doubt that if anyone can defeat this foe, it will be him."

"Then you do have Hevron's power," Seraphina said, with a sigh. "I suppose this explains where he got his power."

"I'm not sure about that," I said. "Well, if I am to guess, I think this power is connected to the entity. As for how the talisman was created or where it comes from, that is still a mystery."

"Caden, I..." Nila said, her eyes going wide before rolling back into her head. Collapsing to the ground, she hit the polished stone hard. Several gasps sounded and getting off my chair, I knelt on the ground beside her. Grabbing her arm, I placed my first two fingers over her wrist and felt at her pulse. Her veins throbbed rapidly and her chest rose and fell in short shallow breaths. Rolling up her sleeve, I saw a long dark vein running down from under her dress.

"Shit," I cursed, looking over my shoulder at Vivienne. "Go get the bracelet, now!"

Without a second's hesitation, Vivienne sprinted from the room.

Seraphina, Tiristin, and Nero all stood around me, their faces white with fear.

"Nero, help me lift her up. Let's get her to a bed."

Obeying my command without question, Nero crouched down and together, we lifted Nila up off the ground.

"Caden, what's happening?"

"She's infected, she's dying."

"No!" The cry slipped past Seraphina's lips and her eyes went wide. "How is this happening?"

"It's going to be okay. She is going to survive this." *She has to.*

CHAPTER TWENTY-SEVEN
TAINTED BLOOD

Slamming my fist against the wall of my room, I shouted in anger. The skin on my knuckles split as a wave of pain jolted my arm up to my elbow. If this was what was to become of my friends, I was better off going at this alone. It was clear to me that it would be better for me to perish than for them to die on my behalf. Punching the wall again, I heard a pop and the bone above my left index finger bowed in. Shaking my hand, I growled and grit my teeth. Pressing the bone with my right thumb and index finger, I popped my finger back into place with another loud crack. Grunting from the pain, I used it to help calm my temper.

My room was dark save for the moonlight which streamed in through my windows. Walking over to the hearth, I removed a box of matches from the mantle and striking one, I tossed it into the prepared tinder. The small flakes and shards of wood caught fire and with the wave of my hand, the square stack of small logs burst into flames. Keeping my hand close to the flames, I let the heat bake my skin for a few moments before I thrust my hand into the fire.

Drawing in the flames slowly, I let the energy soak my hand

and felt my skin and bone knit back together. It took the better part of an hour, but when I pulled my hand out, there was no discomfort as I flexed each finger individually. The infection of dark magic still remained though the pain had lessened some. As I looked at the ink-like infection below my skin, I began to wonder what would come of me should I be successful. What did I actually know?

Staving off both my frustration and despair, I stood and walked to the double doors that opened onto my balcony. Through the glass, I first looked over Seraphina's gardens and recalled how they had looked the first time I saw them. My eyes then looked over at the line of trees at the back which ran up the mountain that loomed high above. The peaks gleaned in the moonlight and their majesty and magnificence made me feel small. Grateful for their beauty, I opened the balcony doors and stepped out into the crisp midnight air. Wind ruffled my hair and the scents of flowers and pine added to the pleasantness.

Calming my mind, I pushed away all of my worries, feeding them to an imaginary fire in the back of my mind. Vasha began to squirm in my pocket, his small paws pressing against my side. Reaching my hand into my cloak, I stroked the small creature. Curled into a ball, Vasha pressed his back against the palm of my hand. He was such a strange creature and as I held him I was beginning to feel a strange connection that was beginning to grow.

Is that what Sheyor feels? I wondered, gently rubbing the top of Vasha's rat head with my thumb. The creature went still, once more asleep. Pulling my hand from my pocket, I placed it upon the balcony and felt the cold stone balustrade.

"Caden," Vivienne's voice said from behind me.

Turning my head to look at her as she joined me on the balcony, I saw that her eyes were red from crying.

"Is she alive?"

"Yes. Barely."

"Did the talisman not work?"

Vivienne reached out and placed the bracelet of white bone on the stone rail of the balustrade. "It wasn't what we thought, just a normal infection. We had to amputate her arm."

"Will she live?"

"The next few hours will be crucial. Tristin isn't sure how far the infection spread. Her wound was near her shoulder and it had killed the flesh of her arm. Chances are, it has already spread into other parts of her body and into her heart."

"Then she should hold onto that," I said, pointing to the talisman.

"If it helped, I wouldn't have brought it back."

A wave of shame passed through me which caused a strange wave of chills to rush through my skull and into my teeth. Growling, I reached out and picked up the talisman. Wrapping it around my wrist, I felt an immediate sense of relief wash over me. The sense of shame returned and my stomach turned to knots as it welled with guilt for being relieved to have the talisman back. Slowly the dark veins of black in my fingers began to fade. Soon I would show no signs of the infection. Just like what had happened with Kori.

"There is still another option that might save her life," I said. "Though I am not sure we can trust Nels enough to not kill her himself."

Vivienne perked up at the idea, her chin lifting up and eyes going wide. "Caden, we have to try."

"It's not certain. Nels might not even be disciplined enough to help heal her. But those who can influence water have a knack for diagnosing disease and infection. When I fought for the Malkethian army, I saw many wounded saved. He may at least be able to tell us how far the infection has spread."

"Then let's go. He may not be able to save her, but I want to give her a fighting chance." Vivienne was already walking away by the time she finished speaking.

Closing the balcony doors behind me, I hurried after Vivienne who was already out of my room and in the hallway. I followed Vivienne through the palace to the southern end opposite the servants quarters. Though just as ornate as every other part of the palace, the walls lacked decoration. At the end of the hall was a door with a guard on either side. They bowed to us as we approached and the guard on the right reached to his belt and removed a large ring of brass keys.

"Here to see the prisoners Sir Caden?"

"Yes. Have they caused any problems?"

"None at all."

The guard unlocked the dungeon door and held it open, gesturing for us to enter. He handed me the keys which I slipped into my pocket. Stepping through the dungeon doorway, I entered a short stairway which descended into the unlit stone room. Seraphina's dungeon was small, with only two cells, both of them occupied. With chains on both their hands and feet, Isar and Nels were together in one cell while Malin occupied the other. With their arms suspended over their heads, they were forced to stand. There was just enough slack in the chains that they could sway. My eyes traced the links in their chains to metal rings set in the ceiling and then down to a large winch.

"Nels," I said, walking up to the door to the cell where he hung. "Nels!"

My voice echoed around the small dark dungeon. The hydromancer shifted slightly and his eyes opened. When he looked at me, his eyes seemed distant.

"Are you a healer?"

He didn't answer my question, instead dropping his head and closing his eyes.

"No," Isar muttered. "He cannot help you."

"Can't or won't," Vivienne snarled.

"I am no healer," Nels said.

The false hope I had created for Vivienne was shattered and she turned away from them, tears streaming down her face. She looked at me with pure desperation.

"Leave them to me," I said, placing my hand gently on her shoulder. "Go, leave me with them."

"No. I'd like to stay." There was venom in Vivienne's voice.

Nodding, I looked back to the winch that held them up. Walking over to it, I took one of the wooden spokes and began to slowly lower the chains. Slowly, their arms lowered and they sat down upon the ground, relief evident on their faces. Vivienne crossed her arms and glared at me in disbelief.

"*Trust me,*" I mouthed, pointing to the winch which held the chains attached to Malin. With a huff, Vivienne went over and lowered Malin's chains so she could sit upon the ground as well.

Removing the keys, I walked over to the cell and unlocked the door. Stepping inside, I looked down at Isar and Nels who were both kneeling. Isar looked up, his eyes no longer filled with hatred but with fear.

"What are you?"

It was a simple question, one I had not anticipated.

"A monster," I whispered. "The same one I've always been."

"How did you control that beast?" Nels asked.

"That is why I am here. Surely in the time you have spent here, you have learned what I have done and where my notoriety came from."

"You defeated a necromancer and stole his power," Isar said, his tone accusatory.

"Not quite. It was never my intention to acquire his power and even now the power is slowly poisoning me as it did him. There is an entity of darkness living beneath this city, one I intend to destroy. My hope is that you will help me." I paused and knelt down beside the prisoners. "This is the moment where you get to make a choice. Perhaps the first choice you have ever truly made for yourself. It was an offer that was once extended to me. Fight with me, help me defeat this evil, and go your own way. Be free of me, be free of Malketh, go live on your own terms."

"Why should we trust that you will keep your word?" Nels asked. "You wouldn't trust us."

"Because I need your help. I don't know if I can do this alone and of all those who I could call upon for aid, you three are my best hope."

"I will not help you. This city can be damned to darkness and oblivion for all I care," Isar growled.

Standing, I took a few steps away and leaned against the cell bars. "Does this man speak for you?"

Looking first to Nels and then into the neighboring cell where Malin was sitting, I waited and hoped for them to answer. The silence droned on, neither sorcerer meeting my gaze.

"Caden, they're not going to help us," Vivienne said. "Let's leave them to die. String them up by these chains and hang them until their arms are torn free of their bodies."

Vivienne began to turn the winch, raising Isar into the air. He thrashed violently and the ground began to tremble. Drawing my sword, I pressed it against his gut and the man went still. The tip of my sword drew blood and it made a shallow cut in his abdomen as he was lifted up. As he was hoisted, his arms began to bow inward and it looked as though his shoulders would pop from their sockets. Once his feet were dangling several inches off the ground, Vivienne stopped turning the winch and locked it in place.

I waited a few minutes, watching Isar struggle with the pain. His arms were strong, but he was weak and soon the strain from the effort became too much and he went slack, whimpering in pain.

"Let him down, Viv."

With reluctance, she did as I asked.

When Isar was once more kneeling upon the ground, he placed his palms on the stone. Small pebbles began to float around his fingers and reaching forward, I placed the tip of my sword under his chin. Coaxing him to lift his head and look at me, I was careful not to drive the blade into his throat.

"Why do you hate me so fervently? Can we not set aside our differences to fight a common enemy?"

"Every time I look at you, I see only the brother who betrayed me. You betrayed all of us on that battlefield and you should have died. Hell, I thought you had died and I mourned you."

"You have every right to hate me for what I did."

"Tell me why? I need to know why you killed them?"

"My intent was only to kill the Malkethian commander. The others weren't supposed to be in the way. I was trying to make it look like an accident. I didn't mean to kill Amod. But I couldn't live any longer as a slave to the Malketh."

"So murdering your brethren was your only choice?"

"You weren't there!" I screamed. "You have no idea what I was forced to do."

"If I had been, they would still be alive."

I shook my head. "There is nothing you could have done to save them."

"Do you even feel bad about killing them?" There was venom in Isar's voice. "Looking up at you now, I don't see any remorse in your eyes. You truly are just a demon who deserves to perish."

"I will always feel guilty for what I did. But I cannot change the past." I paused and let out a sigh. "I am prepared to face judgment. If you are willing to help me destroy the evil hiding deep below, I will go with you peacefully back to Malketh."

"No," Vivienne said. "We won, Caden. You don't need them. Just kill them and be done with it."

I turned to look at Vivienne and smiled sadly at her. "There is a significant chance this ends in my death. I am willing to accept that. But I will not let you or any more of our friends die on my behalf." I paused, turning my attention back to the sorcerers. "They are the best chance I have at a favorable outcome. With their help, we can win. I can't keep running anymore. I will gladly give up my happiness and my life for you. It's the only way."

"I will help you," Malin's soft voice squeaked. "We are the Valon'Keasure, wielders of the primordial magics, bringers of order and peace. I see it as our duty to help you destroy the evil that has been hiding here. Since you also offer yourself up to us for judgment willingly, I see that even more so it should be our task to provide you the aid you requested."

"No Malin, it is not our duty," Isar growled.

"I agree with her," Nels said. "We all saw what he did. If this entity is here, we should destroy it. Then we all get what we want. The evil is gone, the city is safe and will become a part of our great empire, and Caden will come with us."

"I do not trust his word," Isar said. "He will betray us and we will have given him the power to do so."

I looked down at Isar and with my blade still pressed to his throat, I knew there was no way to convince him of my intentions. The only thing I had to offer was my word and that would mean nothing to a man who did not trust me. Pulling back my sword, I sheathed it, then walked back to the cell door. I racked my brain in hopes that I could perhaps find the words that would convince this man.

Is it possible that if I say the right things, he will listen?

An answer came to mind and taking a seat on the ground, I rested my back against the bars of the cell and let out an over dramatic sigh. Then I let out a frustrated laugh.

"Vivienne, release Malin from her chains," I tossed her the ring of brass keys which she easily snatched from the air. Everyone was silent as Vivienne opened Malin's cell door, the rusted hinges squeaking. Vivienne hesitated, but Malin remained still as she unlocked the shackled chains around both of her wrists and ankles. Leaving the sorceress on the ground, Vivienne walked out of the cell and tossed me the keys.

Catching them, I got to my feet and proceeded to unlock the shackles around Nels hands and feet. He too took a moment before climbing to his feet. He stumbled to the side, catching himself on the bars which divided the two cells.

"Viv, if you would please lift Isar back up. If he wishes to remain here, then he will need to be lifted up off the floor."

Vivienne was all too eager as she began to turn the winch. Slowly Isar was raised into the air. The geomancer closed his eyes and allowed his body to go limp.

"Is this what you want?" I asked as Isar was lifted up off the ground. The winch clicked as Vivienne locked it into place. Isar said nothing as he swayed back and forth. "You can remain here. If we return, I will still go back with you and honor my word. Your friend's offer to help has guaranteed this. You don't have to participate and I don't blame you if you would rather stay here. Although you will be in pain, at least you will be safe."

Running my hand through my hair, I scratched my scalp and closed my eyes. Exhaustion was beginning to make it difficult to remain upright and the sudden desire to go to my bed almost overwhelmed my strength. I was ready for this day to end.

"But," I continued, "you could still join us. We will return in the morning for you to make your final decision."

Leaving the cell, I closed the door which locked into place. Clenching my fist, I rubbed my wrist, pushing back the bone white talisman so it was no longer resting on my wrists. Though they were healed from fire, the skin was still tender. I rubbed them, massaging the veins at the base of my palms. Isar was now looking at me with a curious expression, but said nothing. With a grunt, I walked away from the cell and joined Vivienne, Nels, and Malin at the bottom of the dungeon stairs. As we began to climb the steps, Isar called out.

"Wait!"

Pausing, I turned around and looked at the hanging man.

"Can we speak, alone?"

"Viv," I said, looking at her and the two freed sorcerers. "Take them up to the top of the stairs. I will join you shortly."

Vivienne eyed me, clearly uncomfortable with the prospect of being alone with them.

"Please?"

"If they do anything, can I kill them?"

"Yes," I said.

Neither Nels or Malin reacted at all to the threat. Both looked too exhausted to fight and I had confidence that they would keep their word.

"Take me to your friend, Vivienne," Nels said. "Though I am not a healer, perhaps I can help a little."

Vivienne's face still looked suspicious, but an eagerness returned to her expression. She looked at me wearily.

"Go, take them. But have the guards go with you."

The three of them hurried up the stairs and I watched them until they exited through the dungeon door. Walking back down the stairs, I strode up to the cell and looked up at Isar whose forehead had a large bulging vein from the stress of hanging off the ground. He struggled to take in every breath and I waited for him to gather enough strength to speak.

"Caden, what is that bracelet hanging from your wrist?"

Surprised, at the question, I lifted my wrist and pulled back the sleeve of my cloak. Showing off the bracelet, I held it up so the torchlight would allow the geomancer to see it. His eyes widened

AUSTIN COLTON

and he shuddered. It was strange to see such a visceral reaction from the man.

"You recognize this?" I asked, moving up to the cell bars. "What do you know?"

"I've seen things like what you did, far to the east. Men and women who rode on the backs of evil beasts."

A shiver ran down my spine.

"Caden, how did you get their power?"

"I told you. The power comes from the dark entity who lives below this city."

"No it doesn't."

"Then explain to me why he has been able to enter my mind?" I growled, slamming my hand against the cell bars. "When this all started, my friend was injured, her blood tainted by dark magic."

Rolling up my sleeve to my elbow, I removed the talisman bracelet. Once it was no longer around my wrist, the dark lines of magical infection began to creep up my arm. Isar's eyes widened and his mouth parted, a gasp escaping his lips.

"Her body was so severely infected that it was covered in these dark lines. When I killed the necromancer Hevron, I removed his talisman. As you just witnessed, his body was covered with these same signs of infection. I used this talisman to save my friend and she too became a necromancer."

"What happened to your friend?"

"She...I killed her to kill the Shantenbose that was trying to take over her body."

"And you. How long have you been infected?"

"I don't know when it started, but the progress has been slow." Putting the talisman back on, I once again felt sudden relief. The infection retreated, disappearing as my skin returned to normal. "I've been feeling the affects of the necromancy for a while now. But the infection is now. The talisman keeps the infec-

366

tion at bay. I hope that killing the creature below this city will free me of this curse."

"Those we fought in the east, they wore talisman of bone and their bodies decayed quickly upon their death. Within minutes, their corpses looked as withered as the dead we found in Grugon's Pass. Do you remember?"

"The dead we found in the winter, beneath the ice." I shivered, the memories of the cold coming back to me as if they had happened only a day ago. "Where we found the pit of Aqrabuamelu."

"Exactly."

Taking a step back, I let out a groan and rubbed my eyes. "Last winter, we found several crates in the basement of a palace that Hevron was using as a lair. Each contained an Aqrabuamelu."

Isar's head bobbed for a moment, his eyes narrowing. "You are telling the truth. You really have seen this entity?"

"Unfortunately, I have. He has shown himself as the ghost of my friends and he has appeared to me wearing the face of that same necromancer who started this whole nightmare."

"Let me down, Caden." Isar let out a sigh and he shook his head. "I will temporarily set aside our differences to help defeat this evil. We cannot let this spread. You were right. It is my duty and I will not allow it to live."

Walking over to the winch, I slowly lowered Isar down to the ground. Once his feet touched the stone, he remained standing rather than falling down to his knees as he had done before. Securing the winch, I walked over and unlocked the cell door. Isar remained still as I removed his shackles. Each chain clattered to the ground, the sound of metal striking stone loud in the dungeon. Placing the keys into my pocket, I looked Isar in the eye and stretched out my hand. His lips pulled back slightly, as if he were about to snarl, then he clasped my hand.

"I truly am sorry," I said. "I am glad you decided to help."

"Don't push it, Caden. I'm not doing this for you. This is what Graham would have wanted. He taught both of us better than this. It's time we started acting like the men he wanted us to be."

I nodded, a lump forming in my throat. "Let's get out of here."

"You better get me a damned bottle of rum."

"I think that can be arranged."

CHAPTER TWENTY-EIGHT
SWORD, FIRE, AND DEVASTATION

I t took seven days of planning and making preparations before everything was ready. With nothing to do and a few hours to myself before dinner, I found myself in Seraphina's library, once again studying the old Grimiore. The large tome was now as easy for me to read as any other book. Hevron's journal entries were not any more insightful than they had been when Kori and Tiristin had transcribed them, but one thing had become clear. Hevron had been communicating with this entity who he did truly believe to be the Valon of Death. This was both disturbing and enlightening. Looking at the small silver idol of Nirlos, I felt the strange power which emanated from it. Reaching out, I ran my finger along the side, the touch of the cold talisman on my finger sent a small jolt of energy up my finger.

Flicking my finger, I knocked the idol over on the table. I went back to the book and continued flipping through the pages, looking at the different drawings of all the monsters. It was a little disheartening to see so many dark creatures which we could potentially run into below. I paid close attention to the monsters that were labeled as cave dwellers. Stopping on the page of the Omukade, I took a moment to study the details. The large arrow-like head, dual pincers, and armored body looked exactly like the creature I'd killed. The only difference was the legs. They were much larger in the drawing with longer spikes where the legs bent.

Perhaps the Omukade we faced was young.

Closing the book I placed it upon the table and looked aimlessly around the room. I got lost in my thoughts and as my eyes continued to bounce between the shelves of books, I found myself becoming extremely bored. I wanted nothing more than for Vivienne to return so we could pass our final peaceful night together. No matter what happened tomorrow, at least we would have tonight.

A tugging on my cloak's inner pocket caught my attention and reaching in, I removed Vasha, placing him on the table. The rat looked up at me with his beady eyes as he rubbed his nose.

"Hungry my friend?"

Vasha nodded, placing his small paws down on the table. Reaching down, I stroked the back of his head and neck, something the creature seemed to like, then picked him up. Placing Vasha on my shoulder, I left the library and began to make my way through the palace halls towards the kitchens.

"We'll be going down soon and after you can return to Sheyor," I said to the rat as he crawled closer to my neck.

Vasha squeaked in excitement at the mention of his friend. His paws held tightly to the seam in my cloak and his tail flicked back and forth. Reaching up, I scratched his head.

"I wonder what you really are, Vasha."

Descending the servants staircase in the north wing of the palace, I entered the kitchens and kifed a small piece of bread, cheese, and meat from the pantry. The cooks and kitchen boys were all busy, preparing dinner and though I got a few glances from them, none uttered a word of protest.

Passing the ovens where freshly baked bread was just beginning to rise, I felt Vasha's small feet tighten on my shoulder. The rat shivered with excitement, the scents invigorating him. Leaving the kitchen through the doors which led into the dining hall, I took a moment to look at the large oak table which had been prepared for the evening's meal. The table was set with more than twenty plates, enough for the syndicate, the Malkethian's, and the soldiers who would be joining us down into the tunnels.

The double doors of the dining hall were open and striding through them, I began to make my way towards the central atrium. I wanted to look upon the mosaic one final time. There were a lot of servants running about, as well as members of Seraphina's extended family. Returning nods as they were given, I couldn't help but smile as almost every person I passed took a moment to look at Vasha. Most tried to hide their horrified expressions, some not hiding them well.

Sun streamed in through the windows of the main atrium and when my eyes looked upon the tile mosaic, I was once again filled with wonder and astonishment. Falla and Ullu, depicted mid-fight, surrounded by storm clouds and lightning, glowed in the late afternoon sun. The polished lacquer of the fingernail sized tiles reflected the light causing the warm and cool tones of the artwork to be accentuated. Mesmerized as always, I stood and tried to memorize it, holding the image in my mind so every detail could be captured and remembered. If there was one thing I wanted to hold onto, it was something beautiful.

This mosaic had come to represent everything I had come to love about Kings Keep. My friends, this palace, the opportunity to be unburdened with the common needs of life. So much had been provided and there was so much for which I had to be grateful. As I reflected upon everything good that had happened to me, I slowly realized how little I'd actually enjoyed.

Setting Vasha on the ground, I placed his food before him and as he ate, I continued to admire the mosaic. As the sun descended, the light which filled the center atrium faded and I was left to gaze upon the art in semi-darkness. The moment, like every moment, had passed. Yet I did not feel sorrow for its passing. A warmth lingered in my chest, a pleasant memory that I would forever cherish.

I heard Vasha's squeak before I felt him climb on my boot. He reached up towards me with his front paws, opening and closing them like a child asking a parent to pick them up. Reaching down, I lifted Vasha and placed him back on my shoulder. Taking one final look at the beautiful tiles, I walked to the end of the wall and entered the long chamber which was lined by five hearths on either side. All were burning, their fire flickering light upon the checkered stone floor. At the far end, the doors to the ballroom were open and standing inside was a woman with long curly blond hair in a green dress. She stood alone, her attention on the gardens beyond the wall of glass windows.

The sounds of my boots clopping on the polished stone floor announced my presence and Seraphina turned to look at me as I approached. She smiled, a soft sad smile. Her eyes glanced at my shoulder and her smile faded, replaced by a quizzical expression. Then, she turned her attention back to the window and I walked quickly through the ballroom and took a stand beside her.

"Caden, why do you have to carry that rat on your shoulder?"

"Vasha likes to see new things," I replied. I couldn't help but chuckle slightly, realizing my answer was not much different than one Sheyor would have given.

"Just be sure to put him away before dinner."

"Of course."

"Beautiful sunset, don't you think?"

"Quite."

"If you could have one wish granted to you, what would you choose?"

"Any wish? No matter what?"

"No matter what," Seraphina repeated.

I paused, not because I didn't know the answer, but because I wasn't sure if my impulsive response was the best thing I could wish for. To give myself time to think, I decided I would try to pry the answer from Seraphina first. "Will you tell me your wish first?"

"I wish I could change the world with the snap of my fingers." Seraphina chuckled and snapped, the sound loud in the quiet ballroom. "It would be marvelous to have such power, don't you think?"

"I am certain the Valon would agree with you. Though there must be a reason they do not use their power in such a way."

"Or perhaps no such power exists."

"If you did have that power, what would you like to change?"

"The better question is what wouldn't I want to change. If we could have a perfect world at the snap of our fingers, I'd imagine it would be a very different one than this."

"I suppose so. But I'd say any world where there are people, you will find imperfection. It's perhaps the most frustrating as well as the most magnificent thing about us humans. Even if you were able to make a perfect world, I suspect it wouldn't remain so for too long. Unless the thing you remove is the very thing that makes us human in the first place. I don't know about you, but I'm not sure I would want to live like that."

"Way to shatter my dreams," Seraphina said with a laugh. "How come I get the feeling you are going to give me a pragmatic answer."

Chuckling, I ran my hand through my recently cut hair. The short black hair felt good against my hand and it made me feel like a warrior again. "What, you don't want my honest answer?"

"You're stalling. The look in your eyes, I saw that you knew the answer to the question the moment I asked it." Seraphina reached out and placed her hand on my arm. "I'm not going to tell anyone."

"If I could have one wish, I would wish that my friends could come back to life. But since you were looking for a realistic answer, I would wish that I could keep the rest of my friends from dying."

"Oh Caden." Seraphina gave me a sad smile and wrapped her arm around me. "You can't stop death. It's part of life. All we have is to remember to give attention to the wonderful and beautiful things this world has to offer us while we can."

"I know," I said. Taking in a deep breath, I exhaled sharply through my nose, and I gave Seraphina a hug. "Thank you. Truly, I am grateful."

"You're saying that like this is goodbye," Seraphina said with a sniffle.

We let go of each other and she wiped away the tears which were forming beneath her eyes. She forced a smile and laughed.

"No, I am not saying goodbye to you, but I suppose to yet another beautiful moment. One I am glad we got to share."

After dinner, the soldiers who'd been invited to eat with us departed, which left only the Syndicate and the three Malkethian's sitting at the dinner table. Lifting my glass of wine, I drained the final portion before setting it beside my half-eaten dessert. The rich cake was too sweet for my liking, but I forced myself to take another bite. It would be wasteful not to enjoy it, and after so long of living on the most meager necessities, the thought of leaving it made me feel guilty.

"It has been a wonderful evening," Seraphina said, getting to her feet. "But if you will all excuse me, I think I will retire to my room. Please, enjoy yourselves as long as you wish. I will see you off in the morning."

Tristin followed Seraphina out of the room, which left me, Vivienne, Nero, Isar, Malin, and Nels sitting at the table. My friends gave the sorcerer's distrusting glances and everyone seemed determined to avoid eye contact with each other. So far, everyone was being amicable, but the tensions were high and it felt like at any moment things would turn sour.

My cloak was draped over the back of my chair and reaching around, I took a small wooden box from one of the oversized pockets. The dark painted wood box was scuffed and the rolled cigars inside slid towards one side. Placing the box on the table, I flipped open the lid. The cigars had a rich earthy scent to them and were just as potent as the day Calix had gifted them to me. Taking out a cigar and the cutter, I took a moment to smell the tobacco before placing the cigar in my mouth. Clipping off the tip, I produced a flame at the tip of my finger and slowly puffed on the end until it was easy to pull the rich smoke into my mouth. Taking a long toke on the cigar, I held in the smoke for a few moments before exhaling. The smoke drifted up towards the large vaulted ceiling of the dining hall where it dissipated.

"Anyone else care for a smoke?" I lifted the box, proffering it.

"I see you're still fond of bad habits," Isar said, smiling. "Hand one of them over."

I stood, and leaning over the table, held the box out to him. Isar plucked a cigar out, turned to his friends, and gestured for them to take one. Both Malin and Nels took a cigar and like I had, held them up to their noses to smell the earthy tobacco.

"Either of you two want one?" I asked, turning to Vivienne and Nero.

Nero's face pulled back in his version of a smile, revealing his set of sharpened silver teeth. "Indeed."

Holding out the box, I watched him take one, his eyes looking greedily at the box. Shaking it, I urged him to take another. He obliged.

"Viv?"

"No thanks," she said, lifting her glass of wine. "I'm fine with this."

Nodding, I closed the box, then passed around the cutter. Producing another flame above the tip of my right index finger, I lit each cigar before dismissing the flame. Puffing a few smoke rings, I sat back in my chair and looked at each of my companions. The tension had lessened and everyone was lounging comfortably in the high backed dining chairs.

"You've been holding out on us," Nero said. Since he didn't have lips, smoke leaked out of his mouth while he blew smoke from his nostrils. He barked a laugh and bit down on his cigar, his metal teeth puncturing small holes in the tobacco leaves. "Where did you get something this nice?"

"Oh, let's just say from a dearly departed criminal friend."

Nero shook his head. "Well, I suppose I won't ask you to thank him."

"I remember a time when there was always smoke on your breath," Isar said. "Though not from tobacco."

"He still does that," Vivienne said, "when he gets nervous or when he's deep in thought."

Isar laughed, a strange sound to hear from him. At most, it seemed as though he was getting better at tolerating me. When I looked him in the eye, his distrust was still unmistakable. But part of the ally I remembered had returned.

"Caden, did you ever tell them of the time we destroyed the Jezerine Army in under an hour because you had the brilliant idea to send flaming boulders down upon them from the mountain?"

"He's hardly told us any stories," Nero said, removing the cigar from his mouth and taking a long drink from his wine. "But I get the feeling there was more to it than that."

"Indeed," Isar said, pounding the table. "I of course helped supply the boulders."

"Do you try to keep your past a secret?" Malin asked.

"How else do you think I managed to survive so long without you finding me?"

"Of course," Malin said, glancing down at the table. "But you haven't even told your friends?"

"I see little point in telling them every detail of my past. The three of you may look upon the battles you fought for Malketh with pride. For me, all I remember is death."

"But death for the greater good," Nels said. The ash from his cigar fell onto his empty plate as he flicked his hand. He wasn't smoking and I suspected he took it to be polite. "You have not seen the prosperity the decades-long war has brought, but you still know that we extend our hand to all to join us in our prosperity."

"By the threat of sword and fire and devastation. All of which I wrought time and time again. There is no reason to argue this. We do not see eye to eye, nor will any amount of arguing change that. We have lived very different lives and perhaps if I were in your place and you were in mine, we would still see things, not as they are, but as we perceive them to be."

"You use many words to say little," Isar said with a chuckle. "You have always been short sighted and your ability to perceive is distorted by your ego. There is right and there is wrong. You simply claim that truth is determined by circumstance. That is a lie."

I smiled, stood, placed my hands on the table, and leaned forward. "In history there are always three stories. Your side, my side, and the truth. We are often too close to see the actual picture. I simply claim that what I know I have come to learn from my experience." Lifting my hands, I looked down at my palms. "These hands have destroyed more than they have created. Done more evil than good. Tomorrow I hope to change that. Some things are more important than the conflicts of nations."

"So, you admit that evil must be destroyed for good to prosper."

I nodded, though I disagreed with the connection he was trying to draw. Still, I remained silent to give him a chance to speak.

"It's interesting that we both seek the same thing," Isar continued. "In the end, what we want to do is destroy evil, but we believe in different paths of finding success."

"Is there only one true path to walk?" Vivienne asked. She looked up at me and smiled. "There is never only one way to climb a mountain."

"I'm with Caden." Nero said. "You bastards think you're good, but if that is your intent, it is not proven through your actions."

"What would you know about us, southlander?" Malin snarled.

"The proof is in my face!" Nero opened his jaws wide, displaying his carefully crafted metal teeth. He looked like a wolf breaking his fangs and he growled to match. "Your kind has been nothing but brutal, arrogant, and self righteous. I don't know what Caden sees in you, but if I had it my way, we'd be going down there tomorrow without you."

"And you would die," Isar spat. "Just like the pathetic man you are."

Nero drew his dagger and the three sorcerers leapt out of their seats.

"Enough!" I shouted, slamming my fist upon the table. My wine glass tipped over, bounced off the cigar box, then rolled off the side of the table. I failed to catch it before it struck the ground. My glass shattered into a thousand shards. The sound of breaking glass was followed by silence. "Like I said, we're not going to be seeing eye to eye on this. Drop it and go back to your drinks and cigars."

Without any word of protest, everyone took their seats. Though Isar did so with reluctance and Nero waited until everyone else had found their place first. He set the knife on the table, picked up his cigar, and placed it towards the back of his silver molars, bit down and puffed.

Everyone remained silent for a while and when I finished my cigar, I opened the box and lit another. I felt almost bitter that what had been a pleasant afternoon had nearly been ruined by disagreement. My desire to hold onto one good night helped quell my anger and I searched my mind for something pleasant to talk about. Sadly, nothing came to mind. Just when I was about to give up and call it a night, Vivienne opened another bottle of wine and spoke up.

"So, does anyone want to hear an embarrassing story about Caden?"

Frowning, I looked over at Vivienne, a sheepish smile on her lips. Everyone seemed to perk up and I shrugged. Perhaps this type of story was just what we needed.

"About a year ago, back when we were chasing after the Wendigo, we were on our way to a tunnel."

I let out a groan and Vivienne's smile widened.

"Now, we have to hear it," Isar said, leaning forward. His demeanor had changed and he was no longer scowling.

"Go ahead, it could be worse," I said.

"Well, we were down in a ravine by one of the smaller waterways which connects to the River Earn. We found an entrance to a tunnel and while we were trying to break in through a sewer grate, this oaf slips and falls into the river. He was dressed in his red armor and the current from the water which poured into the river caused him to start flailing about. It was sort of like watching a bathing cat, the way he struggled.

Anyway, I had to pull him up out of the water to keep him from drowning. You should have seen the look on his face. Caden, who always seems to have it together, looked like a boy pulled from a well."

"Perhaps not one of my finest moments," I said with a bit of a chuckle.

Everyone around the table chuckled a little and the humor helped relieve some of the tension. Winking at Vivienne, I decided to tell another story.

"That was not one of my finer moments," I said. "But nowhere near as embarrassing as the time I picked a fight with a bull and ended up in the ground covered in shit."

"This sounds promising," Nero said. "Don't skimp on the details."

"Gather around folks and let me tell you a tale of a wayward sorcerer, his knack for getting into fights, and his desperation to fill an empty stomach."

It was late when Vivienne and I left the dining hall. I wasn't the least bit exhausted, but the wiser part of my mind knew I should try to get some rest. We were quiet as we walked through the hallways. I was beginning to feel the inevitable dread build up in my gut and I did my best not to let my mind wander. There was so much out of my control, all I could do was simply face this demon with everything I had.

"You were in an unusually pleasant mood this evening," Vivienne said as we reached the door to my room.

"I wanted to enjoy it."

"Did you?"

Smiling, I nodded. "A great deal of it."

Opening the door I paused, wondering if I should invite her

in. Vivienne glanced from me, to the floor, then back up. Looking into her dark brown eyes, I couldn't help but get lost in them.

"Are you tired?" I asked. "Or would you like to come in for one final drink?"

"Just a drink?" Vivienne said with a smirk. She slipped past me and entered my room. Waving my hand, I produced a flame on the nearby candles. Once their wicks sprung to life, I linked the flames to the others until each candle in the room was alight.

As Vivienne sauntered over to the couch in front of the fireplace, I walked to the liquor cabinet and removed a small bottle of apple brandy. It was not my preference, but it was strong, and I knew that she would like it. Taking two glasses, I filled them, then joined Vivienne on the couch. Passing her a glass, I took a moment to smell the brandy before taking a sip. The sweet flavor was both floral and sweet with a hint of oak from the barrel it had been aged in. The liquor was strong but it burned off all too quickly.

"It is going to be a restless night for me, I'm afraid," Vivienne said with a sigh.

"Well, we can always spend it together."

She took a sip of her brandy before placing the glass on the end table. Vivienne slid in beside me and rested her head on my shoulder, her eyes trained on the unlit fireplace. Reaching out my hand, I cast a small flame from the palm of my hand into the stack of wood. Bursting to life, the fire burned a bright blue.

"Can you make them dance for me?"

"Of course."

Closing my eyes, I created a mental picture of a fox before causing it to spring to life in the flames. The fox leapt from log to log, tail wagging back and forth sending sparks up towards the chimney. Another fox sprang to life, chasing the first. I continued to make them run about, causing the fire to take the shapes of a forest.

"I love when you do this," Vivienne said, wrapping her arms tighter around me and pulling herself closer. I felt myself relax and the images in the fire flickered, changing shape so they no longer depicted foxes, but instead became large soaring eagles. At first, I was taken aback by my choice, but decided not to dwell upon it. The eagle of fire soared out of the hearth and around the room before us for a few moments before I caused it to return. For an hour, I made the flames dance, creating dozens of different animals. At last, I let the flames return to normal.

"When this is all over, will they let me come with you?"

"You'd still want to, even if I am going back as a prisoner?"

"Wherever you go, I want to go."

"I would like that, though I cannot guarantee what will happen. You may have to become Malkethian."

"A small price to pay."

I leaned in and gave Vivienne a kiss. Her lips were soft and she melted into me as I pulled her close. As we kissed, I pushed all thoughts from my mind and time almost seemed to stop. In that moment everything felt right.

CHAPTER TWENTY-NINE
THE CASTLE BENEATH

The soldiers were silent as we approached the burned gates of the northern village fort. As we made our way through the gate, I noticed that the bodies had been cleared away since my last visit. Dismounting from my horse, I looked to Isar who's expression had darkened. The geomancer dawned his helmet, then dismounted. Turning around, I watched as Malin, Nels, Nero, Vivienne, and Terrowin dismounted as well. Each wore stunning armor that covered them from head to toe, and each was armed to the teeth. I couldn't help but flex my muscles, making my own armor creak. It felt good to be back in the scarlet painted steel. My horned helmet cast a strange shadow upon the ground as I took a step away from Stormcloud.

Remaining atop their horses, the company of soldiers who had volunteered to join us waited for their command. The squires, mostly young men who were not quite fighting age, started to dismount their horses and rushed to the supply wagon which was just rolling to a stop in the back. Each of them had grave expressions and most were fidgeting in their saddles.

"We will rest here for an hour," I said, patting Stormcloud's side. The horse nodded her head, then began to eat at the grass. "Then we go down."

"Dismount!" Terrowin called. "Bring forth the refreshment!"

As Terrowin continued to bark orders at the squires, I turned from the company and looked at the walls of the fort. A stillness seemed to hang in the air above it. No birds sang and no insects buzzed. Aside from the wind, the entire place was silent as a tomb. The somberness of the thought almost brought a smile to my lips.

"You seem hesitant," Isar said, stepping up beside me.

"We will need to be at our best," I replied. "Go, grab something to eat. We'll be going in soon enough."

Isar didn't utter a word of protest, but another figure took his place. Nero, who wore a helmet shaped like the head of a wolf, placed his hands on the hilt of his sword and grunted.

"Do you feel him?"

"What do you mean?"

"I sense a presence. Like we're not alone."

"He's expecting us," I said. "He's been calling out to me all morning, almost laughing in the back of my mind."

"That's a troubling revelation."

"I kept it to myself for a reason."

"What do you suspect we will find down there?"

"All manner of dark things could be waiting for us. Getting in won't be the problem. Getting out will be."

"I'm not sure I understand what you mean."

"Nero, he wants us to come, he knows why we're coming. Like I said, he's expecting us and like a spider, he's waiting for us to get trapped in his web."

"Well, it's a good thing we're going in there with you." Nero placed his gauntleted hand on my shoulder. "You're the only man I know who I believe could kill this monster."

"I appreciate the confidence you have in me. But I am also glad you are coming in with me."

"Of course my friend. I would go into the very depths of perdition with you."

Smiling, I clasped Nero on the shoulder. "Go grab something to eat. This will be the last chance."

Nodding, Nero walked away, but only returned to his horse. Undoing the clasp on my own saddlebags, I pulled out the map of the underground and began to leaf through the pages. I was confident I had most of it memorized, but I wanted to be sure. Vivienne joined me and reached into the pocket of her cloak, removed Vasha, and set him on top of the saddlebags. The rat squeaked as it looked up at me and I smiled down at it.

"Are you still certain you can guide us?" I asked, still feeling strange to be putting my trust in a rat.

Vasha nodded and lifted up his front paws. Scooping up the rat, I put him on my shoulder and continued to look over the maps, tracing the lines with my finger that denoted the pre-planned path we would take.

When the hour had passed, I called for the others to gather. The soldiers fell silent and stood in a group, remaining a few paces away from the rest of us. Looking them up and down, I nodded my respect to these men.

"I want everyone to stay close and remain as quiet as possible. I can't promise you that we won't run into trouble long before we get to our destination. These tunnels are treacherous and if any of you wander off, we may not be able to find you again."

The soldiers nodded. Most of them seemed ready to face what was about to come. Every man had been in the palace previously when the Shantenbose had attacked. Each had been told what they would face, and each was bold in their desire to see the evil hunted down and destroyed. In their eyes I could see my own fear reflected back to me. I felt honored to have them fight beside me.

"I don't have fitting words of encouragement, but I do thank you all for your willingness to face this evil with me." I paused, then turned to look over my shoulder at the burned doors of the fort. "Prepare your weapons and torches, we leave everything else behind."

~

The sound of marching soldiers echoed through the tunnels as we made our way down towards the Sunken Foundry. The flickering of torch lights cast long shadows which played tricks on my eyes. Enlarging the ball of flame which hovered beside me, I used it to dispel more of the darkness. Adjusting the heavy sack of coal which hung from my shoulder, I proceeded down the final set of stairs which would let out at the foundry.

Walking quickly but carefully, I moved down the steps and quickly found that I was outpacing the soldiers. I kept glancing periodically over my shoulder at them until we reached the bottom. Holding open the gate, I let each of the soldiers pass before letting it swing closed. The metal clanged loudly, echoing across the large open chamber. The ruined buildings of the Sunken Foundry had not changed and nothing was waiting for us.

"Where to next?" Isar asked, his voice booming as it reverberated around the cave.

I pointed to the other side where long stalactites hid the caves which Osbert and I had used when I had first entered this place. It was difficult to see and raising my hand, I caused the ball of flame to rise towards the ceiling. Like a small sun, it hovered above, its light dispelling the shadows.

"There's a cave system that will lead us further in. Once we are there, Vasha will help guide us."

Glancing at my shoulder, I nodded at the rat which was

386

resting contentedly against my right pauldron. Picking up Vasha, I bent down, and gently set him on the ground.

"We're seriously going to let the rat guide us?" Nero asked.

"That's no rat," Isar said. "He's a Puca and a rather benevolent one at that."

Vasha looked up at Isar and sniffed.

"What's a Puca?" Nero asked, taking a step back.

"It's a shapeshifter." Isar gave Vasha a nod. "Though they typically like to cause mischief. This one is kind and deserves your respect."

"Again, Vasha will lead us through the tunnels. The entrance to the caves is small and will require us to slide through on our stomachs. Once we are on the other side, we should be able to walk single file through the tunnels. At least for a while."

Everyone nodded, though I got a few discontented looks from Malin and Isar. Nels seemed almost relaxed, his breathing slow and his eyes unfocused.

"Everything alright my friend?" Isar asked, placing his hand on Nels' shoulder.

"Yes, sorry. I was just sensing something."

"There is quite a bit of water down here," I said. "The sewers that run below the city are not too far from here and I would guess that in these depths, there are plenty of caves flooded with water."

"It's more than that," Nels said. "I feel an entire network of rivers below, and they all seem to be leading deep, deep underground. Isar, do you feel anything?"

"Not much outside this cavern," he said, squatting down. Placing a thick hand on the stone, he closed his eyes. "The stones feel odd down here. Old and ancient like a ruin."

"No wonder we didn't find you down here," Malin added. "This is more extensive than I had thought."

"We aren't even close to where we are going yet," I said. "Let's get moving. No reason to waste time standing around here."

Vasha darted forward and I followed him to the far side of the cave and getting down onto my stomach, I slid underneath the opening to the cave. Though the other side was black as night, I was still able to see with absolute clarity. Nothing lurked in the darkness and I produced another flame, I broke my connection with the fire which still hovered on the other side of the cave wall.

One by one, the others crawled through the opening and once everyone was through, I looked to Vasha and nodded. The Puca lowered his head and darted forward, taking one of the tunnels that led down rather than up. I felt my anxiety build and my chest was heavy. Though I had memorized that path ahead, we were venturing into what was unknown.

This must be how everyone else is feeling, I thought.

We followed the Puca closely and as we walked I found that it never moved faster than we could follow. Where the tunnels were wide, it would speed up, and where it got narrow, Vasha would slow down. The buried city was odd in that it seemed almost like it had been partially built within a cave. What remained of the buildings were still beautiful and the stonework had a sense of delicate craftsmanship.

Being underground made it impossible to tell how much time had passed and it began to feel as if we had been wandering for hours. The unease that the place caused was growing more intense by the moment and as we went deeper the tunnels began to become more like alleyways. Running my hand against the walls, I felt the stones, touched the mortar, and peered through the empty gaps of windows. We eventually reached the end of one long narrow alleyway and emerged into what may have once been a courtyard. Though the ceiling was stone, the buildings were almost all intact and even some of the glass windows remained. I saw bloodstains on the ancient stone cobbles. The blood was fresh and the scent of death was strong. It was humid and there were other strange scents in the air which mingled with the foul odor of death. In the distance I could hear the sound of rushing water.

"What is this place?" Vivienne asked, walking past me and stopping at one of the bloodstains.

"I don't know," I replied.

Vasha darted up to the bloodstains and lowering his head he began to sniff. After a few moments, the Puca looked over at me and tilted its head. Everyone else looked at me with both amazement and fear.

"Everyone spread out and be ready for anything," Isar said. No one hesitated to obey his command. The geomancer looked at me and lifted his war hammer. Isar motioned to the far side of the street where the path deviated right and left. "Which way?"

I looked over at Vasha who squeaked, then scamped off towards the other side of the courtyard, moving far too quickly for a rat.

"Let's see what he comes back with." I said, reaching into my belt pouch where I had placed the folded map. Removing the papers, I flipped through the pages until I found where the map depicted the Sunken Foundry. Tracing the path we had taken through the tunnels, I found a place that closely resembled the strange courtyard where we stood. The two paths ahead did not look to converge again, at least to where the maps ended. The left path ended at the place where we had placed the marker, but it was still a labyrinth of tunnels away. With how the lines were drawn, I realized why it had looked so confusing before. The lines resembled a broken cityscape rather than a network of tunnels. "If I am reading the map right, we go left."

As I spoke, Vasha came scampering back and leapt up onto my leg. He scampered up my body and crawled into one of the pouches that hung on my belt. A deep roar sounded from within the caves and a few of the soldiers screamed.

My sword was in my hand in an instant and casting my flame high, I once again created an imitation sun which illuminated the courtyard cave. Off to the left street, something large retreated back into the shadows. Tucking the map back into my belt pouch, I proceeded forward, and poured flame into the gemstone cross-guard of Burnfinger. The steel of my sword went from cool gray to deep red in an instant. The light from the blade lit the cobblestones underfoot, making them look molten. I strode forward with my back straight and sword at the ready.

I allowed the ball of fire which hung above us to diminish and once more the far end of the strange underground courtyard went dark. Scratching from long heavy hands followed and whatever lurked beyond in the shadows once again began to move. My eyes searched the darkness and I saw thorny shapes moving closer. Footsteps followed behind me and pausing, I glared over my shoulder. Vivienne and the three sorcerers had their weapons drawn and were following me.

"Stay back," I commanded, gesturing backwards with an open hand. "I will take care of this creature myself."

Not waiting for their response, I turned back around and stalked towards the beast who still clung to the shadows. When I reached the edge of the courtyard, I raised Burnfinger and called out to the creature in the darkness. A hum in the air, like the buzzing of insects ensued, and from out of the shadows strode a tall boney creature covered in spines.

The flesh of the beast was white as bone, its red eyes gleaming in the light of my blade. A dozen fangs, coated in dried blood protruded from cracked lips. The face was long and narrow. Spikes protruded from the cheekbones and ran along both sides of its head, eventually morphing into long twisting horns. Taking a step forward, the long wolf-like paws of the creature had long red claws. The entire creature's body looked like skin had been stretched over twisting bones. Standing more than twice my height, the creature hunched down, strode towards me, and growled.

Through the vibrations of the sound, I felt the familiar sensation which had connected me to the Omukade. This boney monster was no different and closing my eyes, I let out a deep breath and felt within for the Empyrean. As before, when I reached for the power I felt as though I were pressed up against a window. On the other side, I could sense the sea of white filled with tiny black stars. Applying pressure, I forced my mind through the barrier and I was inside the creature's mind, looking down upon myself. Splitting my mind, my vision held two images simultaneously. The first a picture of a towering creature of bone, the second of myself. Striding forward, I raised my sword and sliced off the creature's massive boney hand.

There was no blood and my heated blade seared the flesh causing acrid smoke to drift upwards from the wound. The monster struggled for control and without hesitation, I leapt forward and slashed it across the stomach. My blade pierced the white skin easily, passing through the viscera like a hot knife through butter, and when it hit the bone, I heard a distinct popping. Pain flooded my mind and I stepped back, relinquishing my hold on the creature.

A shrill scream filled the cavern as the creature fell backwards. When it hit the ground, the two halves of the body split apart yet the top half continued to move. Arms flailing frantically, the Bone Wolf clawed its way towards me, the one remaining hand dragging the creature close. With another swipe of my sword, I cut off the top half of the creature's head. As the left side of the skull clattered to the ground, the large horn broke, shattering into several pieces. The brain-matter was a deep pink and continued to burn as the creature fell still. I watched as the head burst into flames which consumed both the brain and the flesh within seconds. Stepping back, I watched as the creature's head turned to ash.

Letting out a deep breath, I drew the fire from my sword and Burnfinger once again was nothing more than cool gray steel. Then the laughter started again in my mind. My vision began to bend and a sharp pain behind my eyes caused me to yelp. The disorientation lasted but for a moment and shaking my head, I stepped back and looked back to the others.

"Caden? Are you alright?" Vivienne called out.

"I'm fine," I said, straightening up. The group approached with caution and I saw wide eyed admiration in the eyes of the soldiers.

"Let's hope that when we do find this son of a bitch," Isar said, "you can kill it as easy as you did this bloody creature."

I scoffed. "I wouldn't count on it."

Vasha poked his head out of my belt pouch and then the Puca leapt out onto the ground. The rat scampered forward and paused as it reached the burned corpse of the Bone Wolf. As the Puca examined the body, I turned my attention back to my companions. Everyone was still holding their weapons, their faces more grim than they had been. For that I did not blame them and I hoped that they would not crumble. This was far from the worst we would see. Meeting Vivienne's eyes, I saw her concern but she gave me an encouraging smile.

"Let's keep going," Vivienne said. "Which way, Vasha?"

The rat squeaked and motioned with one of his paws down the road the Bone Wolf had emerged from. Sheathing my sword, I lifted my hand and produced a flame, drawing upon the coal stored in the sack slung over my shoulder. Vasha moved quickly but it was easy to follow him through the streets of the buried city. As we passed the half crushed and buried stone buildings, I found myself taken aback at the strangeness of the architecture.

These ruins were centuries old, the carvings ornate and more detailed than I had ever seen.

Have the caves preserved them? I wondered.

We walked for hours, and though we would see the occasional decayed corpse, nothing evil tried to lash out at us through the darkness. Keeping myself as alert as possible, I felt my senses become more in tune with the darkness. It was not unlike becoming one with the flame, feeling it live and breathe. Although I could not see everything that lurked out beyond in the small cracks and crevices between ruined buildings, I could feel them there, watching.

Perhaps against my better judgment, I reached out further with my mind, calling towards the entity who's invitation I'd followed. Him too I could sense, but it was not a figure or a creepy crawling thing that I felt. The entity was like a well of power, a great fire of shadow, that pulsed every few minutes. With each pulse, the sensation of satisfaction, greed, and rage began to grow stronger. The swell of all that raw emotion made my skin crawl.

Wiping away the sweat which was beginning to bead on my brow, I looked to Vivienne and the sorcerers. Their faces were also clammy and their breathing was growing labored.

"Does it feel hot to you?" I asked.

"It's more than just heat. I feel all sweaty," Isar answered, "like there is too much water in the air."

Nels reached out his hand and as he moved it through the air, water began to condense on his hands until a glove formed. "There's is a lot of water in the air, but I feel cold."

Malin shook her head. "I am beginning to feel trapped, like there is no air." Her face was growing pale and her hands were trembling.

Vivienne only shrugged. "I don't feel any different. It's just a cave to me."

I looked over my shoulder at the soldiers, all of whom

regarded me much in the same way Vivienne had. None of them looked any different, but I decided it was best to ask. "And all of you? Is everyone still feeling well?"

The answers came in a myriad of nods, grunts, and shrugs.

Pressing forward, we continued to follow Vasha through the streets which were growing wider. The buildings were now more consistently two or three stories high and most were intact. The cave ceiling was also starting to open up and soon it seemed like we had found ourselves in the middle of an underground city. It was similar to the Sunken Foundry, but a thousand times grander. We reached an enormous courtyard and in the center was a large round building, the outer walls lined with columns. The domed roof was of bronze and though the light from my fire was enough to cause a glimmer, most of the structure remained wreathed in shadow. Vasha stopped and motioned with his paws towards the building. Then, the Puca darted away, disappearing into the shadows.

I opened my mouth to call after him, my hand outstretched as I pointed to where the creature had vanished. Sighing, I shook my head then turned back towards the large circular building. We all marched to the large open doors Vasha had pointed us to. The entryway to the building looked like a mouth. Brass hinges still clung to the sides but the wood had long since rotted away. As we entered, the air grew more foul and the stench of rotten flesh was almost overwhelming.

The entryway was wide and the hallway went only a few feet before splitting in three directions. The large arched ceilings of the halls were beautifully carved and I recognized the carvings. Each of the Valon were depicted in their primordial forms, all raw power expertly depicted in stone. Glancing down each of the halls, I saw no movement. My fire cast long shadows and the flickering almost made it seem like something was just on the edge of jumping out at us. Reluctant, I continued forward down the hall. The doors at the end were made of metal which still shimmered slightly in the firelight as we approached.

When we reached them, I stretched forth my hand and placed my palm on the cool surface. The tarnished bronze had turned a green tint and it felt rough. The twin doors had two ring handles and taking hold of them, they made a loud grinding sound when I lifted them. The sound echoed down the hallway behind us. I froze, heart pounding in my chest, waiting for something to respond. The silent stillness of the place was like a weight that had settled over everything.

After a few moments the soldiers began to shift in their armor and the natural sounds helped ease the unnatural tension of the ancient building. Heaving hard, I pulled on the door again. I cringed as the old door scraped and whined as it was tugged open. A strange silver light poured out from the gap and I quenched the flame I'd been holding to focus my attention on opening the door. It took considerable effort to pull open just wide enough for us to get through. Without hesitation, Vivienne took the lead and went in, followed by Isar.

Malin and Nels stood on the other side of the door and motioned me forward. Entering the room, I found that the interior walls were made from the same stone as the hallways, but the stone lacework was more intricate and detailed. The high ceiling above curved inside forming a dome. Strange lights drifted through the air around the room, drifting about like specks of dust. The entire room was filled with these strange lights which drifted high above, shining their silver light down upon us. A few smaller ones drifted down from above, similar to a light snowfall. One passed before my eyes and I realized they were small gnat sized bugs that were giving off the glow.

Vivienne and Isar had only walked a few paces and both stood frozen in place. Looking past them, I saw what they were staring at. A pile of corpses sat in the center of the room. The mangled flesh was gray from death and rot had settled in. Sitting atop the pile was a small figure completely cloaked in darkness. The way the darkness moved was unnatural, seeming to flow in every direction as if buffeted by an ever changing wind. I couldn't help but feel as though the shadow was fixated on me and I didn't dare look away from it.

"I have waited an eternity for this moment."

The voice that spoke was more than a single voice. It sounded as if the wind was whispering to us, a hundred overlapping sounds coming together to form words. The voice echoed around the room and seemed to cause the very stone beneath our feet to tremble.

Before I could react, the snapping of a bowstring sounded and an arrow flew past me, soaring towards the shadow. The arrow passed through the phantom and after a few moments I heard it slam into the far wall, splintering into pieces. The phantom laughed, the shadowy form taking a clearer shape.

"Stand down!" I shouted, raising my sword. "Do not attack until I give the command. This is not him, just merely a phantom."

The phantom's shape solidified and it became a tall thin form of a man in a hooded cloak and silver mask. The creature began to clap as it descended from the mountain of decaying bodies. Pouring all of the flame which I had been holding within myself into Burnfinger, I turned the blade a bright white and leveled it towards the creature.

"Caden, what do we do?" Vivienne said, her assassin's blade in hand.

The other sorcerers stood with their weapons ready, their eyes focused on the phantom.

"Spread out and remain on guard."

I had hardly issued the command before the phantom image of Hevron stretched forth his hand and cast a bubble of evil. The tar-like bubble expanded outward, rapidly covering the ground and surrounding space. The bubble of darkness enveloped me and everything went black. My body went numb and I felt clumsy as I tried to move. I wasn't in the void for more than a moment before I began to feel the presence of a darker, more powerful being that hadn't been there before.

"Here, let me open your eyes," the words seemed to sound from all around me and from within my mind.

This entity was not of shadow, nor of light. It had no physical form nor that of the ethereal. It was a creature of mind, far more powerful than I could have ever imagined. As I took notice of this evil presence, it seemed to take notice of me. The being presented itself to me as an image in my mind. While I couldn't see it before me, I could see him as clearly as if he were standing before me.

The Lich stood taller than two men, its skeletal form long and thin. Its leathery skin was a harsh gray and was stretched across the bones but still hung loose around the joints. There was a hole in its chest, splintered ribs poking through the dilapidated flesh. A darkened heart, black as ink, pulsated every few seconds; each beat drummed loud in my ears. Atop its head was an old golden crown which was made from three interwoven bands. At each crossing of the bands, a large diamond had been set, though several were missing from their fittings. The face of the Lich was nothing more than a skull, with no eyes, nose or lips. The sharp teeth were far from human, with long fangs which hung down either side of its mouth. The eye sockets burned with a purple flame and they looked upon me hungrily.

"Welcome scion of the ancient ones. Oh how long I have waited for one such as you to come and free me from the darkness. So long have I slumbered here that I almost forgot what I was. But now, finally, you are here and I can be set free."

"I have not come to free you, but to see you destroyed. "

"You poor wretched man. Do you think I didn't know that?"

The Lich cackled. "I know you, all of your desires, all of your fears."

The Lich stretched forth his hand and the small body of Vivienne materialized from the mists of darkness. He was clasping a rope which was looped around her neck. The Lich hoisted her up and I watched as her limp body hung before me; legs dangling with her feet pointed to the ground. She looked as if she had been hanging from the gallows for days. Her bruised face was cut in several places, the skin a deep shade of purple, her eyes red and filled with blood, and her mouth hung open with a swollen tongue. I was only able to glance at her face for a moment before I turned away, closing my eyes to try and blot the image from my mind.

It's not real, I told myself.

Even knowing that it was all in my mind, the image haunted me, and I felt a profound and disturbed sickness fill my gut. I wanted to wretch and the longer my eyes remained closed, the more difficult it became to keep my bearing. The strange void seemed to be twisting and whirring around me. Opening my eyes, the strange disorienting motion ceased but I was once again presented with the terrible image of Vivienne hanging from a rope.

"No man who has ever lived has been able to kill me. Hundreds have tried and all of them have failed. This entire city was brought down and buried to try to imprison me. Even now, my bones still remain. You cannot destroy me."

"For what purpose then invite me here? You must not be all powerful or you would have escaped this prison already."

"Foolish boy. The only thing I needed from you was your flesh!"

The Lich laughed and as he did I found my hatred growing stronger. I wanted to unleash all of my power and fury at the demon. Instinctively, I reached within to draw upon the fire I kept inside and found nothing. My rage evaporated, replaced with an empty longing which gave way to fear. There was no power there, I could feel no connection to the Empyrean. It was as if a wall had been placed between me and the power. I pressed up against the barrier, felt the power alive on the other side and could sense it just outside my grasp. This time, it was not like it had been before. As I pressed against the barrier it pushed back and sent waves of pain through my mind. Screaming, I pressed all of my will against the barrier until there was no thought left within me, only pain. When the pain subsided, I was alone in the void of darkness. Turning every which way, I searched for the Lich, seeing nothing.

"Where are you!" I shouted.

"It's time for you to see." The voice sounded from all directions.

The darkness which surrounded me faded and I found myself standing once more in the large circular room. My companions were stirring, their armor creaking as they shifted back and forth. The pile of corpses in the center of the room began to move, their arms and fingers twitching. As the Deadmen slowly began to get to their feet, the sound of the bronze doors slamming echoed around the room. Raising my sword, I looked over my shoulder at the doors and watched as Vivienne and Malin rushed towards them. Together they each grasped one of the large ring door handles and tugged with all their might. The doors didn't budge. Something heavy knocked against the other side and the two women leapt back.

Groaning came from the rising Deadmen and I turned my attention back to them. As they lumbered towards us, many raised old rusty swords. Though their movements were slow, I was familiar with their strength.

"Fight to dismember," I said, trying to sound as confident as possible. "The dead fight with more tenacity than the living and cutting off their heads will not keep them from attacking."

Isar growled, raising his hammer. "Let's kill some monsters."

Reaching within myself, I found the fire burning as it should have. Pouring everything I had into my sword, I watched the blade turn a bright white. I lifted Burnfinger high over my shoulder, then swiped down at an angle. An arc of flame shot forth, striking the first row of Deadmen. The blade of flame cut through their armor and rotten flesh, causing them to crumble to the ground. Bits of burning flesh rained down upon the stones and continued to burn as new Deadmen stepped carelessly over the fallen.

"Just like old times." Isar barked a laugh then slammed his hammer into the ground. Stones shot up from the ground, knocking down another dozen Deadmen.

Seeing our foes fall easily seemed to lend courage to the soldiers. One let out a warcry which was followed by more. Joining in, I shouted my rage and rushed forward, preparing another attack. It was time to destroy these swiving monsters for good.

CHAPTER THIRTY
SEPULCHER

I cut a Deadman across his chest, Burnfinger's white hot blade slicing through the rotten corpse with ease. Dropping to the ground, I stepped over the half burned remains and I slashed the air, casting a blade of flame which struck a dozen Deadmen all at once. Their flesh ignited and exploded before falling to the ground. Burning like oil, the flesh and entrails covered the stones, spreading to the other Deadmen. Drawing upon the coal in the sack slung over my shoulder, I poured energy into the flames and created a wall to help protect our right side. The Deadmen on the other side did not try to cross the wall of fire.

As we continued to fight I began to notice how the soldiers desperately grappled with the Deadmen, struggling to defeat the stronger foe. The fighting corpses moved savagely and with more power than was natural for any man. I watched as one of our soldiers was struck down, his throat slashed by a broken blade. His body hit the ground, and as blood began to leak out onto the stone floor, he got to his knees, lifted his blade, and started fighting with his comrades. The newly created Deadman's face began to droop and his skin shriveled and decayed in seconds.

Fighting with all my strength, I hacked and slashed at the animated corpses. Again, as my fiery sword cut apart the rotten flesh, the corpses burst apart, flaming pieces raining down upon the ground. Continuing to pour energy into Burnfinger, I burned a large portion of the coal in my sack and once again the blade became white hot. Slashing wide, I cast another blade of flame from my sword which traveled forward, slashing apart dozens of the Deadmen. As their bodies were torn apart, their smoldering pieces dropping to the ground, I caught sight of the shadowy form of the Lich. He was hovering in the air, his arms outstretched, a large smile on his skeletal face.

A sound from across the room drew my attention away from the Lich and to my dismay, more Deadmen began to pour in through the doors on the far end of the room. Laughter erupted from above, a sound which chilled me to my bone. Raising my hand, I threw a ball of flame at the Lich who still hovered twenty feet above the ground. The fire struck him, dispelling the figure into bits of shadow which dripped like oil to the ground. Casting ball after ball of flame at the bits of liquid shadow, I tried to dispel all traces of the figure. As the smoke cleared, I saw that the stone floor was poked with holes, the rubble all strewn about.

Lifting my burning hands, I felt more energy surge within me, feeding the power to keep it raging. Something was burning in the ground below my feet and I felt the traces of fire go deep into the earth. Cracks in the ground began to glow from the fire and within a few moments, the floor where the Lich had disappeared looked molten. Holding out my hand, I pulled as much power as I could from the ground and placed it into Burnfinger. Fighting my way through another cluster of Deadmen, I reached the pock-marked floor and drove my sword into the ground. The floor below my feet began to tremble and hundreds of Deadmen rushed towards me. These new men who had come from the far side of the room wore armor of a strange make and their bodies were significantly larger than my own.

As these new enemies began to crowd around me, I threw balls of fire at them. The fire caused their bones to break upon impact and the dried withered flesh to burn like paper. Within moments I was surrounded by a hundred burning skeletons who were striking me with their swords. Dropping to my knees, I once more pulled upon the power and screaming, sending a surge of flame out from my body in all directions. The wave of flame disintegrated the corpses, turning the ground to molten rock which began to flow towards me. A loud cracking sound ensued and the ground I knelt upon dropped down several feet, sending me tumbling forward. Rolling to a stop, I began to lift myself up off the ground when the floor broke again, a large hole opening up before me.

"Caden, get away from there!" Isar screamed. I looked over at the geomancer who's eyes were wide with alarm.

Another large section of the ground broke apart and fell into darkness. The hole which had opened was getting larger by the second as huge sections continued to collapse in. Climbing to my feet, I raced back away from the hole as the ground continued to break below me. As I approached the edge, a large crack opened up and separated me from the others. Isar held out his hand, beckoning me to join him. As I bent down, preparing to leap, the stone beneath my feet collapsed and fell. Tumbling backwards, I hit the broken floor as it sank into the pit.

"No!" The cry slipped past my lips as I fell into the darkness.

I struck several stone landings on my way down through the darkness which helped to break my fall. Something reached out and grabbed me in the darkness, enveloping my body like I was being wrapped in a sheet. I lost all sensation in my body and my mind seemed partially detached. The loss of motor control made me feel like I was riding inside my own body like a spectator. The experience was similar to when I was in the mind of a dark creature, but instead I was inside my own body. Whatever was controlling my body moved it through the darkness with such speed and precision that I landed uninjured upon the ground of the cave below. The rocks and stones still tumbled and fell around me and I watched as they skidded to a halt. As the last few stones grew still, my flaming sword struck the ground, the tip driving several inches into the floor. Burnfinger's fire slowly faded and the cave went still.

A sudden hollowness filled me and I gasped. I once again regained control of my body and the pain which slammed into me temporarily overwhelmed my mind. As my head began to clear, I took in several quick breaths. The sudden shock of regaining connection with my body faded and though I felt immense anxiety, I was able to climb to my feet. Stumbling forward, I paused and looked from the rubble strewn ground to the broken ceiling.

More than half of the floor above had caved in and the stone was more than fifty feet thick in some places. The sounds of fighting came down from above and through the hole I could still see flickering torchlight. My eyes lingered upon the hole for only a moment before I looked back at my surroundings. Walking to my sword, I pulled Burnfinger from the ground and taking in a deep breath, I pulled fire from one of the torches above. A small flickering light shot down from the hole and ignited the gemstone set into the cross guard. Linking the fire to the sack of coal slung over my back, I fed my sword until the blade once again shone a brilliant white. The pack was considerably lighter than it had been and looking under my arm at it, I saw a long tear in the side. Cursing, I adjusted the pack so it hung diagonally across my back, I whispered a silent prayer to the Valon that what remained would be enough.

Holding my sword aloft, I lit the way and began to make my way forward. Eyes that had been growing accustomed to seeing in the dark now seemed to be able to cut through it entirely. The walls of the cave were covered with thousands of skulls. Most of the skulls were recognizably human in shape, but every so often there was one which was larger, more animalistic, or so distorted that I couldn't begin to imagine which creature it had belonged to. These skulls were not randomly placed, instead forming a matching pattern. It was hauntingly beautiful the way a grave-yard could be, yet there was a true and disturbing wrongness to it as well.

At the edge of the skull lined cave was a large hallway carved from the stone. Large pillars lined this hallway, each similarly set with skulls. None of the skulls on these pillars were human. They were of the distorted type, of beasts and monsters that were born from darkness. I recognized the familiar horned skulls of a Wendigo among them. I scoured the room for signs of the Lich and found nothing. With hesitant steps, I crossed the giant cavern and proceeded down the hallway.

My armor grew heavier with every step. Lumbering down the hallway, I walked past rows of pillars and looked down other narrow passageways which lined either side. The darkness ahead called to me and I could feel its power urging me forward. At the end of the hall, it opened up into a large rectangular room with an arched ceiling. The pillars which lined the sides of this room had been carved to look like the statues of men with monstrous heads. Each was in a position where their hands were raised above their heads to give the appearance that they were holding up the ceil-ing. The sculpting of the statues was immaculate and was untouched by age. There was something haunting about their beauty and I felt compelled to marvel at them. After my eyes had traced the lines of each of the statues, my gaze finally fell upon the stone dais on the far side of the long rectangular chamber.

The dais was raised half a dozen feet into the air, stone steps lining the entire front. Upon the dais sat a throne and sitting upon it was the withered body of the Lich. He didn't move like he had when he had appeared before me in the void of evil, and his body was only the size of a man. The boney body and face looked brittle and the old golden crown that sat upon its head was tarnished. There was a purple flame in the otherwise empty eye sockets and it looked as if the creature had been sitting there for thousands of years. The shadowy figure the Lich had taken above appeared before the corpse on the throne and held his hands towards me.

"Take up the crown and all my power will be yours."

The voice spoke in my mind and I felt my entire body shake from the power of it. I stepped forward, unable to help myself as I walked towards the throne. The shadowy figure bowed his head to me as I approached and the glowing purple eyes of the Lich looked hungry. My attention only lingered upon the shadow for a moment as I climbed onto the dais. With eager, greedy hands, I reached out to take hold of the crown.

"Stop!"

The voice broke the spell that was in my mind and I staggered back, my hand dropping to my side. I glanced back into the burning eye sockets of the Lich and though the creature didn't move, I was suddenly filled with anger. Something stirred in my chest and with fury, I whirled around, raising Burnfinger in an aggressive stance.

"Caden!" Isar shouted from the large hallway on the other end of the throne room. "What are you doing?"

Looking at him, I growled, my hands tightening on my sword. "Get back! I can't control myself."

Isar paused, his eyes glancing from me to the Lich and back. "We must destroy it!"

Lifting his hammer, Isar slammed it into the ground, causing the stone floor to crack. My feet became unsteady on the shaking dais and leaping away from the throne, I watched as the breaking ground reached the throne. The stone split and the high back of the throne cracked, the corner falling off the side. When a chunk of the throne struck the ground, it shattered into dozens of pieces which tumbled down off the dais to the floor.

The shadow which stood beside the corpse began to grow until it was almost the size of the statue columns that lined the room. With a massive hand, it reached out towards Isar and beckoned him forward.

"Isar!" The deep voice called out. "Take up the crown and all my power will be yours."

My blood went chill and I watched Isar pause, all color draining from his face. Almost like one of the Deadmen, he began to stalk forward, much as I had.

"No!" I shouted, rushing back to the throne.

Reaching for the crown, my fingers grazed the gold when a large stone struck me in the side. The impact sent a shockwave through my armor and I dropped to the ground. Yelping in pain, my lips pulled back in a snarl and another stone struck me in the side of the head and my world began to spin. Falling to the ground, I watched through blurry vision as Isar sent a third stone into the air. It soared past me, striking the base of the throne.

The front of the throne broke apart and the immobile body of the Lich fell forward. When the dried corpse struck the ground, the withered bones broke and crumbled to dust. Sliding forward, the golden crown skittered across the floor and landed at Isar's feet. Dropping his torch and hammer to the ground, Isar stooped down and picked up the crown.

Placing the crown upon his head, the rest of his body turned white as fresh snow. Even the hair of his beard went white, making them look frozen and brittle. Along with these sudden changes in his appearance, there was one change that was more disturbing. His eyes began to glow with purple fire. The shadow which had been looming above soared through the air and entered Isar's body. As the darkness became one with the geomancer's flesh, his body started to change. The bones below the skin began to shift and grow, causing the man to increase in height by several feet. Long twisting horns sprouted from his head, curling around the golden crown. Isar smiled and lifted his hands and large shadows burst from them, soaring into the walls.

The skulls began to tumble free from their places on the walls as something large pounded them free from the other side. Rolling to the side, I avoided being struck by one of the large horned skulls as it dropped from above. Large boney hands began to emerge from the walls, followed by long spined arms. Five Bone Wolves, much larger than the one I had killed above, began to crawl out of walls, their long spiked tails whipping back and forth.

Moving too fast to see, the Lich possessed Isar crossed the distance between us in an instant. Looking into the creature's glowing purple eyes, I felt as though I was looking into a void. The Lich opened its mouth and growled as he plunged his hand into my stomach. When the creature pulled its hand from me, blood sprayed from the wound, covering its arm. I collapsed to the cold stone floor and watched as my blood pooled around me. Reaching down, the Lich picked up Burnfinger, held him high, the metal point still glowing a bright white, then plunged the blade into my chest.

My entire body erupted with a bright white light and pain was all I knew. That pain erupted into a great flame and I felt every fiber of my being ignite with heat and power. Opening my eyes, the world around me was wreathed in flame, as if viewed through red glass. Flame, the color of blood, flickered up and down my arms, cracking the metal of my armor which started to glow from the heat. Looking up, I saw that no corner remained in darkness, but the figure who stood before me seemed untouched by the light. The Lich walked back for a few steps, joining the Bone Wolves who had fully emerged from the walls.

Sitting up, I looked down at my sword as it stuck out from my chest. I reached up and grasped Burnfinger's hilt and tried to pull the sword from my chest. Removing the blade only an inch, I was overwhelmed once again with blinding pain. A deep roar emanated from within me that was so fierce and bestial, I couldn't believe it had truly come from my throat. Control of my own faculties began to fade and I fell to the ground.

Struggling to breathe, I placed both hands on Burnfinger's hilt. Instead of trying to pull the blade out, I pushed it deeper within me. Wincing in anticipation of additional pain, I was surprised to only feel my own power grow and intensify. Burnfinger's hilt began to melt, turning to molten steel which dripped down the front of my breastplate, melting away a large hole. The steel was hot and gave off an almost euphoric sensation as it sank deep into my flesh. Glancing down, I watched the blade melt and soak into my flesh leaving behind a strange silver mark upon my bare chest. This mark faded and was replaced by charcoaled flesh and flame. Whatever the Lich had done to me by stabbing me with my talisman sword had given me incredible strength.

Climbing to my feet, I opened my mouth and let out a roar. The deep primordial rage which filled me caused the room around us to shake, dislodging more skulls from the broken walls. As they tumbled to the ground, the Lich snarled at me. Raising his finger, the monster pointed at me and screamed, "*Kill him!*"

The five Bone Wolves rushed towards me, their claws digging into the stone as they went, jaws opening wide to reveal rows of sharp fangs. My pulse quickened and raising my hands, I visualized two swords of flame in my hands. An instant after these images had formed in my mind, the fire which burned around my body rushed towards my fingers and formed the long blades. The flames, dark as blood, turned almost solid, the edge sharp as a razor. Rushing forward, I met the first Bone Wolf head on, slashing at him with my swords.

Slicing off the creature's snout, I stepped to the side and watched as the creature barreled into the wall of skulls. Bone fragments sprayed into the air as I leapt onto the creature's back and drove the flame blades deep within the Bone Wolf's flesh. The fire hissed and the insides of the creature began to glow. Letting out a deep breath, I flared the blades and the corpse burst apart. Flaming entrails sprayed the walls and ceiling.

The other Bone Wolves didn't hesitate and fell upon me one after the other. Dancing between their slashing claws and whipping tails, I hacked and slashed the creature's apart. When their claws did rake across my armor, the flames which burned around me caused them to catch fire. I moved like living fire, easily destroying the beasts. Soon I was standing in the midst of burning gore, caramelizing blood burning around my feet.

Shrouded in darkness, the Lich remained still. We looked at each other, and in the creature's burning eyes I could see all of the malice and hatred he harbored for the world. A blade of shadow formed in his hand and he raised it high in challenge.

I could feel the fire raging within me diminishing and wondered how long this newfound energy would last. Merging the two blades of flame into a single sword, I rushed towards the monster, determined to end this fight. Our swords clashed and flame and shadow seemed to become one, spiraling around us. Back and forth we fought, our blows striking fast and fierce. The more we fought, the fiercer we became. After each blow, I felt my power diminish by degrees. As I was reaching the edge of my limit, my flameblade began to shrink. With power enough for one more attack, I sidestepped a strike and thrust my blade forward. Striking the Lich in the shoulder, I drove the flameblade deep until it went through the other side.

Smiling wide, I looked into the creature's glowing purple eyes.

The Lich laughed, wrapped it's hand around my neck to pull me closer, then thrust upward with his own blade. The blade of shadow struck my stomach, piercing my side before breaking out the back of my armor. The blood-red flames which burned around the hole were snuffed out.

"Now, we shall become one."

The Lich pulled the blade from my side and tightening its grip around my neck, lifted me up off the ground. Snarling, the Lich bared its fangs before biting down upon my shoulder. My world was consumed by darkness and all pain vanished in an instant. Floating through the void, I was cold. My first thought was of death.

Is this what is waiting for me on the other side?

No sooner had the thought crossed my mind than did the ground beneath my feet solidify. My feet felt like they had been placed on blocks of ice and I walked through the dark vapor which obscured my view in all directions. There was something familiar about the place and I closed my eyes and tried to remember. I heard something move behind me and spun around. I raised my fists and watched another figure emerge from the thick vapors. He walked with sure footing and his expression was grave. Isar, ten years younger and healthy, stopped several feet away. His beard was grown, the burns on his face gone. Isar folded his arms as he looked at me, his eyes uncertain.

"What trickery is this?" Isar asked. "Are we both dead?"

"No," I answered, recognizing this place. "I've been here before, though I am uncertain what exactly this place is."

The memory of being trapped in this place after entering the mind of the Shantenbose sent a chill down my spine. Kori had been there to rescue me then. Now, there was no one I would be able to rely upon.

"So where are we exactly?"

"It is a void, a space between thought and reality. A shadow realm I have traveled to before after using necromancy."

"How did we get here? I am struggling to remember what happened. You look so young." Isar reached up and touched his own face, running his fingers through his beard. "What is happening to us, Caden?"

"You picked up the crown and the Lich took control of your body. He's taking mine now as well. I don't know if it's already too late for us."

"We have to try and do something."

"How?" I asked, desperation in my voice. "I have done what I can and it wasn't enough."

"You said you've been here before. How did you get out the last time?"

"I had help, my friend pulled me out of it."

"Then there has to be a way."

Isar knelt down upon the ground, placing his hand on the strange floor. After a few moments Isars expression changed. His face contorted with pain, his teeth bared. Grunting, Isar pulled his hand back and let out a howl.

"Isar, what's wrong?"

"I, I can sense him." Isar reached up and placed his hand over his heart. "Can you still feel your body?"

Taking in a breath to control my emotions, I tried to sense my body. Again, I felt nothing. "No. I cannot feel it."

Despair welled up inside. I looked down at my hands and hanging from my wrist was the bone white talisman. It was as it had been before, unmarred by the flame. My fear and frustration faded and a sense of clarity replaced the turmoil within my mind. The Lich had allowed me to use necromancy. He shared his power with me and in so doing, might have provided me a way to escape. I no longer felt lost or afraid.

This fight isn't over yet, I thought, extending my hand to Isar. "Take my hand."

Isar looked up at me, the anguish on his face lessening. Reaching up, he clasped my hand. Heaving, I pulled him to his feet. As I looked into my old friends eyes, I felt my resolve solidifying. I held up my arm and showed Isar the talisman.

"I might have a chance to break free of this place and drag you free. Take hold of my wrist and reach out for the Empyrean."

Isar obeyed and his grasp was tight, driving the bone bracelet into my arm. There was no pain, but I felt a sense of pressure around my hand. Closing my eyes, I reached out for the Empyrean and what I found was different than I had expected. Once more, the well of power had changed. It was not the sea of black filled with white stars. It was not the sea of white with black stars. Instead it was a sea of flame and shadow. The two powers twisted together, mixing in strange patterns. Within the twisting shapes I could feel the power of creation and destruction, of life and death. The true power of the Valon was made manifest.

"Get ready. I'm going to try and pull us both out."

"Caden. If we survive this, I don't want to be enemies."

"We won't be."

With a smile, I closed my eyes and reached out towards the Empyrean. Drawing upon the power, I pulled it towards me. Energy flowed into my body and the cold which had set in vanished. Heat seared my skin and rushed through my body like blood. Every fiber of my being began to tingle from the overwhelming power. When I opened my eyes, I was once more in my body, the Lich's jaws firmly clamped down upon my shoulder. I erupted into blood red and black flame. The Lich released its fangs from my shoulder, pulled away, and screeched in agony. I roared in response which caused the flames to burn larger. Spinning around us, the heat from the fire began to turn the stone into slag. The statues began to melt, the stone forming pools of molten rock on the ground.

Backing away, the Lich dropped to his knees. The glowing purple in its eyes was diminishing and the features were twisting once more. Opening his mouth, the Lich spat black bile onto the ground. The liquid continued to gush from its mouth for a few seconds before it was followed by white chunks of bone.

"Kill me!" the creature screamed. I could her Isar's voice mingled with that of the Lich. "Do it, Caden!"

Raising my hand, I conjured a final flame which swirled together both black and red. Coalescing into a blade, the flame turned solid and I thrust it forward into the Lich's chest. The creature's body exploded. Fragments of flesh and bone sprayed out in all directions, small pieces burning as they struck the ground. Tumbling forward, the head rolled to a stop at my feet. The Lich's eyes glowed for a moment before the purple fire was snuffed out.

Slowly the strange blood red and black fire which wreathed my body faded, leaving me in total darkness. I collapsed to the ground, having no energy left within to remain upright, and felt myself enter the void. Whether it was sleep or death, I wasn't sure, but my mind didn't seem to care either way. Whichever it was, I welcomed it.

CHAPTER THIRTY-ONE

SHATTERED THRONE

When I awoke, I was still lying upon the stone in absolute darkness. I could no longer see in the dark and when I reached inside myself there was no power and no fire to be found. Rolling onto my back, I once again closed my eyes and rested. Though I never truly slept, I teetered on the edge of consciousness. The stillness inside of me was like a balm to my soul. The aching anxiety which had been ever present was gone and I truly realized what a burden it had been. Finally, I found myself feeling content. I had accomplished what I had set out to do. I had defeated the evil which had caused the deaths of those I loved.

Time seemed to pass slowly and my exhaustion was soon replaced by hunger and thirst. Still, I continued to lay on the ground. I supposed that even if I was able to find my way back through the darkness, I would never be able to climb out of the pit. My only remaining hope was that the others had survived.

When torchlight flickered on the walls and ceiling, my first thought was that I was dreaming. Shortly after, I heard the echoes of footfalls and the chattering of people. Sitting up, I looked over at the entrance to the throne room and waited for my saviors to arrive. The first person who came into view was Malin. She was holding a torch in one hand and a javelin in the other. One of the statue pillars had melted in front of the entrance and she easily leapt over the now cooled stone. Landing softly on her feet, Malin scanned the room, her eyes opening wide when she saw me.

Lifting her javelin, Malin prepared to attack. I raised my hand and gestured for her to stop. My fingers were charcoal black and my armor was in ruin. Reaching up, I removed my helmet. The horns had been burned away and charred stumps were all that remained of them. The metal was covered in cooled steel scale, making it look old and withered. Placing the helmet on the ground beside me, I turned my attention back to Malin. Knowing that I must look unrecognizable, I remained as still as possible. Malin regarded me with wary eyes and held her javelin at the ready.

"It's me. Caden." My voice was dry and hoarse.

"Caden's alive!" She cried, waving the torch.

The sound of footfalls were loud as the others quickened their pace. Two more figures came into view and I smiled when I saw Vivienne's face. Nels helped her over the rubble and she leapt down onto the ground beside Malin. Vivienne sprinted past Malin and dropping to her knees, slid to a halt beside me. Wrapping her arms around me, she pulled me into an embrace, tears spilling down her cheeks.

"What happened to you?"

I didn't answer.

Holding onto Vivienne, I looked back to Malin who helped Nels down off the rubble. The two sorcerers looked at me for only a moment before they began to search the room, clearly looking for Isar. It took me longer than it should have to summon enough courage to speak.

"He's gone," I said, my words though soft, were clear in the silence.

Both of the sorcerers stopped, their shoulders sagging.

Vivienne held me close for a moment longer before pulling away and helped me to my feet. Leaning on her for support, we walked several feet to the remains of the Lich. The head, neck, and upper shoulders were still intact, but the larger portion of this body was little more than clumps of charred flesh. The blood which had pooled around the remains was hard and glistened in the torchlight.

Nels and Malin joined us beside the remains as the other soldiers reached the entrance. They called out to us, and Nels waved them away. Remaining on the other side of the rubble, they seemed content just to look into the room. I was happy to find that most of them had survived. Nero was the last to come into view, guarding the back of the group. His arm was wrapped in a sling and he gave me a stiff nod. His eyes scanned the skull covered walls with distrust, as if Nero expected something to leap out at him at any moment.

The sorcerers stood beside Isar's corpse for a time. Both were upset but Nels hid his emotions a little better. I remained silent while they examined the body. Eventually, both turned to look at me. Malin had tears in her eyes.

"I'm glad you all made it," I muttered.

"Sorry it took us so long to mount our rescue," Nels said, his voice hollow.

"I am sorry I could not save him."

"What happened?" Malin asked, her voice tight.

I pointed to the far side of the room at the shattered throne and explained to them what had happened. How the Lich had tried to get me to take the crown and how Isar had ended up with it. No one interrupted me and I didn't hold back a single detail. When I finished, I found myself unable to meet their eyes.

"I'm so sorry. He saved me twice in the end. Saved me from

picking up the crown and again saved us all by sacrificing himself."

"You did what was required," Nels said. "Isar knew that. I believe that had the positions been changed, you would have done the same."

I found myself at a loss for words and swallowed the lump that was forming in my throat.

"How did you survive?" I asked, once again looking at the soldiers. Everyone looked as haggard as I felt.

"When you fell into the hole, we kept fighting." Vivienne answered. "Isar helped us break through the wall and once we were in the corridor it became easier to fend them off. Then he went after you. I don't know how long we fought, but they drove us back and out of the building. It didn't matter how many of the Deadmen we cut down, they just kept coming. I thought we were going to be destroyed. Then all at once, the Deadmen stopped and fell to the ground. To be safe, we cut them all apart and scattered the bodies, but none of them moved."

"Sorry it took us so long," Malin added, "it took some doing to find a way to climb down into the pit."

"We weren't going to leave you." Nels said, placing his hand on my shoulder.

"Thanks for coming for me."

I paused, then with Vivienne's help, got to my feet. I stepped over to the remains of the Lich. The head and shoulders were still intact and the tarnished golden crown was held in place by the twisting horns. Reaching down, I grabbed one of the horns, and tried to lift it up. I only had the strength to lift it an inch off the ground. Grunting, I set the head back down.

"Will one of you take this?"

"Why?" Nels asked.

"I know it's gruesome, but this needs to be shown to the

queen. Everyone should know what happened here and what so many people gave their lives to defeat."

Nels bowed his head, muttered something under his breath, then picked up the Lich head. Placing it on his shoulder, he let out a sigh, and started towards the exit.

"Come on Caden," Vivienne said. "Let's get the hell out of this place."

When we emerged from the tunnel, the scents of the fresh air were a welcome relief. The sun shone brightly in a cloudless sky. A gentle breeze rustled the grass of the fort lawn and brought with it the crisp scent of pine. Closing my eyes, I basked in the warm sunlight for a moment while the others emerged from the corner building. Many of the soldiers collapsed onto the grass, sighing with relief or letting out whoops of joy. Sitting down upon the grass, I rolled my shoulders to loosen them. My body hurt terribly, all of my muscles sore to the point that even breathing was difficult. I feared that if I sat down to rest, I would be unable to continue. Vivienne stood beside me and I smiled up at her.

"Are you feeling well?" I asked.

"I assume I'm holding up better than you." She smiled at me, leaned down, and kissed my forehead. "You rest here a bit. I will go fetch the horses and squires."

Vivienne hurried away, disappearing through the fort gate. I looked around at the others and saw that they too were sitting on the ground to rest. Malin and Nels were sitting together with their backs against the small stone building which hid the tunnel. They had been silent for most of the journey back to the surface and now they were whispering to each other. Leaving them be, I turned and waved to Nero who was adjusting his sling. He got up from where he sat and came over to join me.

"You alright?" I asked as he sat down beside me.

"Fine, just a little uncomfortable. Not my first bone fracture. Nothing too serious."

"Good. I'm glad."

"What about you? No offense, but you look rather terrible."

I lifted my scorched hand, examining my charcoal colored skin. The lines and cracks made me look like I was made from burned wood. Flexing my fingers, I felt a tightness in my joints but no pain.

"Don't worry about me. I look much worse than I feel."

"Is it just me, or do you also feel an immense sense of relief?"

"You're not alone there. I feel almost tranquil. Can't remember the last time I felt like that."

"So, what now?"

"Head back to Seraphina's palace. I'll figure everything else out later."

It seemed like no time at all before Vivienne returned. She helped me to my feet and together we walked across the fort lawn towards the gate. We moved with slow determination and it took most of my focus to put one foot in front of the other. The bottoms of my feet throbbed and every time I stepped on a small stone or knot in the grass, a sharp pain shot up my heel or down my toes. Just beyond the gate, the squires were preparing the horses. Most were ready, and only a few horses were without saddles.

Stormcloud stood in the front of the group, the majestic white horse grazing on the wild grass. Vivienne helped me over to my horse and up into the saddle. Holding onto the pommel of the saddle, I let Stormcloud continue to graze while the others mounted. Vivienne started to make a few adjustments to her saddlebags. She worked quickly and soon was in her saddle, ready to ride back to Kings Keep.

Nels walked up to my horse, holding the Lich head in both hands. "What do you want me to do with this?"

"Will you strap it to the back of Stormcloud?"

Nels nodded and then tied the head to the back of the saddle. He left without saying another word, joining Malin by their horses. I forced myself not to stare at them and instead began to stroke Stormcloud's mane.

"Caden," Vivienne said, holding out a wineskin. "Drink this."

Taking it, I popped open the cork and drank greedily. The cool wine was refreshing and I felt a little more invigorated. Wiping my mouth on the back of my hand, I then used my hand to hammer in the cork before passing it back to Vivienne.

"So," she said, looking at the Lich head which swung from the back of Stormcloud's saddle. "What are you going to do with that?"

"Take it to the Queen."

"Is that where we will go first?"

"I was going to accompany the soldiers back to the Castle, but I think Nero should go back to Seraphina's, tell her what happened and make sure his arm is properly tended to."

"Are you sure you don't want to rest first? I'm certain we can present the Lich head to the Queen once you are feeling better."

"I'd rather just get it over with." I looked up at the cloudless sky and scratched my head.

"If you don't mind, I'd like to go back with Nero. I can see that food and a hot bath are prepared for you when you arrive."

"That sounds wonderful," I said, smiling wide. "Thank you."

Vivienne laughed, pulled open the wineskin, and took a drink.

Within the hour we were riding back down the mountain towards the northern road. My body swayed from side to side as I rode in Stormcloud's saddle. My horse, moving quickly and confidently, took the lead. The clopping of hooves and gentle movements of the strong muscles below me were rhythmic and I slowly felt myself drifting off to sleep. Shaking my head, I gripped the pommel of the saddle hard in order to keep myself awake.

It was early afternoon when we arrived at Kings Keep. We were ushered through the gates quickly and a messenger was sent to inform the Queen of our arrival. Riding down the main road which ran between the gates, we were slowed by the carts and everyday merchants. It was interesting to watch them, so oblivious to what we had just gone through. Surprisingly, I found myself happy to know that we had not failed and these people were now safer than they had ever been, though most would never know it.

When we reached the crossroads, we parted ways with Vivienne and Nero who took the horses of those who did not make it with them. The road to the Castle was less packed than the main road and those who were in the streets moved out of our way to let us pass. When we arrived at the gate, the guards were prepared and hailed us through.

The guards called out to the soldiers who parted ways, taking the side path towards the Queen's stables. Riding Stormcloud, Malin and Nels rode behind me. Glancing back, I eyed the sorcerers who both looked exhausted.

"Have you decided what you're going to do?" I asked.

Neither one of them answered.

"We can leave whenever you are feeling ready. I should be able to recover on the road."

"Caden," Nels said. "We can discuss this later."

Turning back around, I pulled my shoulders back and tried to look as alert as possible. When we arrived at the end of the Castle drive, the front doors were guarded by soldiers who wore brightly polished armor and deep crimson capes. They saluted us as we dismounted and the doors opened. The Queen's master servant

Ervin stepped out of the Castle, long dark red robes flowing down to the ground.

Removing the Lich head from Stormcloud's saddles, I held it out by the horns, careful not to let the dangling neck and shoulder touch me. Emerging from behind my horse, the severed head came into view of the guards and Ervin. Each shied away from it, several turning their heads away. It truly was a rotten thing, but seeing their reaction denoted that I had made the right choice in bringing it. These people needed to know what it is we destroyed.

"Please, if the three of you would follow me," Ervin said, his smile returning. Clasping his hands behind his back, he turned around and walked back into the palace.

I motioned for Nels and Malin to go first and I remained a few paces behind as I followed them into the Castle. The guards pulled the doors closed as soon as I entered, the loud knock of hard oak on stone echoed around the large central atrium. The brass bowl in the center of the room was burning bright. Ervin led us around it and as we passed, I held out my hand, feeling the heat of the fire. My eyes lingered on the coals flickering flames and a small hollowness filled me. Smiling sadly as we passed the fire, I lowered my hand and tucked my thumb behind my belt.

Preceding down the main hall, we arrived at the open doors to the throne room where a long line of guards stood at attention. The red carpet which had been laid out leading to the throne was littered with red flower petals. Many of the nobles who lived in the Castle were in attendance, along with the judges and magistrates who oversaw the legal dealings of the city. Murmurs spread through the crowd as we approached and several people screeched with alarm as I lifted up the severed head.

The Queen, dressed in a long gown of black and red, was looking at me with a blank expression. Her long auburn hair was woven into the eight spikes of her crown which almost reminded me of the horns upon the Lich head I held before me. Her eyes seemed fixated upon the severed head. As we got close, I saw her squirm in her throne before she uncrossed her legs. Standing, the Queen lifted her hand and everyone went silent.

"Welcome Caden, Malin, and Nels. I see that you have been successful in your task. Will you present the head for all to see?" Pricilla gestured for me to join her upon the dais.

Climbing the steps, I took hold of the horns with both hands and lifted the head high. Turning from side to side, I gave everyone time to see the head and watched as most turned away. After it had been shown off, I lowered the Lich head and turned to Pricilla.

"My Queen. Here is the head of the beast that is responsible for the death of your sister. I ask that you make a remembrance of this evil that it will not be forgotten nor repeated."

"Thank you. Please, lay it at my feet."

I did as Pricilla asked, and setting the head down, I retreated back down the steps of the dais and joined the other sorcerers.

"To honor you in this great deed, I rescind your banishment and declare you a hero of the city. And to you, Malin and Nels, the same honor will be bestowed upon the two of you. A monument shall be erected so this deed shall never be forgotten."

"Thank you," I said bowing deeply.

The Malkethian's bowed as well, but remained silent.

"May I also request that those who gave their lives fighting this evil be remembered as well?"

"Of course."

Turning to Nels, I reached out my hand and he narrowed his eyes in surprise. "Will you give me the hammer?"

Nodding, the hydromancer removed Isar's war hammer from his belt and passed it to me. Stepping forward, I placed it next to the Lich head. Pricilla nodded, her lips pressing to a thin line for a moment.

"On this day, let it be remembered that the noble and valiant

Isar gave his life in the fight against this evil. His name shall also be remembered as a hero and savior of Kings Keep."

The Queen bowed her head to me, then sat back down upon her throne. The crowd was silent and I looked out over them. I felt a strange reverence from everyone, and when I looked back at the Queen, I saw her eyes were glistening.

"So that this deed may be documented, will you please give a full account of the proceedings, from the beginning."

I told my story, beginning with my first encounter with the dead bandits almost a year ago. Detailing everything that had passed, I recounted events as honestly as possible. All the while, one of the Queen's scribes wrote down my words, making a record which would be added to the annals of the city.

CHAPTER THIRTY-TWO
NO LONGER

Sitting at Seraphina's dining table, I lingered while the others went out onto the balcony to watch the fireworks. Pouring myself another cup of wine, I drank it slowly, relishing in the soft buzz that filled my head. Hearing the crack, pop, and sizzle of the fireworks outside, I half smiled to myself, pleased to have a moment to myself. My body still ached and after three days, I was beginning to wonder if I would ever recover. Rubbing my chest, I grimaced as pain shot down my sternum and into my abdomen.

When I finished my wine, I got up from the table, sparing a glance at those standing on the balcony, and saw that Seraphina was looking at me. The other members of the Syndicate, along with the Malkethian's were still drawn to the fireworks, but Seraphina didn't so much as spare them a glance. She beckoned me to join her and with a bit of effort, I managed to get out of my chair. With slow careful steps, I walked over to the balcony and joined them. Seraphina didn't say anything to me, finally turning to watch the fireworks. As the Queen's celebratory display continued, I relaxed and enjoyed the show. The final set of fireworks were large red blooms of fire which erupted one after the other. As the sizzling light faded, we were left with a dark starry sky.

Seraphina opened the doors and I was the first to go back inside. Returning to the table, I watched as the servants brought out large plates of cakes and puddings. Thanking them, I sat back down at the table and impatiently waited for the others.

"Come, dessert is ready for us," I said, eyeing the chocolate orange pudding that was set out in the center of the table.

"If you are so eager," Tristin said, "you could have started without us."

"How could you believe I would be so rude?" I joked back.

Tristin smiled and she took a seat beside Nero. The man wasn't wearing his mask, but he'd had a new set of teeth fitted for the occasion that were less wolf and more man. He gave me a nod, reaching for a cake.

Seraphina and Nila took their seats across from me and Vivienne returned to her seat beside me. Nels and Malin were the final two to take their seats, both of them seeming hesitant. They gave each other strange looks before their attention fell onto the desserts.

"Everyone, please enjoy yourselves," Seraphina said, cutting a slice of cake for herself. "I specifically requested that the chef provide everyone's favorites."

Without hesitation, I picked up my knife and cut a piece of the orange chocolate pudding and placed it onto the clean white porcelain plate. I ate slowly, enjoying and savoring every bite. Soon such delicacies would once more be beyond my grasp. Though that thought saddened me, I didn't let it dampen my mood. Things needed to be enjoyed and I'd found that over the last few days, it had been rather easy for me to do that.

"It truly amazes me how different everything feels," Seraphina said, setting down her fork. She took a drink of her wine, eyeing me. "It's hard to believe that you have only been in my life for a year. It feels so much longer than that."

"I second that," Nero said. "I am glad we met."

"What is your plan," Tristin said, her eyes glancing between me and the Malkethian's. "You are still going with them, are you not?"

I nodded my head and looked over at Malin and Nels who were both looking down with contemplative expressions. After a moment of silence, Nels looked up and gave me a half smile. I felt a small tightness in my chest. The hydromancer gave Seraphina a sheepish smile and looked back down at his plate. He had only taken a small bite of his cake.

"We have decided to return without Caden." Nels said.

I raised my eyebrow and looked at Vivienne who seemed just as surprised as I was. Everyone at the table remained silent, their attention first going to me, then to the sorcerers. Nels and Malin shared a few glances, then looked at me. They both gave me sad smiles.

"Why?" Seraphina finally asked.

"What would be the point?" Malin answered. "Caden is no longer one of us. As far as we are concerned, the demon of the north died alongside Isar, both sacrificing themselves to defeat true evil."

"If that is what you think is right," I said, silently relieved. Still, I couldn't keep the smile from my face and I cut myself another piece of pudding. "Are you certain you won't need to bring back proof?"

"I was hoping you would be willing to give us your armor," Nels said, shrugging. "I am certain that will be proof enough that we found you and from the damage, I believe they will find it acceptable evidence of your death."

"Then it is yours. Nero, will you see that it is sent to them?"

Nero nodded, "You can just come to my workshop. I did start

on repairs, but I haven't made much progress. I will have it packed up and ready for you by morning."

"I am not sure I understand," Seraphina asked, her eyes narrowing as she looked me up and down. "Why do you consider Caden to be of no use to you?"

Malin and Nels both looked at me, their eyes filled with regret and sorrow. It was clear neither of them were comfortable speaking about this. Perhaps the very thought made them anxious. It explained their strange behavior and why they had trouble meeting my eyes.

"I am not a sorcerer any longer, Seraphina. I am certain they were trying to be respectful by not being blunt about it."

"Why didn't you tell us?" Tristin asked.

"It's an uncomfortable thought, seeing as how I have lived more of my life as a pyromancer than not. I suppose I have just been adjusting to the idea myself."

"How did this happen?" Nila asked. She seemed more concerned than the others and her gaunt face accented her emotions.

"I've been trying to puzzle that out. My best guess is that when the Lich stabbed me with Burnfinger, I survived because it was a talisman. By combining myself with the weapon, I must have damaged my connection to the Empyrean. It is not a normal thing for someone like me to lose their power, but this was not a normal experience. Do you have any ideas that might shed light upon what happened to me?"

Nels shook his head. "I have not seen this before."

"Neither have I." Malin finally took a bite of her cake, her shoulders relaxing. "And I cannot imagine how you are feeling."

"As far as consequences go, I count myself lucky. Things could have turned out a lot worse. Even still, not everyone made it home."

A somberness fell over the room like a blanket, dampening

everyone's mood. I desperately wanted to lift everyone's spirits. Each of them deserved it, but I struggled to find the words. After a few minutes of silence, everyone started half heartedly eating their desert, and I finally understood what I needed to say.

Standing, I raised my glass and forced a smile to my lips. "It seems only right that we offer up a toast to celebrate good friends and brighter days to come."

Everyone raised a glass and drank.

"Most importantly," I continued, "I wanted you all to know that I am grateful for you and for all the help you have offered me. I did not come to Kings Keep expecting to find anything more than steady work. It was a wonderful reward and a surprise that I found so much more than I was looking for. For that, you have my eternal thanks."

EPILOGUE
NEW MELODY

The dock was loud and busy, sailors hurried about loading or unloading ships. Dismounting from Stormcloud, I took my horse by her reins and led her the rest of the way to the ship. Vivienne followed me, leading a large black stallion with a white nose. Reaching the last dock on the river, I saw Seraphina waiting for us. The regal woman was talking with the ship captain. Captain Gil was stroking his short brown beard and his blue coat was buttoned up. The both of them waved to us as we approached.

"We're just about loaded up," Gil said, walking over to meet me.

The captain reached out his hand and took Stormcloud's reins. My horse tossed her head and I patted her neck. The white mare eyed me for a moment as Gil led her to the edge of the boat. I watched him secure a sling beneath her belly. The horse neighed in surprise and slight distress as she was hoisted onto the ship. Once her hooves were on the deck, she was hitched to a post and several ship-mates patted her down. Gil returned and took the reins from Vivienne. It was quite the ordeal to get Vivienne's black stallion onto the ship, but as soon as he was secured next to Stormcloud, all seemed to be fine.

"It doesn't look like you do this often," I said to Gil as he approached, a half bemused half embarrassed smile on his face.

"Not to worry, we'll keep your horses safe."

"I'm certain you will," Seraphina said. "If you will give the two of us a moment."

Gil nodded, and used the plank to walk onto his ship. He helped as the final crates were loaded and began to prepare the ropes to tie everything down.

"Are you certain I cannot convince you to stay?" Seraphina asked. Her long blond hair curled down beautifully around her shoulders, swaying slightly in the wind. She wore a green dress which matched her eyes. Though she smiled, the rest of her face looked sad.

"No. But this isn't a final goodbye, I don't think. For either of us."

I looked over at Vivienne who smiled. "We'll be back. But some time out of this city will be good."

"Gil has everything you need packed up. When you get to the port, a friend of mine shall be waiting for you." Seraphina pulled a letter out of a small pouch which hung from her waist. "Just give him this and he will take you to the inn."

Vivienne took the letter and tucked it away into the pocket of her cloak. "Thank you, again."

"It truly isn't a problem. If you wouldn't mind inspecting the warehouse while you are there."

"Of course," Vivienne said. "We'll make sure everything is in good standing."

"You take care of him. Make sure Caden stays out of trouble."

"I'm not sure I can promise that," Vivienne said with a smile, then added, "for either of us."

"I can hope," Seraphina said, running her index finger beneath her left eye, "until the next time we see each other."

Vivienne embraced Seraphina then walked up the plank and onto the ship. With a sheepish smile, I let Seraphina hug me as well. When we let go of eachother, I took a step back and smiled. Seraphina's blonde hair swayed in the wind and her sad expression faded slightly.

"What will you do next?" Seraphina asked.

"I don't know."

"Does that bother you, not knowing?"

"For once in my life, I am perfectly happy to go and see what I find."

"May the Valon smile upon you both. They know you deserve it."

"Thanks again. For everything."

"You're welcome. It was a true pleasure."

Bidding Seraphina goodbye, I walked up the plank and stepped onto the ship. Joining Vivienne at the front of the ship, I looked over my shoulder and waved once more to Seraphina who waved back before getting into her carriage. I watched the carriage disappear as the riverboat pulled out of the dock and began to row south. Looking out over the water, I put my arm around Vivienne and she rested her head on my shoulder. It seemed like no time at all before we were past the gate and sailing south through the winding valley.

"It's been so long since I have traveled, I'm so excited."

"Me too, Viv."

"Have you ever seen the sea?"

"No. I've never seen the sea."

"It's wonderful. That is the first place we will go once we get to Rockport."

"I can't wait."

I leaned forward, putting my face close to Vivienne's. I gave her a soft, tender kiss which she returned with a long passionate one. Together, as we watched the city of Kings Keep pass from view, I had a distinct feeling that I would return. This was not a final goodbye, and there was so much more to come. I had always thought that life was like a song and each of us played a part. Perhaps one verse of my life's song had come to an end and it was time for a new melody.

THE END

ABOUT THE AUTHOR

Austin Colton is a jack of all trades who compulsively takes on far too many projects at once. He has found this a good strategy for curing perpetual boredom and a head stuck in the clouds. Austin lives in Arizona, where he writes, paints, explores the great outdoors, and looks for new stories to enjoy. You can view his complete list of works and contact him online at:

AustinColton.com